PROLOG

IVY

"Where do you want your next cut, little thief?" Silas asks as the blade points at my chest, his purge mask haunting me.

Heath hovers over my face, his mask glowing in the dark, as he trails his finger down my body until he's right beneath my sternum. "Here?"

I shake my head.

Silas smiles as he points it at my legs. "No. Here ..."

I gasp when the edge pierces my skin only briefly, causing one droplet of blood to cascade. He groans and leans over to lick it straight off my skin, and the hum that follows creates chills all over my body.

"Devilish little vixen," Silas whispers.

My brain has floated off into the unknown. Sweet, sweet nirvana ... beyond destruction.

I still feel the burn on my skin right where he carved me... still feel the arousal building in my body with the need for more. More insanity.

"You love this, don't you?" Max says, spreading my legs apart.

I nod.

Even though I know these boys are wrong for me.

They're beyond filthy and out of their minds insane.

But I still want them anyway.

I was a runner, an escapee, fleeing from my past, fleeing from the present.

I ran so fast my legs could barely carry me until they started chasing me ... and carried me instead.

They caught my body and used it as they saw fit, chaining my heart and soul to their unhinged ways. I've fallen into their dark pit of desires and don't want to crawl back out. Not even if it kills me.

Heath slowly zips down above me. "Who do you belong to?"

"You. All of you," I murmur.

"Then you're going to be a good little slut and beg for us," Heath groans.

My entire body shivers as both he and Max touch me everywhere, hands creeping underneath my blouse, into my pants, all over my body.

They've distorted my mind beyond comprehension and wrecked my heart until all it wanted was the taste of the hedonistic freedom they offered me.

And I realize now I'm not the only thief. I never was.

These boys have seized all the dark fragments of my soul, and I never want them back.

A devious grin spreads on Silas's lips as he crawls on top of me, hovering dangerously close, and he sucks in a breath. "God, you smell so good when you're scared, my pretty little thief," he whispers into my ear, his tongue darting out to lick the rim. "Now run."

BOYS WHO HUNT

BOYS WHO HUNT

CLARISSA WILD

AUTHOR'S NOTE

I want to preface this by saying if you haven't read any of my books before, have mercy on your soul.

This one has bullying, stalking, masked chases, permanent marking, and so much more stuff that I can't put it all in here, so I've put a list on my website for you to check out.

Boys Who Hunt is titled the way it is for a *reason*.

This book is vulgar, deranged, raunchy, completely unhinged, and over-the-top smutty. Like, I'm not kidding when I say it is drenched in sex. There is plot, too, you know. But also lots of smut. *AND* a HEA of course.

You do *not* need to read the Spine Ridge University books in order to read this, but some characters from that series do make happy cameos.

The boys in this book do have murderous tendencies, just like you will when you finish reading. Honestly, I went all out with this one. Please don't kill me. I know you'll want to, but I need to stay alive to write the next book, thanks. I apologize in advance. (No, I don't. Hahahaha) PS: 4 more books are coming.

TW/CW for Boys Who Hunt can be found here:
www.clarissawild.com/boyswhohunt-tw/

A full family tree can be found here:
www.clarissawild.com/spine-ridge-university-legacy-series-family-tree/

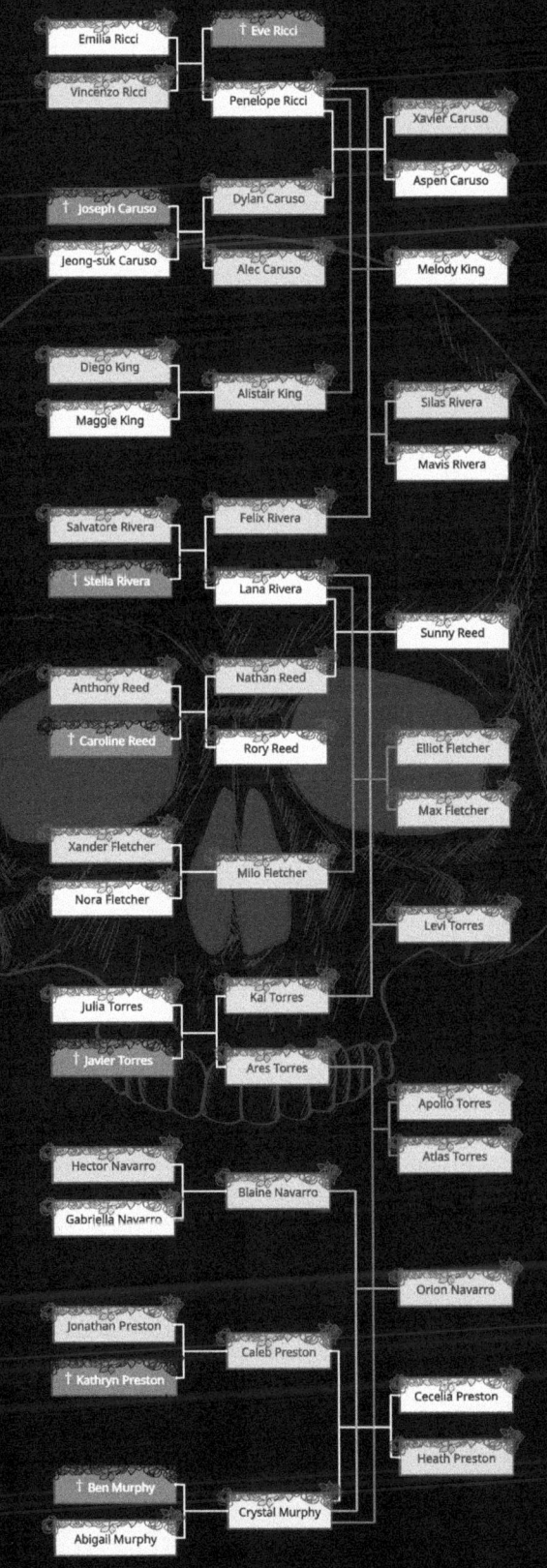

DEDICATION

This is for all the unhinged booksluts who say they don't need three more deranged, masked psycho boyfriends that like to hunt you down...

Liar.

ONE

IVY

Nothing is more priceless than the smug faces of rich boys who think they're untouchable ... just before I've robbed them.

I walk around through the dark, wood-paneled halls of the Skull and Serpent Society, amazed at the wealth on display. Century-old paintings and extravagant statues are covered in drinks and food while masked people dance away to the loud music blasting across the giant mansion, believing they'll stay anonymous. Safe.

But what draws my attention the most are three boys on the expensive leather couch in the back of the common room, drinking liquor straight from the bottle, all wearing LED purge masks that strike terror into the hearts of anyone who even dares to glance at them.

I've been at Spine Ridge University long enough to know exactly who to avoid.

These boys are at the top of my list.

The one on the left—a tall, muscular guy with a piercing in his lip and brow and tattoos all over—casually leans back into the couch as he takes a whiff of his cigarette right through the mask, his painted brown, medium-length hair loosely tucked into a bun, along with those black ear tunnels giving away who he is—Heath Preston, a notorious heartbreaker of Spine Ridge University, and the eldest of the three.

The one on the right, with his lanky but muscular frame and dark-brown hair swooping above his mask has a girl on his lap who's suckling on his knife earring, but his head is tilted over the couch and his eyes are fixated on Heath as he bites his lip. Max Fletcher is the youngest of the boys, an eternal dreamer, and definitely the odd one in the crowd.

But the one that really makes all the hairs on the back of my neck stand up is the one in the middle. The shortest of the three, but the one who's the most fucked up—Silas Rivera.

He flashes the expensive bottle of liquor, running his fingers through his black-tipped ear-length hair and white roots, the little heart-shaped tattoo on his face a stark paradox to the piercing green eyes that flicker through the mask with deadly precision as he aims the bottle at a guest's head and chucks it at him.

The guest jumps aside, and the bottle smashes into a million pieces against the wall.

"No one said Phantoms were welcome tonight!" Silas yells.

The guy runs off through the crowd, and I step aside just in time for him to bolt through the door, leaving a cold gust of wind in his wake.

Silas Rivera laughs maniacally as the guy runs off, and the other partygoers laugh their asses off like it's one big joke. He runs his fingers through his hair and sits back down as a girl approaches him from the side with a box of bonbons in her hand.

"Aw … Cutiepie's getting a box of chocolates." Heath chuckles, shoving his elbow into Silas's ribs.

Silas looks at Heath like he's about to chop his head off.

"For your birthday," the girl says, blushing hard as she barely manages to glance at Silas.

Silas breaks out into a full grin, which reminds me of the Joker, the right edge of his full lips touching the heart-shaped tattoo on his cheek.

Suddenly, he grips her by the throat. "Chocolates. That's what you bring me?"

He snatches them from her hand and chucks them at Max, whose girl stumbles off him like she's scrambling to save her own life.

The noise in the room slowly dies down as they all focus on Silas and his tough grip on the girl's throat.

"I ... I ..." she mutters.

"What?" He leans in with a wicked smile on his face. "Say it."

"I like you."

"You *like* me?" The laughter emanating from his throat is nothing short of ominous. "Get on your knees for me, then."

The girl is slowly pushed down by the sheer force of his fingers squeezing the life out of her neck. I clutch the doorjamb with all the power I have to stop myself from intervening as a knife is flicked around.

He points it right at her face. "Do you like me enough to bleed for me?"

Her pupils dilate. "What?"

Heath leans forward too now, intrigued by the scene Silas is causing. "It's his birthday. Don't want to disappoint the birthday boy, do you?"

Silas holds the knife under her chin, and tears well up in her eyes as he slowly brings it to her lips. The whole room has gone deadly quiet. Even the music has died down.

"Do you want to make me happy?"

She nods.

The vicious smirk disappears. "Open your mouth."

She slowly parts her lips as tears roll down her cheeks. He inserts the knife, lays it on her tongue ...

And then the grin on his face reappears as a fucked-up laugh follows.

He retracts the knife and releases her throat by shoving her away, causing confusion all around.

"Get out. You're not worth my time."

After a quick knife flip, he tucks it back into his pocket as the girl crawls away.

"Fuck you," she mutters as she scrambles to her feet. "Asshole."

"She doesn't seem to like you anymore," Max says, ogling her as she scurries off. Then he chucks one of the chocolates into his mouth.

Silas snarls, "Good."

I grip her wrist as she passes me. "Are you okay?"

She wipes the tear stains off her face and jerks her arm free. "I don't need your pity. Thanks."

She bolts off to the exit, and I understand why. Not only did she get humiliated in front of an entire crowd but he also scared the living shit out of her.

For a second there, I almost believed he was going to cut her, just like everyone here. He had us on the edge of our seats, wondering how far he would go and whether he'd finally veer off the dangerous tightrope he'd been walking all along. Always looking for the next hit to keep him smiling while surrounded by all that money can buy. But all the riches in the world couldn't fill the void these boys have in their hearts.

"Music, hello?" Heath growls, and within seconds, the music booms through the room again, drowning out the silence.

I take a last swig of my drink before I waltz out of the dance room. I've made my decision.

Fuck these boys. They deserve everything coming for them.

I head into the bathroom and lock myself inside before I take off my bag and pull out a hoodie and black surgical mask, covering everything until only my eyes are visible. I open the door and look around again to make sure no one watches me as I head up the stairs. The people attending the party are too busy dancing and chatting to notice me going into the hallway upstairs.

I rummage every room until I find one that's unlocked and not occupied by people having sex, and I head inside. Books line the walls of this room, and the bed in the back seems unkempt. The scent of burnt incense meets my nostrils as I head toward the closet and open every drawer, searching through the clothes. Boxers, black pants, black shirts with skulls and spiders on them, studded belts and necklaces. This must be Heath's room.

I get to the next closet and throw everything out until I find a very expensive-looking box from Cartier. "Well, hello there," I murmur, tucking it into my bag.

I check the rest of the closet, but there's not much else, and I'm definitely not getting the shoes, no matter how expensive they might be.

I open up some more drawers for some leftover dollar bills as well as an actual new, unused phone. Who keeps a phone carelessly in a box like it's a fidget and not a whole goddamn phone that probably cost a thousand bucks?

I doubt he even bought this himself.

Men are rich ... but boys? Boys don't deserve the wealth they've been handed on a silver platter by their loaded parents. They don't even pay for their admission to this university. Silas's mom and dad own the RIVERA clubs across the globe, and his dad is the dean at this fucking college. The parents of these boys bought their spots long ago, while the rest of us have to work our entire lives to earn a scholarship to such a prestigious university.

I stuff the phone box into my pocket before I head to the room right next door.

A ton of skulls are all over the place like someone started a collection, and I don't know whether they're real, but I don't have enough time to care either.

I grab the wallet on the desk, fish out all the credit cards and bills until it's empty, then snag some rings from the top drawer. Then I filter through his closets, opening up a box in the back that makes my eyes almost bulge out of my head.

"Money shot," I murmur. There are stacks and stacks of dollar bills, hundreds of them, maybe thousands.

And now they're all mine.

I take the whole box out and empty it into my bag, which is starting to feel heavy. Then I look around the room and underneath the bed, where I find a particularly strange little box. The lid is closed, but it's easy to break into as it looks like one of those boxes kids use to hide stuff in. I crack it open with one of my smaller keys, hoping to find some interesting loot.

Instead, there's a shiny, plastic red flower inside.

Why is he keeping this in a box?

CREAK!

The sudden noise makes me stop and look up.

What was that?

It sounded like ... footsteps.

Panic bubbles to the surface.

Shit!

With the box still in my hands, I bolt out of the room, but the second I spot Silas's black-and-white hair and those eerie tats running all up the back of his neck as he walks up the stairs, I immediately go back inside and shut the door, holding my breath.

Shit. What the hell do I do?

I check the room and find two windows in the back. One is bolted shut, but the other is opened a little bit.

Can I fit through that?

Silas's footsteps make the wooden floor creak.

There's no time.

Without thinking, I tuck the little box in my bag and run to the other end of the room. With all my strength, I push open the window and slip through, one leg after the other, squeezing my body through the narrow gap, ripping my bag half open at the zipper from the hook on the window.

"Goddammit," I hiss, pulling it through as I land on the balcony.

"What the fuck?!"

Silas's deadly voice makes all the hairs on the back of my neck stand up.

Guess he found the mess I left.

I look over the balcony, but there's no way to go down except a big-ass tree in front of the house.

Should I risk it?

"Whoever's in my room, you're dead if I catch you!" Silas's loud growl is all I need to make the jump.

I grab the tree's branches and catch myself just before falling, but fuck me, my heart's shooting through the roof. This stuff had better be worth it.

I grasp the tree trunk and make my way down each branch, but one of them gives way underneath me, and I tumble to the ground, knocking me out for two seconds.

My head is spinning.

I can't hear from one ear.

I swiftly search my way around the grass, but it's hard to see in the dark.

Shit. Shit. Shit! I don't have time for this.

A door is loudly thrown open mere feet away from me.

Fuck. I have to run.

Without looking, I scramble to my feet and run in the opposite direction with a half-broken bag and a few stray bills flying left and right like a trail left by Hansel and Gretel.

***

Twenty minutes later

I tried the credit cards, but of course, they all got canceled within seconds of my stealing them. If only I hadn't been caught red-handed.

I throw my bike inside the shed in the building and shut the door behind me, nearly ripping off the door handle. The light fixture above me flickers, and I blow out a sigh of relief. Made it through another day safe and sound.

I head up the grimy stairs to the third floor and walk to the end of the hallways and knock on the door there, swiftly fishing some of the money I stole from my pocket.

My neighbor Mrs. Schwartz opens up in her pink fuzzy slippers and pajamas, and I hold out the cash. "For the trouble."

"You're welcome," she says, snatching it out of my hand.

"Anything happen today I should know about?"

"No, nothing unusual. We played with Barbies, drew some pictures, and watched TV. The regular stuff a five-year-old is into." She shrugs.

I nod tentatively. I don't know if I can trust her, but I have nothing else to go by but her word.

"Tomorrow, same time?" she asks. "I can use the cash."

"Yes, please," I say, and she briefly nods. But as I open my mouth again, she closes the door on me, and I'm left nearly eating the wood.

"Thanks."

I breathe out a sigh and turn around.

It's not the best deal I've made, but at least it keeps me standing and allows me to try to make life a little easier.

I shove my key into the lock to open the door to my apartment. The home has a quiet atmosphere, and the curtains have already been closed. A gentle song from the radio in the bedroom makes me smile as I peek in the door and see Cora fast asleep. The whole room is plastered with newly drawn pictures of her and me together, fighting a monster.

I smile and place the red flower I found in the palm of her hand. A small gift from me to make her smile when she wakes up.

My black cat meows, drawing my attention, and I pet him on his little head. "Hey, Bagel. Been a good boy today?" I plant a kiss on his head, and he purrs as he nudges his head against my cheek. "Love you too."

I chuck the nonfunctional credit cards in the trash and place my bag on the table. I grab a chair and sit down, then pull all the stuff I stole from the bag and lay it out in front of me so I can add up the value and count the leftover money. My cheeks blow up with air. This must be at least five grand. That'll last us a while. Normally, I'd only be able to steal enough to pay for dinner and breakfast for her and have some scraps for me, but I truly hit a goldmine this time. Maybe I can finally take Cora to that burger place she's always wanted to go to.

After I've dealt with some other business.

I pluck the remaining hearing aid from my ear and place it on the table in front of me. The void of sound usually calms my soul after a busy day, but now? Now, it creates violent, chaotic turmoil in my heart.

* * *

SILAS

Twenty minutes ago

All the veins in my arms pop as I burst out of the front door and peer around me to find the person who just ransacked our house in mere minutes, but all that's left is a broken branch and skid marks in the grass.

My eyes twitch, and the anger begins to boil over again.

"God-fucking-dammit!"

I rush to the side and look up at the open window through which they jumped, then follow the trail to Priory Forest behind the house.

They fucking ran away like a coward after stealing from me during a fucking birthday party? No fucking way am I going to let that slide.

"You can't fucking hide from me!" I scream, listening to my own voice echoing across the dark streets.

The moment I take one step in the direction of the forest, a hand on my shoulder stops me from moving. I almost pummel him over my shoulder, but then I realize who it is.

"Relax, it's me," Heath says. "What happened?"

"Some fucker just robbed us!" I growl, spitting on the ground.

He frowns. "What?!"

I jerk free from his grip. "Stole my money right out of the box and ransacked my room. Yours too, I checked."

"Fuck. Where'd they run off to?" He eyes the forest. "They could be anywhere by now."

"I need to cancel all my fucking credit cards," I growl, fishing my phone from my pocket so I can get to work.

Heath goes to his knees in front of the fallen branch, inspecting something on the ground. "This wasn't here before the party."

I cross my arms. "I don't fucking care about some tree. No one fucking steals from me on my fucking birthday and gets away with it."

"No one said anything about them getting away with it," Heath says, a dangerous smirk forming on his smug face, one of the few things that can make me feel something other than rage.

He holds up something between his index finger and thumb and shows it to me.

"What the fuck is that?" I mutter, staring at the small skin-colored metallic object with a tiny wire attached. "It looks like—"

"A hearing aid."

A wicked grin spreads on my face. "We might be able to track them down."

"Exactly."

Now it's getting interesting.

I grab the hearing aid from his hand and inspect it in the street-light. The grin on my face only grows bigger and bigger.

I haven't been this excited since I last got blood on my hands.

But fuck me, a chase like this ... who could resist?

A low-rumbling laugh emanates from my chest.

Mark my fucking words, I will fucking track you down, little thief ... and make you beg for mercy.

TWO

HEATH

Max sneaks a peek over my shoulder at the book Mavis is reading to me, but Mavis leans in and smacks him on the head with a rolled-up piece of paper. "Don't be nosy."

"What?" he growls, rubbing his head. "I just wanna know what you guys are reading."

"Nothing you'd find interesting anyway," I mumble while Mavis flips the page.

I've seen some dark shit in my life before but never written down so perfectly in a book. Enchantments and spells for Wiccans and everything supernatural. Mavis really knows where to find them.

"See, this one might work for finding something you lost," Mavis says, pointing at something on the page.

Silas sits down and skewers his apple with his knife before chomping off whole pieces. "So, Mave, who are we going after?"

"Going after who, for what?" Max asks.

"We don't know yet," I answer, toying with the screw-fit tunnel in my ear. "We need more time."

"To do what? Hex her?" Silas snorts. "Like that's going to work."

"Oh, shut up, Silas." Mavis shoves him. "Just because you don't know anything about magic doesn't mean it doesn't work."

Silas raises his brow, brings his finger to his temple, and circles it around.

"Wait, what did I miss?" Max mutters.

I sigh. "Someone broke into the Skull and Serpent Society and robbed us."

"ROBBED US?!" Max yells.

Silas grabs his fork and shoves it between Max's fingers, narrowly avoiding his skin. "Don't be so fucking loud, Fletcher. The entire fucking cafeteria doesn't need to know our security is shit."

"They got away," I tell Max.

"But we found this on the grass." Silas fishes the hearing aid from his pocket and shows it to Max.

"Okay ..." Max grabs it and inspects it up close. "How's this going to help you find the person responsible?"

"There must be some sort of identification code on it, right?" Silas says.

"I can cast a tracking spell," Mavis offers. "You'll find him in no time." She winks at me in the most devilish way, and I almost succumb to her charms again. Almost. But we both know she's just playing with me.

Silas sticks his finger into his mouth and fake gags.

"Oh, grow up," Mavis growls at him before she jumps off the table and closes the book. "You can either accept my help or fumble by yourself. Your choice, little bro."

"Don't fucking call me little," Silas snarls.

"Well, she is right. I mean, you are the shortest of all of us," Max says, but Silas's deadly eyes stop him halfway through his sentence. "It's the truth."

"Whatever. I'm done here." She rolls her eyes and throws her blue-streaked brown hair over her shoulder. "See you later, Heath." She smiles at me before walking off, and I throw back a wink before grabbing my knife to cut slices off my apple.

"You really can't help yourself, can you?" Silas says. "Still trying to get into my sister's pants."

Not this again.

I stop and point the knife at him. "I'm just being fucking friendly because we're friends. That's it."

I don't need him to remind me of my past mistakes.

"Right. And you just read spell books from a self-proclaimed witch because you enjoy it." He scoffs. "Liar."

"Shut up." I throw a piece of apple in Silas's direction. "She's trying to help. That's it."

Max is still busy checking out the hearing aid, completely ignoring what's going on at the table.

"With bullshit that doesn't work," Silas quips. "Besides, she's not interested. She made that much clear last year. Or did your sad-boy heart not want to believe it?"

My eye twitches.

He fucking dares to bring that up?

"Bro, I'm *this*"—I pinch my fingers together—"close to shoving this apple down your throat."

"Try me." Silas folds his arms and leans back. "See how it works out for you."

"Hey, what's this barcode?" Max suddenly asks.

We both grow quiet and stare at him like he's just unlocked the secret to the universe.

"Give me that." Silas snatches it out of his hand and looks at the exact spot Max was inspecting. "What am I looking at?"

"There are three different sequences of numbers on the bottom of the battery lid, in the tab."

Silas narrows his eyes and looks at the hearing aid up close. "Well, fuck me." A big grin spreads on his lips as he tosses it at me so I can see it too. "Guess we'll find this little thief in no time."

***

IVY

I park my shoddy bike in the shed and run across the pavement, checking my watch every second because I know I'm late for my classes. The neighbor took her sweet-ass time before she was finally at my door ready to watch over Cora for me. I really need to find a more reliable babysitter.

Picking up the pace, I skid across the pebble path that surrounds the fountain in front of Spine Ridge University and nearly bump into people. "Sorry!" I add a smile so they're not too mad at me, and I bolt off.

I should really be more careful. Missing one hearing aid messes with my ability to navigate because I'm working with mono instead of stereo sound.

Fuck. When these classes are over, I'm going to look for it.

After I've made sure there's no one at that damn Skull and Serpent Society house on the lookout, of course.

"Hey, Ivy!" River Landon swoops his wavy brown hair aside to show off his handsome smile. He's leaning against a giant pillar near the big main entrance to the university next to his brother, Talon, who doesn't even spare me a glance.

"Sorry, no time. I gotta run. I'm late for class!" I say as I pass them and head inside through the massive doors.

"Wanna hang out later?" River yells.

I turn around momentarily with my right ear pointed at him to yell back, "Hit me up in my DMs!"

He smiles and nods, and I turn around again. But the second I do, I bump into someone face-first, my lips making contact with a very defined chest hidden underneath a white shirt with an ominous skull on it.

My body instinctively leans away as my eyes slowly move up his chest and meet the flickering, hollowed bright-green eyes and that distinctive grin on that diamond-shaped face, making him look like he works in a haunted mansion at the carnival.

Oh God.

Silas Rivera.

I step back, shocked by the fact that I ran into him out of all people.

Get yourself together, Ivy. He doesn't scare you. He's just a fucking bully. A short one too.

"What do we have here?" he growls, narrowing his eyes. "Another stumbling, bumbling, lovestruck girl?"

My eye begins to twitch. "Over my dead fucking body."

The smile instantly dissipates from his face. "You wanna die that badly?" He briefly inspects me, and the way his lip contemptuously curls like he's judging me makes me wanna puke. "I'll bend you over and snap you in half with ease, twig."

I get up in his face and hiss, "Why don't you pick on someone your own size, shortie?"

His eyes almost bulge out of his skull at this point.

Good.

He deserves nothing less for calling me a twig and threatening to kill me over bumping into him.

He buries his hand in his pocket, and I steel myself, but then someone walks up behind him and places a hand on his shoulder, stopping Silas from making a move.

"Silas. Don't you need to go to class?"

It's the dean. It's the actual fucking dean.

Felix Rivera.

I take a step back and look up into those same soul-crushing hollowed-out eyes that mirror Silas's, and my God, the apple really doesn't fall far from the tree ... except for the height difference. And the hair.

"Ivy Clark?" the dean says with a stoic face—like he's asking me if that's my name even though he apparently already knows.

Silas's nostrils flare at the sound of my name.

Fuck. I really did not want that out there for him to know.

He jerks free of his father's grip and marches off without another word. "See you later, twig."

The dean waits until he's out of view before he continues, "Better stay away from trouble like him if you wanna finish your studies at this university."

I laugh it off like it's no big deal even though the pressure is real. "Yeah, of course."

But it's already too late for that. Silas and I have become more than well acquainted after I stole his shit. He just doesn't know it yet.

The dean nods and walks off like he has nothing more to say, and every crowd he passes through separates for him like he's goddamn Moses himself. Two decades have passed, and his name still holds power in these halls.

His offspring is just as infamous, if not more dangerously unhinged.

And I don't understand why he would let him reign these college grounds like he's the goddamn king.

I walk down the halls to my classroom and make my way inside, sitting down on the seat in the front so I can hear the professor best. But when I look around the room and see Silas and his friend Max sitting in the back, my veins run frigid.

We share a fucking class too?

***

MAX

The girl sitting in the front of class is so gorgeous, both my eyes *and* my heart have to do a double take. Her dark-brown hair tumbles over her short white woven top as she types something onto her phone, and she throws it back, allowing me to marvel at her beautiful face with sculpted cheekbones, a sharp nose, and thick, downturned red lips.

Wow.

I tilt my head to watch her put down her bag and take out a few books, her round ass making me lick my lips. I shake my head and close my eyes.

Maybe someday I'll have the same courage Silas has and ask someone like her out on a date. Not that he dates, but he has the arrogance of someone who does.

Anyway, for now, I'll pine over someone I couldn't possibly have anyway.

The girl in front of the class suspiciously homes in on Silas with narrowed eyes, and I immediately look away, feeling the heat.

"Jesus, Silas. You got girlfriends who despise you everywhere, don't you?"

"What?" he snarls back, refusing to look up from the desk where he's torturing a tiny bug by pinning it to the wood with his knife while it's trying to fly away. I don't know why, but I can't stop focusing on the bug trying to desperately get away from him.

"That girl ..." I whisper, trying to point at her without making it obvious I'm pointing at her.

He plucks at the insect's wings. "I'm busy."

"Okay, fine. Never mind." I roll my eyes.

She's already turned her gaze to the professor again, writing down notes as he begins to speak, and she tucks her hair behind her ear as if to listen better to his words. She reaches into her bag, and as she lifts out a book, I spot something glinting in her ear, with the same kind of skin color and wire as ...

My eyes widen.

"The hearing aid."

Silas immediately rips the knife out of the bug, and it zooms off with damaged wings, surviving the worst kind of predator it could ever meet.

The knife lands against my neck, and I gulp at the feel of the blade against my skin.

"What did you just say?"

"It's hers. The girl in the front row."

His eyes follow mine down to where she's sitting, and he gets up from his seat, leaning onto the table with both hands as he zeros in on her like a drone finding its target.

Fuck.
Maybe I shouldn't have said that out loud.

THREE

SILAS

My nails dig into the desk so violently it cracks through the wood as I find her sitting there right in front of me.

The girl who fucking dared to walk into me ...

The girl who called me a shortie ...

Is the girl who fucking stole from me.

"Wait, we don't know if it's her yet," Max mutters.

"Who else could it be?" I grit.

It can't be a fucking coincidence she's wearing only one hearing aid.

Rage quietly takes over every atom of my body as I stare at her, wondering when she'll feel the burn of my gaze. If she even realizes I know who she is and what she's done.

I wait, and wait, watching the clock tick away on the wall while she listens to the professor speak. But after she's filled her notebook with scribbles, she tucks it back into her bag and turns her head to a girl sitting next to her on the benches ... and I clearly spot the empty ear.

Fuck yes.

All this time, I thought I was searching for a guy, and now it turns out to be a fucking girl.

A wild smirk forms on my face.

The wait seems eternal, but it's worth it because the moment she slowly turns in her seat and looks my way, I can see the blood drain from her face.

Yes.

Look at me, Ivy Clark.

I know your name. I know who you are. I know what you've done. And it will cost you dearly.

I can't fucking wait to watch you beg.

The professor finishes his class, and she swiftly grabs her bag and rushes out the door. She thinks she can escape me, but this *shortie's* legs favorite thing in the entire fucking world is chasing something down ... And today, I've found my prey.

***

IVY

I run through the corridors of Spine Ridge University, the sound of students chatting away doing nothing to drown out the noise in my head.

He saw me. He saw me sitting there and looked at me like he knew what I'd done.

I head into a women's-only bathroom and lock myself in a stall to catch my breath. I sit down and close my eyes for a second.

He doesn't know you stole from him.

He couldn't possibly kno—

The door slams open, and my eyes burst open along with it. I hold my breath as someone steps into the bathroom and closes the door behind them. I immediately pull both feet up on the toilet seat and make myself as tiny as possible.

"Ivy ..."

It's him.

"Oh, Ivy ..."

His unsettling, dark voice brings chills to my spine.

"Come out, come out, wherever you are ..."

WHAM!

A door two down from me is knocked open so harshly I nearly squeal, and I cover my mouth with my hand to stop him from hearing anything.

"I'm going to fucking find you, one way or another."

WHAM!

The next door is kicked open, and when I peer through the tiny slit between the two stalls, a shoe retracts. My door is next.

"And when I do, you're gonna be *mine*."

I have to find something, anything, to defend myself with when he gets ahold of me. This guy is insane.

I turn around, gripping the old, nonfunctional water pipe behind me that's bound to break eventually, and the moment his shoe lands against the door, I rip off the piece. The door flies open, and his unhinged smile makes my veins burst with fear and disgust.

"Found you."

The second he lunges at me, I swing the pipe at his face, but he blocks and grips the metal.

"Can't hit me, twig. I'm quicker than you," he taunts, and he tries to pry the pipe right out of my hand.

"What the fuck do you want from me?"

"What do I want?" He laughs maniacally. "Your life."

"Get away from me!" With the pipe between us, I push him out of the stall, forcing him back against the sink, but all it does is make him smile and laugh even harder.

"What the fuck is wrong with you?"

"What's wrong with me?" he mocks. "Maybe you should ask yourself that question."

"I didn't do anything," I say.

I know I'm lying, but I'm not going to admit the truth to the likes of him.

Clutching the pipe hard, he leans in with a tilted head as he stares at me. "You missing a hearing aid, thief?"

He looks me dead in the eyes, and the toxic smirk on his face makes me gulp.

Oh fuck.

Suddenly, he inches forward and bites the air right in front of my nose, making me jolt back. Another sadistic laugh follows.

"You don't know who you're messing with."

He pushes me back with ease as if all this time he was letting me believe I could take him, that I was in control of the pipe that separates his hungry teeth from my skin.

"You stole from me," he growls. "I don't take that lightly. You *will* pay. Whether it's in cash ... or with skin."

Skin?!

What the—

He pushes me all the way to the wall, and it knocks the air out of my lungs as I'm pinned between him and the pipe. Nowhere to go. No way out.

His face inches closer, green eyes nearly boring a hole into my heart.

"Now ... how should I make you pay for your crime?" His breath leaves hot marks on my skin. "With blood?" he whispers. His tongue, wet and dripping with hunger, licks a trail from my neck to my ear. "Or with fear?"

Fuck. He's actually licking me.

Silas Rivera is licking my skin, mouth wide open, teeth ready to sink in.

How am I going to get out of this?

If only I hadn't fallen out of that damn tree, I would've still had my hearing aid, and he would've never known it was me in his room.

"Prove it." It's out before I realize it.

His tongue lifts from my skin. "Prove what?"

"Losing my hearing aid is not a crime. You don't know if I stole from you." I'm not backing down even though I know this is a tough shot. "Prove. It."

Murderous obsession flashes in his narrowed eyes. "How many strokes do you think it would take before you spill?"

I frown. "What?"

Suddenly, his hand dives between my legs, swatting them aside with no remorse as he begins to rub me right through the fabric of my pants.

"One?"

I'm so shocked I don't even know how to respond as his callous fingers circle my most sensitive area like he already owns the place.

"Two?"

He circles once more, biting his lip as though he's enjoying the view of seeing me unravel.

"Three? C'mon, thief, give me a number, and I'll make you see the stars above before I bury you."

"You're insane," I growl.

I try to shove him away, to no avail, as my arms are still lodged firmly behind the pipe he's holding onto with just one strong hand.

"Do you feel this finger, twig?" he says, a chaotic-looking grin on his face. "I could kill you with just this one. So that makes *you* insane for stealing from someone like *me*."

I don't think I want to fucking know how he'd do it.

He adds another finger, and I struggle to stay upright while my knees begin to buckle.

"Now, are you going to fucking tell me the truth?"

"Fuck you," I hiss, trying not to let it affect me, but it's hard, so damn hard, when he's touching me exactly the right way while those green eyes bore a hole into my head to keep me from running.

It's as if my mind no longer belongs to me.

"Oh, we'll definitely get to that fucking part if you don't tell me what I want to know right fucking now."

The door suddenly opens, and a girl stands frozen in the doorway, staring us down like she walked in on a murder, and I don't think that's too far from the truth.

Silas pulls his fingers away from my slit, drops the pipe, and immediately walks away, but not before throwing me a final glare. "I'll see you soon, twig."

His tongue dips out to run along the top of his lip like he's still tasting me. A final lick of the dessert he will devour when he gets the chance.

I gulp as the door shuts behind him, and the girl grabs my shoulder. "You okay?"

I don't want to involve her in this. Those boys are way too dangerous.

But damn, I'm lucky she came in.

Even though I'm in complete shambles just from the way he touched me.

"I'm fine. He was just messing with me."

But I'm not fine.

My heart has never beaten faster than it did just now.

I can still feel the wetness he left with those ruthless fingers, still feel his filthy tongue on my skin, leaving a mark of death.

Like a threat ...

A promise to ruin me.

FOUR

MAX

I lean back against the wall near the main exit of the building and check my watch, breathing out a sigh. They were supposed to be here ages ago. What the hell are they doing?

When I look up again, Silas storms through the hallways, and people actually move aside for him only because they fear being run over. And if there's one thing you want to avoid, it's being in Silas's way.

"You left me!" I lament.

"Oh, get over it," Silas barks over his shoulder.

"Nice to see you too," I retort. "Hope it was fun."

He smacks his fist into the door. "That twig thinks she can get away with it."

Already at the nicknaming stage? That's quick. He must really hate her. But ... why?

She's gorgeous and smart and so very cunning. How does he not immediately fall in love?

We head outside into the sun. Well, it's more like me following Silas as he rampages around campus, but I like following him and Heath around.

Speaking of ...

"Do you know where Heath is?" I ask.

"No. Haven't seen him." Silas fishes his phone from his pocket and starts tapping away. "He should've been here. I almost had her."

"Almost."

He looks up at me and shoots darts with his eyes, making me side-step. "Maybe ask me to help next time."

"Why? So you can fawn over her good looks again?"

I stand stupefied underneath a tree in the grass.

A smug grin spreads on his face. "Yeah, I saw you looking at her."

"No, I—"

He taps my chest. "Don't go denying it now. I know what I saw. I'd recognize that look anywhere."

"What look?"

I shriek and nearly jolt up and down from his sudden voice behind me. "Fuck, you scared me."

But when he places his hand on my shoulder, it immediately calms me.

"Relax. Want one of these pills too?" he muses, showing off the new bottles he got.

"So that's what you were doing," I mutter.

"Gimme that." Silas snatches them from his hand, pops off the lid, and takes at least two.

"Wow, wow, calm down with the pills, bro," Heath says. "My dealer only wanted to sell me three of these bottles. Talk about being squeezed."

"Silas is on edge because he talked to a certain thief today," I say.

"What?" Heath's fingers dig into my shoulders, and it suddenly doesn't feel so nice anymore. "Who? Where?"

"Ivy fucking Clark."

Silas nearly crushes the bottle of pills before Heath finally snatches it back from him.

"A girl?"

"She was missing a fucking hearing aid," Silas says. "It has to be her."

"But ...?" Heath raises his brow.

"She got away," I say.

"I confronted her. Told her I knew she stole from me. She told me to fucking prove it."

My jaw drops. "Holy sh—"

"We have the fucking proof!" Heath growls as he fishes the hearing aid from his pocket. "This is all the proof we need."

"She'll just say she fucking dropped it in the grass." Silas shrugs. "We gotta have something better, something that irrefutably proves she's a thief."

"If she really is the thief, wouldn't it help finding out why she stole from you guys?" I ask.

They both look at me like I'm onto something.

"I mean, we could talk to her. Try to figure it out."

"And catch her in the act," Silas adds.

"I didn't—"

"Good thinking, bud." Heath grabs my shoulder and squashes me against his pecs, and I don't even know what to say. "We're going to make her talk."

"I scared her so much, I doubt she'll say another word to me," Silas says, folding his arms.

"Maybe not to you, but she might talk to *him*."

Heath glances down at me, and I frown, confused.

"Wait, what?"

"Yeah, you can talk to her and make her confess," Silas reiterates.

"What makes you think I'm good at lying to people?" I ask.

"Oh, c'mon, it's not that difficult," Heath says.

Silas's brow rises. "It's not lying if you like her."

"You like her?" Heath asks.

A blush creeps onto my cheeks. "It's nothing, I—"

"He couldn't keep his eyes off her," Silas jests.

"Is that true?" Heath's arrogant smile makes it hard to focus. "Does Max have a crush?"

I roll my eyes. "Fuck me, this is embarrassing."

Both boys laugh.

"It's perfect, bro," Heath says. "She'll never suspect someone who's swooning head over heels at the thought of kissing her."

"Do you really think I could do that?"

"Of course!" He grabs me and turns me around to lock eyes with me. "You go talk to her. Seduce her. Make her trust you." He leans in and whispers, "And when we have her right where we want her ... you will convince her to admit she's the thief."

***

IVY

Years ago

"I'm home!"

Dad's voice rings through the hallways, and I jump up from the couch and immediately sprint to hug him tightly like I do every day when he comes home from work.

He hugs me back, laughing. "God, one of these days, you're going to squeeze the rest of my life out of me with those strong arms."

I giggle as he leans over to kiss me on the forehead. "Dad, I got an A plus on my test! Wanna see?" I'm jumping up and down with excitement as I hold up my paper for him to see.

"Really?" The beaming smile on his face makes me feel proud. "You did great, sweetie. If you keep this up, you'll definitely get into Spine Ridge University one day."

"YES!" I yell.

Suddenly, he begins to cough, and I hold my breath while he struggles and clutches the table next to him. Mom jumps in to whisk him away while he keeps coughing and drops my paper on the floor.

"S-sorry, sweetie, I n-need a f-few minutes," he stammers, coughing up heaps.

The smile dissipates off my face while I look down at the paper, as a splotch of blood slowly spreads on it like venom seeping into the ink...

And into my hopeful heart.

***

Present

I put my bag on the counter and lock the door, but when two warm hands envelop me, I jolt up and down.

"Ivy!"

Smiling, I turn around and kneel for little Cora, whose hands barely fit around my body.

"Hey, sweetie," I murmur. "What are you doing out of bed? It's way past your bedtime."

"I couldn't sleep. I miss you," she says, rubbing her little face into me.

"I missed you too," I say, hugging her tight. "How was your day?"

"Mrs. Schwartz is mean. I don't like her."

I sigh. "I'm sorry. I'll ask her to be a bit nicer."

I wish I didn't have to leave her with my neighbor every day, but I have to work and study so I can at least provide us with a better future.

"Can you tell her I don't like peanut butter on my sandwich?"

I frown. "What? You don't like peanut butter? Since when."

She shakes her head. "Not anymore. I want chocolate cereal and milk."

I rub my lips together. "I get that … it's just that it's very expensive."

She pouts and averts her eyes, and I know she's disappointed. So am I. This life was not the one I had envisioned.

I place my hands on her shoulders. "You know what? Once I get that next check from the club, I'm going to get you some chocolate cereal."

The pure spark of hope in her eyes makes this all worth it. "Really?"

I nod, and she hugs me even tighter.

"Thank you!"

I rub her back, knowing full well I will have to keep my promise now, no matter how much it costs me. The only problem is that check will never provide enough for us to afford that expensive brand of cereal.

This means I'll have to employ different means to get my hands on that kind of money.

She yawns against my shoulder, and when I push her back, she's rubbing her eyes.

"C'mon," I say, and I pick her up. "Let's get you back to bed."

"Wait, but I want Rosey with me!" she pleads.

I roll my eyes and pick up the plastic flower from the table. "Here she is."

She hugs the flower like it's some kind of stuffed toy. Adorable.

I put her down on the only bed we have and lie down next to her on the second pillow, pulling the blanket over us while the small light next to the bed stays on so I can watch her fall asleep.

I cherish moments like these the most, a sliver of happiness in the daily storm of life.

And I find myself slipping away, just like her, into a deep sleep filled with waking nightmares.

Pools and pools of blood.

My vision becomes cloudy as the red puddles growing on the floor beneath me stain my eyes.

I have to get out.

Frozen, I stay put near the wall, shuddering from the breaths my lungs refuse to take.

It's happening again. And again. And again.

"Ivy!" I can hear my name but don't hear anything else even though I can clearly see a mouth moving in the distance.

My head spins violently, but I don't know what to do.

All I can hear is the deafening sound of footsteps coming up the stairs.

THWACK.

THWACK.

THWACK.

Tears form in my eyes and roll down my cheeks, flooding the house with my tears until I can no longer stand. I'm drowning. Drowning in the misery of my own wails. I grasp my neck as I suffocate, reaching out to breathe.

Breathe.

Breathe.

Breathe.

But no matter how hard I try, my lungs refuse to open.

Refuse to give me the life I need to force my legs to move.

RUN.

A crackling noise makes me stir, and I turn around, but a warm fog close to my face wakes me up from my slumber. I sit up straight, sweat dripping from every pore of my body as I swiftly turn on the light.

There's nothing.

No one.

Yet ...

The window is open.

I didn't open it.

I shiver and get out of bed, brushing off the recurring nightmare I just had. I grab my knife from my bag and clutch it tightly as I look around. I check all the closets, all the doors, all the nooks and crannies, under each cabinet, and under the bed.

Nothing.

I take a deep breath and sigh out the remaining adrenaline.

Maybe it was just the nightmare that woke me up, as usual.

I approach the window and peer outside.

A man stands in the shadows down below.

I don't know what he looks like. I can't see his face or make out any features except for his lanky figure.

A gust of wind makes goose bumps scatter on my skin, and I promptly shut the window, sealing it tightly, still staring at the man who refuses to budge.

Maybe I was only dreaming.

Maybe the gust of wind pushed the window open.

Or maybe ... just maybe ... someone was inside my house.

FIVE

IVY

A few days later

"Table six," the bartender says, scooting the tray with drinks toward me.

"Got it." I make my way through the crowd of people dancing to a table on the left of the club where I recognize a girl from university—Sunny Reed, Silas's cousin, is laughing with her friends, all wearing extravagant, over-the-top outfits covered in glitter. Her long, black-and-green hair falls beautifully over her tattooed skin, and she looks like she sparkles in the club lights.

I place the order in front of the group, and they cheer in unison, grabbing their drinks.

"Happy birthday, Sunny!"

"Can I please take these off?" she grumbles, picking at the hat on her head that's covered in bright lights.

"Nope!" another girl says, and she takes a picture. "It's just for your birthday, promise."

"The last one, yeah," she adds. "Because I'll definitely throw myself off the bridge after tonight."

The rest of the girls holler at her, and she grabs her drink and chugs it down in one go, then hands it back to me. "Another one."

"Sure," I say, smiling awkwardly, but the stone-cold look on the face of the girl just won't budge.

I've never seen anyone this pissed off to be a birthday girl.

I shrug and turn around but feel woozy all of a sudden, and I catch myself on one of the booths. My legs have started quaking from the lack of energy, but I have to keep going. No time to slack off. I'll catch up on sleep during some off hours at the university. I need this goddamn money more.

I pick up the next order at the bar. "Table twenty. In the back."

"Got it," I say, swiftly placing everything on a tray before I whisk it away.

Even if the work is tedious, I'm grateful to be able to do this on the side with my studies. It provides just enough money for me to ensure Cora has a warm home and a full belly. Everything else is gravy on top.

And even though this is a RIVERA club, I feel relatively safe here because there's no way Silas knows any of the people who work here at his mom and dad's establishments. There's no way those fuckers would come looking for me here. They're too busy playing the rich and popular guys to even notice a girl like me.

Besides, what I took from them was peanuts of the wealth they have. I'm sure they'll have forgotten about that tiny amount of money I stole before the week is over.

***

HEATH

From the booth in the back of the RIVERA club downtown in Crescent Vale City, I watch the server with the flowy dark-brown hair and the downturned smile bring the drinks and food to customers while weaving her way through the crowd. She's expertly dodging people like she's done this a million times before, but after every delivery, she takes a moment to catch her breath against some piece of furniture while her knees wobble.

It's almost like she's overexerting herself, pushing herself to the limit until she can no longer function. And for what? A few measly dollars?

I wish I understood.

How does a girl who works here have the money to go to such a prestigious university, let alone the time? If she's studying during the day and working at night, when does she sleep?

I'm intrigued.

Too much to let Max have all the fun.

She moves effortlessly between the people dancing on the floor as she serves the customers like her life quite literally depends on it, wearing a fake red-tinged smile and sweet eyes like she's skilled at faking it.

I wonder what else she's skilled at ... and I won't wait for Max to squeeze his way into her life before I find out more.

I roll the hearing aid between my fingers and look away as she approaches the table behind me. I hide my face in my hoodie and turn toward the wall, but when she passes me, I grasp her wrist.

She stops in her tracks and looks at me with that fake smile on her face, and seeing the realization of who I am slowly dawn is nothing short of perfection as her smile withers away into oblivion.

"Out of all the places you could work ... a RIVERA club is the one you chose?" I muse, staring at her from underneath my hoodie.

"What the—"

She tries to jerk free of my grip, but my hand easily encompasses her entire wrist. "No. You answer to me now."

I briefly flash a knife under the table until she's spotted it and immediately stops resisting.

She places the tray she was holding down on my table. "What are you doing here?"

I raise a brow. "I can ask you the same thing. What kind of girl chooses to work at the place of the man she robbed?" Her face turns snow white as a smirk creeps onto my face. "Sit. Down." I eye the seat in front of me until she understands she's not going anywhere.

She swallows and nods, after which I release her, and she gently shuffles into the seat in front of me.

I get it now, why Silas called her a twig. She's so thin I could probably fit my whole hand around her thigh too. Sickly thin. Like she could end up in the hospital if I so much as sneezed in her direction.

"What do you want from me?" she asks, folding her arms.

I grab one of the drinks she was supposed to serve off the tray. Taking a sip, I recoil at the taste.

Apple juice? Who orders apple juice at an adult club?

"I want to know why you stole from us."

She snorts. "Good luck figuring that out."

My eyes narrow. "So you admit it?"

"I don't admit to shit." She scoffs. "You came here to spy on me, didn't you?" She sucks in a breath. "How did you know where to find me?"

She's quick. I like that. "It was easy to figure out once Silas told me your name. A lot of Spine Ridge University students come here. They talk." I pause to glare at her intently. "I make them."

Her eyes glance toward the knife I'm still clutching underneath the table. There's not a hint of fear in her deep brown eyes, only rage, and it puts a smile on my face because now I'm only more intrigued.

"Now ... care to tell me why you stole from us?"

She merely stares at me like she can't believe I had the audacity to follow her here and ask her to tell me the truth.

She sits back in her seat with folded arms and says, "No."

Her eyes sparkle with defiance, and it rouses my cock.

"Like I said, I didn't do anything."

This girl ...

Even with the threat of us looming over her, she refuses to give in. I like her.

"You have something that belongs to us," I say. "I have something that belongs to you."

I fish in my pocket and take out the hearing aid, placing it on the table in front of her.

Her eyes widen as she realizes what it is.

"Go on. Take it."

"This is a trap, isn't it?" she mutters. "You wouldn't just give this back to me."

"I have nothing more to gain from keeping it," I answer. "I've already learned everything I need to know."

Her face slowly turns ghostly, and I can't help but wonder what kind of thoughts swirl through her head. If she's wondering whether I know more about her than just where she works.

The answer is yes.

She tries to snatch the hearing aid off the table, but I grab her hand and stop her when she's covered it with her hand. Even if there is no fear in her eyes, I can feel it oozing off her skin, the terror exciting the darkest parts of my soul.

This is the only part where Silas and I are alike.

"You think you're safe, hiding out here in a crowd. But there is nowhere you can hide from us. We know it was you." I lean across the table. "And whether you tell us the truth or not, you *will* pay for your crime."

She stares me down for a second, refusing to back off. Then she jerks her hand free, along with the hearing aid, jumps off the seat, and marches straight toward the exit of the establishment without even saying a single word to the man who hired her.

Guess I really frightened her.

A wicked smile forms on my face.

Good.

***

IVY

"What are you doing?" the barkeeper yells as I grab my bike out of the stand.

"I can't do it anymore. I quit."

"What?!" He looks at me like I've lost my mind, and maybe I have. "But I need you tonight! It's fucking packed in there!"

I sigh and take a moment. "I'm sorry."

The disappointment on his face hurts, but there's nothing I can do. I can't go back there.

I can't ever go back there because they'll be waiting for me, and I can't fucking risk it.

I jump on the bike and race off before I change my mind.

Fuck.

I have to get out of here.

The wheels spin as fast as possible as I make my way across several intersections and weave through traffic, getting as far away as I can from Club RIVERA. My heartbeat is shooting through the roof as I pedal wildly, crisscrossing the streets in the dark, barely avoiding an oncoming car. I stop for nothing, not even a red light, and nearly getting myself killed almost feels like the easier option.

Until that sweet little face pops into my mind again, and I immediately slow down.

Cora ... she's waiting for me to come back, to hug her and tell her everything will be okay. She depends on me.

And I'm failing her, over and over.

I have to go home.

I breathe through the pain and swallow back the tears as I keep biking through the city, but every car and every motorcycle that passes me makes me do a double take.

What if they're following me?

What if Heath only gave me back the hearing aid and said all those things to gauge my reaction? To see how far he could push me before I snapped?

To watch me leave ... and follow me straight to my own damn home?

No.

I shiver in the cold and head right into one of the many city parks, where I stop near a bench and sit down. I pull my phone from my pocket and ring the neighbor until she picks up.

"Hey. It's me."

"How long 'til you're home?"

"I ... I can't."

"Can't what?"

"Can you watch Cora and my cat for me?"

"What do you mean? Like ... at night?"

"Yeah," I say, still shivering.

"Oh fuck—"

"Please." I'm not opposed to begging. "I can't come home."

"Why?" She sounds like she's suspicious of me.

"It's not safe."

She grumbles for a moment, and I can tell it's hard on her too, but I can't tell her the truth or she'd never help me out.

"Please, I wouldn't ask if it wasn't important," I say. "Just for a few days. I promise I'll be back."

She sighs out loud. "Fine. But you owe me. Big time."

A load falls off my shoulders. "Thank you. I'll pay you."

"You'd better."

"Yes, definitely," I assure her. "I'll give you double."

"Good. Because I have other things to do."

"I know. I'm sorry. Thank you. Thank you for helping me out."

"Yeah, yeah." She hangs up the phone before I can say anything else, and tears immediately spring to my eyes.

That's it. It's done.

No more Cora.

At least not for a little while.

And even though I should feel relieved for not having to take care of a young kid for a while, the tears still stain my eyes at the thought of disappointing her, too.

I promised her I'd keep her safe. I promised her I'd make a life for us.

And now I lost the only job I had to get us some extra much-needed cash because of those fuckers who stalked me there. All because my hearing aid fell out.

I fish it out of my pocket and stare at it for a moment.

Those boys are ruining my only chance at staying at this university, ruining my job, ruining everything I worked so hard to achieve. And for what? Money that means the world to me yet is pocket change to them.

They're almost making me regret stealing from them.

Almost.

But I need that money more than them.

I need it more than I need my sanity.

And if this is the game they intend to play with me ...

Then I will fucking give it my all to bring them down.

SIX

IVY

My eyes can barely stay open.

I hid in a park behind a tree last night and didn't have a single ounce of sleep.

But I'm here.

I'm here on Spine Ridge U campus and going to my classes, just as I swore. Nothing will make me give up that easily.

"Hey, Ivy! Come sit with us!" River Landon waves at me from the grass where he's having lunch with the friend group I frequently join since I came to this university.

Fuck. I really did not want to sit down today when I didn't bring anything with me to eat. But with River calling me over, I'll have to go over there.

"How are your classes going?" Océane Pearce smiles at me, her dark skin so radiant in the bright sun that it dazzles even me. "Getting used to Spine Ridge U yet?"

I shrug and smile back. "It's okay. I'm slowly easing into it."

The twins, Xavier and Aspen Caruso, share a family-sized salad. One picks out the cucumbers and pickles, while the other vehemently avoids them and eats only the raisins and apple slices. Xavier tries to steal one of the apples, but Aspen swats his fork away. "Fruit's mine. That was the deal."

"Bitch," he whispers under his breath, swatting at her fork too.

She spits a piece of raisin in his face.

"Gross!" Xavier wipes off his face, and Aspen scrunches her freckly nose in amusement.

River laughs. "Y'all can't ever be nice, can you?"

"Girl's been bothering me since she stole half my mother's fucking womb from me," Xavier growls, and Aspen punches his shoulder in response.

"So much love between you two, it's infectious," River jokes, running his fingers through his dark-brown hair.

"What are they fighting about now?" Talon, River's older brother, asks as he stands over the group.

"Sharing air," Océane jests as she gets up and pecks Talon on the cheeks. "Where've you been?"

"Extra class," he says, smugly kissing her on the lips, claiming her in front of everyone. "Ready to get out of here?"

"Bet," she says.

"Where are you going?" Aspen asks, throwing back her medium-length red hair she once told me was not natural even though it totally looks like it. "Somewhere fun?"

"Talon's taking me out on a date." She smiles brightly, her curly black hair waving in the wind. "See you all later. And Ivy, we should catch up soon. Message me, okay? We'll make plans for a night out." She winks.

"Got it!" I reply.

Talon throws his arm over her shoulders as they walk off.

"Those two have been slobbering each other's faces off the entire day," River groans.

"He's just staking his claim," Xavier says. "Who wouldn't with that catch?"

Aspen makes a face. "Bro."

"What? She is a catch." He looks at me. "You can't deny that."

I nod. "True. She's gorgeous."

Xavier makes a weird gesture with his hands. "See?"

Aspen rolls her eyes, but Xavier's already lost in his thoughts. He looks dazed as hell, staring at something in the distance. I follow his gaze to find Sunny Reed with her super long black-and-green hair waving from side to side as she struts around campus with her usual grumpy expression. Her friends tail behind her, trying to catch up like they're trying to catch a whiff of air from the queen herself. When she turns, one of them pulls up her phone and takes a picture while she leans against the fountain with a killer smile.

"Xavier," Aspen says, but he's not even listening. "Hello, earth to Xavier." She waves her hand in front of his face.

"What?" he mutters.

I laugh. "You're staring."

He looks away with furrowed brows. "No. I'm just tired of my classes, that's it." He swiftly dips his fork into the shared salad bowl and pulls out five cucumber slices, shoving them all in his mouth with some lettuce. "Want some?"

I shake my head. "No, I'm fine. Thank you."

"Aren't you hungry?" River asks.

"No, no, I've already eaten," I lie.

I always lie.

If I didn't ... they'd know I never have food here. Ever.

And I don't want them to know I'm not rich like they are.

Whatever is in the cafeteria costs money, which I don't have. I don't bring food from home because there is none. I save everything for breakfasts and dinners for both Cora and me; that's it. I used to eat at work sometimes, but now that's out of the question. I was used to two meals. Unfortunately, my stomach doesn't agree with my need to fit in with the societal norms here at Spine Ridge University.

Almost everyone here is rich. Save for the couple of people who have a scholarship like I do. And most of them form a clique together to study and work their asses off so they don't lose it.

I just want to blend in. Fake it 'til I make it.

I clear my throat and look around the college grounds when I notice a particular lanky brown-haired boy with a knife earring slowly walking toward me.

And then turning around the second our eyes connect.

***

MAX

Two minutes ago

I'm jogging outside on campus terrain, enjoying the warm sun after a long day of classes. I pause for a moment to take a deep breath, but when I spot a familiar dark-brown-haired girl from the corner of my eye, I have to blink twice to make sure I'm not dreaming.

The girl Silas chased into the bathroom is sitting on the grass with a bunch of her friends. What a coincidence.

I tilt my head and watch her tuck away her bag while some people in the group eat. She smiles, awkwardly clutching her belly while chatting with them, and when they offer her a bite, she politely declines with more smiles.

I wonder what they're talking about or if they even know what kind of guys she's got chasing her. But I wonder most of all what she's thinking about, if she's worried about Heath and Silas, or if she's too busy trying to survive to even care about them.

My phone buzzes, and I check who it is.

Heath: You've got a free hour, right?
Me: Yeah...
Heath: Go talk to her.
Me: I can't lie.
Heath: Try. For me. Please.

I rub my lips together and sigh. It's so, so fucking hard to say no when he asks me like that.

Not that I'd be able to resist talking to a girl like her. It's just that first step that makes me want to run in the opposite direction. She's too beautiful. Too ... mysterious.

I swallow away the nerves and approach while she hasn't seen me yet, but the second I get closer, she looks me right in the eyes.

I freeze, turn around, and walk off.

What the fuck are you even doing, Max?
You pathetic, nervous motherfucker. Get your shit together.

I run another lap around the Skull and Serpent House, but when I get back to the grass, she's gone, along with her friends.

Fuck. I missed my chance.

Goddammit. If you only just gathered the courage to—

"Hey."

I squeal and drop my bottle of water. "Fuck!"

But when I turn to see who spoke, I forget all about the bottle. And my open jaw.

It's her. She's right here in front of me. And even more beautiful up close than I could ever imagine with that silky-smooth hair, olive skin, and plump lips that would make anyone want to kiss them.

And she's talking ... to *me*.

"Hi?" she repeats, making an odd face.

But I still don't know what to say. All I can do is stare. Stare at that gorgeous face, those dark, smoldering eyes I could just ... drown in. Good God.

"Hello? Do you speak English?" she asks again, making signals with her hands, and I realize she's trying to use sign language.

"Oh yeah," I say, blushing like crazy. "Sorry."

"Wow. Okay. Confusing." Her face is all scrunched up because I'm being weird, and I know I am, but my God, even her face like that is nothing short of perfection.

"This might be a weird question," she says, "but are you following me?"

My eyes widen. "No, I—"

"I saw you walking straight at me and then turning around while I was still sitting in the grass, and now you're here again."

Well fuck. Caught red-handed.

"What do you want?"

I don't know what to say. My mind is broken. Completely and utterly broken just from talking to someone like her.

She snorts. "You always sneak up on girls and then pretend you can't talk?"

"No. Not girls—"

She tilts her head and folds her arms. "Boys too?"

"Well, I mean, sure, I don't mind boys." I close my eyes and mentally slap myself. "No. What I meant was that I'm awkward. Not that I sneak up on anyone. I didn't mean to. It just ... happened." I laugh it off as I scratch the back of my head, but at this point, I just sound dumb. "This is not at all what I wanted to say to you."

She frowns, and the way all the hairs in her eyebrows curl and draw together is rather cute. "Then what did you want to say to me?"

Every second feels as though all the beats in my heart are musical notes written in the wind, hoping to flutter into her ears.

She rolls her eyes and bends over to pick up my water bottle at the same time I am, and our hands collide midair. The electricity is instant, and I retract my hand as she grabs the bottle and attempts to give it back.

"So ... care to tell me why a dude from the Skull and Serpent Society is sneaking up on me?" She narrows her eyes. "Because you do realize I *know* you're friends with *them*, right?"

Well damn. For a second there, I almost forgot Silas and Heath existed.

"I just wanted to talk to you," I say.

"Yeah, right."

"No, I mean it." I clear my throat. "I saw you ... before they even noticed you."

She gives me a skeptical look before bursting into laughter. "Good one."

She passes by me and walks off, so I saunter behind her, determined to see this through.

I follow in her footsteps. "Wait. It's not a lie. I'm not here because of them. I want to get to know you."

"Really?" she scoffs. "Why do you even think you want to? Because Silas chased me around?"

"Because you seem nice, and you're... gorgeous."

She pauses for a second. "You think I'm *nice and gorgeous*?" A laugh bursts out of her like she tried to keep it together but failed.

God, why am I such an idiot when it comes to girls? I always know what to say to the guys, but girls? Girls scare me.

"Look, I don't mean this in a bad way, but I don't trust you. You're friends with Rivera and Preston."

"So?" I shrug. I don't see the problem.

"This isn't going to work." She turns around again, but I don't give up that easily.

"Wow. Hold on. You're going to deny me just because of who I hang out with?" I ask.

"Yup. You got that right."

"I'm not my friends," I say.

"But you're close."

"That doesn't mean anything."

"Yeah, it does." Suddenly, she stops in her tracks and looks right at me. "You know why they're after me, right?"

I shrug. "I don't care."

She makes a confused face. "You don't care that I stole from your society?"

I empty my pockets and take out the change. "Steal whatever you want. I'm broke anyway. I don't have anything, so I can't lose anything either. Except my heart."

She snorts. "That doesn't make any sense."

"I know, but neither does my attraction to you, yet here I am."

Her face turns pale as snow, and I realize I may have said that out loud.

Oh fuck.

Suddenly, her stomach growls, and she holds her hands in front of her belly. "You didn't hear that."

"Yes, I did." I smile and place my hand on her shoulder. "I promise you, I am not interested in whatever reason those guys are after you. Just ... let me take you out for a late lunch or early dinner. It's on me."

She eyes me up and down like she's trying to determine the weight of my words.

"I know a fantastic place downtown, Sammy's Sandwich Shop. He has the best teriyaki chicken sandwiches you could ever taste. Like, they make you want to eat ten of them. I'm not kidding. Drool-worthy."

She snorts again, so I add a smile.

"Please?" I murmur. "I know we got off on the wrong foot. But will you please let me take you out for a sandwich?" I ask. "No strings attached."

She sighs out loud and sizes me up again. "Okay, fine."

I make a fist and hiss to myself, "Yes."

But her chuckle clearly gives away that she heard it too. "Just food." She raises a finger. "That's it."

"Got it," I say with a big grin.

She snorts. "You are one persistent motherfucker, you know that?"

A proud smirk forms on my face. "You don't even know how much." I wink. "Meet me by the fountain in an hour."

***

An hour later

I put on my jacket and comb through my hair in the mirror, ensuring I look nice before I waltz out the door. But the minute I do, Heath grabs my shoulders and stops me in my tracks.

"Wow, where are you going dressed up so nicely?"

"Out," I reply.

He frowns. "With who?"

"You *know* who." I make a face. "*You* told me to talk to her."

"Oh ..." His brows wriggle, and he bites the piercing on his lip. "Why didn't you say so?"

I sigh. "Because I don't want you to ruin it."

"Ruin what?" He snorts, and he points at my chest. "Remember why we're doing this."

I roll my eyes. "Yeah, yeah, we're catching a thief."

"Exactly." He fishes a wad of cash from his pocket and stuffs it in my hands. "Keep this. Bring it with you to wherever you're going. Make sure it's visible at some point."

I frown, confused. "Oh-kay..."

What is he trying to do here?

He leans in and whispers, "Don't ask why. Just do it."

His voice lulls me into submission. "Fine."

"Good boy."

My heart beats in my throat, but then he releases me and shoves me out the door. "Have fun with that little thief."

SEVEN

IVY

I'm waiting near the overgrown entrance gates with my bike in my hand when a motorcycle stops right next to me, and for a second, I glare with furrowed brows until he takes off his helmet.

"Max?!"

"In the flesh," he says with a big grin.

"A motorcycle?" I'm impressed. "I didn't peg you as a guy who'd drive one."

He pats the seat behind him. "Hop on."

"What, me? On that thing?"

"Yeah, why not?"

I lift a hand. "No thanks."

I'd rather not jump on a motorcycle with a stranger, and especially not one who's part of the Skull and Serpent Society.

"Well, that's too bad because it gets cold going this fast," he says before putting on his helmet again.

Suddenly, he doesn't look so dorky anymore with that leather outfit. Damn, it really fits him nicely.

"See you down at Sammy's Sandwich Shop, then." He lowers the visor and hits the gas. "Race you there!"

I laugh as he bolts off, and I hop on my bike. The drive down the mountain is easy; it's the way up that always makes me question why I ever enrolled here. But I love the carefree days like these, letting the wind sweep through my hair as I race toward Crescent Vale City down below.

When I'm finally at the shop, of course Max's motorcycle has already been parked out front, and he's sitting smugly by a table, waving at me like I'm fashionably late.

I roll my eyes and wave back, then head inside.

"Nice of you to finally join me," he jests.

I sit down on the seat next to him. "Ha-ha. I'm just glad I didn't die going down the mountain."

"Hey, I drive safely and responsibly," he retorts. "You're just scared, and you won't admit it."

"Sure, I'll admit it." I shrug. "I don't get on motorcycles with strangers."

"Whoa." He puts his hand against his heart. "You think I'm a stranger?"

His obvious sarcasm makes me laugh, and I give him a playful shove.

"No worries, I get it," he says.

"I didn't think you'd be the kind of guy into motorcycles, though," I say.

He leans back. "I just love the freedom my bike gives me. Swerving down the roads, enjoying the breeze." He sighs. "Anyway, are you hungry?"

He calls the server over, and we both order our sandwiches. My stomach is still rumbling, and when it finally gets here, the smell alone makes my mouth water.

I only came along because I was hungry. I don't want my friends to know I don't have the money to buy my own. I struggle to keep up the image, but I don't want them to find out the truth. Especially not now that my life has gotten even more difficult. All the money I had leftover I gave to my neighbor Mrs. Schwartz so she would agree to watch over Cora and keep her safe.

Safe from *them*.

But now I'm sitting here in a sandwich shop with one of them.

Can I even trust him?

The sandwich he bought for me looks amazing, but I'm hesitant to taste it.

"Go on," Max eggs me on. He smiles, the dimples in his cheeks too cute to look away. "I know you're hungry. Just eat. I promise, you'll feel much better afterward."

I take a deep breath and pick up the sandwich. My growling stomach begs me to give it something to digest, and it's very, very hard to ignore with this delicious bread filled with teriyaki chicken right in front of me.

Fine. Eating one sandwich won't hurt, right?

I take a bite and nearly cry happy tears from how good it tastes.

"And?" Max asks. "Good, right?"

I swallow it swiftly, only to chomp on the next bite like a starving animal, nodding between. "God, it's so good."

He smiles proudly. "See? Told you."

"You come here often?" I ask.

"Once a week. Maybe more."

"Wow. I'm impressed," I say, taking a sip of the iced tea he also ordered for me.

"I'm a simple man. When I find food I like, it's all I can think about for like a whole month before I move on to the next thing."

"Interesting."

"I have a very particular palate," he says, laughing at himself. "That's what happens when your dad is a chef. You get picky."

"Your dad's a chef?"

"Yeah, and famous too. Chef Fletcher. You never heard of him?" He takes another bite of his sandwich. "He's on all those cooking shows."

"Oh no, I don't watch television." I take another bite too, trying not to look embarrassed. If he only knew.

"What? Like ... none?"

I shrug. "No time." It's partly true, at least.

"Here." He pulls up his phone and shows me a YouTube video of his dad, and his smile honestly reminds me of Max so much.

"Aw ... that's cute," I say. "He seems very nice."

"Oh yeah, he wouldn't hurt a fly on the wall," Max says. "He's the coolest ever, and most of my half siblings would agree."

"You've got more than just one?" I frown.

He nods and counts them out loud on his fingers. "There's Elliot, my brother, then there's Levi Torres, my older half brother, and Sunny Reed, my older half sister. My mom has three partners. They're poly."

I take a sip of my drink. "Interesting."

Didn't even know that was possible, but to each their own.

"What about your parents? What's your family like?"

"My parents?" I nearly choke on my food. "Oh, uh ... I don't ..." I take a deep breath. "They're not around."

I don't like talking about it because it forces me to face the fact that the one person who always had my back is no longer here. And that fucking hurts.

***

Five years ago

As I head home, I pass by the cemetary, glancing inside the fenced area before brushing off the wind that hits the bruise on my skin. Tears well up in my eyes, and I pull down my sleeve to stop the cold from entering. But another gust that blows through my hair and into my hearing aid makes me stop and stare.

I blow out a breath before I finally decide to head inside.

There is no stone, no marking. No pebbled path or expensive-looking ornament. Not where I'm going.

All that's left for me to stare at is the grass where the soot was discarded and a life was forfeited.

And for what? What grand purpose did his death serve?

My fingers dig into my palm so deeply it begins to bleed.

It shouldn't have to be this way. It was too soon. I'm too young to grieve. Too young to take care of a mother who would rather drown in the idea of romance with dangerous men than live without the love she craves so desperately.

How do we keep going?

My heart weeps, but my tears refuse to budge.

"Why ...?" I say through gritted teeth, my knees slowly sinking to the grass. "Why do I have to do this without you?"

I lower my head and touch the grassy ground underneath me, wishing I could rip out this heart so it wouldn't have to hurt anymore.

"I miss you, Dad..."

Fuck cancer.

***

Present

"Oh, I'm sorry." Max puts down his food. "I didn't mean to pry."

"It's fine. You couldn't have known." I smile to ease the tension, but my throat feels dry. "Besides, I don't need them. I can take care of myself."

"I can tell," he muses. "I mean, you go to this prestigious university and manage to hold your own."

"I wouldn't say that too loudly," I muse, taking another bite.

"But you've got your own place, right?"

"Yeah, but it's not much."

"But you worked hard for it," he says, taking a sip of his iced tea.

"Right ..."

"I think that's amazing. You don't need your parents to succeed," he says, making me feel a little prouder of my accomplishments.

"Thanks," I say, finishing my food. "I appreciate it. The food as well."

"Don't mention it," he says. "Besides, can't let a lady go hungry." He adds a wink, making my heart flutter a little.

Maybe not all of the Skull and Serpent Society guys are evil. "You know, you're not half bad."

He laughs. "Thanks. You're not half too bad yourself either."

I snort and playfully shove him. "You know what I mean."

"Yeah." He pulls out his phone. "Before I forget, lemme give you my number so you can always reach me."

I frown, confused about how we got to this point so easily already, but I'm not going to say no either. I take out my phone and copy his number.

"Thanks."

"My pleasure." He keeps staring at me with those soulful eyes like he's taking in every inch of my face, and something about that makes me look away so he doesn't see me blush.

"Those things in your ears..."

I frown. "Oh. They're hearing aids."

I take them out and show them to him, and he seems intrigued. I can see his mouth move but can't hear anything, so I sign to him.

Can't hear you.

He sheepishly looks at me for a few seconds before he hands them back, and I swiftly tuck them into my ears. "Sorry," he mutters. "I didn't realize."

"It's okay."

"So you can't hear at all without them?" he asks.

I shake my head. "Barely. I may hear some loud noise, but that's it."

"Does it bother you at all?"

"No. I was born with it, so this is all I've ever known."

He leans on his hand as he seems even more fascinated. "Wow, so you got those when you were a kid?"

"Not these specifically since they're too big for kid's ears. But I did have similar ones when I was a kid, yeah."

"But I just saw you sign."

"My parents wanted me to learn how to speak in both languages so I could always navigate the world, even without my hearing aids."

"That's wonderful. I love how you just did that with your hands so fluently. Now I wish I could use sign language too."

A smug smile forms on my face. "It's never too late to learn."

"You know what? You're right. Maybe I should start."

I take another sip of my iced tea, feeling good about this whole thing. Maybe he could be a friend after all.

"Can I ask you something?" he says, pausing for a second. "Why did you steal from them?"

My eyes widen.

"If you're able to attend Spine Ridge, you don't need the cash, right?"

The sudden shift in his tone doesn't go unnoticed.

"I have a scholarship." I get up from my seat.

"Silas found your hearing aid." Even his face has darkened significantly.

Panic boils up to the surface, so I do the first thing I can think of: Run. "I need to go to the bathroom."

I bail before he can say another word and lock myself in a stall in the women's bathroom. I sit down and bury my face in my hands. I shouldn't have come here with him, but my hungry ass was too enamored with the possibility that someone could want to buy me food to realize it might all just be a trick.

My phone buzzes, and I check my messages.

Neighbor: I need more. The kid is whining for food, and I don't have enough in my pantry, and yours is empty.

I bought enough groceries to last us at least three days, so I don't know where she put it all. But I can't let Cora go without food either. I sigh out loud.

Me: I'll send some money so you can go buy something. Don't worry.
Neighbor: Good, because this kid is eating the table right now.

Cora's always putting her teeth into everything. The kid just likes sensory play. It's nothing weird to me, but I guess my neighbor isn't used to it.

I check my wallet. Empty. Of course.

Then I check my online bank account. Pennies.

Goddammit, this fucking scholarship is never going to cut it. Most of the money goes straight to Spine Ridge U, and what's left for me is not enough. Losing my job at the RIVERA club because of those fuckers really fucked with my income.

I need to make sure Cora's taken care of, and for that to happen, I need money. Now.

I get out of the bathroom and look around to see if Max is still there, but he appears to have left his drink unattended. I glare at the men's bathroom, and the door just closed shut.

He must've gone to the bathroom too. This is my shot.

I walk to where we were sitting, trying to be as inconspicuous as possible while the shop owner and all the other customers aren't looking as I slip my hand down the pockets of Max's jacket. I pull out a soft leather pouch and fish a couple of bills out, then tuck it back into his jacket. All within mere seconds.

I scoot back my chair and walk out the door with a racing heart, knowing full well I just robbed the only guy who was nice to me. But he's part of their society, part of their friend group, part of the rich upper class. I don't feel sorry. I need this money more than he does.

So I slip away before he realizes I've disappeared.

***

MAX

When I return from the bathroom, the chair she was sitting in is still empty.

"Oh, that's odd," I mutter to myself.

I keep my eyes fixated on the women's bathroom, hoping to see her walk out too, but when I get back to the seats we had, I notice my wallet is hanging partially out of my jacket.

I fish it out and check the contents.

There are fewer bills than what I came here with.

"Oh no," I murmur. "What have you done, Ivy?"

My phone buzzes, and I check the messages.

Heath: She took the bait. Good job, Max.
Silas: I fucking knew it was her.

My stomach begins to churn uncomfortably.

Silas: She's ours now.

The car outside begins to skid across the pavement, and I peer outside, straight into Silas's piercing eyes.

Fuck.

EIGHT

IVY

I ride my bike as fast as I can up the hill where Spine Ridge University is situated. The steep and curvy road follows a mountain path surrounded by pine trees. Every day, I made this trek up and down the mountain to attend the university while I still slept in my own home. But now that I have those Skull & Serpent guys after me, I can't risk going home and putting Cora's safety in jeopardy, so I've opted to stay somewhere else for the time being, somewhere far less cozy.

Joining a sorority this late in the year was out of the question, not to mention that I can't pay the associated costs. My only option was an abandoned house halfway up the mountain road, colloquially known as The Shack.

There are a few empty rooms and lots of stains on the flooring and walls, but there's one relatively clean room upstairs with a dirty bed where I've put a new sleeping mat and a blanket on the floor. It's better than sleeping on that filthy bed or out in the cold air, and it's already getting darker outside.

But with every push of the pedal, my eyes can't help stray to the car persistently driving behind me. There are no streetlights for me to see who it is, nor are there lights turned on inside the car. But I can definitely tell it's driving far slower than it should be ... and it's been like this for the past fifteen minutes.

I glance over my shoulder again and try to peer inside the vehicle, but no matter how hard I pinch my eyes, I can't fucking see.

"Goddammit," I growl, nearly crashing on my bike, but I catch myself by swerving around the road.

I come to a stop in front of The Shack and swiftly chuck my bike into the grass before I head inside and shut the door. With labored breathing, I make my way to the living room and lean over the couch, ripping away at the wood that blocks the window until I've managed to peel off a corner. I peer through the hole I created and nervously look around the premise and all the overgrown bushes and weeds.

But then I spot that same car, parked a few feet away from the house.

I do a double take. Something flickers between the trees in Priory Forest and I suck in a breath.

Is it a flashlight? No.

An LED purge mask. Not one, but two.

And the guys wearing them are dressed in all-black streetwear, including chains and a white Skull and Serpent Society logo on the front of their shirts.

Silas and Heath ... are marching straight toward me.

Panicking, I crawl backward, falling off the couch headfirst.

"Fuck," I groan, rubbing my head before I get to my feet.

I have to get out of here, fast. But how? Where?

I run into the kitchen and rummage at the door, but it's locked and bolted shut.

"Shit!" I growl, and I run back through the living room and bolt upstairs, skipping several steps.

Right as I enter the bedroom door, there's a loud banging noise downstairs.

I shut the door and hide under the bed.

WHAM!

The front door is knocked open, and I jolt up against the wooden slats of the bed.

"Oh, Ivy ..."

His voice makes all the hairs on the back of my neck stand up.

"I'm baa-hack!"

It's really them.

"Miss me?"

An unsettling laugh makes me shudder underneath the bed.

If I stay here, they'll definitely find me, but where else am I supposed to go? The doors are locked. The only way out ... is running straight into their arms.

"You know you can't hide from me, right?"

Crack. Crack. Crack.

His footsteps as he heads up the stairs make my heartbeat shoot through the roof.

"Little thief, little thief ... let me come in."

Fuck.

I fish into my pocket and search for the only thing that can help me right now. My little pocket knife that I always carry with me.

"Not by the hair on my chinny, chin, chin."

That was definitely Heath. His voice is much, much lower than Silas's ... and much more ominous.

Crack. Crack. Crack.

Silas laughs. "Then I'll huff, and I'll puff, and I'll blow your house in."

WHAM!

The door to the bedroom is slammed open, and I hold my breath.

They're here.

I swiftly cover my body with the blanket I bought underneath the bed.

"I'm impressed at your ability to lie, twig," Silas says.

"Almost had me fooled too," Heath adds as they enter.

I can see their black-laced boots as they waltz around the room, searching every nook and cranny. The closet is thrown open, all the contents that were left spilling out onto the wooden flooring. Objects are smashed against the walls, windows are torn open, and not even the bed is spared.

That's when I spot him. Bent over. Looking straight at me.

Heath.

Strands of his painted brown hair fall over his face as he gazes around, and I can see it all right through the fabric of the blanket. Our eyes actually connect. But for some reason ... he doesn't see me.

He grunts and stands up again, and the footsteps sound farther and farther away.

Did they leave?

I wait a few more seconds, my ragged breath the only sound I hear as I clutch my knife so hard it feels like my fingers might break.

After a while, I push the blanket off me and look out from underneath the bed. They're not in the room anymore. I have to be quick.

I crawl to my feet, kick off my shoes, and run to the stairs in my socks, praying they won't hear as they search the other rooms. One. Two. Three steps down.

CRACK.

My pupils dilate.

"There!"

Heath's voice sets me off, and I race down the stairs as fast as I can and storm out the door. I can hear them bolt down the stairs behind me as I run to the side of the house where I left my bike, but my eyes widen as I come to a full halt.

The front wheel has been taken off.

Oh God.

The front door slams open.

Shit, no time to think.

I run off into Priory Forest, not even checking where I'm going as I need to get away from them as quick as possible. I fall over a couple of rocks and catch myself on the ground, grazing my skin until it bleeds, but I still keep going. Because when I glance over my shoulder, two dark figures are chasing my tracks, their masks like warning signals beaming through the woods.

"Keep running, little thief!" Silas's voice booms through the woods. "I'm still going to catch you."

He's insane. He's completely, utterly insane!

I go to the left and zigzag downhill through the forest, trying to shake them off by disappearing in the sea of leaves, but every time I look, they're still there, running after me like hounds who've been set loose ... and I'm the prey they're going to catch.

"Run all you want, but there's no escaping us, Ivy," Heath calls out.

I glance over my shoulder.

THWACK!

A knife whooshes right past me and lands in the tree beside my face, barely avoiding my skin.

I rip it out and keep running as I tuck it into my pocket. If they don't stop coming after me, then at least I'll be ready when they pounce on me.

"Yes, that's it. Run, little thief," Silas growls. "Do you even know how badly it turns me on?"

A maniacal laughter follows that makes me acutely aware of every step I take.

My feet hurt from running across gravel and uneven ground with only socks on, but I refuse to give up. I have to get out before they find me, but they're slowly catching up to me with every passing minute.

I only have one choice—lay low and hide.

From the corner of my eye, I spot an alcove with an overhanging rock overgrown with bushes, and I make a beeline for it when they're momentarily out of sight. I jump underneath and throw a whole pile of leaves on top of my body while I make myself as tiny as possible.

The wind blows through the trees, making them sound alive as they creak with movement, the howling noise making me shiver. But I stay put with my breath held and my body stiff as can be while their footsteps close in.

"Oh, twig, where are you hiding?" Silas yells.

"Come out now, and we might go easy on you," Heath adds, but I can hear them snigger at each other.

Lies.

Even though I can't see them, I can hear them circling the area, kicking leaves aside with every step. And then ... nothing.

The wait seems forever.

Did they bolt off in a different direction?

My eyes open slightly, and I gaze around through the debris I stacked on top of myself while hidden in this alcove.

Maybe I managed to shake them off?

I take in a deep breath as my eyes skid across the forest floor. I don't hear a single step.

"Nothing excites me more than hunting a wicked ... little ... thief."

His voice is the first thing I hear before sparkling green eyes connect with mine ... floating right above me. A devilishly sharp grin grows behind the mask as Silas leans over the stone.

"Boo."

NINE

MAX

I jump on my motorcycle, put on my helmet, and race across town. There's no time to waste. They've already caught her, I'm sure of it.

Heath should've told me they'd follow me to the sandwich shop, but of course he didn't.

Does he even trust me?

I already thought it was weird Heath handed me those bills. I should've put two and two together. He wanted me to be her honey trap.

I make my way up the mountain slope, zigzagging across the road to avoid fallen rocks. It's hard and perilous with that steep drop-off right beside the road, but I know how to stay out of danger. At least when it comes to nature.

I push the throttle to go faster and faster, trying not to lose my grip as I pass The Shack, a long-abandoned house on the hills rumored to be filled with the ghosts of murder victims.

But when a scream emanates from the woods behind the house, I hit the brakes.

"Ivy," I mutter to myself.

That was definitely her.

I turn my motorcycle around and race toward the house, then head off the beaten path and into the woods. Brambles and bushes hit me around the ears, and a scrape on my shin makes me hiss. This forest is too dense to continue by motorbike, so I park it against a tree, take off my helmet, then run farther on foot.

I'm too far away for them to see me, but I see *them*.

Two masked men, hovering near a stone alcove in the middle of the woods.

I slide behind two trees and hide, observing from afar ... wondering what they're going to do to her.

Wondering if it would ruin her to know that it excites me to watch.

***

SILAS

One shriek from her throat is all I need to feel alive.

Before she's even managed to move a single muscle, I jump off the rock and grasp her by the legs to drag her out of the alcove and into the open forest. She kicks me and scratches at the ground, nails digging into the soil, but all it does is get me fired up.

She fishes a knife from her pocket and swings at me, but I knock it out of her hand with ease.

"Nowhere to run to now, little thief," I say. "You're *mine*."

She doesn't know who she's messed with, but now she'll definitely find out the hard way.

"Let go of me!" she shrieks.

She's flipped on her belly from all the thrashing, but it won't stop me. Nothing will.

I laugh and call out to Heath, "Found her!"

He runs out of the forest. "Good catch," he says as he runs up to me and takes one of her legs to help me drag her away from her hideout.

"This little thief thought she could wait it out," I say as I crawl on top of her. "But I know how to hunt my prey."

She grabs a rock off the forest floor and attempts to smash me in the head, but I pin down her wrist before she even has the chance.

A filthy grin spreads from ear to ear as I admire my prize, and I lean in to whisper, "You're a violent little thief."

"Fuck you!" she growls, attempting to slap me as she flips on her back, but I swiftly dodge.

"I like the mouth on this one." Heath laughs as he goes to his knees near her head and holds down her wrists. "I can't wait to hear what it sounds like when she moans our names."

"In your fucking dreams," she hisses.

"No ..." With a mere inch between her skin and mine, my hand travels all the way from her belly to her neck, my lips hovering so close to her face I can almost taste her fear. "You won't need to sleep to feel my presence. I will make every day a living nightmare." I grip her throat and squeeze until she squeaks. "Until you give me back what you stole from me."

"I. Can't."

My eyes narrow. "What's that?" I lean in with my ear to her lip. "I can't hear you."

"Don't. Have. It."

Her eyes are slowly turning away, so I release the pressure, and she sucks in a breath.

"Liar," I grit.

"It's not a lie!" she yells back. "I didn't—"

"Steal?" Heath interjects, holding up a few bills. "I just fished these out of your pocket while Silas was busy teasing you."

"You don't have proof," she says. "That's my money."

He laughs and grabs his cell phone, shining light through the bill until our marking becomes visible, and I can literally see all the color drain from her face. All that blood pooling somewhere else ... somewhere much, much lower, and I can't wait to fucking taste it.

"We marked them."

Her eyes widen. "Max."

The fucking shock riddling her face is the greatest thing ever. Fuck, we should've done this much sooner.

"That's right, twig. This is our proof. We tricked you like you tricked us." I lean in to whisper into her ear, "Time's up ... payday is here."

"What?" she murmurs.

"No one steals from us without paying a hefty price," Heath says, digging his nails into her wrists.

"I don't have the money!" she yells.

"Oh, now you admit you stole from us?" Heath's brow piercing moves as his forehead muscles pinch.

"What do you mean 'you don't have it'?" I plant my fists beside her face. "What the fuck did you do with *my* money?"

She gulps. "It's gone."

"Where?"

"Used. For bills and food."

Heath frowns, while my brow begins to twitch.

"Bills and food?" I snort, but it swiftly turns into full-blown laughter. "Bullshit, that was five grand. There's no way you spent it all." I fish my knife from my pocket and hold it under her neck. "Where is it?"

"I'm telling you the truth," she grits, eyes filled with rage. "I don't have it anymore."

"What about the phones?" Heath grits.

"I sold them for more cash," she replies.

I frown. "What about the little box underneath my bed?"

"What?" she mutters.

"The red flower," I say through gritted teeth.

"Why would that be important? It was plastic."

I grip her tightly. "Tell me what you did with it!"

Her eyes widen in shock. "I gave it to a girl ... on the streets."

My teeth nearly grind off a chip.

She gave my flower to a random fucking girl on the streets?

"It wasn't yours to give away," I hiss.

"You should've known better than to steal from Serpents," Heath growls.

With my blade, I tip up her chin far enough and force her to look into my eyes. I have to admit the droplets of blood rolling down her skin entice me.

"You think I do any of this for the fun of it?!" she yells. "You think I stole from Max because I enjoyed it?!"

"Yes. To see the look on his face when he realized his money was gone," I reply.

"Laughable. Like I don't have something better to do than look at spoiled assholes."

My eye twitches, and I shove the blade farther into her skin. "Watch it."

Heath snorts. "Don't taunt him, little thief. You'll get more than you bargained for."

"You don't fucking know me," she says.

My eyes narrow as I push the blade deeper into her skin. "No? Well, we're about to get very acquainted." I draw a line from her neck all the way down to her heart, watching her squirm underneath me. "Remember what I told you in that bathroom?"

She swallows, blood droplets rolling down her delectable skin. "Are you going to pay me back with money ..." I push the blade into her shirt right where her nipples are. "Or with skin?" I cut through the fabric with expert precision until the only thing between the blade and her is her bra. "Now tell me ... What do you prefer, little thief?"

***

IVY

What am I supposed to do? How am I going to get out of this alive?

I can't get away from them. Heath's got me pinned, and Silas has all his weight on my thighs.

"I don't have any money, and I can't pay it back. I don't have a job anymore thanks to you!" I yell, gazing up at Heath, hoping it'll help to pin the blame on him.

"He came to visit me at Club RIVERA during my shift. It's because of him that I had to take extra precautions and leave Club RIVERA abruptly."

Silas narrows his eyes at him, and I glance between them.

He ... doesn't know?

"I gave her a warning she'd remember," Heath says.

So they operate separately from each other? This could be my only advantage.

"I have nothing to give you," I swiftly say. "But if you can get me a job, I—"

"*Nothing?*" Silas repeats, hung on that single word.

He raises a brow, pushing the knife farther into the thin layer of fabric separating the metal from my bare nipple.

Fuck.

His teeth glint in the dark, a smile so vicious it's almost more frightening than the knife in his hand. "I thought I made myself clear. You're not getting out of this. And if you don't have the money to pay ..."

He wants my skin.

He wants to make me bleed, crack me open, and split me in half ... kill me.

I shudder as he brings the knife to my mouth and slowly lowers the bottom half, blood caking my lip.

"You will have to earn every fucking dollar back," he whispers as the knife pushes into my mouth and across my tongue. He wets his lips as he slowly drags it out across my tongue, leaving a trail of blood. "What will you do, twig?"

I have nothing left to offer ... nothing except ... Myself.

"Anything," I say, letting go of my soul along with those words.

Because both of these boys know as well as I do what it means.

What that word unlocks ...

What it will cost me.

Everything.

His eyes flicker with interest. *"Anything?"* he parrots like he can't believe his ears.

A tear wells up in my eyes, but I push it back and nod softly.

There's no taking it back.

This is it.

This is the trade-off.

That money I needed so dearly to keep my head above water cost me my body. My freedom. My soul.

He grins, baring sharp, wolf-like teeth before his smile slowly turns into a diabolical laugh. "You don't know what you're offering."

"You want to play with me, don't you?" I grit. "Then do whatever you want. I don't care. My body ... for the money."

"Don't tempt him," Heath says.

"Too late," Silas growls, pulling the knife from my mouth. "I accept."

Heath laughs, the sound filling the forests around us with echoes. "I'm curious how far you're willing to go," Heath says, leaning over to look me in the eyes. "Because we're not going to go easy on you."

"What?" I stammer, seeing the excitement in their eyes.

Silas rips the mask off his face, revealing his bloodshot eyes and the insane grin that makes my blood run cold. "You're mine now."

TEN

SILAS

A thief ... offering her body to *me*?

And here I was thinking I couldn't laugh harder. I've never been offered a better toy in my life.

"Tie her up," I tell Heath.

"Wait, what?" she protests, but I cover her mouth with my hand.

"You offered ... and I've taken the deal. Now I wanna play with my new, dirty, little thief."

I wink at Heath, who rips his own belt through the hoops and swiftly ties it around her wrists, kneeling on the long end of the belt so it's secured in place. This fucking thief is not going anywhere ... and it's time to pay for her fucking crimes.

"You've got guts, twig, I admit. But you seriously don't know what you signed up for ... so let me show you how depraved I can get. Maybe then you'll regret stealing from me."

The flicker of fear in those deep brown eyes makes my cock rock hard.

Then she bites down on my finger.

My nostril twitches, and I push my finger deeper into her mouth, savoring the pain.

"You wanted a taste? Here. Taste my fucking blood, thief. You won't get another chance."

She spits out my finger and yells, "You're fucked up."

I laugh. Loudly. Wildly.

What else should I do when someone tells me the fucking obvious?

"You thought I didn't know?" The look of terror on her face gets me going. "The only one here who didn't was you, apparently. But you're about to find out how truly fucked up I can get."

I pull my fingers away from her teeth and slowly wrap them around her neck one by one, watching her struggle to suck in the oxygen like a fish out of water. I choke her until she practically begs me with her eyes to give her the life she's so desperately trying to hold on to.

Sometimes, maybe one second of the day, I wish I wasn't such a fucked-up lunatic who enjoys the pain of others. But then that one second passes, and I'm back to my crazed self. I don't fucking give a care in the fucking world what anyone thinks about that, and especially not this girl.

"Are you going to be a good little thief or a bad one?" I growl. "Nod if you'll behave."

She moves her head up and down, and I release the pressure just enough to allow her to gasp.

God, that fucking sound makes my dick twitch.

"Good girl," Heath groans, clearly enjoying this by the size of the bulge in his pants.

"Already rewarding her for good behavior?" I say. "And we haven't even started toying with her yet."

"Gotta give her some motivation," he retorts, wriggling his brows.

I like how his brain works.

I put my knife against her chest and push it into her shirt. "Now ... how much were you willing to give me again?"

RIP!

I cut through the fabric with ease, exposing her tits to the dark of the night and our wild eyes. And fuck me, they are small and pointy, just how I like them.

"Nice tits, twig," I groan.

"Fuck you," she growls.

I stick the pointy end of the knife into her chest, right between those pretty tits.

"You always this foulmouthed to the person holding the knife?"

She makes a face. "You won't kill me."

A filthy grin spreads on my cheeks. "How are you so sure of yourself?"

"Because you took the deal," Heath interjects.

I narrow my eyes at him. He's not supposed to take her side.

"Do what you want," she says, averting her eyes. "I don't care."

So easy to throw away her body like it means nothing to her ... I wonder why.

"You." I point my knife at her face. "Eyes on me."

"Fuck y—"

She stops the second I grip her nipple and twist, swallowing down the scream she really, really wants to let out.

"Give me your scream, little thief."

When she doesn't react, I lean over and cover her nipple with my mouth instead, lavishing it with licks and nibbles until she's squirming beneath me.

"See? You know how it works. Now let me hear." I bite down.

A squeal follows, and it makes my cock nearly break through my pants.

Fuck me.

This is what I live for, what I'd literally kill for.

"That's our good girl." Heath leans over to lick her other nipple like he's enjoying a lollypop.

"Had enough yet?" she asks.

I lean sideways so she can see me. "You think this is it? We've only just started."

I lower myself down her body until I'm right between her legs, which I force apart.

"What are you doing?" she asks.

"You thought you could steal from me without giving me something in return?" I slide the knife down her belly and into her pants. "I'll take, and take, and take from you and use your body as I see fit until you have nothing left to give, and even then ..." A dirty grin spreads on my face. "I'll take more."

POP!

"Until every last inch of your body belongs to *me*."

I tear away the button that keeps her pants together, and in one swift yank, I have them down her thighs. Pussy never fails to excite me, but this one right here ... this is what I'll fucking savor.

"Don't claim her all for yourself," Heath groans, rubbing himself right through his pants.

"You can have her mouth ... this pussy is mine."

I cut through the fabric of her panties and rip them off, watching her face begin to glow with heat. She jerks on the belt around her wrist, but it's no use. Heath is right there to keep her in place.

I lean in to take a whiff of my prey, the delectable scent of pussy making me hungry, greedy ... animalistic.

"This pussy is begging to be punished ..." I murmur, fanning hot air across until she begins to squirm. "And I know just how."

I firmly grab the knife and hold it over her skin while I lower myself and take the first lick. I can taste the fear, and what an aphrodisiac, fuck.

I push the knife into her skin and watch the blood droplet roll down into her slit.

"Fuck!" she hisses.

I lap it up and spread it all over her clit, which thumps under my tongue.

"I'm going to make you wish you never laid eyes on my prized possessions," I say, licking her until she begins to squirm while firmly clutching the knife as it slowly pierces her skin. "By marking you as *my* prize."

***

Marking ... me?

I can't even process what it means before Silas digs the sharp end of the knife into my skin beneath my belly button, making me hiss.

"Yes, that's it ... make those sounds," he groans.

He licks my clit at the same time, causing excitement and fear to ripple through my body simultaneously. Warm blood trickles down my skin, and each of my blood droplets is caught by his eager tongue.

This is insane. He's crazy. Completely, out of his mind demented.

He's going to mark me as his?

The knife drags down my skin, the pain so sharp I let out a whimper, and Silas literally moans into my slit.

"Fuck yes, that's it." He laps me up like there's no tomorrow, causing equal amounts of pleasure and pain, and with every passing second, I become more and more confused.

"Scream for me, little slut. Let me hear you scream."

I refuse. I can take a cut. He won't get his fix, not from me.

"Go on, make a sound," he whispers into my pussy as he looks up at me from underneath thick eyelashes, rolling his tongue around to catch all the droplets. "I know you want to."

"Fuck you," I spit instead, watching his eyes twitch. "What the hell are you drawing?"

I may have lost my body, but I still have my defiance, and I'll be damned if I let go of that.

But Silas merely laughs. "You'll see when I'm done with you."

His tongue rolls around my slit again, and it feels so good I temporarily lose focus on the fact that he's piercing my skin.

"God, I'm so going to fucking enjoy seeing you punish her," Heath groans, leaning over to lavish my nipples with more kisses and licks.

It's incredibly hard to focus, but Silas reminds me of his torment by coaxing out more blood. He enjoys seeing me ache because, with every stroke, he gazes up to see the look on my face, all while licking me like his life depends on it. And I'm lost in a confusing clash of soreness and bliss because of that damn tongue of his.

Suddenly, two fingers enter me, and I gasp.

"I can feel your wetness, little slut," he groans. "You're enjoying this, aren't you?"

No, I'd never, ever admit that to myself or to him. Never.

I jerk around in the belt because right now, I wish nothing more than to slap him in the face so hard he'll see fucking stars for daring to remind me of my own pleasure building up.

Heath snorts. "It's no use, thief, I know how to tie a knot."

"Fuck you," I spit at him.

"Say that again, and I might just fucking do it," he retorts.

Silas's knife pushes even deeper into my pubic area, and I tilt my head back to bite my tongue. The way his tongue circles my most sensitive spot and his fingers roll around inside me almost makes it feel like he's a goddamn expert, and it's so hard not to react. Every inch of pain he gives me is accompanied by mind-blowing pleasure, and I can't tell the two apart anymore.

This is what he wants ... to wreck me, completely.

And he's only just begun.

Each letter he carves makes me bite my lip so I don't let out a sound. But goddamn, is he making it hard on me.

I'm panting, trying to catch my breath, but then Heath starts to fumble with his zipper right above me.

SLAP!

I yelp and nearly buckle from the sizzle of a flat hand on my pussy.

"Eyes on me, slut," Silas growls. "Look at me while I lick this pussy like no one else ever fucking has."

"You deranged motherfucker," I growl.

He merely laughs. "I like this dynamic we've got going on here. But you will lay still and take it like a good girl, won't you?" He runs his fingers through the wound he just created, and I hiss from the ache. He lifts his fingers to his lips, and his tongue dips out to lick the blood, *my* blood, off the tips.

Holy shit.

"Because you agreed to be my little plaything," he says, a wicked grin on his face, "and there's no coming back from that."

Another painful gash is applied, and deep down in the dark corners of my mind, I begin to wonder what it is he's drawing on me. And whether it's supposed to feel so goddamn good to be hurt.

But it's no use. I can't see, and no matter how many times I'd ask, he wouldn't answer.

"How much more?" I ask.

"You will take every inch of this blade and my fucking tongue before I will ever let you off the hook," he growls.

He flicks my clit with his tongue until my eyes nearly roll into the back of my head. "Please," I mutter as I close my eyes.

"Hear that, Heath?" he murmurs from between my legs. "That sounds like a thief begging for mercy."

But when I open my eyes, there's a dick right in front of my face. It's huge, at least seven, maybe eight inches of thick, veiny hardness with multiple piercings, including a reverse Prince Albert through the tip.

Heath tilts his head, a bemused smile on his face. "Like what you see?"

"Fuck you," I hiss.

"Better put that filthy mouth to good use," Silas groans, swiveling his tongue around until I can barely focus.

Heath grips my chin and forces my head back. "Open up, thief. Let me see if you can take my cum as easy as you took my money."

He pushes down on my lips, and before I know it, he's pushed the tip all the way across my tongue and into my mouth.

He barely fits in my mouth, not only the length, but the girth too.

"Make her gag," Silas growls.

Heath pushes even farther, going past my uvula and into my throat. God, I can feel each and every one his piercings as they rub against my tongue.

"Fuck, you have such a tight little throat," Heath groans, tilting his head back. "Almost makes me forget..."

Forget. Something I wish I could after tonight, but these boys will never let me.

But what could he possibly want to forget?

My teeth scrape against his length as I try not to choke while simultaneously trying to ignore the tongue gyrating between my legs ... but it's no use. These boys have my head spinning, and the longer it goes on, the deeper I sink into their madness.

***

HEATH

I've felt my fair share of tongues before, but never one so filthy and willing to spew rage. Most girls who come into the Skull and Serpent Society house practically beg me to take them to my room and fuck them in every orifice. But this girl? She hates our fucking guts.

Which is why it's the most arousing thing I've ever done. Fuck.

My dick slips so easily down her wet throat, and I can't help grasp her neck to feel my length deep inside her. The thrill of toying with our prey has me groaning out loud.

"Fuck, we should've done this sooner."

I pull out for a second to allow her to breathe, and she gasps for air, but the second she tries to spit out more swear words, I thrust right back in.

"Don't use that tongue for swearing, put it to better use," I say, gripping her face tightly. "Wrap it around my cock and suck."

She struggles with my size, but it only makes me harder.

Silas laughs. "That's it; slip that cock down her throat and make her choke on it."

"I know how to fuck a pretty throat when I see one. You focus on licking that pussy."

"I'll do what I damn well want to," he retorts, and he punctures her skin with his knife again, writing the next letter onto her skin while he laps up the blood like an animal in heat. "And this slut will take whatever I have to give."

He slaps her pussy, and it makes her jolt up and down, her moans reverberating through my dick, and my balls tighten from how good it feels.

"Her sounds are the icing on the cake," Silas says, flicking his knife around.

"I'll give her some icing," I say, grinning like a crazed motherfucker as I slide in deeper and deeper.

She gargles, and I pull out for a moment.

"One. Two. Three."

Her eyes widen. "I—" I grin and shove right back in again, watching her struggle with the limited amount of oxygen I allowed her.

What she doesn't understand is that her body no longer belongs to her.

It belongs to *us* now.

I thrust and thrust, spreading her own saliva all over her face before I dive back in again, making her filthier with every stroke of my cock.

Oh yes, I will very much fucking enjoy playing with this newfound toy.

Maybe this girl … will finally make me get over it.

This girl right here with her filthy mouth and her greedy little lips, sucking me dry as she tries her best to atone for her sin. Every one of my thrusts is matched by a swirl of Silas's tongue around her most sensitive spot, causing her whole body to spasm from the stimulation.

"Yes, that's it. Earn back your fucking innocence," I growl, burying myself to the hilt just so I can grab her nipples with both hands and twist. When I pull out, she sucks in the air like it's her final breath. "Whose body is this?"

"Mine," she retorts.

Silas marks her skin with the blade, making her muscles strain, only for her to relapse into arousal the second his tongue hits her clit. "Wrong."

"Open your damn mouth," I tell her.

When she does, I spit inside and push her mouth shut. "Now swallow." After a few seconds, she finally does what I say. "Good girl." A smug smile spreads on my face. "Now, who does this mouth belong to?"

She coughs. "You."

"And who does this fucking pussy belong to?" Silas slaps it for good measure.

"You." She makes a face, almost like she hates the mere idea of saying it out loud.

She bargained for this, and she will learn what it means to make a deal with evil incarnate. We don't fucking play nice.

"Now ... give me one more scream," Silas growls, and he carves the final letter into her skin and sucks up the blood like a goddamn vampire.

I pull out of her right when he finishes and discards the knife. Her moan echoes through the woods, along with his roars as he pulls his rock-hard cock from his pants and covers her pussy with cum.

ELEVEN

IVY

Fuck. Did Silas just ... come?

I can't see a thing with Heath hovering over me, but my skin burns and aches.

"Now take me deep," Heath groans before thrusting back into my mouth again.

He scrapes the back of my throat as he enters, forcing himself all the way down until he hits the base and then some.

His hard-on pulsates inside me while I struggle in the restraints he put on me.

I can't breathe, can't think, can't even make a sound as my senses are bombarded from both ends.

One inside my throat, and one still swiveling his tongue around my pussy like he wants to devour it whole.

"You're going to come for me now," Silas groans.

"What?" I mutter between thrusts, but Heath keeps me too busy to form a proper sentence.

This wasn't part of the deal. They could do what they want, but that doesn't include me giving them—

"Did you honestly think I would be satisfied with your blood alone?" he growls into my skin, nibbling at my clit. "Either you come ... or I will make you, and you won't like how."

Shit. I don't think I have a choice, but this asshole thrusting into my mouth makes it so hard to concentrate.

"And you will do it with my cock down your throat too," Heath adds, spitting right into my face. "Because you're our good fucking slut."

I gasp for air as he pulls out, only to squirm from the way Silas licks me.

"Fine. Have it your way," Silas says.

He pulls his fingers out of me and picks up the knife instead.

"What are you—" My words are interrupted by a strangled moan as he inserts the handle of the knife into me. "I told you to come. And you will fucking come for me."

I can't believe he's fucking me with the back end of his knife.

That he's licking his own cum off my slit, mixing it with my blood like he enjoys the taste of us both together.

That he's slowly turning my mind inside out with pure depravity.

And that I'm slowly getting near to that edge of no return.

"Do it. Come for me, and you might live to see another day," he groans, flicking the tip of his tongue across my clit so good I swear I might pass out. The knife is inside me, prodding and poking against my G-spot until all that leaves my mouth are whimpers between each of Heath's thrusts.

Heath slowly pulls out, only to impale me once again, and my entire body feels like it's on fire from the sheer need coursing through my veins.

What is wrong with me? Why do I feel aroused?

"You look so good when you're being ruined," Heath says, leaning forward to grab my breasts. "Now swallow me down like a good girl."

I gulp and gulp and gulp until his cock begins to thicken, and my body can't withstand the licks any longer. My muscles tighten as Silas hits that spot with both his tongue and his knife, twisting and turning the handle until I release all the pent-up desire into a tsunami of wetness and ecstasy as I come undone.

"Fuck yes, she's coming," Silas says.

"I'm going to fill you up, little thief," Heath groans before warm semen shoots down my throat. I'm helpless to stop it as the salty taste fills my mouth, and the spurts gush down into my stomach, his orgasm feeling never-ending.

When he finally pulls out, I cough and heave to suck in the oxygen.

"Stay. Swallow it down," Heath warns, firm hands keeping me steady. "Or I'll make you regret it."

I push myself to keep it together even though my legs are literally trembling. My brain has floated off into the unknown. Sweet, sweet nirvana ... beyond destruction.

I can still taste him on my tongue, still feel the burn on my skin right below my belly button... still feel my clit thumping with a need for more.

More of whatever fucked-up shit this was.

But my body is completely wasted and exhausted. It feels like I could fall into a thousand-year sleep and still not awake refreshed.

Heath unties my wrists and stands while Silas remains between my legs. Their cocks are already tucked back in by the time my eyes manage to flutter back into focus, and all I can see are their foul grins.

"This was it, right? You've had your fix now," I murmur in a drowsy state.

Silas's eyes flicker in the dark. "This is only enough to keep me at bay ... for a day."

Heath laughs. "Maybe two, if you're lucky."

Somehow, someway, a tear still manages to escape my tired eyes.

Silas crawls on top of me, eyeing me. "Are you crying?"

"No," I growl, shivering from the cold wind.

This isn't a tear of sadness but a tear of anger at how easily I succumbed to pleasure and damn near wished to beg for more.

Have they broken me so quickly already?

Silas leans in, his face and those haunting, hollow eyes so close to mine it makes me hold my breath. His tongue dips out, and he licks up the single tear rolling down my cheek, biting his lip after as though he's savoring the taste.

"I'll cherish every one of those tears," he murmurs. A wretched smile follows.

What the ...?

He gets off me before I have a chance to respond and fishes something out of my pocket. My phone.

He and Heath swipe my number and swiftly enter it into their own phones, then Silas throws the phone onto the ground next to me. I look down at my stinging belly, the bloodied marks on my skin making me feel woozy despite the rush of oxytocin still flooding my veins.

Why would I still feel arousal, even now, after he's long removed his tongue from my sensitive parts?

"Seems like she's still riding the high." Heath gawks at me from above like he's admiring plundered prey.

My eyes flutter down toward the bloodied marks Silas etched into my skin, permanently reminding me of what I gave away.

"Your debt isn't nearly paid ..." Silas says as he picks up his mask from the ground and puts it back over his face. "See you Friday in the Skull & Serpent Society house. Eight o'clock. Don't be late."

***

MAX

With a hard-on tenting my pants, I turn around to the other side of the tree and watch Silas and Heath walk away, leaving Ivy in the forest, completely wasted. She doesn't move, doesn't even say a word.

Is she ...?

I swallow back the nerves and wait until they're out of view before I step out from the woods. With a raging boner, I approach her. Her body lies limp between the leaves, like a beautiful flower whose petals are scattered on the ground, stained with a mixture of blood, spit, and cum.

I kneel in front of her, licking my lips at the sight of her body, and I lean in to listen. Short puffs of air leave her mouth. She's alive.

I breathe a sigh of relief and pick up her phone, checking what the boys did before I tuck it back into her pocket. I softly push my hands underneath her body and pick her up from the ground. I can't help but marvel at her pretty face, those luscious lips, that beauty mark near her eyes, and all the individual hairs on her eyebrows as I carry her with me. She looks like a doll in my arms, and I blow a bit of air into her face to see if she wakes up, but it only makes her dark-brown hair tumble to the side.

Has she fallen asleep?

I hold her close to my chest as I walk toward my motorcycle. She groans in my arms, and her eyes momentarily flutter open.

"M-Max?"

I look down and smile. "Shh ... it's okay."

I place her down on my bike and sit down in front of the wheel while securing her arms to my body. "Can you hold on tight for me?"

She murmurs some words I can't understand, but at least she's semi-awake enough to stay on the bike as I drive off into the dark of the night.

***

IVY

When my eyes flutter open again, the burst of sunshine radiating through the window makes me blink voraciously. I'm in a warm, soft bed that smells like ... home.

I sit up straight and look around. I'm actually in my own bedroom.

And I definitely didn't walk here by myself.

I rub my face, listening to the weird noises coming from the living room.

What the ... what happened to me?

All I remember is dozing off in the forest after Silas and Heath used me, and then ...

I cover my mouth with my hand.

Max.

He was there.

I can still remember his smell. The feel of his body against mine. His heartbeat was so fast as I lay against him while sitting on his bike.

I walk to the living room, where the television blasts cartoons.

"Hi, Ivy." Cora smiles. "You're awake!"

It's as if I just walked into a fever dream.

How did I even get here?

Did ... Max actually bring me to my apartment?

How did he get inside?

My whole body begins to shiver.

Fuck. I shouldn't be here. It's not safe.

"Did you buy the cereal?" Cora asks, pulling me from my thoughts.

"No ... not yet."

She pouts. "Aw..."

"But I will. I'll get it for you today," I say.

I don't know how I'm going to do it, but I will.

Cora's eyes grow bigger. I didn't even realize I had a shirt on until she points at it. Or that there's a bloody stain near my pubic bone. "You're bleeding!"

"Oh," I mutter, swiftly taking off to the bathroom. "Don't worry! Lemme just take care of this first."

I take off the shirt and look at it with a frown. I haven't worn this in ages.

How did I put this on? Did I even do this myself, or ...?

A cold shiver runs up and down my spine.

There are red markings all over my skin.

I grab a towel, wet it under the faucet, and dab my skin until the blood is gone and the letters are clear.

THIEF.

That's what's now eternally etched into my skin, thanks to Silas Rivera, a vicious, demonic boy ... And I gave him permission to do it, to defile me, use me, hurt me in any way he wanted.

All of it ... just so I could keep *her* safe.

I look at the door as my hand balls into a fist.

"I will protect you," I whisper softly so she can't hear. "With every last shred of my dignity."

"Are you okay?" I can hear her squeaky voice through the door, and it nearly breaks my heart in two.

"I'm fine." I clear my throat and throw the shirt in the washing bin, then grab a fresh one from the bedroom closet. I reappear through the other door like a magician. "Tada. See? Fine." I do a weird little dance to make her laugh.

"You're so funny." She dances with me and shows off. "See this? I learned this last night from that man."

I freeze. "What man?"

She sheepishly looks at me. "The man who brought you home."

"Max," I mutter.

"Yeah!" She jumps up and down like his name alone makes her happy. "He taught me some cool moves before he left!"

"How did he come into the house?" I ask.

She points at the front door, and I can feel my blood running cold.

I suck in a breath and pat her on the head. "Finish your breakfast now, Cora. It's about time for me to go back to the university."

"Aw ..."

I swiftly put on a blue skirt and a black top, along with my jacket, and I stuff some high heels into my bag for later. "I'll see you again in a few, okay?" I kiss Cora on the cheeks. "Be nice to Mrs. Schwartz. She'll pick you up in five minutes. And if she gives you a tough time, just feed a few of those hot dogs she always gives you at lunch to that wiener dog of hers."

"Mr. Squiggles?"

"It gives him the runs." I wink, and her loud giggles are the last thing I hear before I close the door behind me.

TWELVE

HEATH

"Where is she? Why isn't she here?"

"She's at a boarding school," Mom says, curling her long blond hair around her finger.

My eyes widen. "WHAT?!"

My nostrils flare as I listen to my parents talk about Cecelia like she's no longer with us. Like she's dead and buried, and there's nothing we can do about it.

"It is for the best," Dad says, running his fingers through his dirty-blond hair.

"Bullshit," I growl. "You sent her away."

"Heath ..." Mom sighs. "Please, don't fight about this."

"When were you going to tell me you sent away my goddamn sister?" I make a fist with my hand, staring at the coffee in front of me. I thought they invited me over to the house to catch up on things, but this ... this is a bombshell I was not prepared for.

Mom sighs, pouting her rosy lips. "We couldn't. Not until after she'd already left and—"

I slam the table with my hand. "No! Cecelia loved it here. She never wanted to leave. She told me she wanted to go to Spine Ridge University too, and now you're telling me she'd leave without telling me? No. I don't fucking believe it." I scoot my chair back. "You shipped her off to some boarding school, fuck knows where!"

"Heath, stop," my father growls. "You don't get to talk to your mother like that."

"Where is she?" I respond.

He keeps his mouth shut, biting the piercing in his lip as if that'll keep him from telling me the truth, but it only makes me laugh. "Really?"

"If we told you, you'd drive over there today," Mom says.

"Damn right, I would," I say, shoving the coffee aside. "I'm done here."

"Heath ... please. Talk to us," Mom says as I get up.

"No, I'm done here. I didn't even get a chance to say goodbye to her. You can kiss your early Thursday morning coffees every week with the family goodbye." I march out the door before they can say anything else to convince me to stay.

Cecelia was always there for me when I needed her. I couldn't wish for a better sister. But this? This is a backstab.

It can't be fucking true. It can't.

As I rush to my car, I pull my phone from my pocket and message her.

Me: *Is it true? Are you really at some boarding school?*
Me: *Where are you?*

There's no response.

Me: *Cece, did they fucking ship you off?*
Me: *Tell me right now if I need to come and pick you up.*
Me: *I swear, I'll come get you. Just say the word.*

I start the car and race off before my parents come out yelling at me to come back into the house and talk. I'm not interested in whatever the fuck they have to say. Not today.

I light a cigarette from my pocket, taking a few deep drags.

Goddammit. This is too much, even for me. She always, always told me when she was up to something. Whenever she'd go on vacation, she'd let me know first. And now I have to find this shit out through our parents? Things are not adding up.

I race down the streets, not giving a shit whether it's a red light. I know how to pay attention, and the faster I go, the more alive I feel. What are the police going to do, fine me? Let them. I have enough money to do whatever the fuck I want. I don't need anyone's permission, and I definitely don't need my fucking parents keeping shit from me.

I take another drag of my cigarette and race up the mountain back to Spine Ridge University, completely fucked out of my mind with rage. I park my car near the Skull and Serpent Society house and jump out, taking another big drag of my cig. The kick just doesn't do it anymore, but when I spot a particular brown-haired girl biking through the main gates, I stop and gawk. She's wearing a blue skirt that barely fits her, a short black top, and high heels that are surely hard to walk on. Yet she chose this outfit specifically for her first day back after her punishment. That's definitely a statement.

She's headed right for Max, who's casually reading one of his study books for an upcoming test on a bench outside.

"Well ... this should get interesting," I mutter to myself, chucking the cigarette aside.

I fish my phone from my pocket and PM him.

Me: *Thief headed your way. Look up.*

He grabs his phone and freaks out... Right before she steals the book from his hand and stares him down, fiery eyes and all.

And I've suddenly forgotten just how enraged I was.

I guess this is going to be a fun day after all.

***

MAX

"What the—"

"Come with me," Ivy growls, holding my book hostage.

Oh shit.

I grab my bag and follow her as she struts off. "Hey! Wait up!"

She doesn't respond, and I can barely keep up. Man, this girl can walk fast. How does she do this? I have to actually run to catch up, but I don't want her to run away with my book. I literally have a test tomorrow that I can't flake out on.

"Give that back, please," I say. "I have a test."

But she still ignores me.

When I try to snatch it from her hand, she expertly throws it around from one hand to the other, avoiding my grip each time until we're already inside the Spine Ridge University main building and headed up the stairs.

I attempt to grab her, but she keeps evading me, always one step ahead. She's like a mad fox dashing from left to right, faster than I can keep up. She enters a hallway on the second floor and disappears into a door with tape all around it. This part of the building is under renovation since it's old, and it's probably not safe to be here.

Yet I can't help but follow her inside.

It's dark in here, with only a sliver of sunlight peeking through the closed blinds. A couple of chairs and tables still inside have been thrown over, and the paint is chipping off the walls in this room.

"Damn," I mutter to myself.

Suddenly, the door is flung closed behind me, and before I know it, she's gripped me by the shoulders and shoved me against the door. A knife is shoved under my throat, and I lean back into the wood, gulping.

"You tricked me."

That doesn't sound like a question.

"Admit it."

"With what?" I ask, confused.

"Don't play coy with me," she grits, obviously upset, but all I can look at are those deep, dark eyes I just want to drown in. Shit, I can't even focus on what she's saying.

"You only invited me to that sandwich shop to catch me in the act, didn't you?"

"What? No, I—"

"Don't lie to me," she hisses, pushing the blade even further. "I'm not afraid to use this."

"I'm sure you aren't," I reply, raising my hands. "I really wanted to take you out on a date. That's it."

"Right. That's why that money was marked. That's why Silas and Heath came after me. That's why they fucking marked me."

My heart begins to bleed.

I can't tell her.

I can't say the words out loud.

I was there.

I watched and wished I was the one licking her off instead of Silas.

But what kind of messed-up guy would want that?

"I didn't know they marked that money, I swear," I say, swallowing with the metal pressed to my skin. "Heath forced me to take it. I didn't know what it was for. Or that you were going to steal it. Why did you?"

"That's none of your concern." She grabs my shoulder and flings me away from the door. "You thought I'd be an easy victim? That I'd play along nicely?"

I shake my head, but while backing away, I bump into a chair and fall. The knife immediately meets my throat again. And I'm not gonna lie, it's kinda hot.

"Answer me," she growls.

"No," I say. "I never thought you were easy. I never thought you were anything but ... perfect." Her eyes flicker with interest. "I've been nothing but enamored with you ever since I first saw you. You have to believe me."

She tilts my chin up, forcing me to look her in the eyes, and my God ... I'm blinded by her beauty.

She inches closer and closer, her warm breath fanning my skin, and I can barely resist leaning in. I want to kiss her so badly. But would she let me?

"You were the one who found me last night, weren't you?"

I should lie.

But I also shouldn't tell her this.

Heath and Silas would kill me if they knew.

"Yes."

Fuck

.

***

IVY

My lips shudder as I suck in a breath, looking down at the boy who fell into the chair while his puppy-dog eyes are permanently glued to my face. "How did you know where I live?"

There's a reason I didn't go back to my house, and then this fucker suddenly pops up like he already knew where I lived.

"Are you sure you want to know?" he asks.

I nod, the knife still firmly lodged into his neck.

I can't trust him. I don't. Yet ... something about the way he looks at me, like he would bow at my feet, keeps me intrigued.

Keeps me wanting to know more.

"Tell me."

He gulps.

"I've been following you home ... ever since I first saw you."

Wow. But that feels like ages ago.

"The first time, I came in through the window."

My eyes widen.

He's ... been stalking me?

That means I wasn't dreaming when I felt like someone was watching me that night I came home to Cora wandering out of bed.

"It was you," I murmur.

So I was right all along.

He knows where my house is. It's too late to hide. Too late to save Cora.

"I promise I won't tell a soul where you live," he says. "I also brought your bike back after I took you home. I put the wheel back on and fixed it."

What is this? A plea for forgiveness?

My grip on the knife tightens. "How did you get into my home?"

He gulps. "I stole a key the first time I came into your home."

Damn. I should've hid them better.

"Why? Why did you do it?" I ask.

"I couldn't help it. I had to see you. Over and over again," he says, straining against the chair like he's trying his very best not to lean in to the knife. "It's never close enough."

I have to say, it's kind of a kick to have a guy like him, with the power he has and the frat house he belongs to, practically fawn at the idea of being close to me.

And even though I'm angry as hell that he knows where I live and sneaks into my house ... I really want to know where this could lead.

If I could take back some of the power those boys have siphoned off me.

"I'm addicted," he murmurs.

"How addicted?" I hover so close to his face I can practically taste his desire from the air he breathes. "Show me."

His dimples show up again as his lips part, and a tongue dips out to lick the top of my lip. And for a second, I just look down at him fawning over me, those caramel eyes taunting me, pushing me over the edge. And then I return his lick with a kiss.

THIRTEEN

MAX

When her lips collide with mine, I'm in heaven.

There literally isn't a better place than this.

Just that one kiss and I know for sure...

I'm in love.

A kind of crushing love that threatens to tear open my soul because she isn't the only one I love, but I still let it happen. I still fell so hard, and I don't wanna stop.

I return each kiss she gives me with a more desperate one, latching onto her lips like I won't ever get another chance. I need to taste her, need to feel her, need to have her close to me, no matter the cost.

I know I messed up, and I know Ivy will hate me for it ... and most definitely Heath.

I'm a stalker, a voyeur, a liar.

And she ... she is an angel ... and a thief.

When she leans back, she looks into my eyes, searching for answers I can't give her. I don't know why she kissed me. All I know is that I want more.

"Please," I whisper. "More. I need more."

Her lips linger near mine, coyly teasing me, tempting me to lean into the blade like she wants to test me and see if I'd go the distance. But I'm not afraid of the pain she could cause.

The blade etches into my skin as I close the gap, a warm trail of blood slithering down my skin as I kiss her once again, too desperate for more to care about my own safety.

The knife drops from her hand and clatters onto the floor as she grips my face and kisses me hard. I whimper into her mouth, growing hard from her mere presence. But then she actually sits down on my lap, and I feel like I'm about to die from happiness.

"How much more do you need?" she asks, a foxy smile appearing on her face as she grabs my hands and brings them to her ass. My cock is tenting in my pants from feeling her rub up against me. "Do you want this?"

"God yes, I want you," I murmur, stealing more kisses whenever I can.

"Haven't you already had your fix when you snuck into my home?" she asks, gently biting my lip. "When I was so out of it, you could just take from me what you wanted while I was still half naked from what your friends did?"

She begins to gyrate on top of me, teasing me so much I actually moan.

"No. I wanted to. I thought about it, but I stopped myself," I say.

"Why?" Her hand dives down between my legs, rubbing my package, and fuck me, I could come right then and there. "Your friends take what they want from me just for stealing from them. Why don't you?"

"I told you I'm not like them," I say. "Rob me until I'm as poor as dirt, I don't care. As long as you leave my heart intact ..."

Her eyes flicker with interest.

"If you stole my heart, I'd have nothing left to give to you." I suck in a breath when she squeezes my dick. "I couldn't bear it."

A filthy smirk forms on her face. "A stalker with a heart? That's new."

"I just love watching you sleep ..." She zips me down and pulls out my dick, making me moan from arousal when she looks down at my ample size. "I love ..."

"Go on ..." she whispers into my ear while slowly jerking me off.

"Fuck, I love your hands. I love your lips. I love your tits, your hips, your ass. I love your back talk. I love how you hold nothing back, how you fight back. I love everything about you."

"Hmm ..." Her tongue dips out to lick the side of my neck, and my cock bounces up and down from the lust coursing through my veins.

"Oh fuck," I murmur, my head tilting back.

"Hands behind your back," she whispers into my ear.

When I do, she slips my belt off my pants and loops it around my wrists and the chair, sealing me in.

Suddenly, she gets off me, leaving me high and dry, and I'm almost tempted to get up with the whole chair attached to my body, but she points and says, "Stay."

That's all I need, like a goddamn fucker on a leash.

"You want to watch?" She raises a brow as she sits down on the table opposite of me. "Then watch."

She raises her skirt and parts her legs, revealing her panties, which she swiftly slides aside. My mouth begins to water at the sight of that delectable pussy, wet and glistening with need.

Good God, the amount of begging I would do to get a taste of that.

She starts rubbing herself right in front of me while keeping her gaze fixated on me, almost as if to tell me something. As if she wants me to know she holds all the power. And I'd be lying if I said it wasn't true.

"You want this?" she asks.

I nod, mouth wide open, tongue running along my lips. "Fuck yes, I want it so badly."

She circles her most sensitive spot, spreading her juices all over, and my dick bounces in response. "Beg."

"Please ..." I murmur.

"More."

The more she circles her slit, the more I feel like a starved man. "Please, I need it."

"Need what?"

"You. I need you." I whimper while my cock still bounces up and down from what she's doing to her own pussy. "Please. Let me have you."

Her downturned lips curl upward into a smile as she continues playing with herself, her fingers rolling around her clit until it's swollen.

My saliva practically rolls off my tongue, and when she actually sticks a finger inside, I'm lost.

"I can't take this. Please."

Still, I don't move.

"Show me how badly you want this then. Come for me without touching yourself."

I'm so close. If she'd touch me just once, I'd explode all over her.

She dips in and out of her pussy, spreading wetness all over before rubbing her clit once again, her breathing growing more rapid with every passing second. My tip oozes pre-cum, and I can feel my desperation to release building inside me.

"Please, I wanna come," I mewl, my dick bobbing up and down. "Please. Touch me."

"No," she groans, still circling around her most sensitive spot while forcing me to watch. "You wanted to watch? Then watch me come."

Her fingers go faster and faster until finally, a soft moan escapes her lips, and I can literally see her drip all over the table. The view sends me over the edge, and I moan loudly as cum bursts out of my cock, spurting all over the floor and my pants. But it's still not nearly enough to satiate my desire for her.

"Fuck," I groan with frustration from the half-finished orgasm.

She smiles wickedly and gets off the table, pulling down her skirt again. "Now you know what it feels like."

I'm out of breath. "What do you mean?"

She pulls up her top and lowers her skirt from the waistline, showing the scar Silas left in her skin beneath her belly button, close to her mound.

Thief.

She tips up my chin. "To be used."

And she picks up the knife and walks toward the door, but as she clutches the handle, she adds, "Don't ever tell those fuckers where we live *or* about Cora. Got it?"

I shake my head. "I won't, I swear."

"Good."

The door closes, and I'm left with an overwhelming sense of satisfaction ... as well as a great hunger. She used me to gain back the power she lost to Silas and Heath, and I'm not even mad. This is the first time in my entire life I've ever been able to come without anyone even touching me. I sink back into the chair.

She left me here. Panting. Desperate for more.

Wow. What a woman.

Suddenly, the door bursts open, and my eyes widen when it isn't her who's looking at my dick.

It's Heath, and he looks shocked. "What the—"

My cheeks flush with heat.

"Shit." I try to free myself while awkwardly bumping up and down in the chair with my ass.

"Wow ..." Heath shakes his head, judging me. "She did this, didn't she?"

I nod, my flaccid cock still twitching every time he glances at it.

He approaches me. "Where is she?"

"Gone," I reply, sitting up straight to look him in the eyes. "Can you help me out, please?"

He lowers himself to my level, placing both hands on the back of my chair as he narrows his eyes. "First, you're going to tell me what happened."

"We had a little ... chat."

He snorts. "That's one hell of a chat, Max."

He sniffs the air and inches close, too close, making me lean back into the seat. Fuck. I can barely take it when he gets this up close and personal, let alone after I just had an encounter with Ivy. I'm still a fucking mess, and his presence only complicates that further.

"You let that girl walk all over you ... for some pussy?" he asks.

"I couldn't help myself. She's—"

His fingers curl around my throat. "You went behind my back. Are you into her? Is that it?"

He squeezes off my oxygen, but all it does is bring my cock back to life. And I know he sees. Just one small half of a second, but I know he glanced.

"Why?"

"I'm trying to win her trust," I reply.

I know it's a lie. I'm lying to both of them, and it's eating me alive. But I'm already in so deep now ... I can't come back from this.

Heath releases me from his grip and steps back, looking me up and down like he's judging the state I'm in. He sucks in the oxygen through his nostrils and then smiles, patting me on the shoulder. "That's my boy."

Then he undoes the belt around my wrists, and I breathe a sigh of relief.

He tilts his head. "Now, go clean yourself up."

FOURTEEN

IVY

The next day

Anonymous: Remember what I said. Eight sharp. Don't be late, twig.

My grip on my phone tightens.

Silas.

I change his name in my phone to Psycho and tuck it into my pocket, so I can focus on my studies, but his warning still looms over my head. I check the library clock, feeling my heart sink into my shoes the closer the arrow gets to twelve—the time for my supposed punishment by the Skull and Serpent Society boys.

"You okay?" Aspen asks, closing her book. "You've been off all day. What's going on with you?"

I sigh. "I have an appointment with someone at eight."

She raises her brows. "Ooooh! Something important? Or is it a secret? Is it a date?"

I suck in a breath. I don't want to alarm her, but if I don't tell her, she'll find out anyway. "Silas wants my ... help."

"*Silas?*" She frowns like she can't believe her ears. "Silas Rivera? As in the guy with the black-and-white hair and the heart tattoo?"

"Yup," I say, rolling my eyes. "Unfortunately."

"Why are you hanging out with *him* of all people? He's shady as hell," she says.

"I don't want to, believe me, but I ... owe him," I respond.

"Ew." She rolls her eyes.

"Exactly my thoughts."

"Silas is such a fucking freak. I can't believe we're even related at all."

"What?" My jaw drops because this information came out of the blue.

"Yeah. Didn't you know?" She makes a face. "He's my half brother."

My eyes become even wider. "No, I didn't. But how? Aren't your parents still together?"

She nods. "Yep. My mom, Penelope ... she has this poly thing going on since forever with my dad Dylan, as well as Felix and Alistair. To me they're like extra dads, but it feels odd, for sure. Especially for me and my siblings and half siblings."

"Wow." I close my book. I'm too invested now.

She rubs her lips together. "Yup. It's normal for us. We're not alone, though. Silas and Max are cousins too."

My jaw drops. "What?!"

"It's true. I thought you knew that already since you've been hanging with Max." She takes a sip of her water like she's just given me the greatest tea ever, but it feels fishy.

"Wait, how do you know about that?"

"I saw him approaching you in the grass but then turning around, all sweaty. Why did you think I pulled Xav and River with me to go hang somewhere else?" She nudges me with her shoulder. "I got you, girl."

"Thanks." I blush, not knowing how to respond.

If only she knew what I knew.

But I can't risk my friends being pulled into my troubles.

"Oh shit, hide me," she suddenly says, ducking for cover under the books.

"What's happening?" I ask.

"Levi Torres," she whispers. She hastily points at a guy with dark hair entering the library, who's wearing a button-up white shirt to hide the scorpion tattoo peeking out near his neck, his middle-parted fringe falling over his face as he looks around.

"Wait … Levi Torres? Max said something about him being his half brother."

"He's been egging me on to go on this camping trip with a bunch of friends."

"And why is that a bad thing?" I ask.

"Because he's Levi fucking Torres," she hisses. "Do you see those damn abs?"

I take another look at his toned body. He's definitely defined in all the right places. "I get it."

"See? Why would I go on a camping trip with that trap walking around in my vicinity?"

I laugh. "I don't see how that's a bad thing, to be honest."

She frowns from under her book cover. "No, no, no. I'm out of here. Talk later, okay? Good luck with Silas."

She rushes off, passing a few bookshelves to curve around the route Levi is taking. I didn't even get to say goodbye. She just ran off like she wanted to avoid being in the same room as him.

I check the clock again and swallow back the nerves. Ten more minutes. If I'm late … they'll come for me. I have no choice. I have to go.

I push myself off the chair, close my books, and tuck them into my bag, then head out the door. I make my way to the Skull and Serpent Society, feeling like every goddamn person on this campus watches me enter that building. Or maybe I just feel hyperaware of every scrutinizing gaze as I walk up to the door and push the bell.

After a while, a guy bearing a striking resemblance to Max opens the door, and it makes me do a double take.

"Uh … hi?" he says.

I clear my throat. "Sorry, I have an … appointment with Silas." I rub my lips together. "I'm Ivy. I don't know if he told you?"

He just looks amused. "Another one, huh?"

"Another what?"

He grips my arm and pulls me inside, closing the door before I can even say a word.

"He really doesn't know how to quit," the guy says, snorting. "It's like he can go on for days."

I'm still confused what this is about. I hope it's not what I think it is.

The guy sticks out his hand. "Elliot Fletcher."

I frown. "Fletcher? You're Max's brother?"

He pushes up his glasses. "Oh, you know Max?"

"We're friends," I lie. I'm not sure exactly what we are, but that's the least of my concerns right now.

"Interesting." He crosses his arms, looking at me like he's onto something. "You're that new girl, right? Max talked about you, but I didn't think Silas would steal you from under his nose."

"Max told you about me?"

He takes my coat and hangs it. "Max talks. And talks. And talks."

I snort. "Sounds like him."

"It is what it is." He winks. "So ... two boys wrapped around your finger, huh? I won't tell, but I do love the drama."

"Oh, I'm not into them," I say, trying to shake off the rumors before they start.

His brows furrow. "Really? Because you said you were here for Silas."

"So?"

"He only invites girls over he intends to fuck."

My pupils dilate.

He walks off through the hallway while it feels like someone just knocked the air out of my lungs. "He's upstairs, toward—"

"I know where his room is," I interject.

"Good luck."

He heads into the kitchen while I walk up the creaking steps of the Skull and Serpent Society, the dark walls feeling like they're slowly entrapping me the closer I get to his room, where music is being blasted. I can smell the weed from the other end of the hallway, and it makes me cough.

Before I knock on the door, I take a deep breath.

This is it. No way back now. But I'm here, as told.

My nostrils flare and twitch as I force my hand up and knock.

The music in the room stops abruptly, and it makes my heartrate shoot through the roof.

"Come in."

Silas's unhinged voice makes goose bumps spread on my skin.

I step inside and search until I find him in a black pair of cargo pants and a white shirt sprawled on the black velvety couch, smoking pot.

A smile spreads from ear to ear on his face, causing the heart tattoo underneath his eye to wrinkle, but it abruptly disappears within seconds. "Good. Now close the door."

I'm already irritated as hell as I kick it closed with my foot under his watchful gaze.

"Come here," he says.

I walk closer to the table in front of the couch and stop, folding my arms.

"I was wondering if you'd show up." He tilts his head, his short hair falling over his sunken-in eyes. "It would've been so fucking fun to drag you out of your hiding place myself."

More goose bumps erupt on my skin at the reminder of what he and Heath did the other night in Priory Forest. "Too bad for you."

He narrows his eyes, and his lip quirks up. "I would've made you enjoy it."

Made me.

That's what he likes. Control.

Fucking psycho.

He holds out the marijuana. "Want a drag?"

"No thanks."

"You obviously need it."

"I'm fine," I grit.

His eyes narrow, and he looks amused by my effort to keep my shit together. "Are you?"

I swallow back the lump in my throat. "What do you want from me?"

His brow rises, and he puts down the blunt. "Did you forget your fucking debt to me?"

He fishes a knife from his pocket, while his eyes nearly bore a hole into my head.

"I didn't," I say. "But you never told me why I had to be here at eight o'clock."

THWACK!

The pointy end of the knife lands right between my feet.

He eyes something lying on the table in front of him—a black-and-white outfit with ruffled shoulders and a skirt that's way too short for anyone, let alone me.

"Put that on."

"What? That thing is way too short for me. No."

He narrows his eyes. "You think that knife is the only one I have?" He flashes three more just from one of the other pockets in his cargo pants. "Put. It. On."

Fuck him. He only wants to degrade me. What's he going to do? Put me in ridiculous outfits and parade me around in front of his friends like some sort of toy he won?

But if I don't agree ... he'll definitely make me.

Your debt isn't nearly paid ...

I can still hear the words singed into my head.

He won't stop until he's satisfied, and I've agreed.

Fuck.

I snatch the outfit off the table, judging it, and slowly but surely, my jaw drops. It's a goddamn maid outfit you'd find at a kink shop.

"What's this for?"

"You got fired from your job, right?" He smirks and picks up his glass of Coke, taking a sip. "You can earn back the money you took right here in this house."

I snort. "As your *maid*?"

He puts the glass down. "You have a problem with that?"

My nostrils flare.

Is this a joke?

The chill in the air definitely tells me enough. "You're insane. I'm not going to—"

"You will," he interjects, those piercing green eyes staring me down. "Or do you want me to remind you of the deal you made with me?"

Fuck that fucking asshole. I was right; he does want to make me feel like less than.

"Now ... are you going to do as you're told?" he asks. "Or do you want me to make you?"

My fingers dig into my palm so hard it cracks and bleeds.

Fine. He wants a show? I'll give him one to remember.

FIFTEEN

SILAS

Grinding her teeth together, she finally brings her fingers to the back of her red dress and slowly unbuttons it. My gaze is on her like a hawk, and I lean back on the couch, legs wide open, my dick already growing hard at the sight of her undressing in front of me like the good slut she's meant to be.

She sucks in a breath through her nostrils as her dress slowly comes undone over her shoulders. She pulls on the fabric, loosening it until it slowly drops to the floor.

And fuck me, does she look like an appetizing little lollypop I can't fucking wait to lick. She thinks the scowl on her face will deter me, but she's dead wrong about that.

Her feistiness is what keeps me interested. Keeps me focused on that beautiful scar I made as she steps out of her dress and kicks it aside, then stares me down.

"Bra too," I say.

She runs her tongue along her teeth, clearly fighting tooth and nail not to call me every swear word in the book right now, and I fucking love it.

Her fingers hook under the straps, and she pulls it down. Then, she clicks loose the metal and pulls it away. Her tits are gorgeous, mouth-watering, and so perky that I just want to grab them and cover them with my lips. But I'm not going to reward her for doing zero work.

"Put it on." I point at the dress, which is way too small to cover her whole body ... the perfect size for her.

She reluctantly steps into the outfit and pulls it up until it's strapped in place, her tits barely fitting in the tight heart-shaped bralette. Her ass peeks out from underneath the black skirt, the fringes clearly showing off her red lace thong. A perfectly designed outfit for all my wicked needs.

"Satisfied?" she deadpans.

My tongue runs across my lip. "I'm not nearly satisfied enough."

She gulps, gathering herself like she's trying not to be affected. But I know how to fucking play with girls like her.

"Grab that bucket. Fill it with water." I point at the bucket in the bathroom. "There's dishwashing soap in the cabinet."

She throws me a sneer before turning around and waltzing off with that thin stick figure of hers, her ass wiggling back and forth in the short maid dress, and my boner nearly breaks out of my pants.

Fuck.

She fills the bucket with soapy water and returns. "Now what?"

"Grab the brush too," I growl.

She throws me another glare with narrowed eyes, mocking me, before turning around and doing exactly as she's told. Perfect. Just the right amount of sass to make me want to fuck her brains out.

She throws the bucket down on the floor, and the water sloshes over the edges onto the hardwood floor.

"What do you want me to do with this?"

She's playing coy with me now. "You know what to do."

"You'll pay me for this, right?" she asks.

I merely stare at her, wondering what she thinks this agreement she made with me truly means.

"On. Your. Knees," I hiss.

The annoyance on her face is such a fucking turn-on as she slowly goes to her knees and dips the brush into the liquid, then rubs it all over the floor.

"Clean every inch of it. I want it spotless."

She cleans the area in a circle around her until she's forced to lean up on her knees and elbows, and when she does, I have the most perfect view of her perky ass barely covered by that red thong.

And fuck me. That about does it for me.

"When is it enough?" she asks.

I grab my glass of Coke and take a sip. "When I say it's enough."

With rage in her eyes, she grips the brush and starts digging into the floor with it so harshly the bristles nearly break. Just like her after I'm done with her.

I glug down my Coke while watching her struggle, and I spit back a small part into the glass, then pour it out onto the floor. She leans up and throws me an abhorred look, the fire in her eyes burning with the same kind of fury that burns in me.

"Now, clean this mess," I say, pointing at the puddle of Coke near the table. When she tries to get up, I growl, "No. On your knees and crawl."

Her eyes twitch, but the smile on my face only grows as she still obeys my every fucking word.

Yes, that's the face I'm looking for, thief. That's the one that gets me going, that makes this worth all the fucking money in the world.

On her knees, she crawls to me in her maid outfit until she's right at the table with the brush. But the second she tries to place it on the floor, I snatch the brush away and watch her reaction.

"Clean the floor, twig."

She snarls, "How? You have the brush."

"How do you think?" My tongue darts out, and I slowly lick my lips until the realization finally hits her. "Lick. It. Clean."

My cock throbs from the sheer number of hateful darts she aims in my direction.

"That's it, little thief. Give me all your fucking hatred. I can take it …" I growl, grabbing her chin to make her look at me. "As long as you play the victim, I'll play the fucking monster." A grin spreads on my face. "Now clean it."

***

IVY

Grinding my teeth until a chip breaks off, I bend over and lick the floor clean, tasting the same Coke that was just in his mouth.

I have never felt more degraded in my entire life, but I can't stop either because I signed up for this. My body is theirs to use and play with as they see fit.

Fuck.

I should've known he would put me through the worst kind of stuff.

I lick up the liquids, trying not to think about it just having been in his mouth as I clean the floor with my actual fucking tongue until it's all gone. But his groan ... God, the groan that follows makes my entire body clench.

"Good girl," he says, placing the brush beside him on the couch like it's some sort of treasure. "See? You can do it."

"Fuck you," I spit, looking up at him while hate slowly poisons my heart.

He grips my throat, and I gasp for air. "Beg. Beg for it, and maybe I'll allow you to feel what it's like to be fucked by my cock."

What?! The arrogance.

I spit in his face.

I don't know what else to do to gain back some semblance of power.

His fingers slowly uncurl from my throat, and he wipes the spit off, then holds his fingers in front of his mouth ... and spits. With his other hand, he grips my cheeks and pinches them. "Open your mouth."

Slowly, my lips part, and his fingers inch closer to my mouth, rubbing my lips with our mixed saliva until he pushes them in. With his eyes locked onto mine, he pushes his fingers in deeper and deeper until his knuckles hit my teeth. "Lick."

Rage fills my bones.

Yet I still do what he asks, licking off his fingers until I can taste both him and me on my tongue for what feels like forever.

Victory drags out a smug half smile on his face, making me want to repeat it all over again. But if I did, this game of back-and-forth would never end. This is what he wants. For me to realize there is no way out, no way to take back what I gave away: My freedom to do whatever I wanted.

And I handed it to him on a silver platter.

As his fingers leave my throat, I cough, but his other hand slowly tightens around my neck. He towers over me, dick tenting his pants, and I can't do anything but let him squeeze off the vein in my neck until I'm lightheaded.

He inches closer and closer until he's a hair's breadth away from me, and his tongue dips out to lick my top lip. Just a hint. Just a taste. Just a single touch.

And my pussy is already throbbing.

Fuck no, Ivy! Don't allow it to affect you.

"Stand up," he says, a filthy grin on his face as he pulls me up from the floor with a firm grip around my throat.

He guides me back until I'm right in front of the couch, and he sits down, his gaze as well as his hands slowly gliding down my body all the way from my nipples, which peak out of the dress, down to my belly button hiding behind thin white cotton.

His fingers crawl underneath the short skirt of the maid's outfit, leaving goose bumps in his wake. He pushes up the dress until my thong is exposed, stopping only once the scar he left is visible.

His eyes travel up to mine, and their hunger makes me swallow. "This scar ..." His finger slides across the mark he created on my skin. "It looks so goddamn good on your skinny bones. You'll learn to fucking love it."

"The fuck I w—"

His devilish tongue rolling across the scar has me choking on my own damn words. He circles it around every letter, following the pattern, drawing out THIEF once more on my skin while fucking moaning. His fingers curl around my thong, and he slowly tugs it down. Before it's even hit the floor, his fingers are already coaxing out the wetness between my legs.

Fuck.

"Wet already, little thief?" he groans, vicious excitement on his face.

I bite my lip in order for the moan to stay inside my mouth as he rolls his fingers around my pussy.

"You like being treated like my personal, slutty toy." He grins. "Admit it."

"The fuck I will," I say.

He shoves two fingers inside me, and I gasp, nearly falling over on top of him, steadying myself only on the tips of my toes.

"You're a thief who deserves nothing less. Every time you dare to talk back to me, I will make you eat your words and moan for me instead."

He swivels around inside me and presses my G-spot, making me suck in a breath.

How did he find it so quickly?

"Every time you try to hide from me, I will drag you out with my tongue spearing your pussy, do you understand?"

When I don't answer, he fishes a knife from his pocket and presses it into the scar, making it bleed again.

"Answer me." He pulls out his fingers, abruptly ending the pleasure.

"Yes," I reply.

THWACK!

The knife sticks into the wood between my feet, buried all the way to the hilt.

Smiling, he leans in and licks up the droplet of blood, groaning like he's obsessed. "Little thief ... get on your knees." The words almost come out animalistic, and the mere sound of them forces me to sink right in front of him until my knees hit the floor.

"*On* the fucking knife."

"What?" I gasp.

With his hands on my shoulders, he guides me over the hilt. "Don't act like you didn't hear me. I know you can." He eyes my hearing aids. "Now sit. Down."

He slowly forces my body to lower until the hilt enters my pussy, and I hold my breath.

I can't believe I'm doing this. That I'm letting him do this to me. That I'm so goddamn wet just from his touch.

Fuck.

"That's it. Take it all the way."

It's cold and hard inside me, yet I'm as wet as can be as I sink deeper.

"I told you I'll make you love that scar," he says, moving his hand up to my chin so he can make me look at him. "And you will fucking worship the knife that gave it to you."

He zips down and pulls out his hard-on right in front of me. I didn't think I could be any more shocked than I already was ... but I was dead wrong.

It's much longer than Heath's and riddled with piercings from top to bottom.

"Now open those dirty lips, little thief, and I'll teach you how to love this Jacob's ladder right down into fucking hell, too."

SIXTEEN

SILAS

I bring her lips to my cock and ram inside, not waiting one second before I sink in deep. I love the look on her face, the absolute hatred seething from her dark, soulful eyes as I bury myself inside her wet throat and claim it as mine too.

"Hate me. Despise me. I don't fucking care as long as you're on your knees for me." I pull back out for a moment. "Now ... are you going to tell me *why* you fucking stole from me?"

She shakes her head.

Of course she wouldn't tell me. "Guess I'll have to fuck the words out of your mouth instead."

I plunge right back in again, leaving no second left wasted.

There is nothing quite like a good punishment session, but definitely nothing like the submission of a girl who would kill me with that same fucking knife.

I know she can feel my obsession with her entering her very fucking bones.

"Are you making that knife nice and wet, slut?" I groan, pushing her down on top of it while I'm still inside of her mouth. She gargles as I pull back and let her breathe for a second.

"Go ahead. Take a breath. I won't allow a second one before you've come."

"What?!" I dive back in before she can say another word.

"I'm tired of words, twig. That tongue licks better than it talks; now use it," I growl, deepening my stroke.

"I know you can feel each and every piercing scraping the back of your throat. Do they remind you of your place, little thief?" I grin when she scowls. "That's it ... choke on my cock, slut." I lick my lips as she struggles with my size. "Bite me, and I'll make you drink the fucking blood from my cock."

She struggles to take me, but I still thrust deeper, reaching down between her legs until I feel her wetness. She clenches, but I swat open her legs and flick her clit until her whole body begins to quake.

"That's it, spread that wetness all over that knife," I growl, enjoying the feel of her tight little throat and that tongue as it sucks on my length. I grip her chin and push her off my shaft. She sucks in the oxygen like an addict on drugs. "Say thanks."

"Fuck you."

I push her head back down all the way to the base. "I warned you, you'd regret it. Now choke on my goddamn cock like the good little slut you want to be."

Her panicked eyes find mine, but I merely bring my fingers back down between her legs, flicking her clit to confuse her even more. I want her on the brink of destruction, almost ready to jump off herself, and I'll be the one to give the final push.

She is *my* plaything, *my* toy. *She is mine.*

***

IVY

I can't believe I'm doing this.

That I'm letting Silas *fucking* Rivera claim my throat like it belongs to him.

And that my pussy throbs with an indescribable need.

I've lost it.

Completely lost it as I bounce up and down on this knife, wishing I didn't feel that surge of pleasure washing over me. Nearly wishing I hadn't stolen from him.

But I did, and this is the price I have to pay.

He forces himself inside me, his cock thick and pulsating with greed. Every ridge, every piercing, I can feel it all as he buries himself deep inside my throat, depriving me of the oxygen I so desperately seek.

Shit, I can't breathe.

I can't breathe, and he wants me to know.

My body no longer belongs to me.

It belongs to him now.

And I willingly gave up control.

The realization hits me like a truck as he pulls out again and makes me look at the tip of his dick as it bounces up and down in my face like he wants me to worship it.

"Do you see how powerless you are?" he groans before thrusting back in. "Take me deep, little slut. Let me hear you gag."

I choke and heave, feeling him throb deep inside me while my tongue struggles to envelop him.

And even though I want nothing more than to curse him to the end of the earth, my pussy still grows wetter and wetter. No matter how many times I remind myself this knife I'm fucking gave me a scar, I've already lost control.

And with every flick of his fingers across my clit, I get closer and closer to the edge of oblivion.

I can't stop.

I don't want to stop.

My mind slowly turns on itself, crazed with overpowered lust I've never felt before.

"Yes, look at me," Silas growls as my eyes find his in the midst of insanity. "Show me what you look like when you give it all to me."

***

"You thought you could steal from me?" I groan, my shaft twitching against the back of her throat. "Then you pay for it with an open mouth, ready to take my cock while coming all over my hand."

I flick her clit until she finally explodes, after which I finally let her take in another breath by pulling out.

She sucks in the oxygen and heaves at the same time. "Fuck!"

"Beg, and maybe I will, twig."

She frowns. "I didn't mean—"

I shove her head back down. "What did I say about back talk?"

She takes me so well despite gripping my knees as if that'll make me back off. I'm impressed. The more she fights, the more turned on I get, and with each stroke, her nails dig into my knees. "Yes, that's it. Bring out those fucking claws. Hurt me like I hurt you."

When I pull out of her, I spit on her face and spread it all over, then dip it into her mouth, swiveling around her tongue. "Lick. Show me what you can do with that filthy tongue of yours."

She does what I say, but the defiance never leaves her dark, hate-filled eyes, and the longer I stare at them, the more I'm beginning to realize I found the perfect prey for my crazy needs.

She won't give up, even when I tell her to. She's not afraid to fight back, even if it hurts. And she won't beg me until I make her.

"Yes... this is it. This is what I need. *You.*"

I get up from the couch, grab her face, and thrust back in again, face fucking her until her saliva coats my shaft and her moans reverberate through the room. Her gagging sounds make my balls tighten, and I roar out loud as my cum coats the back of her throat and then some.

When I pull out, she coughs and falls to her hands and knees, cum and saliva dripping out onto the floor.

"Finally ..." she murmurs.

"Finally, what?" I grab her hair and make her look at me, the grin on my face growing wider the bigger her eyes get. "You thought I was finished?"

I walk behind her and force her back down as I come to my knees, pulling her off the knife. She gasps when I stuff two fingers inside her, feeling her up. "You're so goddamn wet."

I tear the knife out of the floor and take a whiff before I bring the handle to her mouth and say, "Bite on this."

"Wha—"

I stuff it between her lips so she can't say another word.

"Clean it," I growl. "Taste your own excitement for me so you remember why you asked for this. You begged me to take your body in exchange for your crime. Did you expect to enjoy it so much, little thief?"

She frowns, almost ready to spit out the knife.

"Now bend over, and don't drop the fucking knife while I fuck this pussy."

***

IVY

How dare he? How dare he remind me of my own damn wetness for him?

I want to swear, scream, shout, yell at him, but all my tongue lets out is a strangled moan as he rips into me, his cock so deep inside my body I feel untethered from gravity itself.

"Yes, that's it, take me deep like the fucking slut you are for me," he groans as his shaft pulses inside me, still as hard as when he was inside my mouth.

Shit. I can't believe he can go another round. Does this guy ever have enough?

He grips my hair, twisting it into a knot as he rides me, forcing me into him over and over again. "This pussy was begging for my cock, wasn't it? You're so fucking wet for me."

"I hate you," I hiss, not knowing what else to say to let him know I would've never, ever, given any of this to him if it wasn't for that goddamn debt.

"Yes, give me all your hatred, slut. It only makes me want to ruin you more," he growls, fucking me raw.

His dick is so goddamn big, and each piercing rolls against my insides with each thrust, causing unimaginable pleasure to ripple through my body.

"I'm not your fucking slut!" I growl back through clenched teeth, which still hold the knife.

"You're mine, and as long as you owe me this debt, twig, I'll call you whatever name will make me want to coat you with cum. Now take it like a good girl, and maybe I'll finally be satisfied after I've filled this pussy to the brim too."

He shoves my head down into the puddle of cum on the floor and grips my thighs, pulling me closer to him with every thrust. "And you'll beg me to do it."

"The hell I will," I growl back with clenched teeth.

His fingers dive underneath my belly, pushing my legs apart until he finds my clit from the top, and within seconds, I'm gasping for air, not knowing how to breathe with his fingers flicking me into insanity.

"You think you can keep this from me? I told you; I'll take everything from you, whether you like it or not. And by the time I'm done with you, you will thank me for it."

The taste of his cum still lingers on my tongue, reminding me of the hold he has over me. He thrusts in deep and circles his fingers around so expertly my eyes nearly roll into the back of my head.

"Feel that?" His middle finger presses down on my clit, slipping left and right with intent as if to remind me of my place beneath him, hungry for a fix. "That's what being mine feels like."

He pulls out and spears me again, and my body begins to shake with uncontrollable need.

"Don't fucking drop the knife, twig," he warns. "Or there will be consequences."

I struggle to keep it clenched between my teeth, the taste of my own pussy juices a firm reminder of my position, my subjugation, my greed for more as he thrusts and thrusts.

"That's it; fall apart all over my pierced cock like the slut you are," Silas groans.

Right before I come, he stops circling, and my throbbing pussy reminds me of how little power I have while a drawn-out groan escapes my mouth.

A wicked laugh fills the room, and he grabs the brush off the couch.

WHACK!

The hard wood leaves a heated mark in its wake, and I moan out loud.

"Make that sound again ... but remember what I said. Don't drop the knife."

WHACK!

He hits my other ass cheek, the slap awakening a side of me I didn't know I had. Because that slap definitely reverberated in my clit.

Oh shit.

"Are you going to scream for me, twig?" he asks. "Do it. Let the whole fucking house know what kind of a slut you are."

He whacks me again and again, spreading the ache all over my ass until I can't separate his thrusts from the spanking anymore. Pain and pleasure blend into one just like before, and my body literally quakes with need. My nails literally dig into the wood as he impales me while my orgasm looms closer, and my teeth clench together so hard the knife begins to cut into my tongue.

"Now beg. Beg me, thief."

My brain has turned into complete mush. "Please ..."

I cry out in both pain and bliss as the next strike makes my clit thrum, and I come so hard I nearly see stars.

"Fuck yes, just like that," Silas groans before thrusting in like an unhinged madman.

A guttural groan leaves his throat, and I can feel the ropes of cum shooting into my pussy before he pulls out and coats my red-stained ass too.

My whole body feels like it's gone off the deep end—like I'm floating in nirvana or somewhere beyond.

He chucks the brush aside. A proud chuckle escapes his mouth as he gets up from the floor, admiring me from above. I can't even move my legs or arms. Or anything, for that matter.

He bends over near my face and pulls the knife from my mouth, tucking it back into his pocket. "Look at you ... so fucking perfect."

Suddenly, he grips my face with both hands and smashes his lips onto mine. He laps up the blood from my lips before driving his tongue inside in full force. I'm defenseless to stop him, helpless against the onslaught of lust still flooding my veins, and desperate for more of whatever the fuck kind of hit he just gave me.

He kisses me feverishly, clutching my face with both hands as his tongue roams around my mouth, licking off the blood stains and saliva until nothing is left.

And I hate how much it gives me life. I hate it so much I bite his lip, but even that doesn't make him flinch. Instead, he smiles against my mouth as his own blood dribbles into mine.

"I lied," he whispers. "You did get another chance to taste my blood, thief. And I can't fucking wait until next time when I'll have another taste of you."

The filthy grin on his face pulls me back into the here and now. Standing, he drops a few hundred-dollar bills before I can even process what just happened. "Now clean. It. Up."

SEVENTEEN

IVY

Silas has walked out of the room to answer a phone call, leaving me to myself. I don't know when he'll come back or if he'll come back at all. Not that I care.

My hand slowly reaches across the floor, and I grasp the bills, crushing them in the palm of my hand. I hold them as I get up from the floor and tear the outfit from these thin bones. I cast everything aside and grab my own clothes, putting them back on before rubbing my face with the towel in his bathroom. I look at the girl in the mirror, the submissive girl I've been forced to become.

My fist lands on the glass, which cracks beneath my skin, and blood erupts from the crevices in my hand.

Dammit.

I let my rage overpower me.

I wash off the blood and exit the room. Luckily, Silas is nowhere to be seen.

I breathe out a sigh of relief as I head toward the stairs but stop in my tracks the second I come face-to-face with Max. "Ivy?"

The bewildered look on his face makes me rush past him.

"Wait!" he yells.

I run down as fast as I can, tucking the money into my pocket before I head out the front door.

"Ivy, please. What happened? You're bleeding." I can hear his footsteps behind me, but I ignore them.

"Did someone hurt you?"

Your friend.

"No."

"Let me help you," he says.

But when he nearly catches up with me, I turn around and say, "I thought I made myself very clear last time that I don't trust you."

His lips curl. "But ..." He holds up a bag of noodles. "I have food. Wanna share?"

I make a face. "You really don't understand, do you?" Food will never fix this. Food can't prevent me from unraveling. "Your friends are destroying me. You think food will make it okay?"

"No, but ..."

I sigh out loud and turn around. "I'm not hungry. Now, please go away. I want to be alone."

Finally, he doesn't follow me anymore, but my heart still aches as I leave to grab my bike. He's so eager to please that it's hard to deny him, but he's part of that society, part of that deranged friend group, and I can't trust any of them, no matter how nice they pretend to be.

What if it's all a ruse? A way to get me to spill the beans? He tricked me once before with that money. What's to say he won't do it again?

As I bike, I pause momentarily near The Shack.

Should I still try to spend the night there instead of at home?

Those fuckers already have me in their pocket. It's not like hiding out is any use.

But what if they still end up following me home?

I swallow back the nerves.

I race down the mountain and let the fresh air take away the sins imprinted on my skin until the noise from the city drowns out the voices in my head.

Thief.

I gulp.

I don't want to hear his voice, but every time I turn, it's like a silent whisper in the night. And the more I hear it, the more emboldened I get. With a scowl, I park my bike near the grocery store, grab a cart, and go inside.

With each step, the reality of what I did sinks in deeper, and I fish into my pocket and take out the money Silas threw on the floor in front of my face. This money ... it's tainted. It feels wrong to even touch it.

Like I've sold my body and turned myself into their whore.

Fuck those boys.

I rip open the fridge door and take out a big carton of milk. I grab eggs, bacon, pancake mix, syrup, and some Eggos. I pick out the freshest berries and head into the breakfast aisle, where I grasp the largest box of chocolate cereal I can find and dump it into the cart. Then I head to the register and pull out the bills Silas gave to me, slapping them on the counter along with two bags for carrying all this shit.

If I'm going to be someone's whore, then I'll eat to my fucking heart's content.

I go back outside and hang the bags on my steering wheel before I hop on and try to hold my balance while biking across the city. Finally, I get to my building, but first, I double-check my surroundings and wait a while to see if anyone has followed me here before I head inside.

The remaining bills crunch up in my palm as I struggle not to throw them into the bin in the hallway, but that would destroy the only remaining value of my sacrifice. So I hold it as tightly as I can, forcing myself to walk up to Mrs. Schwartz's apartment, where I place down my bags so I can knock on the door.

She opens up, and the cat immediately runs out, purring, as she rolls around my legs, along with Cora, who hugs me tight. "You're here!"

"She's given me the runaround, Jesus." Mrs. Schwartz rolls her eyes. "How much longer do I have to do the nights too? I can't keep this up." She moans and rubs her back.

"Please, can I sleep in our bed, Ivy? Please?" Cora begs, holding my legs like she's afraid she'll be sent back.

I really didn't want to risk it, but her sweet little face beaming up at me makes it hard to say no. "All right."

She squeals and hugs me even tighter.

Mrs. Schwartz holds out her hand without saying a word, and I place two of the bills on top.

"For the effort," I say.

"Thanks." She eyes me down like she thinks I've become a drug dealer. "Where'd you get all those hundreds?"

"Pole dancing." I laugh it off.

"Hmpf." She sticks up a cigarette. "Didn't think you'd dance for them boys. Oh well. Guess these halls are full of freaks."

She closes the door on us without saying another word, and I shrug at Cora, who seems awfully confused by her behavior. I'm just glad I have a decently reliable nanny.

"Let's go home," I say, picking her up in my arms and unlocking the door to our apartment.

Bagel dashes inside, searching for his favorite spot by the window.

"It's so boring staying with Mrs. Schwartz. She doesn't have a lot of toys and only wants to watch TV," Cora says as I put her down on the couch. "But I do know how much all the jewelry costs from the sales channel now."

I chuckle. "That will come in handy when we get rich."

"Oh! Then we can finally get that chocolate cereal!"

I grin and pull up the bags of groceries, planting them firmly on the kitchen counter. "Don't have to wait anymore ..." Her eyes begin to glow like stars as I pull out the cereal she's been dying to taste, and she jumps off and snatches it out of my hands, hugging it like it's her world's best friend. "Thank you!"

"Told you I'd get them."

She runs to hug me next, nearly dropping the box.

"Promise is a promise," I whisper, patting her back. "And look what else I got."

I empty the bag on the counter, and my ears are blasted with a shriek. "Berries? Eggos? Omigod!"

"So ..." I grab the pan and a spatula. "Who's hungry for a late-night dinner with Eggos, pancakes, and cereal?"

She sticks up her little hand. "Me!"

**

HEATH

"Why can't we hang out at my place?" Mavis asks as we head up the stairs. She's still nose-deep in one of those Wiccan books of hers. "I wanted you to listen to the new band I found. They're amazing."

"We always hang there," I reply. "And you can play the same songs on my setup. Besides, I need to talk with Silas. Stay here."

Mavis frowns, folding her arms as she leans back against a wall near the stairs. "I didn't want to see his filthy room anyway."

His door is open, and when I look inside, I'm surprised he's not there.

It's nine p.m. Did Ivy not show up like she was told?

Or did he already finish toying with her?

"Where is she?"

"Gone." He pops out of the room where we keep all our weapons. I frown. "Gone as in ...?"

He raises a brow. "I let her off the hook. Don't start insinuating things. I'm insane, not stupid."

Good. I was almost starting to worry I might have even more on my hands.

A kill outside campus, that I can solve.

A kill on campus? Under Dean Rivera's nose? No way that'll slip by him.

"What'd you do with her?"

"Everything I fucking wanted and then some," he growls, a wicked glimmer in his eyes. "But I'm not nearly done yet."

"Who the fuck are you talking about?" Mavis asks, pushing herself off the wall.

"The thief," Silas says.

"Wait, it's a *her*?" She approaches us. "Holy shit."

"We're making her pay for stealing from us."

"How?"

Silas cocks his head, a smug grin slowly spreading on his face. "I have my ways."

She scowls. "Ew."

"Her saliva's still on my floor," Silas hisses.

Mavis clenches her eyes like she can't even look at him without wanting to vomit. "Don't give me the gross details I didn't ask for. Do whatever the fuck you want, but keep me out of it."

I laugh at their banter. "What were you doing in the weapons room?" I ask Silas. "Overthinking your sins?"

"Shopping."

"Shopping for what?" Mavis asks.

He ignores her and pulls his phone from his pocket. "Mom called. Apparently, we were supposed to be there tonight for dinner with the whole family. She sounded pretty pissed we weren't there."

Her eyes widen. "Oh fuck. I forgot." She immediately runs down a flight of stairs.

"Ugh," I grumble.

"Upset you can't have another fucking date night with my sister?" Silas growls.

"That's not—no."

God, I fucking hate when he brings that up.

"That was once. *Once.* And I'm over it. Forever."

He crosses his arms, smiling smugly. "Oh really?"

"We have a far more interesting plaything," I say, grinning.

A spark of rage flashes through his eyes. "I already fucked with her."

"Doesn't mean I can't, too," I retort.

"Whatever." He shrugs. "I'm off. Mom and Dad are probably gonna kill me."

"Is that why you were looking at the weapons? To defend yourself when they come for you?" I joke.

"No." He sucks in a breath. "Because I need a release after tonight. Are you with me?" he asks.

I nod, licking my lips at the prospect. "Fucking bet on it."

"I'll call you when I'm done." He grins at me as he passes by. "Bring the machete."

EIGHTEEN

SILAS

"Finally, I cooked this new recipe, and none of y'all had the balls to actually show up!" Mom throws the leftover sludge she "baked" in the oven on the dinner table, the rancid smell nearly making me throw up on the spot.

"Mom ..." Xavier begins.

"No, I want none of it! I tried my best, okay? At least you could've tried it. Did any of you even remember we had a date planned?"

She looks at Xavier, Aspen, Melody, Mavis, and me like we're her long-lost children she hasn't seen in years even though it's been maybe two weeks tops.

"Sorry, Mom," Aspen says. "It just ... slipped my mind." She adds a chuckle for good measure.

"I don't think any of us did it on purpose." Mavis smiles.

Mom throws her purple hair over her shoulder and tilts her head. "Really?"

"Penelope, please give those kids a break. They're doing their best at school," Alistair, one of my mom's boyfriends, says as he walks in with tousled hair and a certain swagger in his step. His knuckles and the sides of his hands are still covered in pencil streaks from all the drawing he's done today for his comic book.

He's not my dad, but my mom decided to raise us half siblings together. Only Mavis is my actual sister.

"Dad, don't go easy on them," Melody jests, poking me with her elbow.

If she wasn't already fragile enough, I would've thrown her halfway across the room.

"We're here now, aren't we?" I say, folding my arms.

Mom stares at me, incensed. "True, but that doesn't excuse—"

"Who wants to make the biggest fucking pyre in the yard this world has ever seen?" Dylan, my mom's other boyfriend, yells as he walks into the kitchen through the back door in the kitchen, wearing only flip-flops and a pair of Havana shorts, oblivious to her rage.

Mom merely stands there, flabbergasted he'd even try to upend her.

"Me!" Aspen quickly yells, bolting to the door.

Right as she passes Dylan, he pats her on the back. "That's my girl."

"Really, Dylan? Fucking really?" My mom's eyebrows begin to twitch.

"What?" Dylan shrugs. "I bought all this wood. It would be a shame if we didn't use it."

"Dylan..." Penelope grits, seething.

"Me too," Mavis swiftly says, rushing to the back door.

"And me," Xavier replies.

"I'm in too," I say, definitely feeling the heat.

I didn't just get my temper from my dad, who's already out in the yard gathering the logs.

Melody tags along. "Don't forget about me!"

"Not you too," Alistair groans. "Oh fuck. This is not going to end well."

Mom begins to scream and picks up a piece of her own sludge pie with her bare hands. Dad immediately drops everything and runs towards the back door, shoving Dylan aside. "What happened?"

Too late because Mom just threw her own food ... right at his face.

She pauses and blinks, her face growing white. The rest of us are frozen in the backyard, staring through the back door at the horror that just unfolded. My dad's face turns redder by the second—not from embarrassment but from rage.

Fuck.

"Penelope ..." Felix growls as he wipes the sludge off his stone-cold face.

She seems absolutely mortified. I'd be, too, if I'd thrown lukewarm food at my dad's face. He will literally kill people over that shit.

All of us kids get up close to peer inside and see what's about to go down.

"Get out. A bomb's gonna explode, and as much as I love a good blowout, you do not want to be caught in the crossfire of this one," Dylan says, shooing us away with a grin on his face.

Felix's lips curl up. "Motherf—"

Alistair puts his hands against his mouth. "FOOD FIGHT!"

He picks up a handful of the pie and throws it at Dylan's face, which hits him right in the teeth. Dylan splutters and coughs, and everyone bursts out into laughter.

"Okay, that's it." Dylan, and practically everyone else, storms at the table to grab a handful of food, throwing it around at whoever is in their vicinity. And after five throws, even my mom pitches in, chucking bits and pieces at whoever gets in her way.

"Here! Have a fucking taste of my pie!" she yells, laughing out loud just like the rest of us. "Doesn't it fucking taste good?!"

I manage to dodge most hits, trying to empty the pan before they all come after me.

"Aw, this was my good shirt!" Xavier pulls the fabric over his head.

"Stop whining, bitch." Mavis throws a full hand at his chest, making everyone else laugh.

"I'm so glad you all came home. It's no fun without you guys!" Melody says, throwing small hands left and right despite hitting very few people.

I'm still clean, but the second they all look at me with suspicion, I turn around. "Oh fuck no."

I bolt outside through the back door with everyone on my heels.

"Come here, you little shit!" Felix roars, throwing the biggest load of pie.

I laugh maniacally. "Fucking catch me if you can, cowards!"

Maybe this dinner wasn't so bad after all.

***

HEATH

Max is on the couch in the common room of the Skull and Serpent Society, reading a book intensely. I throw my bag down on the floor and grab his shoulders, but he swiftly closes the book and tucks it away under his ass.

"You scared me, Heath," he says, looking over his shoulder.

"Why? What're you reading?"

"Nothing," he says with big doe eyes.

I roll my eyes. "Fine. You don't wanna tell me, then don't."

He scratches the back of his head. "It's nothing you'd find interesting anyway."

"Thanks," I say, squeezing his shoulders as I lean in. "So, have you talked with Ivy recently?"

He tenses up. "No. Why do you want to know?"

"I'm curious if she still lets you get close to her."

He lowers his head. "She doesn't trust me because of what you did."

"What *we* did." I pat him on the chest. "You're part of our group, remember?"

"Right, but I don—"

I grab his face and turn it sideways until those submissive eyes bore into mine. "You always do what I want. Don't you?"

He gulps. "If you ask me nicely."

"And if I don't ask nicely? What will you do then?" I'm so close, he's beginning to sweat, and I lean in to bite the air between us, making him jolt up and down in his seat. "Cry?"

He jerks his head free from my grip, and I'm thrown off by the sudden defiance, which is unlike him.

"Fine. Whatever you want. Can I read now?"

I sigh. "Why don't you just come along with Silas and me tonight?"

"Where are you two going?" he asks.

I pick up the bag, and the metal inside makes a lot of sound. "We've got something special planned."

His eyes home in on the bag before they narrow. "Like what?"

A grin slowly spreads on my face. "Something fun ... and wicked."

He licks his lips. "I... I'll pass, thanks."

"Aw, c'mon. You never come along." I throw my arm around his neck. "I'd love to have you there."

"I'm busy. Sorry."

I frown, disappointment marring my face. "Fine. Suit yourself."

I walk off, my stomach churning with resentment. He's never been this apathetic about hanging out with me, and it dulls the happiness I nearly felt at the prospect of showing him just how devilish I can be.

I open the bag and pop open the pills I got, taking out two and swallowing them whole.

If I can't feel even a little bit thrilled, then I won't feel anything at all instead.

But what is up with Max's detached attitude? Something's not right, but I can't pinpoint what. Outside, I stare at his motorcycle and think it over for a moment.

Maybe ... just maybe...

I fish my tracker from my bag, stick it to the inside of his luggage compartment, and pull up the tracker app on my phone.

Then I hop into my car, chuck the bag on the back seat, start the car, and race off.

Fuck, this car is the only thing that makes me feel alive, makes me feel anything at all. Adrenaline surges through my veins, the fuel that keeps me going. I don't know why I am this way. All I know is that I need the kick to survive. To feel something other than dead inside.

I pop open the bottle and take another pill, feeling the high slowly come on.

It's not enough.

I need more, so much fucking more.

I turn on the heavy metal music and hit the gas to chase the darkness, nearly catching flight as I race down the mountains and head into the city. I know exactly where I'm going, and I don't wait for red lights to turn green before I pass an empty street.

At the edge of the city is a giant mansion with a huge fence around it, and I park my car near the gates, pressing the button on the wall.

"Hello?" a voice calls out.

"Heath here. I'm picking up Silas."

"Of course, Sir. I will send him down."

Send him down? He's upstairs? At his parents' house?

Frowning, I wait until Silas finally comes out of the house and walks up to the gate. "Just in time."

"Looks like you had a great time in there," I say.

His family waves at me from the distance, and I wave back with a fake smile.

"It wasn't as bad as I thought it would be," he says. "Until Mom decided to force everyone to Melody's room and gush about her paintings." He rolls his eyes. "I've already seen them a million times."

I look at his shirt, which is decidedly... pink. And has a unicorn on it. "Wait a minute ... Weren't you wearing something else?"

"This is the only thing Mom had that I could fit into. Don't ask what happened." He jumps into the car. "Did you bring an extra hoodie?"

"No, just the masks," I reply.

He sighs out loud. "Fine. I'll keep this on. Are we ready?"

I eye the bag in the back, and his wicked smile makes me grin too. "Let's go fuck some shit up."

***

MAX

Ten minutes later

From my motorcycle, I look through her window, checking for any movement, anything out of the ordinary. I'm antsy, desperate to know if Silas and Heath planned on doing something to her tonight, but it appears they chose another target instead.

I have to admit, when Heath said he and Silas had planned something wicked, I was worried it would involve her. Not because I don't like watching what they do, but because every time I talk to her afterward, there's more hatred in her voice than before.

Hate is Silas's business, and every time he touches her, he injects it straight into her veins.

I blow out a sigh, but the second the light comes on, I switch into hypervigilant mode.

She's never awake at this time of the day.

I know because I've watched her do her routine with that little girl every goddamn night since I set my eyes on her.

What is going on?

I bring out my binoculars and watch her through the window. She's putting on a hoodie and slings a bag over her shoulder that appears quite heavy.

The lights go off, and I tuck my binoculars away, then wait, and wait, and wait ... And there she is, exiting the building to hop on her bike and race off.

Something's not right.

She'd never leave that kid alone unless it was important enough. Unless it could put them in even more danger if she didn't go.

I swiftly put on my helmet and race after her.

NINETEEN

IVY

I check the kiddie monitor and make sure it works before I head out the door and hop on my bike. As long as she's asleep, she'll be safe I won't stay away for more than fifteen minutes, tops. I'll just bike to the industrial side of the city and pop in and out of warehouse five hundred eighteen.

I count down the time it takes me to get to the location by checking my watch every now and then, and I push the pedals as fast as I can. No time to waste. The only one watching over Cora right now is Bagel, and if an intruder steps in, Bagel will flop down on their toes and ask for pets instead. Traitor.

Sweat rolls down my back as I come to a stop beside the warehouse.

I fish my phone from my pocket and look at my messages to remind myself why I'm here in this secluded area of the city.

Anonymous: Come to Warehouse five hundred eighteen. Eleven p.m. Bring cash. Come alone.

I swallow back the nerves and check the kiddie monitor next. She's still fast asleep. Good.

I put my hoodie over my head and tighten the straps. With surging adrenaline, I enter the warehouse's open door, clutching both bands of my backpack strapped around my shoulders tightly. The only light comes from the small streetlight behind me, and it casts an eerie shadow deep inside the warehouse. I wouldn't normally come here unless my life depended on it, but unfortunately, that's exactly the case.

Get in, get out. That's it.

My senses are on high alert as I look around in the dark. My breathing comes out in short puffs, the chilly night air making me shiver as I dig my hands into my pockets and feel the safety of the metal handle of my knife, my only form of protection.

At the end of the hallway, a man stands, lurched over a makeshift fire he put together from pieces of logwood stored in this warehouse.

"You brought the money?" His voice brings chills to my bones.

I approach him, but he holds up a hand. "That's far enough."

With a racing heart, I pull my bag off my shoulders and take out the wads of cash I stole from the boys. When I told them I spent it all, I lied, but it was a necessary lie.

"Put it down on the floor."

I slowly place the stack on the concrete floor in front of me, but I don't let go of it yet. "What guarantees can you give me that we'll be safe?"

"Did you think you'd still be frolicking around in that apartment of yours if you weren't?"

I swallow down the lump in my throat.

He knows where I live.

Fuck!

I knew that fucker's reach was huge, but not that he'd be able to track me within a few months already.

"As long as you keep paying, I won't talk," he says.

"How much?"

"Five grand. Each month."

"Five?!" My nostrils flare. "I can't—"

"You'll make it happen." He chuckles, stepping forward into the light of the fire. An eerie-looking scar goes all the way across his lip. A scar I recognize from my past life, one that brings terror to my bones.

"Because you made this choice. And now you'll live with the consequences. Won't you?"

With furrowed brows, I nod.

"Good. Now step away, and I promise you and your little Cora won't get in trouble."

I pull away from the money and slowly step back, but my hands still dive into my pockets as I contemplate whether to take my chances and flee with the money.

It'd be one witness down, more money for me, and our location kept secret.

"Don't even think about it," he says. "I already told one other insider. In case you'd try something on me."

Fuck. So that plan is out the window.

I pull my hands from my pocket. "You keep your end of the deal, and I'll keep mine."

"I already told you the terms of our agreement." A devilish smirk forms on his face. "Now leave. Before you get in more trouble than you're already in."

I scowl but still turn around, telling myself it'll all be fine.

I'll just have to find a new place to rob every month. That's it. I can do that, easy. Right?

***

MAX

I follow her all the way to the warehouse without her noticing and park my motorcycle a few blocks down, then trail her on foot.

She never noticed I already installed the tracker on her bike.

Not because I want her to be afraid or feel stalked but because I need to know if she's safe. If I can't be near, then at least I'll make sure she's okay.

What the fuck was that all about?

She gave this gnarly-looking guy a wad of cash, and he couldn't even promise he'd protect her and the kid... from who?

A shiver runs down my spine, and I swiftly make my way back through the streets before she catches me here. However, a few screams up ahead make me turn my head.

What the … ?

There's a bloody trail on the ground as well, and when I follow it, it leads into an alley. Two guys with knives stand in the dark with only a small flashlight to mark their prey. My eyes widen. "Heath?"

Both of them look at me like they're seeing an uninvited guest.

"I thought you didn't wanna come?" Heath asks.

Silas turns to him, lowering his knife. "You asked him to come?"

"Of course, I did," Heath says.

"I thought he hated this kind of stuff," Silas replies.

Oh shit. What do I tell them now?

I can't say anything about Ivy being here too, or they'll definitely want to know what she's up to.

"Um … I finished reading the book and then decided I actually did want to come."

"Why didn't you just call me?" Heath asks as he pulls out his phone to check.

I shrug. "Forgot."

"How did you know where we were?" Silas asks.

"I followed Heath," I lie. "Right after you left the building."

He grins as he lowers his phone. "Oh, well then, why didn't you fucking say so?" He approaches me.

"Because I like to watch without people seeing me," I say, laughing awkwardly.

Heath pats me on the shoulder. "Well, c'mon then, ogler." He drags me along with him. "Here." Heath plucks a mask from his bag and stuffs it into my hand. "Put this on and come join in on the fun."

***

IVY

I swiftly exit the building and hop on my bike, getting the fuck out of here before that asshole decides to come after me because he's got his money now. I race through the streets so I can get out of the industrial area as quickly as possible. This dimly lit neighborhood is no place to be at eleven o'clock at night, and I barely know this place. I can't remember if I took a left or a right here, so I opt for a left instead, only to come to a dead end.

But something on the other end of the street makes me hit the brakes.

A man is lifted against the stone walls of a building, at least two feet off the ground, with four fucking knives stuck in his hands and feet. His screams echo across the street. Three men stand in front of him, two in all black, the other with a ... pink unicorn shirt?

I blink twice to see if I'm getting this right.

The pink-shirt guy lifts a giant machete, and my jaw drops.

Inch by inch, he slowly cuts the man like he's carving off pieces of flesh, draining him of his blood.

My eyes widen in shock.

Holy shit.

The man's head turns sideways, and his eyes suddenly dart to me. "Please! Help me!"

I stand there, frozen to the ground for a split second, as the three masked men turn their heads like vultures, eyes sparkling with vicious murder on their minds.

One with black-tipped hair and icy green eyes, one with brown hair, and a third with longer brown hair in a bun and a piercing in his lip and brow.

Oh fuck.

I hop back on and make a U-turn, racing off on my bike as fast as I can. I'm not sticking around. I just caught those three fuckers from the Skull and Serpent Society in the process of torturing someone, and I'm not about to be their next victim.

TWENTY

SILAS

"Who the fuck was that?!" I grind my teeth. "Max, go after that fucker while I finish the job."

He frowns. "Wait, why me?"

"Have you done anything at all since you came here?" I grit. "No, so get to it."

Max rolls his eyes, lowers his hoodie, and runs off.

I swing the machete around and let the man suffer in agony for a few more seconds, his blood dripping down from his lips onto the pavement. We roughed him up real good before we strung him up here on this wall and sliced him open piece by piece.

"You think he got the message?" Heath looks the body up and down.

"Probably ..." I begin, "not."

The fucker deserves nothing less for plucking kids off the streets and selling them. Heath got onto his track through his drug seller when he tried to offer some free drugs disguised as candy to unsuspecting kids.

Too bad for him, I don't fucking play with that.

"P-Please, please, h-have mercy," the man stammers.

"You didn't have mercy on any of those kids you took from the streets," Heath growls.

I caress his face with the machete. "How many did you sell? Five? Ten? A hundred?"

"More," he replies, gulping the second I reach his temple.

I grin like a total psycho. "Was it worth all the money to lose your fucking life?"

I lift the machete.

"No, no, no, please!"

I hit him straight in the heart, cutting through him from sternum to pelvis until nothing but a sack of flesh is left of him. And man, does it feel good to kill him. It would've been far more fun if I could've toyed with him a little longer.

Finding a victim as deserving as him is a hard find.

Normally, I have to get by with punishing petty thieves or even those who merely looked at me the wrong way.

I swipe my machete clean on his shirt and take out all my knives. His body flops to the ground, and I give it a good kick to turn him over. I go to my knees and rummage inside his chest until I find his heart, and I rip it out, staring at it. Fucking gorgeous.

* * *

MAX

I run around the corner and spot a bike disappearing into the night. It goes left and right, and then left, but when I turn the corner, it's gone. I look around and check all the ways the bike could've gone.

Ivy, please, let me find you. I need you to be safe.

I walk around the neighborhood, each of my steps reverberating between the many warehouses that line these streets. On the ground are skid marks that look fresh. I look up in the direction she went—a road to my right with several dumpsters behind each door leading into a warehouse. Behind one of them, the spokes and an inch of a wheel peek out.

Oh, Ivy. You shouldn't have come here.

Grinding my teeth, I watch the feet disappear behind the dumpster.

If I bring her to Heath and Silas now, they'll definitely mess her up too just for watching them kill. And I can't fucking let that happen.

I take a deep breath and approach her, but the second I raise my head above the dumpster, she nearly swats off my head with a wooden stick like it's a bat and I'm the baseball.

"Wow, wow, calm down."

"Stay away!" She keeps swinging that thing like she's trying to hit something. "I swear to G—"

I grab the stick mid-swing and stop her, and I take off my mask to show her it's me. With big eyes, she ogles me. "I'm not going to hurt you. I promised you. And I will keep that promise."

"They were torturing someone!"

I smash my hand in front of her mouth. "Shhh! Don't let them hear you."

She bites my palm, and I yank it back, hissing as I shake my hand.

"You're with them," she says. "Why are they doing this?"

"I can't tell you. I'm sorry. But I will get you out of this."

"Then what were you—Wait, how?" She frowns and points at me. "You all saw me."

"No, they didn't. They think you were some rando, which is why they sent me after you. But I'm not taking you back to them."

"I wouldn't let you," she says, swinging the stick around like she's trying to show off.

"Good." I smile. "Now grab your bike and get out of here."

With furrowed brows, she eyes me up and down, still holding the stick tightly like she's afraid it'll be her last resort.

"Quickly, before they get suspicious."

Finally, she drops the stick, makes a beeline for her bike, and races off.

When she's out of sight, I breathe a sigh of relief and put my mask back on. Even though I know I'll have to face Silas's and Heath's wrath now. It was worth it.

***

Heath Max suddenly walks back into our alley, and I look up with furrowed brows.

He didn't bring anyone with him.

What the...?

"I couldn't find them."

My teeth slam together.

Fuck.

Silas nearly crushes the guy's heart he ripped out in his bare hand. "You let a loose end get away?"

"They had a bike, but I don't see it anywhere. Probably hiding out somewhere." He shrugs.

"And you just gave up?" Well, this just dampened my already darkened mood.

Silas stuffs the bloodied heart in a plastic bag and walks up to his car. "They saw us. We need to rip them to shreds."

"But do they know us? We're wearing masks. No way they recognized our faces," Max replies.

Hmm. "Dude has a point," I say.

"Whatever. If this comes back to bite us, you're gonna take care of it." Silas points at Max.

Max puts his hand against his head like a military soldier and salutes him, making me grin.

"It's settled then," I say. "Now help us put the body in the trunk."

*　＊＊＊*

IVY

Twenty minutes later

I close the door to my apartment and turn all the locks, clutching the wood while breathing wildly. I just saw them murder a man in cold blood.

Jesus, I looked them dead in the eyes.

Even with those masks, I instantly knew it was them. But did Silas and Heath recognize me?

Will Max keep his word?

I suck in a breath through my nose and head to the windows, checking every corner of the street despite it being pitch black outside. I need to know if they followed me. If there's even an inkling of danger out there, I'm grabbing the kitchen knives and the gun I have hidden in a safe box on top of my closet where Cora can't reach.

My heart races a million miles an hour as I check every window for their car, but there's no sign of them anywhere.

Did I get away safely?

It almost feels too good to be true.

"Mrppp."

Bagel brushes up against my legs, and I pick him up and pet him. He always manages to calm my nerves. "I love you too, Bagel."

I put him back down, check on Cora, and breathe a sigh of relief. She's still sleeping and safe as can be. I take off my hoodie and put on my white tee and a fresh pair of undies before I crawl in bed too, hugging her tightly. She curls up to me and mumbles a little in her sleep, and it makes me smile.

We're safe for now.

***

One year ago

Leaning back in my seat, I take a sip of my Coke while staring at the piece of cake on the plate in front of me. It must taste delicious, I'm sure, but if I take a bite, that means the cake will eventually be finished, along with this day.

I don't want it to end.

"It's so delicious," Mom mumbles, taking a small bite out of her cake, like she's afraid someone will say something about it if she takes a bigger bite.

She tucks her hair behind her ear, the green mark on her face visible for just a second before she readjusts her shades.

"Aren't you going to take a bite?" she asks.

I put down my Coke and pick up my fork, still glaring at that piece of cake. Just one day. That's what it symbolizes. One day of calmness before the storm erupts.

But I don't want to disappoint Mom either. I take a small bite and swallow it, waiting for her content smile to appear.

"Good, right?"

"Love it," I reply, smiling back.

"See?" she says.

"Mom ..." I mutter, putting down my fork. "I've been meaning to tell you, but I didn't know when would be the right time. So I thought, why not on your birthday?"

She pauses, her fork hanging between her fingertips. "What?"

I suck in a deep breath through my nostrils before finally gathering the courage to pull the paper from my bag that I've been holding for too long, and I place it on the table in her direction so she can read it.

"I have a scholarship. I got accepted into Spine Ridge U," I say.

Her eyes fill with tears, and she gets up to hug me right over the table, smushing both of our cakes, and it catches me off guard.

"Oh, I'm so happy for you, Ivy, I could scream." I wrap my arms around her too. "Why didn't you tell me?"

"This was my dream for so long. I didn't know how."

Or when it would ever be a good time.

"I'm so proud of you. You did it," she murmurs into my ear. "And I know your dad would be too if he were here."

I swallow away the lump in my throat. "Thank you."

I almost feel guilty for telling her.

She refuses to let go. "You deserve this. And don't let anyone, and I mean anyone, take this away from you. You understand?" Her tone suddenly got a lot more serious, and it brings goose bumps to my skin.

"I won't," I mutter. "But ... I don't want to leave you—"

"Don't. Don't say the words. If you don't say them, it doesn't exist."

If we don't say the words we want to say out loud, we can keep living the lie.

But we all know a lie is as sustainable as a self-eating void.

"You go to that school," she says. "Whatever it takes."

I smile. "I will."

***

Present

I sit up straight from the sound of rattling near the window. I blink a couple of times to get out of my nightmares and back into reality. I don't know how much time has passed. It feels like forever.

I brush away the sweat dripping down my skin as I look around, but there doesn't appear to be anything here.

I yawn and get up, walking into the living room in only a bit of underwear and a white shirt. I lock the door to the bedroom with the key to make sure Cora's safe at all times before I head to the kitchen. Bagel is rummaging with his bowl, so maybe he woke me up.

I fill it with more food, and he purrs with thanks. I turn around again but suddenly spot a figure sitting on the couch.

I freeze.

The person turns around, his face hiding in his hoodie, so I bolt to the button on the wall to turn on the light, but not in time before he's already cornered me against the wall. My shriek is cut off by a hand covering my mouth.

"Shh ..." The whisper is soft. Almost ... friendly. "Don't want to wake Cora."

What the—

I spin on my heels.

The crazed yell I was about to throw out there is swallowed down as I stare straight into Max's sweet eyes.

"You're here ..." I mutter, confused. "How—"

My words are cut off as I realize why.

The key he stole from me.

"I needed to know if you were safe. But then ... I couldn't leave anymore." His Adam's apple goes up and down as his eyes skid across my face, almost as if he's looking for answers to questions I don't understand.

"Do Silas and Heath know you're here?" I ask.

He shakes his head.

"I can't stop thinking about you," he says, lowering his hand off the wall. "Even when you hate me, I still lie awake every night, wondering if you'd ever forgive me."

"I don't ... hate you," I reply, swallowing down the nerves.

His eyes fill with a kind of hope that makes my heart flutter, and a gentle smile appears on his face but then swiftly disappears. "You should. I'm not good for you. I know that. You don't know what I've do—"

I plant a finger on his lips, narrowing my eyes. "You didn't rat me out to them."

He lowers his eyes. "I couldn't."

He protected me.

"But they'll hurt you if they find out," I say, "won't they?"

He nods, biting his lip, and for some reason, it's so fucking alluring that I lean in to press a kiss to his lips. Just one.

Just one tiny kiss is enough for me to see him unravel right before my eyes.

Suddenly, he grips my face with both hands and smashes his lips onto mine, kissing me so intensely I forget how to breathe.

I shouldn't be doing this with a friend of the boys who've blackmailed me.

I definitely shouldn't, but I can't fucking stop.

I've never been kissed this passionately before—like he's pouring out all of his love into this one kiss as if he'll never get another shot.

Suddenly, he pulls away and steps back. "Sorry, I don't know what came over me, I—"

I place another finger on his lips. "Don't."

"I'm bad for you. I'm a Skull and Serpent Society member. I'm in your house uninvited. I stalk you. You have a kid. I'm endangering both of you by being here. I should—"

I plant both hands on his chest and shove him backward more and more until the back of his knees hit the couch, and he falls.

I settle down on top of him and lean in, whispering into his ear, "Do you want me?"

"Oh God ... yes." It nearly comes out in a moan.

I press my boobs against his chest, and he gulps as I grab his hands and put them over my shoulders while I press silky soft kisses all over his neck. "Then touch me."

His hand lowers down my body, across my breasts, squeezing, moaning when I leave a hickey. "Do you think they'd wonder where you got it?"

"Heath will be mad, for sure," he replies.

I grin. "Good."

And I push his hand farther down until he reaches my panties. "You know how I like it. You've seen me do it." I lean back up. "Now touch me."

He rubs me right through the fabric of my underwear, his gaze on me at all times as though he's enamored with the way I look when I'm enjoying myself, and something about that just feels so goddamn good, I can't help but gyrate on top of him.

As he circles my most sensitive spot, his bulge begins to grow underneath me, so I push down as I roll my hips around to egg him on. I lean back on his knees as he increases his pace, and I whisper, "Yes, just like that."

"Oh fuck, I've dreamed about this," he says.

I smirk. "What do we do in your dreams? How do you take me?"

"In my dreams, *you* take *me*."

TWENTY-ONE

IVY

Max grabs my hand and brings it to his neck until my fingers are around his veins.

"Use me."

My nails dig into his skin. I tighten my grip, and he whimpers, his cock throbbing beneath me.

"Yes. Please. More. Give me more."

I grip his hand and force my own panties aside with his fingers until he gets the message, and when he's finally flicking my clit, I nearly die and go to heaven right there and then. God, he really knows how to pleasure me, how to make me want more without ever saying even a single word. He's just that eager to please.

I cut off his oxygen supply slow and steadily, just like Silas and Heath did to me, while his eyes are solely fixated on me. He continues to rub me vigorously as if spurred on by my need to punish him for what his friends did.

I'm using him like they used me, and he's begging me to do it.

This ... this is what power feels like.

Exhilarating.

***

MAX

I have never wanted a woman more than I want her.

I know it's insane since I barely know her ... but I know that I *want* her. Badly. Wildly. In any way shape or form, she'd be enough for me, as long as I could have her.

Even if it means sacrificing my own goddamn breath.

I can feel her rage pour out from her fingertips straight into the veins in my neck as she squeezes tightly. But I don't care. I can't breathe, can't even think about anything other than pleasing her. It's the only thing that matters to me right now.

She didn't tell me to leave, and I physically can't will myself to get up and walk away. Not from her.

Even though I should because I'm not what she thinks I am. If she only knew what I agreed to, she'd never forgive me. Maybe that's why I want her to make me suffer.

"Make it hurt," I croak.

Her fingers loosen from around my neck, and she slaps me. Hard.

"Focus. Use your fingers."

This. This is what I need. For someone to tell me what to do, to use me, to wield me like some goddamn body made for her pleasure alone.

I need *her*.

I need her because she won't take it for granted.

She won't hurt that one part of me I've kept locked away deep inside.

My fingers roll around her pussy, her wetness covering all of my fingers, and I am desperate for her approval as I look into those dark-brown eyes while she slowly begins to fall apart. Her enjoyment is visible on her face, and I marvel at just how much more beautiful she is when she's close to nirvana. How amazing it is that she would give this privilege to me.

Good God.

I think I'm falling for this woman.

This woman who fights so hard to keep the simple life she lives while others keep trying to take it away.

I am in awe.

Completely and utterly obsessed.

My free hand drifts to her beautiful body as I can't control myself any longer. My fingers slide along her neckline, her pretty bones, her soft belly, and those perfect breasts that fit into the palm of my hand.

"God, I fucking adore you. You're too perfect, too—"

She slams her hand in front of my mouth. "Enough talking. More fucking."

Fucking?

Oh God, yes.

She rolls her hips around so wildly I whimper into her mouth. It's too much. Too much to feel her wetness on my fingers, to have those gorgeous tits up in my face, to have her squeeze the life out of me just for her enjoyment.

I can't hold it.

I moan loudly as my dick begins to throb ... inside my pants.

Warm juices roll down my thighs, filling my pants.

Oh God.

She furrows her brows and leans away, her eyes slowly traveling down my body while I pant. "Did you just ...?"

She tugs at my zipper.

I gasp. "Wait—"

Too late as my cock already bounces out of the underwear she just ripped down, still erect and spurting cum everywhere.

I moan as her fingers touch the tip, and she giggles. "You came just from touching *me*?"

"I'm sorry." She gets off my lap. "I can't help it." She kneels. "You're just too sexy, and I'm—"

My words turn into a loud moan as my entire length disappears into her mouth. "*Fuuuck.*"

She licks my shaft, spreading around all my juices, lapping them up like she enjoys the taste, and fuck me, I'm so goddamn turned on. My cock refuses to go down as she keeps licking me. Her tongue feels divine.

"Go on, moan for me then," she says, taking me deep.

I can't help but let the groan spill out of my mouth. She's just that good.

But the arrogant grin on her face really seals the deal.

Fuck.

"You like this, don't you?" I ask. "Making guys want you." Her tongue really distracts me. "What else do you like?"

"I like making guys moan instead of talk," she jests, circling her tongue around the tip before sucking me off.

"Fuck, that'll do it," I say.

She's avoiding answering my questions, but why? Does she still not trust me?

Suddenly, she gets up and straddles me. "You think you can keep up with me?"

"What, why?" I ask, but before I can answer, she's already pushed that beautiful pussy down on my cock, and my God, it feels like I've died and gone to heaven itself.

Fuck me, she fits so perfectly around me, it's insane.

"Now I see what you mean with talk less, fuck more," I say.

She smiles and thrusts down onto my lap, making me groan out loud. "You're here for sex, aren't you? Then fuck me."

But that's just it. I'm not only interested in her because of the sex.

I want more, so much more, but would she ever give it to me? Do I need to beg?

"Please," I whimper.

She brings my fingers back to her pussy. "You came without my permission. Now keep fucking me for as long as I need it to come too."

"Yes, ma'am," I reply.

She slaps me.

"Fuck," I groan. "Do it again."

She slaps me again. Harder this time.

"Don't call me ma'am. My name is Ivy."

Another slap has me delirious with need, as she bounces around on my lap. "Yes, Ivy. Fuck me."

My balls are getting ready for a second load, but I force myself to keep it together, even when my fingers are touching the most precious gift a girl like her could ever give to me. On my cock, she slowly begins to lose herself as I match her rhythm. I spoil her pussy with my fingers, wishing I could lap her up instead, but I'm already consumed by the fact that she lets me do this. That she wants *me*.

At least, for now.

***

HEATH

When we're done with the body, I drop Silas off at the Skull and Serpent Society house before I make my way back down the mountain road again.

I fish my phone from my pocket and check the tracker.

Funny ... Max has been going back and forth to this address this entire night.

The same address he's been going to on and off.

What could be there?

I hit the gas and race through the streets until I finally reach the address he's supposedly at. His bike is out front next to a building, but he's nowhere in sight. I look up at the windows. There's light coming in from one of them.

Interesting.

I park my car and hop out, checking out the ratchet neighborhood with only worn-down buildings.

Why would Max go here out of all places?

On the right side of the building, there's a small alley and a bunch of shoddy looking fire escapes leading all the way up to the highest floor. And I can clearly see the light spilling from the side of the window on the second highest room in the building.

I grab the fire escape and hoist myself up, not even breaking a sweat as I head up all consecutive stairs until I reach the right height. I peak through the window to catch a glimpse. And from the corner of my eye, I spot two people inside—a girl with dark-brown hair, wearing only a white tee, straddling a dark-haired guy wearing a hoodie. And I instantly fucking recognize him.

Max.

TWENTY-TWO

MAX

"Say my name again," she moans.

"Ivy, please," I moan along with her. "I need it."

"Hmm ... you need it enough to give me back my key?" she muses.

My cock pulses inside her as I can feel her contract, and it's so hard to hold back. Of course, she'd use the key against me right at this very moment, when I'm at my most vulnerable.

But my God, this wet fucking pussy is like heaven, and I'd literally give her everything she wants if she'd ask me to.

"Yes, yes, I'll give you anything. Please!"

"Make me come first," she says, still rolling around achingly slow, as her clit begins to thump.

"Fuck yes, please, let me feel you come," I whisper.

She arches her back, her hair flowing back over her shoulders, granting me the most beautiful sight of her perfect body, and I splay my hand across her belly as her pussy begins to contract around my shaft.

She moans out loud, wetness pouring out of her, and the sheer intensity of it makes me so fucking hungry for more.

"Fuck ..." she murmurs, before lunging back down on top of my shoulders with both hands, her lips crashing right back onto mine. She plants lusty kisses all over my mouth and chin, and I'm lost in ecstasy just from the honor of watching her unravel.

Her fingers slowly find their way back to my neck, gently squeezing tighter and tighter until all the oxygen leaves my throat and all that's left is an empty gasp. And I love how her nails feel when they dig into my flesh as she begins to bounce on my lap in just the right rhythm, covering my entire length with sweet pussy juices. She moves from the front to the back with expert sways until my eyes roll into the back of my head, and a bunch of stars appear on the fucking ceiling while I come undone again.

God.

Those eyes of hers. That's what I see in them. God. Or should I say a goddess?

Her fingers unravel from my throat, and I suck in a breath. "Wow …"

She grins against my lips, planting more sweet, sultry kisses, each one slower than the one before, until I'm bamboozled and … completely lovestruck.

She sinks off my lap and pulls her panties back in place, while I lie here motionless and absolutely spent.

She clears her throat, and leans over to tuck my dick back into my pants. "There. You got what you wanted."

"What do you mean?"

"Just sex, right?" She winks. "That's it."

"No, I … I want to get to know you," I say, sitting up straight.

"What's there to know?" She shrugs. "I live in a dump. I'm a workaholic. I need money. I'm poor. I fight to survive."

"What about Cora?" I ask.

She frowns, her eyes suddenly growing distant. "I don't want to talk about her."

With a forlorn look on her face, she glances at the bedroom where the girl is sleeping and it only makes me more curious to peel away the layers of the mysterious girl in front of me.

I put my hands on her thigh bones which protrude through her skin. "I won't ask you to tell me anything you don't want to tell me."

"Good."

I gaze up into her soulful eyes which are filled with suspicion, and I understand.

She has no reason to trust me, even if I protected her. I am part of their group, I'm a bad guy who enjoys watching people get hurt, I'm the betrayer, and she doesn't even know the worst thing about me.

I am in on their ruse.

And me being here ... I don't know if it's because of my own needs ... or because Heath told me to infiltrate her life.

"I just ..." She sighs. "I can't catch feelings for anyone at Spine Ridge U. It's not an option."

My heart flutters.

Feelings? She has feelings for me?

"I think it's best if you leave," she says, turning away.

Sadness overcomes me, because this ... this is not at all what I'd wanted when I first laid eyes on her. I'm torn between my adoration for her, and my admiration for the person I've known all my life.

How am I supposed to choose?

"And don't tell Heath and Silas about me seeing them kill that man," she says.

I shake my head. "I won't."

"I'll hold you to that."

***

IVY

I close my eyes and rub them. I shouldn't have done this. I don't know why, but I got carried away in the moment. I let my horniness for a man so desperate to please me take control over my actions.

Fuck.

I walk off, but he grabs my hand. "Wait." The way he looks at me is just so ... unsettling to me. Like he would worship the ground I walk on. But nothing I've done warrants that kind of devotion. And definitely not from the guy who's friends with those demons.

"I want you to know I don't give up easily," he says.

I snort and shake my head.

Fuck. Why'd he have to go and say something so sweet?

I head to the kitchen to grab some water. "You should."

I don't know what it is that I'm feeling right now or why I'm so conflicted.

Am I really starting to feel something for this guy?

He gets up off the couch and puts his hoodie back on. "Not when it comes to you."

My soul feels struck by lightning, and I gape at him as he comes up to me. He places the key to my apartment on the kitchen counter. "A promise is a promise."

I don't know what to say.

I thought he came here out of his own selfish needs, that all he wanted was sex as a reward, just like the other two. But maybe ... maybe there's something more between us than either of us are willing to admit.

He opens the front door but pauses halfway through. "I won't stop watching you."

And as he closes the door, my heart beats wildly out of control.

***

HEATH

My face darkens as I lean against the wall on the fire escape.

Ivy fucking Clark. So it was you who got away tonight.

My hand balls into a fist.

And Max is willing to lie to me ... for this thief's pussy?

I'm so fucking mad I could beat a hole into this wall, but I stop myself before I do. This is on him. I told him to make her fall for him, and he apparently succeeded, but he wasn't supposed to hop over to her side. He chose her over us, over *me*.

Max's motorcycle zooms off, and I listen to the sound of the engine disappear into the distance. I almost, almost wanted to go after him. But his time will definitely come. First, I want to see what this thief has been up to.

Finally, I know where she lives.

I peek inside the window again. She's flopped down on the couch, looking exhausted from their fuck session. I keep my eyes solidly on her as she falls asleep right there and then, legs splayed across the couch like she couldn't be bothered to get up.

My nostrils flare.

That's gotta be some excellent fucking pussy, then, if it was worth betraying me for.

My eyes glide over her body, those perky tits and taut nipples, and those panties that are still wet. My tongue dips out to wet my lips.

Maybe I should go and find out exactly why he found it so fucking easy.

I shove the knife between the crevice of the window and hook my fingers underneath, then crack it open. I slowly climb in foot after foot and grab my knife. I'm surprised she didn't lock the window. Or maybe she just forgot because of Max.

With my knife clutched firmly, I look around the apartment. So, this is where our infamous thief lives. She wasn't kidding; she is poor as fuck. There's barely any furniture, and it's all run down like hell.

There's a room to my left, but the door is locked. I could break in, but then I'd wake her up, and a fight would definitely ensue. I'm far more interested in her now that she's asleep. I can hear her breathing all the way from across the room. There's just something so ... attractive about a Sleeping Beauty. Like she's simply there waiting for me to touch her.

My knife is aimed at her heart, and I freeze when she groans and her legs move. She's still fast asleep despite the danger currently invading her house.

I inch closer and closer, feeling the pull like a moth flittering to a flame just to see how close it can get. And the second my fingers make contact with her skin, an electrical current shoots up through my veins.

Fuck.

I watch her eyes flick and wait to see if she wakes up, but she doesn't, so I slide my hand down her body. First across her neck and arms ... then down her chest and belly, where I slowly creep up underneath.

I point my knife straight at her neck, imagining what she'll do if she wakes up.

Would she be scared? Would she try to snatch it out of my hand? Or would she be embarrassed at the fact that her whole body just erupted into goose bumps under my touch?

I snort from how easily I can make her body mine. The fabric moves along with my fingers as she lies on the couch, far away in dreamland, and it makes me wonder what she's dreaming about. If she can feel my fingers crawling up her skin until her tits are exposed.

My cock grows tight against my pants, and my mouth waters, and I can't help but lean over and roll my tongue over those hardened nipples. Still, she doesn't rouse from her sleep. Max must've fucked so hard she couldn't even stay awake.

Does that boy have such a good cock? Or is she just easily destroyed?

I slip my hand down her waist, across her navel, and down across the scar embedded into her skin, and even then, I still slide lower until I reach her panties. Her thighs briefly squeeze together but then relax as I start to circle her clit. The moans she lets out in her sleep are exquisite, like a silent whisper straight from her filthy dreams.

It spurs me to roll my fingers around until her legs slowly begin to widen for me.

"Do you even know how you've gotten under all of our skins?" I murmur, but it still doesn't wake her even though my knife is still firmly lodged between her neck and her chest. "Or was that your plan all along, little thief?"

My eyes flicker to my own fingers as her panties grow wetter and wetter underneath, and a filthy grin forms on my face.

I've been looking for something more for so long ... but maybe the one thing I need is right beneath my fingertips.

And if Max is so goddamn pleased by pleasuring her, then it's time for me to find out exactly why that is.

TWENTY-THREE

HEATH

I circle around and around, watching her body get more and more excited despite the fact that she's still fast asleep, so I slowly slide the fabric of her panties away and slip inside.

She's so goddamn wet, it makes my cock bob up and down in my pants. But it's her moans most of all that make me crazy with lust.

"You're a filthy one, aren't you?" I whisper, my tongue darting out to lick her neck right above the blade. "Even in your sleep, you still want it."

I flick her clit until it's engorged, then dip into her wetness and watch her lips curl up as a soft moan slips out. Still, she doesn't wake from her deep sleep.

I bring my free hand to my pants and pull out my cock, stroking it while I toy with her. I deepen my finger thrusts, coaxing out more wetness as I touch her G-spot. Wetness from her own juices or Max's cum? I can't tell, but her moans reveal the truth.

Her hand slips from underneath her head and nearly touches me as it flops down the couch. Her nipples tighten even more, and I grin from the way my fingers are affecting her so much.

Does she think of riding Max's cock in her sleep?

Or does she secretly imagine it's Silas or me she's fucking?

I know we've already invaded her mind.

Her body yearns for more, more than what Max could ever offer her. It needs someone who isn't afraid to make it bend, to twist it into knots just for the sake of pleasure.

Max doesn't know how to make her ache.

How to make her want to drop to her knees and beg.

But I do.

I pull my fingers out and bring them to my mouth. The taste is divine, and I groan with excitement, my cock ready to claim what I conquered. No wonder Silas loved licking her so much.

I place my knife down on the scar Silas left, push her legs farther open, and slip my head between until my tongue hits her pussy. She moans again as I begin to roll it around and taste her sweetness on my fucking tongue. And I realize then and there I've never wanted to lick a pussy more than this fucking one right here.

I dig in, lapping her up like there's no one stopping me from claiming what I want.

I fucking know Silas marked her as his. I know he considers her his toy.

But he's not here, and she made a deal with both of us. What does it matter if I get to enjoy the spoils of our fucking hunt for myself?

My tongue rolls around and dips inside. I can still taste Max's salty cum lingering inside her, but it only turns me on even more to know he was here. Just like back in class, he couldn't help himself, but I can.

I just choose not to behave.

I wriggle my tongue across her clit and feel it throb underneath. I grin into her skin as her body begins to tense against my tongue, almost as if it's just as willing to let me pleasure it without actually being aware.

If she only knew who was between her legs right now, she'd probably put my fucking knife to my own goddamn neck.

But I have never felt a hunger like this before, this craving to make this woman's orgasm mine and mine alone. Fuck anyone who came before, fuck Silas, and fuck Max for keeping this from me.

I lick her up and then some, rolling my tongue around this sweet fucking pussy like I haven't been fed in years. My fucking God, I can't get enough.

One hand squeezes her thigh while the other fists my hard-on, jerking off like I've never had a more delectable pussy in my life.

The taste of her and him combined is surprisingly even hotter than I could've imagined, and I stick my tongue inside and swirl around until her wetness is all over my mouth and she's quaking with need.

"Fuck, you'd better not fucking wake up now," I murmur, and I replace my tongue with two fingers so I can lick her clit instead.

Her hand finds its way to her nipples, and she squeezes it subconsciously, making me grin.

"That's it, little thief. Can you feel me claim your orgasm like I claim your fucking dreams?" I whisper, gripping her tightly. "It'll never be enough now that I've had a taste."

I circle around and around, watching her entire body tense up and finally release the pent-up orgasm. A gush of wetness flows out of her, and I lap it all up because there is no taste as sweet as the biggest sin that I just committed.

But fuck the rules and fuck whoever thinks it'll stop me from enjoying this forbidden fucking fruit. And fuck me for not being able to resist as I jerk off so hard while she comes that I can't stop the orgasm from rolling over me, too.

And I come to a stand right as the cum bursts from my cock... all over her dainty little fucking body. I keep going, rubbing it all out until her tits, pussy, belly, and even her face are covered in my spunk.

When the rush finally subsides, I release my cock and step back, watching the cum drip down her lips and onto the floor. A dirty smirk spreads on my face. What a wicked fucking sight to behold.

This ... this orgasm might've been the first I've given to her.

But it will definitely not be the last.

And I can't fucking wait to be back.

***

MAX

In my dreams, Ivy is still riding me, licking my lips with that tantalizing tongue of hers, but as I open my mouth to moan, the sound refuses to come out. And with every thrust, her fingers squeeze tighter and tighter and tighter.

I can't breathe.

But these nails aren't sharp, and these fingers aren't gentle. At all.

My eyes burst open as I suck in a breath that refuses to enter my lungs. Because two strong, calloused hands have wrapped themselves around my throat, a devilish grin all I see as the blur between dreams and reality fades.

"Is this what you like, huh? Do you want it rough, Max?"

Heath?

His hair falls over my face as he looks me dead in the eyes while I lie in my bed, utterly confused at what's happening.

"You want to be smothered? Left breathless?" he whispers. "Used like a toy?"

My pupils dilate, and my lips part, but no sound comes out.

He knows.

"Yes, I fucking know exactly what you did last night," he says, leaning in so close I can feel his breath on my skin. "Who you were with."

I shake my head, willing my cock to go down before he sees.

"It's too late to deny it, Max." He lowers his gaze. "I watched you fuck that little thief."

What?!

He watched me?

How?

"I—I..."

His eyes narrow. "You're sorry?"

"Please," I squeak.

Finally, his fingers pry away from my neck, and my lungs suck in the oxygen. I try to throw the blanket off me, my cock still hard as a rock just from that dream ... and from his fingers, but he swiftly sits down on top of me and slams my wrists down on my pillow.

"You're not going anywhere," he growls. "Not until you fucking tell me exactly what you've been doing."

"I did what you told me to," I say. "You wanted me to seduce—"

"I didn't tell you to go to her apartment and fuck her in the middle of the night without us," he seethes. "You *knew* where she lived and you didn't tell me."

I suck in a breath, trying to focus while he's so up close and personal. And angry.

"I was just trying to—" I frown, interrupting my own train of thought. "Wait, how did you know I was there?"

"You think you're the only one who knows how to track people?" He smiles. "You led me right to her."

My jaw drops. "That phone tracker."

He taps my forehead. "Guess that fucking brain is finally working again after all that pussy."

I can't believe he put an actual tracker on my bike.

"I trusted you," he says, leaning up, releasing my wrists, but his words hurt more than his hands ever could. "And look where it led me. Right into that thief's apartment." He averts his eyes. "I thought you were a friend, that I could fucking trust you."

I swallow away the lump in my throat. "You can."

His sharp gaze finds mine again. "Then tell me why she needs that money."

I lick my lips. I don't want to ruin what I have with Ivy. It's too important. But I know Heath wants more information, and I don't know what to do.

He shakes his head as he gets up off my bed. "Thought so."

"She doesn't have it anymore. She's telling the truth," I say, trying to offer at least something.

"Right ..." he says. "And I'm supposed to believe that how?"

"Because I told you," I say, sitting up straight.

"Like you haven't lied to me before," he says.

My brows draw together. "I haven't."

"Hm..."

He looks away and I breathe a sigh of relief.

"Then who is Cora?"

Fuck. He heard us talk about her?

"Her neighbor," I lie.

I promised Ivy I wouldn't mention Cora. I can't break this promise too.

"She didn't want to talk to you... about her neighbor?"

I shrug. "It's complicated."

His eyes narrow and the pause that follows makes it feel like my bed just got turned into an ice bath. But he swiftly averts them again, as his fingers caress his own lips, like he's savoring the taste of something he ate.

"She said she was falling for you, didn't she?"

A blush creeps onto my cheeks. "I don't know if—"

His eyes suddenly find mine in a split second. "Are you in love with her?"

I gape at him, as I don't even know how to respond to that.

"Thought so," he says, fishing a key from his pocket.

The same key I placed on her kitchen counter before I left her apartment.

And he casually throws it up and down in the palm of his hand as he waltzes off, slamming my door shut behind him.

Well fuck.

TWENTY-FOUR

IVY

I wake to a salty taste in my mouth.

Frowning, I lean up and blink a couple of times.

Why am I on my couch? Did I fall asleep here after Max left?

I yawn and still taste the salt, so I rub my face ... only to find something sticky.

What the...

I bring my fingers to my nose and smell.

Wow.

That's definitely cum. No mistaking it.

Did Max come back into my house?

I stand and look around. The key is missing from my kitchen counter, even though I'm sure he placed it there before he left. I shiver.

Maybe he came back to steal it again and then got overwhelmed with more desire?

I check out the rest of my body. There are splotches of cum left everywhere on my skin.

Damn, I didn't know he could come three times in a row. And while I was asleep too.

I pull out my phone and message him.

Me: Did you come back into my house and come again?

It takes him a while to respond, and he keeps deleting messages over and over.

Max: No...

That sounds like a lie to cover up the fact that he was hungry for more. I grin at the thought.

Me: No need to lie. I know the key is missing.

He keeps typing and deleting his sentences, backing up on whatever he was about to say.

Then he stops replying entirely.

Guess he's too embarrassed to admit it.

I shrug it off and swiftly jump under the shower to clean up before I wake Cora to get dressed too. I give her breakfast and prepare her bag, then drop her off at Mrs. Schwartz, and bike back to Spine Ridge University. Every day, my muscles are getting leaner and leaner just from all this damn biking I'm doing, but I'm not going to give up just because it hurts a little.

Going to this college was a dream come true. A dream they'd have to tear from my cold, dead hands if anyone ever wanted me to quit.

Even as a little kid, I was always boasting to my mom and dad about how I was going to go to this school and build my own company from the ground up and become rich. They cheered me on, and I worked so damn hard to achieve this goal.

No amount of blackmail, bullying, or boys with questionable sexual needs, is going to keep me away from here.

I park my bike in the stands and wipe the sweat off my forehead, then chug some much-needed water and head to my first class of the day.

I enter the class room, and Mr. Alec Caruso, my teacher for this class, welcomes me. "Hello, Miss Clark. Nice to see you in good spirits today."

"Hi," I reply as I pass him by. "Just in time."

"No worries, I haven't started class yet." He winks. "Find a seat."

A particular aura hangs in the back of the room, and my eyes immediately gravitate toward its center. There sits the vicious green-eyed boy with his black and white hair and his violent temper. The twitch in his lip when he sees me makes me swallow away the lump in my throat as a grin slowly begins to spread on his cheeks.

Does he know I witnessed him kill?

Did Max rat me out and tell him?

I swiftly turn to the side and sit down as far away as I can from Silas. I'm not going to give him anymore ammo. But the second I grab my books and put them down on my desk, something hits the back of my neck.

It's on the floor, so I pick it up. It's a tiny piece of paper all crumpled up, so I unfold it.

After your classes, you come to me.

I turn around in my seat and stare him down as courage bolsters me to stick up my middle finger. The smirk on his face only widens.

I turn around again and listen to Mr. Caruso as I pen down more notes so I can at least study the material after this class, because Silas is trying to make it impossible for me to pay attention.

Another paper hits me in the back of the head, and I grab it and read the note.

You wanna do this the easy way or the hard way?

I write something on the back and chuck it back at his face.

Didn't know you were so attention-starved, you needed blackmail to get ladies to come to your house.

His nostrils flare when he reads it, and just that one bit of annoyance is enough to make my day.

Suddenly my phone buzzes.

Psycho: Yet I didn't even need more than three words to get you on your knees. Begging. Moaning. Coming all over my floor.

My hand nearly crushes the phone in my hand.
That asshole!

Me: You think I did any of that because I want you? In your fucking dreams. You're a girl's literal worst nightmare.
Psycho: We'll see about that once you're on the floor again with that dainty fucking ass of yours.
Me: Asshole.
Psycho: Thief.
Me: Keep reminding me, maybe I'll finally decide to rob you until you have nothing left.
Psycho: You don't even dare to look at me, so I fucking doubt it.

I immediately turn around and stare him down, making sure he gets the message.

Me: I'm not afraid of you.
Psycho: Oh ... is that a fucking challenge? Because I'm always up for a game of cat and mouse to bring the terror.
Me: Try me.

I don't know why I typed that, but it's too late to unsend it. And judging from the smug look on his face I am already beginning to regret it.
Fuck.
I just invited him to chase me again just like that night in the woods. I should've kept my mouth shut after he antagonized me.
I turn around again so I don't have to look at his psycho face while brewing with hatred.

Psycho: Five p.m. After your classes are done. You'll be cleaning my room.

Me: I don't hear a question.

Psycho: It wasn't one. You need money and I need you to clear your debt. See you tonight, twig.

I turn off my phone before he sends me more lewd messages. Fuck. I really shouldn't have picked up those papers, but it's too late now. He's got his hawk-eyes on me, ready to dig his claws in and pick me up like prey.

But he didn't mention anything about last night. About me, watching them kill.

So maybe Max really didn't tell them after all.

***

SILAS

When class is over, I'm almost sad I'm no longer able to antagonize her with just a goddamn look. As I get up to grab my books, my phone buzzes. It's Dad.

"What?"

"Come to the third floor. I need to speak with you."

I roll my eyes and click off the convo. Whatever.

I shove people out of the way and get out of class, then head up all the fucking stairs to the dean's office where my dad's waiting. He's leaning against his desk when I close the door.

"What's up?"

His darkening gaze makes me realize this is serious business.

"Last night, your mom's men found bones buried in the woods near the house." His penetrative stare forces me to sit down. "Human bones." He squints but I stare him down. "Do you happen to know anything about that?"

I shrug. "I don't fucking know what y'all are up to. What's it got to do with me?"

"Silas ..." he grits. "Don't lie to me."

"Lie about what?"

He rolls his eyes. "You think I don't know what you do? How long do you think we've been cleaning up after you?"

I swallow away the nerves.

Fuck.

Was it that obvious?

He grabs a cigarette and lights it right here in the room, taking a deep drag. "You're callous."

"It's gone, isn't it? No one fucking saw."

"Our men saw," he says, taking another drag. "And they will pin this on you if they ever go to the cops."

"Then I'll kill 'em too." I shrug.

His jaw tenses. "It's not that easy."

"Yes, it is." I tilt my head. "They're your men. If you can't trust them ... why are they near our family?"

He takes another deep drag, staring me down like he's disappointed in me.

But we both know why I am the way I am.

"Who was it?"

"A nobody," I respond.

"Where did you find him?"

"Why does it matter?"

"Because I need to know if there are any loose ends," he grits, slamming his fist on the table. "Goddammit, Silas. I told you to be more careful."

I look away. "I took care of it."

"And my men had to clean up after the mess you left," he says. "That's not going to happen again, do you hear me? You can't jeopardize your mother like this. What if the cops find out?"

"They won't," I retort. "Because you'll take care of it."

His nostrils flare and it takes him a while to respond. "No. Not anymore."

I frown. "What?"

"You." He points at me. "You will stop."

I clutch the chair's elbow rests. "No."

He can't ask this of me. He knows why I do this.

"Yes," he reiterates. "You will."

I stand and kick the chair away. "The fuck I will!"

"You have no choice." He takes another drag before marching over to me and grabbing me by the collar of my shirt. "Stop playing around. This isn't some fucking game, kid. You take the wrong guy, and you're done for. Over. You don't know the kind of monsters that live in this fucking city and what they do to protect their own. Your mother and I have been fighting tooth and nail to keep our kids protected, and goddammit, I won't let you screw this up."

"I *need* this," I say through gritted teeth.

"Take out your anger on something else," he says, grabbing my shoulders instead. "Go to a shooting range. Go join an axe-throwing group. Fuck, you can even join that dojo that friend of Heath's father owns. What's his fucking name ... Blaine Navarro. He'll give you something to take your anger out on and let it go."

I jerk free of his grip. "I don't want to fucking let it go." I laugh out loud. "You think I do this because I'm angry?"

"Silas ..."

"No, you don't get to give me this talk. I fucking know what you and Mom did back in your days."

Shock riddles his eyes.

"Yeah, Heath told me about his father's big shoot-out at the Torres casino, one in which you took part. You act like you're some goddamn good guy, but you're not."

"I never said I was, but I did it for the right reasons."

"Fuck the right reasons," I spit back. "I don't need a fucking reason to kill."

I turn around and storm toward the door.

"Silas, you're not going to dump any more bodies on my property, do you understand?"

I pause as I grip the door, my nails digging into the wood. "I am this way because of *you*."

And I bolt down the stairs before he can say anything else.

TWENTY-FIVE

IVY

As I walk through Spine Ridge University's main building after my classes are all done, Aspen hails me and drags me into the friends group.

"Finally, I found you. Where've you been?" Aspen asks. "Thought you'd ghosted on me."

"Sorry, I got carried away with ... work." I chuckle. "But you can PM me anytime."

I hold up my phone and show her my profiles.

"Oh, I'm gonna add you," Xavier says as he butts in. "Never hurts to add another lady." He makes click-clacking noises with his tongue.

Aspen grumbles with embarrassment. "Jesus, Xav."

"What? A man's got needs."

"I thought you had the hots for Sunny—"

He smashes his hand in front of my mouth, shushing me. "Don't. Don't ever say that out loud again."

I make a face when he finally removes his hand. "Okay, sorry."

"Ignore him. She does the same," Aspen says, rolling her eyes.

"Hey, she's not ignoring me. We just haven't ... talked. At all. Yet." He shrugs.

"Wait, not even once?" I snort. "Wow."

He narrows his eyes at me. "Y'all think you're so funny."

"Bye, Xav," Aspen yells as he leaves. "He's been pissy since the family dinner. Don't worry about him."

"Family dinner?"

"Yeah." She pulls up some photos and holds them up for me to see, and my eyes nearly bulge out of my head.

"That's your family?" I mutter.

"Yup, all nine of us. My mom's got a polyamorous relationship with three guys. To us, it's normal. We're just half siblings, but we love each other to death."

"Oh, interesting ... Max said the same thing about his family."

She nods. "It's a theme, for sure."

But in the photo she's holding, Silas's deadly eyes are all I can look at. Even when he's with his family, he has the same stone-cold face, as though he has zero feelings, not for anyone or his surroundings.

But that pink unicorn shirt he's wearing in the picture ... that's all the proof I need to know I wasn't seeing ghosts the other night when I thought I'd seen them kill a man in cold blood.

"Except Silas. He can suck a bag of dicks for all I care," Aspen says, tucking her phone away again.

"You two don't get along?" I ask.

Couldn't hurt to get more information.

She shakes her head. "We're like the opposite of two peas in a pod. I'm happy; he's insane. I like college; he wants to avoid it at all cost. I'm friends with Mavis; he thinks she's weird. I like hearts and flowers and butterflies and the sun." She shows me the unicorn slapped on her chest. "And he likes death."

He definitely likes death, and that unicorn shirt she's wearing sure seems familiar.

Suddenly, her eyes zoom in on something while her pupils dilate, and it immediately makes me turn around.

Levi Torres just entered the hallway, swagger on point as he casually tosses his bag over his shoulder and dumps a freshly smoked cigarette into the bin, then runs his fingers through his short, smoky hair.

"No, don't look!" Aspen hisses, and she grasps my shoulders and turns me back around again.

I snigger into the palm of my hand.

"Well anyway, gotta run," she swiftly says. "Class is starting. See you later, okay?"

"See ya!" I say, but she's already run off.

Whatever that is about, I'm not going to mess with it. I have enough shit to deal with on my own.

Heath suddenly passes by me, his mischievous eyes briefly connecting with mine, and the air runs thick with both tension and intense heat as I'm reminded of the last time we saw each other ... when he had his thick cock down my throat in the forest.

I clear my throat.

"Done any late-night biking these last few days, thief?" he suddenly asks. "You might want to cover your tracks next time." He glares at me over his shoulders before walking off.

And my whole skin erupts into goose bumps right there on the spot as the realization slowly dawns on me.

Heath knows it was me who watched them kill.

***

HEATH

Hours later

I take a quick lunch break between my classes at the Skull and Serpent Society house because I don't like the taste of the food in the cafeteria. Four more sushi rolls lie in the fridge, and my mouth already waters at the sight of them.

I snatch them out and place them on a plate, then sit down on the couch and munch down on them. I don't even need soy sauce; they're that delicious. These might even cure my depression one day.

"Are you eating my lunch again?"

I nearly choke on the fish as I lean up right when Elliot Fletcher walks in.

"No, it's fine, go ahead, I'm not hurt or anything," he says, waving it off.

"Sorry. Didn't know it was yours."

"Yeah, you did." He laughs it off. "But you don't care."

I shrug. "I was hungry."

"Just say you want me to bring some for you next time I visit Dad's restaurant."

"Bring me some next time, please," I say immediately, then shove more sushi down my throat. "It's delicious."

"I know." He opens the fridge and takes out a sandwich instead. "This yours?"

I shake my head.

"Then I guess we're both stealing food today." He snorts and falls down on the couch next to me. "Have you talked to Max lately?"

I take another bite. "Yeah, why?"

"Does he seem ... off to you?"

I narrow my eyes at him. "What do you mean?"

"I don't know. He just doesn't talk to me anymore the way he used to."

"Dude, it's been like what ... a week?"

He shoves me with his elbow. "C'mon, I'm serious. Even a week for us is a long time." He sighs. "He normally tells me everything."

"Maybe he's just working through some stuff and needs some time to think," I reply.

I'm not going to tell Elliot what we've been doing with that girl Ivy. He'd probably try to shank me on the spot just for involving his brother. He's a soft soul, except when it comes to protecting his family.

"He's fine," I add. "Don't worry."

"Okay. If you say so," he says.

Suddenly, the front door slams shut, and we both abruptly stop eating as two bloodied legs appear in view. Elliot's sandwich drops onto his jeans as Silas walks in with his body caked in blood. He just walks past us without even looking and drops a bag on the floor near the stairs.

"Holy shit ..." Elliot mutters.

I immediately put down my sushi and walk out to gape at him as he saunters up the stairs.

"What happened to him?" Elliot asks behind me. "Should we even ask?"

"I don't know. Stay here. I'll deal with it."

He raises his hands. "Okay, sounds fine by me."

Silas is already upstairs, so I follow his red footsteps and find him standing in front of his bed, dripping blood onto the small carpet. His hands are curled into fists, his eyes monstrously cold.

I swallow. "You okay?"

He doesn't answer.

"Are you hurt?"

He shakes his head, the blood still rolling down the palm of his hands.

"You killed again, didn't you?" I ask.

His eyes twitch as they connect with mine, a wicked smile appearing on his face. "I couldn't help myself."

I sigh out loud. "Go shower. I'll clean the weapons and tell everyone to leave the premises so we can deal with this." He begins unbuttoning his shirt, so I turn and leave, but I grab the door on my way out. "Did anyone see you?"

"No. I made sure of it."

I doubt that, considering how he came in, but whatever. We'll spin a good story for those who saw him.

"And the body?" I ask.

"Gone. Incinerated." The smirk on his face widens. "Fucking ashes in the woods," he replies, letting the shirt fall to the ground.

I shake my head. Even now, he can't stop himself from killing literally anything and everything that walks. Something must've ticked him off, but he'll never tell me what.

"Fine. Whatever. You do whatever you want as long as I don't have to deal with your mess."

"Ivy will be here soon," he says as he walks to his own bathroom, leaving a bloodied trail. "She'll clean my mess for me."

***

IVY

I'm standing in front of the Skull and Serpent Society house, wondering why I'm even back here again. Not that I have a choice in the matter. Silas made that much clear.

Well, at least this way I can pay off the debt without being killed in the process. And I wonder if he's going to pay me again for the effort.

I blow out a breath and approach the door, but when I knock, it's already open.

That's odd.

I go inside and close it behind me.

"Hello?"

No one replies.

Has everyone left?

I softly tiptoe around, but there doesn't appear to be anyone inside the building, not in the kitchen, the common room, or the hallways, so I head upstairs instead. The boards creak under my feet as I approach the only light coming from down the hallway ... Silas's room.

My heart beats in my throat as I push open his door.

No one is inside.

Where is he?

In the middle of the room sits a bucket filled with soap and that same damn brush again that still makes me heat when I look at it.

I walk inside and take a deep breath before I look around the room to see where the dirt is at that he wants me to clean up so badly. If this is even a cleaning job at all. Because as far as I'm concerned, he just wants to use me as a glorified whore.

But when I pick up the wet brush from the bucket and rise, my eyes fall upon a thick, red stain in the carpet near his bed. I get closer for a good look, bending over to touch it.

Blood.

The brush drops from my hand.

He didn't hide the crime.

He wanted me to find it so I would see what he's capable of. As a warning and a threat.

If I don't do what he says and clean up after his mess ... it'll be me next.

I swallow and dip the brush into the bucket, rubbing it over the bloodied mark again and again. Sweat slowly builds up on my back as I get to work, rubbing the blood out of the carpet, adding more soap, and brushing it again. When it's turned more pinkish than red, I lift the carpet and roll it over to get to work on the stain on the floor. But there's a whole set of droplets—no a path—that leads all the way to the bathroom. Footsteps.

With my brush, I follow the path, cleaning up the footsteps until they're erased from existence, and when I get to the bathroom, the door appears to be cracked open. My eyes find the small slit, and I can't help but look inside. Steam has filled the room, and I can barely see anything, except the figure standing underneath the shower, his black tipped hair with white roots dropping rivulets of water ... and blood.

Not just tiny amounts.

Bucket loads.

All while he's rubbing his own muscular body with his hands, washing off the blood. And even though I shouldn't be gawking like this, I still can't avert my eyes as I come to a stand in front of the door, peeking at Silas. He's got tattoos all over his body, like a snake that crosses his left shoulder and shoulder blade, and a very intricate pattern that runs from his side all the way down his thigh. Each inch of his body is tight, muscular but lean, and even though he's not as tall as the other boys, I'm pretty sure he could win a fight with any of them just with his muscles alone.

His hands slowly move down his body, and when he grips his big dick, I do a double take. Even though the blood is still caked on his skin, he begins to jerk off with closed eyes, almost as if he's fantasizing about something. Or someone.

I swallow away the lump in my throat.

Suddenly, something covers my mouth, and I squeal, but the sound doesn't exit my throat.

"Shhh ... Don't make a sound." *It's Heath.* "Don't want him to hear you while you're a voyeur to his filth, right?"

Fuck.

My whole face heats up as he slowly takes his hand off my mouth. "I wasn't—"

He grips my throat instead. "Yes, you were. But I don't mind. The question is ... does he?"

I try to suck in the oxygen, but it's impossible.

"You've got a nasty habit of sneaking up on people ..." he whispers into my ear, body pressed up against mine. "So I thought I'd return the favor."

"Why?" I manage to squeak out.

His other hand snakes up my sides and dips into my skirt, and I shudder in place.

"Because I've seen the effect he has on you ... I can feel your body quaking just from looking at Silas play with himself," he murmurs, diving between my legs until he finds that sweet spot. "I can feel your wetness."

He rolls his fingers around my pussy, and I struggle not to collapse against the door.

Why ... why do these fingers feel so familiar?

"Stay still," Heath whispers as his fingers slowly loosen from around my throat. "Don't fucking move."

I can feel him invade me, inch by inch until my whimpers come out in short gasps.

Good God, how does he do this so well right from the get-go? It's like he's an expert ... not just at pussy, but with mine specifically.

"You think he's the only one who knows how to play a girl like you?" He licks the rim of my ear, a dangerous grin forming against my skin. "I'm the worst kind of player you could ever meet."

"But I came here to clean, didn't I?" I reply, trying to change the subject.

"You came here because you were told. Because you're our fucking toy, and we can do with you what we want."

"Fuck y—"

"No," he interrupts. "You watched us last night, so you can do it again, right?"

My eyes widen.

"You think I didn't know it was you? I know Max let you go." He flicks my clit until I'm all hot and heady. "How he came into your apartment and kissed you." He dips inside again. "How you fucked him on the couch." Another one of his fingers is added. "How you let him come inside you." He thrusts in so hard I see stars.

Oh fuck.

"How?" I ask.

He smirks against my ear. "You think I don't know how to make Max talk?"

My heart hurts.

Max promised me he wouldn't tell. I trusted him.

"But Silas doesn't know," he says. "And if you want me to keep your little dirty secret, you will be a good little slut for me and take these fingers deep."

He pushes even farther, coaxing out the goose bumps with each plunge, and my eyes nearly roll into the back of my head.

"No." He grips my cheeks, forcing my head to stay up. "Keep your eyes on him."

"But I—"

"What do you see?"

The slit in the door is only large enough for one person to peek through, and I'm trying to focus, but it's hard with two fingers rolling around inside me, coaxing out the wetness.

"He's covered in blood," I say.

"And?"

I bite my lip watching Silas grip his cock while moaning. "He's jerking off."

His fingers curl and find my G-spot, and I nearly moan right there and then, but he silences me with his other hand.

Silas still hasn't seen us. Yet.

"Why do you think that is?"

He takes his hand off my mouth, and I say, "He's turned on by blood?"

Heath's lips hover over my neck, making me shiver with both need and hatred for how good he makes it feel.

"Murder."

My eyes widen.

Oh fuck.

He gets turned on by killing someone?

"That's it, watch him do it. Watch him play with himself while he fantasizes about death."

I'm helpless to stop the onslaught of lust coursing through my veins.

This is insane. Silas is a murderer who gets off on fantasizing about his next victim.

Could it be me?

I shudder in place and clutch the doorjamb, desperate not to give in, but Heath's fingers undeniably dominate all my senses.

"Yes, that's it. Give me your goddamn orgasm," he whispers, pushing his body and hard-on up against me.

"Fuck," I murmur, unable to focus on both his fingers and Silas, whose pierced cock is dripping with pre-cum.

Heath circles my clit with his thumb and presses on my G-spot, but it's his whisper into my ear that ends me. "Now."

I moan out loud, unable to contain the wave of ecstasy that floods my body as I writhe in his arms.

Heath holds me tight as the orgasm rolls through, his dick bobbing up and down against my ass, encouraged by his victory, and fuck me, I'm almost about ready to drop down for him and let him do whatever he wants to me.

Until Silas's piercing green eyes suddenly find mine.

"Oh fuck."

TWENTY-SIX

HEATH

I swiftly take a vibrator I pulled out of the closet the moment I saw her from my pocket and stuff it up her pussy during her orgasm.

"Keep that in there," I whisper. "No matter what happens now."

"What the f—" Silas steps out of the shower, still rock hard. "You're watching me?!"

"He forced me," she says, still quaking from both the orgasm and the vibrations.

I laugh. "You were already looking at him before I caught you in the act. And you're still hinging on a second orgasm. Look at you."

With a red face, she stumbles back against the couch. Silas approaches her ass naked, blood still caking his skin from his second kill.

"You're not going to kill me," she says, and when she bites her lip, I know she can feel the intensity build. "You want me."

He stops right in front of her and a smirk slowly forms on his lips. "You know me so well already? I'm impressed."

Suddenly, he shoves her, and she flops down onto the couch. "What did you let him do?"

I lick my fingers, and her eyes home in on them like she's shocked I enjoyed a small taste of what she had to offer. Too bad for her I've not nearly tasted enough to satisfy my cravings.

"I didn't *let him* do shit. He fingered me," she says with a scowl on her face.

"And don't pretend you didn't enjoy it," I say, showing off my wet fingers.

She doesn't even know this is my second time already, but I'll keep that little secret to myself for now.

She folds her arms. "Whatever. It's not like I have a choice."

I push the button in my pocket and watch her unravel. Nothing is prettier than the sound of desperate whimpers, as she tries to make it stop by digging in her own panties.

"Don't," I warn her, and she stops wriggling her legs. "Touch it and I'll only make it worse."

Silas's head tilts sideways as he inspects her.

"You put a vibrator inside her, didn't you?" he asks, sporting a grin.

"I wanted her to suffer a little longer," I reply. "Besides, I kind of enjoy the way she sounds when she comes."

"Good ..." Silas suddenly grips her throat. "You were supposed to clean."

"I did." She eyes the stained carpet.

"So you've seen what I'm capable of then," Silas says, tilting her head up so she's forced to look him in the eyes.

But the unabashed look on her face catches me off guard. "You wanted me to see that blood, didn't you?"

**

SILAS

She truly had no idea how fucked up I really am, but it seems she's starting to catch on.

The scale of my depravity is beyond her imagination, and I don't ever stop until it's too late.

"You killed someone," she says, almost in disbelief I'd be so callous about it.

"Someone?" I snort. "A body. Nothing more, nothing less."

"You don't even see them as people." She grimaces.

"*Them?*" My eyes twitch.

Does she know more about my murderous habits than I thought?

Her entire face slowly begins to lose its color.

My fingers tighten around her neck until she can no longer suck in those desperate breaths. "Tell me ... who else have you seen me kill?"

"No one—"

"Don't lie to me, thief," I growl, my fingers digging into her precious skin. "I know a liar when I see one."

Her whole face turns red as the buzzing increases, and I briefly glance at Heath to see him pressing some button, as if he's trying to keep her from talking.

And it makes me squint, so I release her throat just enough to talk.

"Fine. I was there. Last night," she says after a while, but then her eyes home in on Heath. "And he knew."

That motherfucker ...

I look his way and rage literally pours out through my fucking mouth. "You knew she was the one who watched us kill that fucker?!"

She snorts. "Max told him. Because he found me."

Suddenly, the door bursts open as Max storms inside, glaring at all of us with widening eyes.

And my blood has never run colder.

Max looks shell-shocked. "Oh fuck."

They kept this from me? Deliberately?

I march over to Max and grip his shirt. "You fucking found *her* when I told you to go look for whoever was watching us kill?!" I shake him. "You found *her* ... and you let her escape."

"I couldn't—"

"Are you even our friend?"

"Yes!" Max exclaims.

But I don't fucking trust a word he says.

He let her off the hook, which means there's something more going on than I fucking know about.

"Then why the fuck are you even here, huh?" I ask.

"I told him not to come because we were busy ... with a girl." Heath rolls his eyes.

I pull him closer, hissing in his face, "Max, I swear to fucking Christ, if you don't tell me the truth right now—"

"Heath sent me a PM minutes ago about seeing her ogle you in the shower," he says swiftly, and he holds up his phone for me to see.

Heath: Guess who's watching Silas shower naked? I'm going to have so much fucking fun playing with her ... and you won't even be there to watch.

I frown. "Why the fuck would he send you this?"

Heath's skin begins to glow. He snatches Max's phone from his hand and chucks it into the corner of the room.

I focus my gaze on Heath. "Why didn't you fucking tell me you knew all this?!"

"Because you would've killed him for letting her go," he says. "And I won't allow that."

Now my eyes twitch even more.

That arrogant son of a bitch.

"You think you can control me?"

"No. But she's the one you're after, not Max." He points at Ivy who's writhing on the couch. "Be mad at her for sneaking up on us."

My nostrils flare.

He's right about that. We told Max to spy for us, and instead he decided to double cross us.

"Please ... turn this thing off," Ivy suddenly moans.

"Ivy ..." Max's eyes grow soft.

Too fucking soft.

What the fuck is going on here?

"I'm sorry," Max says, turning to look at both of us. "I'm sorry, okay? I couldn't."

My teeth grind together. *Does no one in this house fucking trust me?*

"Fine, you're fucking forgiven ... as long as you help me deal with her now." I tilt my head and look at her squirm on the couch from the vibrator. "And I know exactly how."

"You're monsters," she says as I approach her.

I burst out into laughter. "That's a fucking compliment." I grip her chin. "You talk about any of this, the blood, the murders ... and it will be the last thing you ever say. Do you understand?"

She swallows, nodding with disdain.

"Good." I bend over to look her in the eyes, a mischievous grin forming on my face. "Now tell me, how good were Heath's fingers just now? Better than my tongue? Who made you wetter?"

"Fuck you," she hisses. "That's all you care about?"

She pauses to swallow away the continuously building lust. "After killing two people?"

"Ivy, don't," Max tries to shush her.

I snort. "You think I've killed only ever two people?"

Her eyes flicker with shock, and it takes her a while to respond. "Why? Why would you do it?"

I can still hear the buzzing between her legs, and it's obviously distracting her.

"They aren't deserving of the life they've been given." Droplets of blood roll from my hair and land on her face, and it almost makes me want to lick it off. "Their only use in this world is to serve as my victim. That's it. And you ..." My fingers slide up her neck until they reach her lips, and I drag them down, enamored by how much hate she exudes. Hate, just for me. And fuck me, those hate-filled lusty eyes are the biggest turn-on ever. "You get to clean up after me."

"You get off on this, don't you?" she says with a sneer.

Oh, she doesn't even know how much.

I just love the way she tries to defy me over and over. This is the kind of tenacity I've been looking for, the kind that can make even a cold-hearted son of a bitch like me excited as hell. Especially when she's still writhing on my very fucking couch because of that vibrator Heath stuck inside her.

A devilish smile forms on my face. "I'm not the only one in the room."

She glances at Heath as if I'm talking about him, so I laugh. "Not just him ... You too."

Her eyes twitch. "In your dreams. I hate you."

I blink at her dark, soulful eyes, and fuck me, I never noticed just how beautiful they are ... and how much they want to make me kill even more. "You. Were. Wet. For. Me."

Her tongue darts out to wet her top lip. Just once. But I noticed.

"And the more you hate me, the more I will make you beg for me."

***

IVY

I swallow, trying not to let it affect me that he's this up close and personal, that he's using his fingers to imprint the feel of my face, my chin, my lips onto his crazed mind. But it's hard, so damn hard not to waiver. There's a deranged killer right in front of me, one who wants nothing more than to own me, use me, play with my body ... and just a single breath could be the trigger to unleash his insanity.

Finally, the buzzing between my legs is turned down a few notches, and I breathe a sigh of relief.

"Don't worry, slut, I'll turn the damn thing on full tilt soon again," Heath muses.

But Silas blocks his view and keeps my gaze locked on his.

"You did a very bad thing." His thumb dips into my mouth. "You couldn't help watch me while I jerked off in the shower... while covered in blood. You didn't run. You didn't scream. You were fascinated." He slides in deeper and deeper until my eyes begin to water, and I can literally see the glimmer of possessiveness appear in his eyes. "You're just as messed up as I am, and you want this."

He slowly pulls out and watches my reaction as he brings his fingers to his lips and licks them off.

And it actually makes my pussy throb.

Fuck.

Why does this insane asshole have this effect on me?

He suddenly grabs a fistful of my hair, forcing my head to tilt back. "Now ask me what you want to ask."

"Why do you kill?" I don't know why, but I have to know.

His cock bounces up and down from the question alone. "Because it's fun."

"Who do you kill?" While we're at it, I might as well ask everything I want to before the chance is gone.

"Anyone and anything, but the bad ones are the easiest targets because they're the easiest to dispose of. Thieves. Monsters. Abusers. Mostly people who won't be missed, but if they get in my way, I will take their life." He leans in even farther until my breasts are pressed up against his shaft. "You're not asking what you really want to know."

"Don't you feel guilty?"

A chuckle leaves his mouth. "Guilt is a thing for people like you, isn't it?" He taps my head. "You assume everyone feels the same as you, that everyone can feel love, affection, sadness, fear, devotion." He bends over and looks me dead in the eyes. "I feel *nothing*."

I look up into his darkened eyes. "What are you?"

"You know the fucking answer." He grips my face with both hands. "Say it."

It comes out in a short breath. "You're a serial killer. A psychopath."

The grin on his face widens until it scares even me. "Psychopath ... I like that addition." His fingers splay across my cheeks, forcing my jaws to open. "But I'm not the one who wants money so badly I'd sell my soul for it."

I swallow. "Body. My body is yours. I never said my soul was too."

Half of his grin dissipates from his face, making him look like the devil personified. "You think I will stop after I'm done with your body?"

Fuck.

He briefly glances at both Max and Heath. "Now, are you two ready to prove yourself to me?"

What does he mean?

Silas's fingers steady my face as they slowly crawl up to my ears. "Now, am I psychopathic enough to make even a sneaky thief run like hell?"

I frown. "What? Why?"

"You thought you could outsmart me. Spy on me. Watch me become the monster of your nightmares. But the darkness belongs to me, and you are just a visitor in my hellish domain. Now run, little thief, and let me show you what a pitch-black soul looks like."

My eyes widen as he rips the hearing aids straight out of my ears, leaving me with only four out of five senses. Before I have the chance to steal them back, he chucks them at Heath.

His lips move, and I try to read his words while my heart begins to race in my throat.

"*Run and I'll catch you. Fight and I'll win. Beg ... and maybe I'll show mercy.*"

He lifts three fingers and counts down.

"*Three. Two. One.*"

Then he nods at Heath ... and the lights are all switched off with a single push of a button.

Pitch-black darkness. Total silence.

All that's left inside me is fight, flight, freeze, or fawn. And I choose to flight.

TWENTY-SEVEN

SILAS

There is nothing that excites me more than the thrill of the fucking chase.

She dared me to play a game of cat and mouse in class... and now the chase is finally on.

I can hear her feet skid on the wooden floor as she dashes out of the room and into the hallway, and the wicked grin returns to my face.

Fuck yes, now this is what gets me going.

"What now?" Max asks like he's desperate to prove himself.

I can hear her downstairs, darting across the hallways, jerking every door she can find. Pottery is thrown over as she bumps into all the tables, cabinets, and chairs. Even without a scream, I can hear her agitation as I slowly make my way downstairs, listening to every sound she makes.

"Let's go catch us a sneaky, voyeuristic little thief," I say.

Heath's lip curls into a half smile. "Give her a head start. Five seconds."

"Fuck that. She got enough of my time already by watching me shower and sneaking up on us while we made our kill," I retort and march past him.

"And you're going to help us catch her," Heath tells Max.

A devious grin spreads on my face as my heart races with excitement. "Time to make her pay."

***

IVY

My heart nearly beats out of my chest from the adrenaline coursing through my veins.

There's no light, no sound, and now I'm being chased by three monsters in disguise.

Demonic fuckers.

I move through the rooms, but it's damn hard like this.

I can't see. I can't fucking see a thing.

Shit!

I could yell, but there's no one else to hear me except Heath, Max, and Silas. All of the Skull and Serpent Society members are gone.

Did they send them away just to toy with me?

Those motherfuckers...

I run across the hallways and try to open every single door I can find, but all the exits are locked. I turn around and run but bump into a chair next to the door, causing me to fall over face-first onto the hard floor.

I crawl up, but my hands detect a rumbling not too far away. I can feel it in my bones.

Thump. Thump. Thump.

I can feel their footsteps like vibrations in the wood.

Lights swiftly flicker on and off like a beacon in the dark.

Their masks.

I swiftly come to my feet and rush off into the opposite direction, heading into a door on my left. I have no clue where I am or where I'm going as I touch my way through the rooms, feeling up all the furniture. A couch. A table. A chair. Some kind of counter. A bump on the floor makes me nearly fall over again.

I turn around and try to see as best as I can, but there's only an all-consuming void around me. Two hands slither their way around my waist. I shriek.

Who is it? Heath, Silas, or Max?

Who can I trust?

Who will betray me?

I grab the nearest object, something that feels like a candleholder. I throw it, but of course it misses because I can't see shit, and I can't hear anything.

So I just run like hell to the next room until I bump into a kitchen counter with my waist, coughing up air. Feeling my way around the edges, I make my way to the other side to try to rip open the drawers, but there are none.

Shit.

A violent buzzing between my legs makes me moan, and I slap my hand in front of my mouth.

Don't make a sound. Don't let them hear you.

I run off to the other side of the kitchen and feel my way to the curtains. Light spills in from the outside, so I hide behind them and stay as silent as possible.

Thud. Thud. Thud.

I can feel their footsteps on the floor.

And even though the buzzing in my pussy continues to distract me, I stay as still as a mouse, trying not to be found.

Wetness slowly trickles down my legs, and I rub my lips together to prevent the moan from spilling out too.

Fuck.

Their masks flicker on and off again, like demonic entities floating through the room.

I wait until the thuds slowly diminish before I make a run for it with a curve around the furniture to make sure they don't catch me if they're still here.

But it's dark, and if I can't see anything, they can't either.

This is my only advantage.

I can feel them coming. They can't feel me.

I tiptoe around the hallways and rummage through each drawer I can find, searching for a key. There has to be one somewhere, right?

But no matter how long I search, I can't find anything.

Shit. Shit. Shit!

The buzzing suddenly intensifies, and I collapse against a door, helpless to stop the onslaught of lust building in my body once again.

Fuck these fuckers for actually making me horny.

For making me *want* to give up.

I push myself up from the floor and rush back through the hallways, then go straight up the stairs. But on the third step, the buzzing between my legs forces a moan out of my throat. And my feet are caught in a snare.

Hands grasp at my ankles.

My fingers latch onto the wood, and I pull myself up.

The hands coil around my legs, twisting me, forcing me down I'm slowly toppled over.

I kick, but my legs are pushed down as someone crawls on top of me.

I can't see; I can't hear. All I can do is feel. Feel the hands cover my body, slip between my legs, grasp at my breasts while relentless buzzing pushes me to the limit of my own excitement.

RIP!

The fabric of my top tears to pieces as my breasts spill out, and two mouths cover them whole. I moan into the void, but all I feel is the vibrations in my throat melding into one with the buzzing between my legs.

A twisted nibble at my nipples has me writhing on the stairs.

RIP!

My pants and panties are torn away in one go.

Two hands hold down my wrists while two others tie them together with a rope. A hand covers my throat, and I shriek, but my lips are covered with a mouth. Ruthless, cold, brazen kisses smother me in the darkness, and the only way I can tell them apart is by their tongue.

Penetrative. Invading.

Silas.

He claims without questions.

Thrusts without warnings.

Takes without apprehension.

But in complete darkness, my face is stolen by another hand, another set of lips on my own, as my breath is hampered by a tongue driving inside. Twisted. Demanding.

Heath.

He's wild and unrelenting.

Coarse and indecisive.

When his lips unlatch, a final kiss is placed on my mouth, one so gentle and soothing, I nearly forget I've been thrusted into a dark and devious game. *Max.*

A sudden tug at my arms makes my body yield as I'm dragged up the stairs and into the hallway.

I don't know where I'm going. Pitch black is my only companion. My back slides across the wooden flooring as I'm pulled toward a room, still struggling to keep the moans at bay from all those damn vibrations.

Suddenly, I'm lifted from the floor with my arms above my head, and the rope tied around my wrists is wrapped around something hard above me, forcing me to stand. My legs are forced apart, and something is placed between them, my ankles strapped in place until I have no more motion in any of my limbs.

Finally, the light is turned on again, and I blink a couple of times as my eyes struggle to adjust.

Silas hovers right in front of me, the lethal smile on his face making me have a visceral reaction as I recoil against the restraints that hold me, to no avail.

I look up at my wrists, which are tied to a metal ring dangling from the ceiling in a room I don't recognize. My gaze immediately goes down, and when I find the bar between my legs, I gasp in shock.

"Like the leg spreader?"

I can see Silas's lips move but still can't hear him.

I look around the room, which is filled with all kinds of furniture I've only ever seen on a BDSM site. A whole shelf is filled with all kinds of whips, chains, paddles, and another with tons of toys, and then another with a bunch of hooks and plugs and bars of all kind.

In the back is a chair with a hole in the seat, a big wooden horse, and a black cross.

"Welcome to our playground."

Suddenly, the hearing aids are pushed back into my ears from the back, and my eyes veer to the right to see who it is.

"Did you enjoy your trip into sensory deprivation?" Heath asks.

"Fuck you," I retort.

Silas grabs my throat. "Watch it, thief. We can take those senses of yours away again without so much as a fucking finger flick."

His free hand rises until it nestles right between my slit, making me jolt in the straps as he begins to rub my most sensitive spot.

"Talking about finger flicking ..." he murmurs, rolling his fingers around until it becomes harder and harder to breathe. "Some senses can even be heightened by lack of exposure." He circles my clit until I'm nearly panting. "And overexposure."

"Fuck," I murmur.

"That'll do it," he says, licking his lips as he slowly pulls his fingers away, leaving me feeling bereft and confused, even as he steps away.

Fuck, what have they done to me?

Suddenly, Heath spins around me with a tilted head, watching me suffer in these restraints as the buzzing between my legs reaches a pinnacle.

He's so close. I can feel his breath on my skin, and his tongue dips out to lick my top lip. "Desperation tastes so sweet from your lips," he murmurs. "Give in, little thief."

"Fuck." I shiver. "You."

He laughs. "I'll grant that fucking wish."

He amps up the volume until I'm literally squealing out loud from the orgasm forcibly washing over me. I'm helpless to stop the tsunami of shivers flooding my body with lust.

Fuck him and that vibrator for feeling so damn good I can't even make it stop.

"That's enough." Heath pulls the vibrator out, and an exasperated moan exits my body in a way I didn't even know was possible. An animal, that's what I sounded like, and those three fuckers definitely heard, judging from the absolute lusty grins on their faces.

And I ... I nearly came just from him pulling it out.

Asshole.

"You made quite a mess there, Ivy," he groans, gripping my face so tightly my lips are forced to open. "Go on. Taste yourself."

He dips the vibrator into my mouth all the way until his fingers join in too, forcing me to taste my own wetness, my own unraveling. And the satisfaction on his face makes me want to bite down.

"Bite, and I'll return the favor," he warns as if he can read my mind.

He swiftly pulls out, chucks the vibrator aside, and marches toward Max, who just stands in the middle of the room, staring at me like I'm something to admire despite the predicament I'm in. "But little miss thief isn't the only one who needed to come clean."

"What do you mean?" Max asks, but Heath grabs his shirt and drags him to me.

Silas snorts. "What the fuck are you doing, Heath?"

"Dealing with this here and now," Heath growls. "You found her snooping on us, then let her go. Now let the world hear why."

"Heath, you know why I did it—"

Heath rips his own belt from his pants and wraps it around Max's arms, tying them behind his back so his wrists can't move. Then he forces him down. "On your knees."

Max is fumbling as he gazes up at me. "I ... "

Heath leans in to whisper, "Say it. Out loud. Tell her."

He swallows, gazing up at me from the floor like he's being torn to shreds. "I'm in love with you."

TWENTY-EIGHT

HEATH

There it is.

The fucking nail in the coffin.

Ivy's jaw drops. "You're in love ... with me?"

"What?" Silas struts around the room, still naked. "How? When?"

"I don't know, it just happened," Max mutters.

"No, it didn't just fucking happen," I growl. "He fucked her."

Silas's eyes turn nearly red with rage. "He what?!"

He steps forward, but I block his way. "Let me fucking handle this." I pull Max's head back by his hair. "Look at her. Look at the girl you wanted to give your fucking heart to."

"Heath, don't do this," Ivy says.

"You think he's sweet?" I ask her. "He was in it from the beginning!"

Her eyes widen, and he looks away in defeat. "Tell me it isn't true, Max," she whispers.

"It is. I told him to seduce you, and he did. He played the game perfectly."

She shakes her head.

"He's *my* fucking puppet ... and somehow you fucking wound him around your little pussy."

I use my free hand to swipe along her slit right in front of his face, rubbing that sweet little clit until she's all wet and struggling to stand in those restraints. The sound of her moans makes my cock twitch, and I grab him by the hair and force him closer.

"Look at her, Max. That's what you wanted to do, right?" I grit. "You loved to watch, so fucking watch."

His breathing is a ragged mess, so I dip my fingers into her and watch her writhe. "Doesn't she look pretty, all tied up, waiting to be used? Doesn't it just make you want to lick that wetness right off her thighs?"

His tongue dips out to wet his lips like he just can't fucking control himself, and it pisses me off.

"This is why I didn't fucking tell you, Silas," I growl. "The boy has been pussy-whipped."

Silas crosses his arms. "I can see that."

"Fuck you," Ivy growls, so I add another finger just to watch her recoil against the restraints. She moans, her pussy tightening around my fingers so good, I just know she's on the verge of another big orgasm. But I'm not going to give it to her yet.

"It's no use, little thief. You're ours now," I groan as I pull out. "And you will pay for stealing what belongs to me."

"*Us*," Silas interjects.

But my brows twitch at the thought.

"Please ..." she begs, but I'm not sure who she's begging.

Me ... or Max.

And something about that makes me clench my fucking teeth so hard they nearly break.

I bend over to whisper in his ear, "Do you know what she tastes like?"

He shakes his head.

"Aren't you going to save her from the lust coursing through her veins?" I grin against his ear. "Go on ... show us how much you want her."

I stand and wait until he slowly inches closer.

"Max ..." she mutters.

"I have to," he replies, gazing up into her eyes like he's a good fucking boy.

And I'm fucking over it. "Do it."

His head falls forward, and he buries himself between her legs, rolling his tongue around that sweet pussy like his life depends on it. And fuck me, is it a sight to behold.

He groans into her, lapping her up real good until she's practically moaning out loud.

"Fuck!" she yelps.

His tongue swivels back and forth across her clit, spreading her juices all over, and I tilt my head and lick my lips at the sight. Max struggles from the belt I've put around his arms, nearly falling into her completely, and the thought makes me fucking smile.

"You wanted her so badly? Then fucking take her," I growl, shoving his head farther into her. "Go on, lick. Lick that pussy until she begs for more."

"Oh fuck," he moans, a bulge forming in his pants.

"What's wrong? Can't hold back the excitement?" I growl, and I rip down his zipper to let it spring loose. "Here, I'll fucking help you."

His tongue hungrily drives inside, and he licks her out like a madman, increasing his pace as her moans begin to heighten.

"Please, I can't hold it," she whimpers.

"Then come like the slut you are," I say, gripping her chin to make her look at me instead.

And as her mouth opens to moan out loud from the orgasm, I slam my lips into hers, driving my tongue into her mouth, claiming the fucking orgasm he gave to her.

And fuck me, it's the most delicious fucking kiss I've had in a long time.

Max's sudden whimpering makes me pull away. "Oh fuck."

I frown as my gaze lowers.

Cum spurts all over, on the floor, his pants, even his own damn face.

My lips part in shock. "Did you just fucking come?"

Silas's laughter fills the room. "He couldn't even keep it together when she came all over his mouth."

I grab his shoulders and drag him away from her. "You fucking simp," I growl as I force him down on a chair in the middle of the room and tie his arms to the chair with the same goddamn belt. "I told you to fucking lick her, not to come from her fucking taste."

"I couldn't help it. She just tasted so good, and then I saw you kiss her and—"

He abruptly stops talking, swallowing whatever words he was about to spit out as he gazes at me, a blush appearing on his face.

I grip his shoulders and look him dead in the eyes, but he refuses to continue.

"Let's give this pussy what it was begging for. What do you say, Heath?" Silas asks, and I turn my head to watch him strut over to her dangling body.

She hisses, "You motherf—"

He tugs at her nipples until she squeals out loud.

A smirk slowly forms on my face. "You had your fucking fun with her ..." I tell Max. "Now watch me have mine."

***

MAX

With a raging hard-on, my body strains against the chair, wishing I could scoot closer.

But Heath would kill me if I tried.

All I can do is watch as they both play with her. Silas by tugging and twisting her nipples, coaxing out the moans, while Heath dips his fingers in and out of her wet pussy, before circling her still swollen clit.

And my cock twitches from watching them toy with her, my mouth watering at the thought of another taste.

At least he could've put me out of my misery by letting me jerk off.

But what makes me worried most of all is that Ivy won't even look at me.

"Ivy. Please," I say.

Silas grips her face, forcing her gaze to his. "She's not looking at you, Max. She never was."

Fuck.

"Heath, please, untie me."

Heath laughs. "Why should I? So you can think of your own goddamn pleasure again? I don't think so."

"Please," I beg, the cum still dripping down my shaft. "I can't take this."

"Yes, you can. Now fucking stay and watch while you starve for that pussy."

"Enough talking," Silas says, and he presses a button to make her body lower until her knees are bent and her face is on belly level. "It's time to teach this girl a lesson about who she's fucking with."

"What are you doing?" Ivy mutters.

But he pinches her nose and forces her lips to part so she can breathe.

"Using the body you offered to me out of your own goddamn free will. Now open up, thief, and take my cock like a good little slut."

He doesn't even wait until she's opened up her mouth fully before thrusting in completely, and the utter surrender in her eyes causes a visceral reaction in my body as my dick pulses with more delicious shock waves.

Fucking hell, why do I love watching them fuck her so goddamn much that it hurts?

"Please ..." I try to scoot closer.

"Stay," Heath barks, and I sink back into my chair.

He positions himself behind her, gripping her thighs, and thrusts in.

But it's the o-shape her mouth makes that really reminds me of my fucking place in this threesome.

And that there literally is nothing I wouldn't do to be near her.

Even when it means my two friends are fucking the girl I want so desperately.

***

IVY

When Heath impales me, it feels like the lights have all gone out again. He thrusts in so deep I can feel him everywhere, pulsing deep inside, his moans making my pussy throb without my permission.

"Does that feel good, little thief?" Heath groans, pulling out, only to thrust back in again. "It'll feel even better after I've made you come on my cock alone."

"What?" I gasp, pulling away from Silas.

But Silas grips my face with both hands. "Oh no. Eyes on me, slut."

He drives into my throat, coating my tongue with his pre-cum.

Tears sting my eyes as I'm impaled on both ends, struggling to breathe, struggling to even think straight. Both of my ends are taken at the same time, my mouth plundered by a demon with no conscience, and my pussy being invaded by a devil obsessed with making me feel things I don't want to feel.

They push and pull me around using the contraption above my head, like the balls on a pendulum, back and forth onto each pierced dick.

"This pussy is fucking divine," Heath rasps, gripping my ass like they're handles. "Is this why you fell so hard, Max? Did this fucking pussy make you succumb?"

Max's Adam's apple moves up and down as he begins to sweat in the chair mere feet away. I can't even look at him without feeling guilt rush through my veins.

But I shouldn't feel this way.

It's because of his obsession that I'm now being used.

These boys are wielding my body as a tool to teach him a lesson.

Heath pulls out and swipes his shaft back and forth across my slit, causing rippling aches throughout my body. "See this, Max? See how fucking wet she is for me?"

"Yes, fuck yes," Max moans.

"You want this too, don't you?" Heath says.

"Please, I'd give anything," Max says, the desperation in his voice making goose bumps scatter on my skin.

"Too fucking bad she's all mine." Heath thrusts back in with no remorse, and a loud moan escapes my mouth.

"None of you deserve me," I growl.

"You hear him begging now," Silas replies, "but when we're finished with you, you will be begging *us*."

My body is dragged from side to side as I tiptoe around on the floor, trying to maintain balance. My wrists hurt from the twisted knot, but I can barely focus on it because of each thrust inside both my pussy and my mouth. Max gyrates in his seat, his shaft still upright, still dripping, and he still groans with pent-up desire.

Silas's cock hits the back of my throat while I forget to pay attention, and I cough and heave when he pulls out, making him laugh. "You're enjoying this, aren't you?"

I grind my teeth and look away.

He grips my chin. "Did the cock catch your fucking tongue?" With his thumb, he forces my lip down. "Good. Keep it that way. I'd much prefer a fuckable mouth over a mouth that talks."

"Oh fuck, this is too hot," Max murmurs from his chair.

Silas pushes his hard-on back across my tongue, scraping along my teeth as if he doesn't care.

"You want to bite? Then do it. Make me bleed, thief. I know you want to."

Anger pushes me to bite just like he said I would. But the smile on his face is something I didn't expect.

He groans. "It'll only make me want to thrust deeper."

He mercilessly slams inside all the way to the base, grips my nipples, and twists them so hard the scream makes its way past his shaft.

"Yes, that's it. Scream for me, slut!"

"Please! Please, please let me touch her!" Max begs, his chair inching forward with each desperate scoot.

Heath merely laughs at him.

When Silas finally releases my nipples, the stinging sensations reach all the way between my legs, and I try to push them together to keep the throbbing at bay, but the spreader bar is in the way.

"Fuck no." Heath spreads my ass cheeks and spits, letting it drip down into my crevice. "I know you're turned on by this. I can fucking feel it. Stop fighting it."

"Fuck you," I spit when Silas finally lets me breathe.

He grips my throat. "I allow you a breath, and this is what you choose to do with it?"

"Just because I allow you to take my body doesn't mean I can't say what I really think about you," I respond.

"And that's where you're wrong, little thief," Heath says.

"You didn't allow us anything ..." Silas's fingers dig deeper into my skin. "I don't need anyone's permission to take what's already mine." His face inches closer to mine. "Hate me as much as you desire, but your body will always be mine. Today, tomorrow, every hour of the week, I will command it as I see fucking fit." His tongue dips out, and he drags it across my lips. "And you will hate to crave every fucking second of my claim on your body until you become just as willing to lay down your fucking soul."

"Lies," I spit back.

His eyes glisten with heightened interest. "The only lies here are your own when you deny me what you promised."

"I said you could have my body in exchange for the money I stole, not—"

"You said *anything*."

My eyes widen.

"And I want ..." He groans as his tongue slowly dips inside my mouth. "*Everything* from you."

TWENTY-NINE

IVY

His tongue drives inside, twisting around mine as I struggle to keep the moan at bay. Heath's relentless fucking only forces me farther into Silas's mouth, his tongue lashing across the roof of my mouth, his lips greedy, demanding, insatiable.

And I can't fucking breathe.

Not just because of his unending kiss, but because of how much more it makes my pussy throb.

Fuck.

"Yes, she's coming. I can feel it," Heath groans, thrusting in so deep, my mouth begins to water.

And a moan still slips out between the cracks of our lips as Heath touches my G-spot with that pierced dick and makes me come right there and then.

Waves and waves of ecstasy roll over me, my body shivering, lips clenching to Silas in an effort to stay in the here and now. In vain. I'm floating off into nirvana, sweet and utter bliss as Heath's shaft pulses inside me.

"Fuck, I'm going to fill you up." A loud roar follows, and a warm jet fills me to the brim with cum. His fingers still dig into my skin as he calls out, "Max ..."

But all I can focus on is Silas's tongue probing my mouth, nearly laying claim to my fucking soul with just the tip of his tongue.

"Yes, please ... I'm at your beck and call," Max responds.

But I'm still lost to Silas's shameless kiss. When he finally pulls away, his lips still hover close to mine, and it almost feels like a loss, like something has been stolen from *me* this time around.

However, the grin on his face immediately pulls me back into reality. "You taste so fucking sweet when you come all over his cock."

"Fuck," I moan.

He waltzes to Heath, pushing him aside. "My fucking turn."

Heath heads toward Max with a half-hard dick. He fishes his knife from his pocket and cuts through the belt keeping Max in place on his chair.

"You want her?" he asks.

Max nods a few times.

Heath points at me. "Then fucking crawl to her."

Max drops to his knees and comes toward me while I struggle not to fall over from Silas poking my ass with two fingers.

"Lick her out," Heath growls at Max.

Max's eyes briefly connect with mine.

"Max, please ..." I murmur.

Still, he moves underneath me and grips my thighs, spreading them apart so his face fits between, and when his tongue hits my clit, a moan still slips out of my mouth.

God, these fucking boys will be my undoing.

"Clean up the fucking mess I made," Heath tells him as he hovers over both of us, shoving Max's face further into me. "Fucking eat her out."

Heath's cum still dribbles down my legs as Max's tongue slides up my skin, picking up every goddamn droplet before driving straight into my pussy. And holy shit, does it feel good.

"You're enjoying that a little too much," Silas says.

THWACK!

The slap on my ass cheek makes me squeal.

Another hit to the other cheek sends me to the moon and back.

"Finally got your fucking tongue back I hear." He grabs an actual spanking paddle from the cabinet I stared at and uses it on me. "Then let me hear you scream, thief."

He spanks my ass until it glows, and I writhe in the chains that keep me secured. "Asshole!"

"Hmm…" he groans as my skin begins to heat. "Good idea." He chucks the paddle aside and spreads my ass cheeks.

"What?" I gasp, turning my head to see what's going on. My face flushes because of the way he looks at me.

"Eyes up here." Heath grips my chin, forcing my face to turn his way again. "Lick me like Max is licking you."

He parts my lips and pushes his tip against my mouth until I'm forced to let him in, and I can taste my own wetness on his goddamn length as it slowly slips down my throat.

"She's so goddamn wet," Max groans.

A finger disappears in my backside, and I jolt from the sensation.

"So fucking tight," Silas says.

Heath's dick pulses in my throat as though it's preparing for another turn, and the deeper he goes, the more it makes my eyes water.

"Oh fuck, I can feel her pussy contract every time you dip in," Max moans between my legs, slathering me with licks and kisses like he adores every inch of me.

"Hmm … so you are a liar indeed," Heath says, burying himself inside me to the hilt before squeezing my nose shut so I can't breathe. "She's enjoying this as much as we are. Aren't you, thief?" He slaps my cheek. "Such a good fucking slut for us."

Fuck them. I'm not admitting to anything.

This is a business transaction. A necessary exchange in order for me to survive. My body for their money—that's all it is.

Right?

Silas adds another finger, pushing them both in and out of my ass until I'm tiptoeing around on the floor, grinding my teeth.

"Does it hurt, twig?" Silas asks, feeling me up.

Finally, Heath pulls out, allowing me to suck in a much-needed breath.

"You like that, don't you?" I bite back at Silas.

"Yes ... very much." Silas pushes in even farther and doesn't stop until he's knuckle deep inside me. "And I will make you love it too."

"You wish," I retort.

A devilish laugh escapes his mouth, and he pulls his fingers out. Something sharp is suddenly slid across my skin. "Tell me, thief ... have you ever had your ass fucked with the back end of a knife?"

My pupils dilate.

Did he just say ... ass fucked?!

But before I can even say a word, the handle of his knife enters my backside and makes me moan. Out loud.

***

SILAS

Her sounds are like music to my ears, and I push in the handle even farther.

Every time Heath fills up her throat, I slide the handle of the knife in deeper so she won't be able to resist moaning. Even if he pleasures her, the sounds she makes are mine and mine alone.

I only share because it's so fucking fun to watch her lose herself to hatred.

But I'll make her fucking fall in love with the hate.

"Are you going to scream for me, little thief?" I bite my bottom lip as I push it, the blade making the palm of my hands bleed. "You know how much I fucking love to hear it."

"You're a psycho," she hisses when Heath lets her have a second to catch her breath.

I wipe my blood all over her ass and my dick. "A psycho you can't help but moan for."

And as I pull out the knife and chuck it on the floor, I replace it with my cock still wet from her saliva, slowly filling up her ass inch by inch.

"Oh fuck!" she moans.

"That's it, I know you can feel every ridge of my Jacob's ladder, every piercing as it pushes past your opening, and every fucked-up need of mine forcing its way into your body until all that's left of *you* is *me*."

"Oh God," she whimpers as I slowly deepen my stroke.

"That's right. I want to invade your every waking thought, every dream, and every nightmare just like I'm invading your body, until every memory of me will turn you into a puddle of need ready to receive," I add, and I push in balls deep.

Heath plunders her throat without effort. "Fuck, this tongue feels so fucking good, wrap it around my shaft and suck, slut."

Max's tongue drives into her, spearing her like I'm spearing her ass, mixing the two together in a delicious mix of pain and pleasure until she's writhing from all the sensations.

She's so goddamn tight. "Are you an ass virgin, twig?"

"A what now?" she says, gargling between each of Heath's thrusts.

I snort. "You haven't ever taken a cock up your ass, have you?"

Her nonresponse tells me enough.

"Good. I'd hate to have to kill every son of a bitch who ever tried to take it. This ass is mine."

With every thrust, I push her further into Heath, further into depravity, further into the darkness that resides in both of our fucked-up nonexistent hearts.

"Her pussy tastes so good, I could lick it every fucking day for the rest of my life and still feel like I'm starving," Max says.

"Not so quick, Max? Who said I'd allow it?" Heath says. "Now lick like your life depends on it."

"Yes, she's worth it all," Max murmurs beneath her.

"You hear that, little thief?" I ask. "You've got us all fucking addicted already."

"Fuck you, I never ask—"

Heath plows into her mouth with a grin on his face, interrupting her words. "All I want to hear from you are choked moans." I hold out my hand. "Max, hand me the paddle."

He throws it to me, and I slap her ass as I begin to thrust.

THWACK. THWACK. THWACK!

She squeals along with each of my thrusts like she's slowly becoming addicted to the pain. And that's exactly the edge I want to fucking leave her on as I grip her thighs and spear her with my cock.

She mewls as we both take her deep.

THWACK!

"You ready for it, slut?" I grit. "Take it deep now, and I'll reward you with some cum."

"Fu—"

She can't even finish the word before Heath thrusts in balls deep and explodes inside her throat once again. I can hear her choke and gargle his cum, but it's her feverish moans that bring me to the brink.

"Beg, little thief. Beg for it, and I'll give you the fucking peace you crave so badly."

"Please!" she whimpers, at the end of her rope.

That's it. That's what I fucking need.

Her breaking apart for me. Splitting open at the core. Her soul ripe for the taking, mine to fucking claim.

I grip her ass and plunge into her bottoms deep, filling her ass to the brim with cum while roaring out loud.

"Oh fuck!" she moans, falling apart all over Max's tongue.

"Yes, please, give me your orgasm. You taste so fucking good," Max mewls like the sicko beggar he is.

He's actually jerking himself off underneath her and comes in tandem, soiling my floor.

"Did you just fucking come again?" Heath grips his hair and shoves him further into her when I pull out. "Clean your fucking dinner plate first."

"Yes, Sir," Max moans, going to town.

I laugh and fish out my phone to take a pic of her while she hangs in the balance, completely wasted from all the orgasms and the hard fucking on her toes.

"You took a picture?" she mutters, all hazy.

"Yes, little thief, I did," I reply, and I grip her hair and make her look at the phone. "Look at yourself hanging there like a dirty little doll for me to use and play with. Just like you begged me to."

"Why?" she asks.

I lick my lips at the sight of her rage. "Next time I get the urge to kill someone, I might look at this and decide to claim you instead."

THIRTY

IVY

I can't believe he actually took a fucking picture for posterity after I already gave him my fucking body. But what's even worse is the fact that I'm still high from whatever the fuck that mind-blowing sex just was.

As Heath unties my wrists from the hook, Silas fishes a wad of cash from his pocket and drops it on the floor between my feet.

"What's that for?" I ask, while Max unstraps my ankles from the bar.

"You needed a job, right?" He tilts his head. "This is your job now."

What?!

That's it.

I shove Heath away, push Max in the chest to make him fall backward, and I steal Silas's knife that's right beside him, turning around to aim it at Silas's chest.

"Whoa, getting spicy now?"

I cut but miss as he steps back, but I keep slicing until I've cornered him against the wall, the knife at his throat.

"Get back!" Heath growls at me. "Don't make me—"

"Don't, Heath," Silas says with a smug smile. "I wanna know where this vicious thought of hers leads."

"I'm *not* a whore," I say through gritted teeth.

"Yet you eagerly gave your body to *me*," he responds. "You're not just anyone's whore ... You're mine."

My nostrils flare. "I don't *want* to be yours."

"Too late," he says, inching closer to the blade, almost like he's enjoying it. "And I think you know that. You can't kill me," he says as the blade etches his skin.

"No?" I reply, blood rolling down his skin. "You deserve it."

He smirks. "I do ..." He leans in even farther, his tongue dipping out to actually lick my top lip while the blood rolls down. "But you're not a killer."

I grind my teeth over and over until finally I push away. I hate, hate, *hate* that he's right, and that he knew before I did.

I snatch the money off the floor and throw it at his face. "Keep your filthy money. I don't want it."

"Oh, now the thief is getting all righteous?" he scoffs.

I snatch the oversized bathrobe off his door and swiftly put it on, then walk out the door, completely ignoring him.

"Ivy, wait!" Max calls as I race down the stairs.

"She'll come back soon enough. Don't fucking worry," Silas calls from the top of the stairs. "She needs us."

I stick up my middle finger as I waltz toward the door. "The fuck I do!"

"The money is going somewhere, thief ..." His voice is dark, heavy, threatening as he clutches the banister while staring down at me with those hollowed-out eyes. "That trail will lead to inevitable death."

I pause and glance at him, wondering if he's trying to tell me something.

"The only question is who will be the reaper?"

A reaper.

A murderer without a conscience.

A killer who could end all my troubles once and for all.

A shiver runs down my spine, but I still march off and slam the front door shut behind me.

***

I walk across the street, hoping no one will notice me walking in a bathrobe, but it's too late. People are already staring, and I just know they want to ask me the reason so they can gossip about it later. I'm not about to answer some questions like some head of press, so I head straight for the first building in my path.

Alpha Psi. The sorority Océane belongs to.

I knock on the door a few times and wait. When someone opens, I immediately ask, "Is Océane here?" Before they even have the chance to question me.

"Um ... sure, let me go get her." The girl looks confused as fuck but still leaves the door open for me as she walks off.

Minutes later, Océane comes to the door.

"Ivy?" She looks me up and down. "What happened?"

"Can I borrow some clothes, please?" I ask.

Her brows furrow. "Um ... sure."

I know we're not the best of friends, but I appreciate her helping me out. "Thanks."

But when I enter, Talon's stern gaze catches me off guard.

"Um, hi," I mutter to him.

He just stares at me like I interrupted their private time, then turns his head back to the other girls who are all chatting in the kitchen.

Océane closes the door after I'm in and places a hand on my shoulder. "Are you okay?" she asks. "Why are you wearing this?"

"I ... I'd rather not talk about it."

I can't lie, I wouldn't even know how to explain this anyway. It's not like I hiked up the mountain and tore my clothes, then found a random bathrobe lying around. But I don't want to tell the truth either and risk exposing myself as a fraud, a thief, just like Silas marked me as.

I clear my throat and add, "Sorry."

She nods. "I understand. C'mon. Let's go upstairs."

She takes me up to what I assume is her room and opens the drawers. "Just grab whatever fits you best."

"Are you sure it's okay?" I ask.

"Mm-hmm." She nods a few times. "It's fine. I have enough anyway."

I pick a soft white blouse and a pair of dark skinny jeans, along with a fresh pair of panties.

"Do you think I could also take a shower?"

"Yeah, of course. It's over here." She opens the door across from her room and shows me the stalls. "Some rooms have a private bathroom, but mine doesn't, unfortunately."

"It's okay. This is perfect, thank you," I say.

"If you need anything, just let me know."

I nod, and she closes the door, leaving me to it.

I walk into a stall and turn on the warm shower so I can put my hand underneath. The heat of the water makes me feel alive—like I could scald off the tainted mark on my soul.

I swallow and drop the bathrobe, but the mirror on the wall behind me instantly reminds me of the viciousness of these boys I've involved myself with. My clothes are torn to shreds, and all that's left are reddened spank marks on my ass … and the hickeys on my pubic bone.

I swallow away the lump in my throat.

Max left those, and it makes me wonder if it was a desperate attempt to leave an equally lasting mark on me … after Silas already claimed me as his.

A blush spreads on my cheeks, but I swiftly push the thought away and step under the shower, washing away all of their sins and mine.

Max played me.

I thought he liked me, genuinely liked me.

But it was all a game from the start.

I brush off the pain and focus on rinsing off the grime. Even if I can still feel their tongues, their cocks, their complete and utter claim on my body, I tell myself it doesn't matter. That I can give my body away to boys like them without ever taking the fall.

But I'm slowly realizing none of this will be without a grave cost.

I turn off the shower, dry off, and put on the clothes I grabbed from Océane's closet. My flat ass doesn't nearly fill up the jeans, but the waist fits well enough that it won't slip, so I'm grateful. The blouse is perfect for my size, and when I look in the mirror, I almost feel like myself again. Almost.

I throw the dirty robe in the towel bin and head out, but the moment I take one foot outside, I come to a full stop. Talon's right in front of me, his hand firmly propped against the wall, like he doesn't intend to let me pass.

"What's up?" I ask, trying to lighten the mood.

"I don't appreciate that you came here," he says.

"O-kay..." I cross my arms. "This isn't your sorority, though, so it's not your problem."

"No, but it is my girlfriend's sorority, and it's my job to protect her."

I frown. "From me?"

"From the shit you bring to her doorstep." His dark-brown eyes intensify. "Those fuckers from the Skull and Serpent Society have attached themselves to you for some reason, and I'm not about to stand by and watch you involve her in whatever is going on with the four of you."

My face turns white hot. "I can assure you, I'm not interested in any involvement—"

"They have your number, and they've been talking about you nonstop in class. I know the truth, skinny."

Damn.

He taps my chest. "Don't bring my girlfriend into their shit. You got it?"

I swat his hand away. "I'm not doing anything. She offered me help, and I accepted. That's it."

"What's going on?" Océane suddenly approaches, and Talon swiftly lowers his arm and backs off.

"Nothing," he says, clearing his throat. "Just checking to see if she's okay."

I scowl. "Right."

"I'm gonna go to class." He kisses her on the cheek. "See you later, 'kay?"

He waltzes off before I can say anything else, almost like he doesn't wanna get caught.

"Did he say something to you?" she asks.

I shake my head. I'm not about to start another war here on campus grounds.

"Was the shower okay?"

"Yeah, perfect," I say. "Hey, I've been meaning to ask ... do you think I could borrow some cash? Just two hundred, that's it." When her brows begin to furrow in apprehension, I add, "I'll pay you back, I promise."

She sighs. "If you really need it, sure." She pulls out her wallet and takes out a few bills. "Here."

I swiftly tuck it into my pocket. "Thanks. I won't let you down."

"As long as I get it back by next month. I need to buy a present for Talon."

"Of course," I reply, smiling.

I don't know how I'll pay this back yet, but I'll make it happen, regardless.

"It's his birthday?" I ask.

"No, it's just our monthly anniversary." She winks. "I wanna throw him a private party somewhere. Speaking of parties, wanna come with me to a party at the Phantom Society tomorrow? Not one of my friends can come, and I don't wanna go alone."

"Wait, not even Aspen? But she loves parties," I say.

"Nope." She slams her lips together. "Something about burned homework and her parents being angry."

"What about Xav?"

"Oh no, I'm not even thinking about it. Sunny's also gonna be there, and I'm not looking for the drama attached to whatever is brewing there. Besides, he doesn't like the Phantoms."

I snort. "There's no way Xav would make a move on her."

"I'm not gonna risk it. I'd rather just hang with you and Talon." She smiles. "If you're okay with it, of course."

I don't know what to say, so I just agree. "Sure. He won't mind if I tag along?"

"Of course not. He can get a little possessive, so that's exactly why I need to take him to these parties. Loosen him up a little." She jests. "Besides, you don't have a dick, so he doesn't consider you a threat."

I shake my head, laughing. If only that were true. "As long as he doesn't look at me like he wants to kill me, I think I can handle it."

"Cool. I'll tell him to simmer down the glare. You need anything else?"

"No, I'm good," I reply.

She places her hand on my arm again. "You can always come to me if you need help, okay? Don't be shy."

Her warmth radiates through her voice, and it reminds me of my mother so much tears actually well up in my eyes, but I push them away. "Thanks. I feel much better now. Honestly."

At least now no one can see the ravage those boys left me in.

Océane walks me to the front door.

"Oh, and if you see Heath Preston, tell him Mavis Rivera was looking for him."

The mere mention of his name makes all the hairs on the back of my neck stand up. "Why'd you think I'd see Heath?"

"I've seen you enter the Skull and Serpent Society. Aren't you friends? People have seen you talking in the school hallways, so word got around."

I swallow away the lump in my throat. I don't even know what to say. He's not my friend, but I know him in ways I never thought I would. But I can't deny I know him either.

"I'll ... tell him," I mutter as I walk away feeling numb.

"Great. Thanks." She closes the door, but the only thing that roars through my head is how the whole school must already know more than I thought they did.

Everyone's seen me talk with them.

They don't know what was said, but it doesn't matter.

Word gets around.

And everywhere I look, people are gawking at me, whispering, gossiping.

She's *that* girl.

The girl those popular boys are obsessed with.

The girl who put a target on her fucking head.

Might as well shoot me now and get it over with.

***

I swiftly head home and knock on Mrs. Schwartz's door with the bills still in my hand. She immediately opens up and snatches them from me.

"That's not enough for that hungry gremlin, and I'm not talking about the cat."

"I'll give you more soon, I promise," I say as I take Cora's hand and leave.

"I didn't clean the litterbox, so there's poop all over the floor."

I sigh. "No worries, I'll take care of it."

"You're welcome," she snarls before shutting the door.

"She was not nic—"

"Cora, not now," I interrupt.

I can't have her slandering the only person who's willing to help me on a daily basis.

I head into our home and close the door behind us before I go to eye level with her. "It is what it is, okay? I'm trying my best to get us out of this."

"But how much longer do we have to stay here?"

Her little pouty face makes me feel guilty. "I know you miss your old home. But we can create a new one here. Together."

She hugs me so tight, tears well up in my eyes as she begins to cry. "Can't you stay with me all day long?"

Some tears roll down my cheeks. "I can't, I'm sorry."

"But why?"

"We need money to live here, and I can't earn any if I stay home."

She sighs, so I grab her shoulders. "But we can stay up late tonight and watch a movie together on my cell phone. You up for it?"

The sweet smile that reappears on her face makes all my troubles worth it. And I don't even have to say a word for her to squeal. "YES!"

Within an hour of turning on the movie, she's already fallen asleep in my arms, and I bring her to bed and tuck her in tight.

But when my phone buzzes, and I pick it up, all the hopeful joy is instantly drained from my heart.

Anonymous: Five grand. Tomorrow. 2 a.m. Same place.

My eyes widen, and I ram the buttons to PM him back.

Me: I need more time.
Anonymous: You had enough.
Me: This wasn't our agreement.
Anonymous: Terms changed. Time's up. Tomorrow night ... or you know what will happen.

My nerves get the best of me, and I chuck the phone away in anger.

Shit. How am I going to get five grand by tomorrow?

I run my hands through my hair and scratch while pacing around the living room, wishing I could force my brain to come up with a solution. I could steal from the Skull and Serpent Society again, but they're probably expecting me now.

Shit, shit, shit! What do I do?

Wait.

I run to my phone and pick it up from the floor to check my past messages from my friends.

Tomorrow. Yes. It should be doable. It's crazy, but it might just work.

In the kitchen, I grab my notebook and a pen and start penning down all the money I still need in order to stay safe and alive ... All the money I will have to steal.

And I know just the place.

***

HEATH

In the middle of the night, I turn the key into the lock as silently as possible and lean my ear against the door to listen. No noise except for the soft buzzing of what sounds like a crooked fan.

I pull out the key and slowly push open the door to peer around. The lights are all out except one next to the couch in the living area. No one is here, so I enter and close the door behind me.

Sneaking in, I take care not to bump into anything so I don't wake up the ghosts that haunt this place. The fan in the bedroom is on high speed as I slowly approach. I grip the wooden slats and peer inside. There she is, lying in bed with her eyes closed and her petite body tucked underneath a tattered blanket.

The ghost who haunts my dreams.

Ivy Clark.

A smile perks up my lips, and I fish my hairband from my pocket and tie up my hair. Then I approach Ivy in the darkness. I tilt my head to watch her chest rise and fall with every breath she takes, and it's quite literally breathtaking.

For a moment, I stay there, listening to her breathing while my heart begins to thud.

This is the girl who's gotten Max so goddamn weak he fell to his knees for her. Yet ...

My lips hover close to her skin, and I take in her sweet, fruity scent through my nostrils. My dick throbs at the memory of having her body, but I don't understand why.

I've never wanted like this, hungered for more like this, or been brought to the brink of desperation where I'm almost tempted to lick this supple skin beneath my teeth.

Fucking her tight little pussy was the best feeling ever, and it still didn't satisfy my cravings.

Is this why Max kept coming back? Why he couldn't stop himself from falling for the girl he was supposed to trick?

My nostrils flare, but this fucking girl sleeping in her bed, blissfully unaware of my presence, has captured my gaze. I'm so enamored I can't look away.

There's something huddled underneath her arm.

I lean over and carefully peel away the blanket to look, and my jaw slowly drops.

A girl.

Does she have a child?

I frown as I look closely at the girl, whose little finger is wrapped around her dark hair. She's so tiny, and those red apples on her cheeks make me smile.

Why? Why does it make me smile?

Suddenly, she coughs, and I take five steps back, disappearing through the bedroom door again before either of them open their eyes. But a paper on the kitchen counter grabs my attention on the way out, and I pause to pick it up. There's a list of places and stores, as well as a fuck ton of numbers written down, like she made some kind of calculation. Along with a few dollar signs ... and the word "owed."

Does she owe someone money? Is this the reason she kept stealing from us?

I flip the page and gawk my eyes out at the hasty drawing scribbled on here with arrows and illegible writings all over, and with all those stripes and squares it almost looks like a map.

Or more specifically, a map of the Phantom Society.

I fish my phone from my pocket and take a couple of pictures of both sides before I put the page down exactly the way I found it. Then I exit the apartment and close the door behind me, locking it with the same key I used to open this Pandora's box with.

A long-drawn-out sigh leaves my mouth before I head down the hallway and grab my phone, dialing Silas's number.

"Hey. Guess what we're doing tomorrow evening?" I pull the hair-band from my hair and let it all fall over my shoulders. "Crashing a party at the Phantom Society."

THIRTY-ONE

MAX

"Why are you looking so gloomy?" Dad asks, rolling up his sleeves as he prepares to dice some veggies. "C'mon, where's that fucking Fletcher smile?"

I throw him a stupidly fake smile while trying to make sure no one else but him sees. I don't want the customers in this high-end restaurant during their lunch break to flee at the sight of my stupid grin.

"That's my boy." He scoots a whole plate of sushi underneath my nose. "Bon appétit."

"I'm not hungry anymore."

His brows drop as hard as his jaw does. "Since *when?*"

"Since my life got so goddamn complicated." I groan and flatten my face on the bar, barely avoiding the sushi.

"Max ..." Dad says. "What's going on?"

"I don't know if I wanna talk about it. If I should."

"Then eat."

"No."

"Then why did you come here?" he asks.

"Why?" I frown and lift my head. "I come to your restaurant every week."

"Exactly. So either eat or talk or get out and do something else." He throws the towel he just used to wet his sushi over his shoulder.

I groan again and put my hand under my face to support myself while I languish in self-misery. "It's this girl."

He places two flat hands on the bar and stares at me. "A girl? Tell me all about her. What does she look like? What's her name? What does she like? Where does she live?"

"Wow, wow, calm down," I say.

"No, I need all the details. You've never mentioned any girl before." I can almost see the hearts floating in his eyes. "I can't believe it, my boy is all grown up and falling in love." He wipes his forehead and pretends to faint.

I snort. "Oh God. Do I sound like that too?"

"Like what?" He picks up one of the sushi he gave to me and chucks it into his own mouth. "Mmm, delicious."

I roll my eyes. "Anyway, I kinda messed up."

"Messed up what?"

"With the girl."

"Oh, right. Spill the beans." He leans onto the bar and winks. "I can help."

"Can you?"

"C'mon, give me a chance."

I sigh out loud. "Well ... I sort of fell in love with her the moment I saw her."

"Oh wow." A big smile forms on his face. "You really are just like me."

"What, you fell in love with Mom the first time you saw her?" I frown. "But she's an angry b—"

Dad slaps his hand in front of my mouth. "Don't. Don't say that shit out loud." He leans in. "She can hear you."

Now I'm frowning even more. "She's not here."

He points at the cameras in the corners.

Oh. Is that how she keeps tabs on us?

"It makes her feel better if she knows we're safe," he adds, picking up his knife.

"Obsessive."

He cuts through the carrots. "I prefer to call it 'affection.'"

"Right. Anyway, my girl is not like that. But she is cunning. And beautiful. And ... so damn spicy."

"Spicy," he repeats before plopping some wasabi in front of me. "Try this."

"Dad. I'm trying to talk about the girl."

"Why is she trouble for you, then? You've only mentioned positive things."

"I thought I didn't like girls. I thought I liked boys. And it makes me so confused."

He snorts. "Max, you do realize there's such a thing as bisexuals?"

"What?" I stutter.

"You can like both."

My entire face turns red. "Oh ..."

Why didn't I consider that option?

"So, I don't see any issue so far," he says.

"She stole from my friends, Silas and Heath, and now they want to make her pay for it."

"The Rivera and Preston boys?" he says, like the surnames make him do a double take. "Okay, that complicates it. But it's not a deal breaker."

I narrow my eyes. "A thief? Not a dealbreaker?"

"Yeah. Didn't I tell you how your mom and I met for the first time?" He puts down his knife. "Me, Nathan, and Kai were trying to rob this guy. He deserved it, trust me. Then your mom came to try to murder him, but she found me instead, and we ended up fighting on the pavement in front of his house, and her shoe nearly stabbed me in the heart." He sighs in a woeful way. "Oh, I was smitten on impact."

I make a face. "Really?"

"Really," he responds like it isn't the most unhinged story I've ever been told.

I can't believe what I'm hearing. My mom and dad are casual murderers, just like Silas and Heath.

Does it run in the family? I mean, my mom is Silas's aunt. Wouldn't surprise me if every one of our parents had secret lives during their college days.

"You never told me any of this."

"I didn't? Oh." He proceeds to chop like nothing ever happened. "Maybe your mother told me not to. Oops."

What the...

"But about your girlfriend, your friends want to hunt her down?"

A blush spreads on my cheeks. "She's not my girlfriend."

"Yet."

"It's complicated."

"I don't see how."

"My friends made me trick her, okay? They forced me to help them catch her by making her fall for me so she'd tell me the truth about her thievery, and one thing led to another, and now I'm involved, and she just found out."

"Oh ..." He pauses. "Well, she probably didn't like that."

"No." I flatten my face on the surface of the bar again, slamming it so hard it definitely left a dent. "What do I do? How do I fix this?"

"Buy her flowers. Tell her the truth. Apologize." He pushes another plate of veggie sushi under my nose, drawing me in with those delectable scents. "Eat some sushi and think about it."

I lift my head and look at his beaming smile and the unproblematic look in his eyes. For some reason, his advice, no matter how simplistic, always manages to strike a chord.

"Maybe I should do just that," I reply.

He rubs my hair, messing it all up. "Good."

Suddenly, the main doors burst open, and my mother's other lovers, Kai and Nathan, step inside. Technically, they're all each other's lovers, with all the poly stuff they've got going on. "Goddamn, I'm hungry," Nathan says. "What's for dinner, Milo?"

"The same as always," my dad replies, shrugging. "Why do you even ask?"

"Courtesy." Nathan approaches and gives him a kiss on the cheek. "You're looking good, as always. Now bring me my California rolls."

Milo grins. "Yes, Sir. On the way."

"Make it a double for me," Kai tells him, as he sits down beside me. "The casino still doesn't have a good sushi place, and it sucks."

"Maybe it'd be a good idea to invest in a new restaurant ... like mine, for example." Dad winks.

Kai rolls his eyes. "I know, I know. I just have to get Ares on board."

"How is your brother?" Nathan asks.

"Good, in a very Ares way, I guess."

"What does that mean?" I ask.

"He's not the talkative type," my dad fills in, winking. "He just barks orders, that's it."

"Max, your mom told me to tell you not to come to the RIVERA clubs anymore," Nathan suddenly says.

"What? But we go there on the regular. I'd hate to miss out."

"I know, but she's trying to keep things clean on the books, and every night you guys attend, extra liquor seems to vanish from the register."

I blush and raise my hands. "Not me."

"I'm just saying ... can you relay the message to Silas and Heath?"

"Why can't you tell them yourself?" my dad asks.

"Because you know how Felix acts when I try to correct his kids, okay?" Nathan responds. "I don't like dealing with him. You know that."

I snort. "Didn't think petty arguments were still a thing at your age."

"Excuse me?" Nathan's eye twitches.

My dad begins to laugh, then spanks him on the ass. "He called you old, bro!"

"You fuckin—I'll make your ass shrivel up next!" Nathan growls at him, chasing him back into the kitchen, while my dad simply giggles like he's twenty again.

I wonder if this is what they were like back in their day.

"Anyway, gotta run." I stuff more sushi into my mouth before I hop off my seat. "I have some flowers to buy and a girl to woo."

"Good luck on the wooing," Kai says. "Tell us how it went."

I run off before they ask me anymore questions. "Sure. Later!"

***

The moment I enter Murphy's Magnolias, the scent of flowers instantly fills my nostrils, putting a smile on my face. The little bell above me rings as the door closes, and a woman in a soft blue dress steps out of a storage room.

"Hi! Can I help you?"

"Um ... yeah, I'm looking for a bouquet. A big one."

"Of course." The beaming smile on her face is infectious. "What's the occasion?"

Here comes the blush again. "An apology."

Her eyes glisten. "Wait, you're Milo's kid."

"Yeah." I scratch the back of my head. "I'm Heath's ... friend."

"Oh, that's wonderful! I'm so glad he finally made some more friends. Other than Silas and Mavis." She laughs as she grabs a few flowers and pushes them into a bundle in her hand. "Let me make you a custom one."

"Thanks," I say. "So has Heath never mentioned me at all?"

She shrugs. "Maybe? He doesn't talk a lot about any of his college friends, actually. I only know about Silas and Mavis through Penelope." She makes a beautiful bouquet filled with roses and blue hydrangeas. "Not since his sister left, anyway ..." She sighs.

"Well, in any case, could you give him a message for me?"

"Um, sure," I reply.

He's their kid. I don't understand why she can't do it herself, but I'll listen.

"Tell him his dad and I still want a chat. Please have him call me," she says.

I nod as she hands me the bouquet. "Sure. Thank you." And I swipe my card.

"I'm sure she'll accept your apology." She winks.

⁎

It takes me at least three tries to gather the courage to actually knock on her door. I swallow and hold my head high as I prop up the bouquet with a smile so wide it might break my face.

But the door never opens, and Ivy never appears.

Weird.

I knock again and hold my breath, hoping she just didn't hear.

But the third knock is when a door behind me opens.

"She's not home."

"What?" I mutter.

Behind me, a granny with flipflops and her gray hair in a perm blows out some smoke from a cigarette between her fingers. "You're looking for Ivy, right?"

"Yeah."

Who is this woman?

"I'm the babysitter," she says, coughing like she's trying to hack up her lungs through her mouth. "You look like you've got some extra money on hand, judging by that giant bouquet."

I frown. "This is for her."

"I don't want your flowers, silly little boy." She takes another whiff of her cigarette. "Gimme a hundred and I'll tell you where she went."

"Why would you—"

"You look like someone she trusts." She eyes me up and down and I feel weirdly violated.

Still, I fish the hundred from my pocket and hand it to her. She swiftly tucks it away between her boobs, and I pray I won't ever have to touch that paper again.

"She's at some party. Ransom ... no ..." She taps her head a few times. "Phantom boys ... Phantom group ... no. Dammit. Phantom something."

My eyes slowly widen. "Phantom Society."

The Phantom Society are rivals with the Skull and Serpent Society, and they're wildly unreliable. There's no way she'd go there, unless...

Shit.

"Yeah, that's the one. Anyway, she told me she'd be back by eleven. That's all I got."

I bolt off back through the hallways. "Thanks!"

"What, that's it?" the neighbor barks, but I'm already gone.

I have a thief to catch.

THIRTY-TWO

IVY

"Are you sure it's okay we're here?" I ask Océane while I tug on my yellow dress to try to keep it in place. "It looks like a frat party."

She nods and leans in to yell through the noise. "Talon's a Phantom."

"Oh, really?" No wonder he didn't like Felix and Heath.

"They know me," she adds. "Besides, the Phantom Society throws amazing parties."

She turns around and nudges me with her ass, so I do the same and we dance back-to-back to the music, vibing away. It's been a long time since I last let myself go like this, and honestly, I could do this more often if it wasn't for the cost.

But I'll pay Mrs. Schwartz all the money in the world for just a night of this.

Nothing feels better than shutting off my brain and letting the music take over, even if we're forced to wear these white half-masks that remind me of the *Phantom of the Opera*. The Phantoms think it adds an element of danger to the excitement, but all it does is confuse me.

"Ivy?" Aspen's voice makes me stop and do a double take as she peeks beneath my mask. "Wait, it really is you. You're here!"

Guess I'm not the only one who's confused.

She throws her arms around me. "Eep, I'm so glad you're here!"

"Hehe, yeah, I just thought, why not?" I reply. "Wait, I thought you weren't supposed to be here? Something about homework."

She shushes me. "Don't say that out loud. I'm not here, so if anyone asks, you didn't see me, okay?"

"Right." I wink.

"Just don't tell anyone."

I make a key-turning-in-a-lock motion near my mouth. "My lips are sealed."

"You should've told me you were coming, dude, I would've waited," Océane tells Aspen, sighing.

"And risk my brother finding out I was going?" Aspen snorts. "He definitely would've told my parents."

Océane raises a brow. "Which brother?"

Aspen shrugs. "Both."

"But Xavier isn't even in the Skull and Serpent Society ..." I say.

With her lips smashed shut, she just eyes me and then averts her gaze to a bunch of muscled masked dudes standing near the door, chatting with new guests.

"Is it Levi?" I mutter.

Aspen smashes her hand in front of my mouth. "He'll hear you. Don't summon him."

I laugh when she finally removes her hand. "Over this noise?"

"You don't know him. He has ears like a hawk."

I glance at the boys, who sometimes glance back, and every time they do, Aspen disappears either behind me or behind Océane.

"Why don't you just talk to him?"

Her face turns white as snow beneath the mask. "Ha-ha, absolutely not."

"They used to be best friends," Océane says. "Or so I've been told because I see none of it."

"We grew apart." She shrugs. "Doesn't matter. As long as no one draws attention, he won't notice me, and I can just enjoy the night."

But I can't stop staring at the three dudes in the doorway, with their lean-cut muscles and olive skin. One has short pitch-black hair and icy-gray eyes, while the other has curly blond hair and such an androgynous-looking face, I'm mesmerized. The third has black hair, a middle-parted fringe, and a scorpion tattoo. *Levi*. But I don't recognize the others.

"Who are those other guys?" I ask.

Océane throws her arm over my shoulders. "The blond guy with the curly hair, the sharp cheekbones, and the bushy brows, that's Orion. He's in the Tartarus House, though. The guy standing next to Levi, the one with the broad shoulders and that blackout tattoo on his neck and arms, is Apollo. He's in the Phantom Society."

"Apollo?" I snort as I take a look. "What kind of a name is that?"

"Oh yeah, it gets worse," she says. "His younger brother's name is Atlas, but he's not here at the university yet. Their parents obviously went with a theme."

"Greek gods?" I make a face. "Cringe."

"They act like they are, though," Aspen says, ogling her eyes out. "And look at those muscles. I can't remember Apollo being this ... well-endowed."

"Girl, you grew up with them. What do you even mean?" Océane jests. "Your parents are friends."

"That doesn't mean I saw them every day. Maybe every other month. I'm just saying ... he filled out." Aspen bites her lip, then looks at us, giggling. "What? A girl can fantasize about anyone and anything."

"Right." Océane rolls her eyes. "You just can't stop drooling over those Torres boys, can you?"

Aspen's jaw drops. "I am *not* drooling."

"So wait, those Torres boys, are they all related?" I ask.

"No, Apollo and Atlas are Levi's cousins," Aspen says.

"No wonder he's the only one with a normal name."

Océane laughs. "Glad I'm not the only one who noticed."

"I think they're all fine as fuck," Aspen says.

"Stop letting those ovaries do the talking." Océane rolls her eyes.

"Easy for you to say, you already have a boyfriend to jump," Aspen replies.

"That's not important."

"Yeah, it is."

"I know how to appreciate a nice physique without lusting after it," she says.

"Appreciate a nice physique?"

Talon's stern voice makes us all look over our shoulders with dread.

He's standing right behind Océane and looking madly obsessed. Or borderline psycho, I can't tell.

"Don't tell me you were ogling those Tartarus and Phantom Boys. They like the attention too much. Especially from pretty girls like you." He grips her shoulders and leans in. "I might have to break their legs to take them down a notch."

"What?" I gasp.

"He doesn't mean it," Océane says.

His fingers dig into her shoulders. "I don't?"

She sighs out loud and says, "Talon's gonna go grab me a drink. See ya, guys." She grabs his hand and leads him through the crowd, but his gaze seems fixated on her.

"He's madly in love with her, isn't he?" I mutter.

"He's something all right." Aspen snorts. "Anyway, I'm gonna go find the bathroom. You coming too?"

I shake my head. "No, I actually wanna look around for a bit. See if I can find more familiar faces among the sea of white masks."

"Oh, well, good luck then. I'm going to go find Mavis after this, so if you need me, call me, okay?"

We hug and each head in a different direction.

But I'm not interested in finding anyone in particular.

In fact, where I'm going, I'd rather not anyone recognize me at all.

***

HEATH

We pick up the white masks lying near the entrance of the Phantom Society building and put them on before heading inside. The building is huge, and the glass dome in the middle of the roof lets in an eerie light from the night sky. With its wooden paneled walls and tapestries, the place itself looks haunted by ghosts of the past. A perfect place for someone interested in the occult, and I smile at the thought of digging in to all the books this place has to offer. Mavis would have a field day.

"Now I remember why I never came here," Silas scoffs, looking around. "All these fucking creeps."

"Like you're any better." I snort.

"What? They're all liars and cheats."

"And the Skull and Serpents are killers. We all know the gossip."

He tilts his head and smirks. "It's not gossip if it's true."

I roll my eyes and take two champagne glasses off a server walking around with a tray, and I shove one into Silas's hand. "Here. You need to relax."

"I'm calm." He looks around like he's trying to find someone.

"You don't look calm," I reply.

"Where is she?" he mutters.

"We have plenty of time for that later," I say, whisking him away from the stairs and into the crowd. "Let's mingle first."

"We can't catch her if we're not there to witness it," he grits.

"Don't worry about it. I got it covered."

"How?" He frowns. "What the fuck aren't you telling me?"

"Well, hello to you too." Two strong hands land on each of our shoulders, forcing us to turn around and face the giant with his scarred-up face partially hidden behind a mask. "If it isn't my two favorite Serpents."

Apollo Torres. A monster so cruel he might even put Silas to shame. Both of them have no conscience, but Apollo? He doesn't even get angry. Zero emotions, ever. And best of all? He's my goddamn half brother.

He leans between us, a vicious smile on his face just as menacing as Silas's, if not worse. "And here I was thinking you two hated the Phantom Society."

"We do," Silas retorts.

"I'm fine with anyone," I reply. "As long as there's a good party."

"Same, bro," Apollo says.

"I'm not here for the party," Silas replies.

"Oh?" Interest sparkles in Apollo's killer eyes. "Do I smell an ulterior motive?"

Silas knocks his hand off his shoulder. "Another time."

"I'm bored." Our other half brother, Orion Navarro, approaches while swirling a glass of wine. "Nothing fun ever happens at these Phantom parties."

"Oh, c'mon. I know you're just spoiled with those oversexed Tartarus House parties." Apollo slaps him on the back.

"There's girls, booze, music. What else does one need?" I reply, shrugging as we saunter around through the crowd.

Apollo's smoldering laughter fills the room before he abruptly quiets and whispers, "Murder."

Silas stares him down, not in a scared kind of way, but in a territorial kind of way. And I don't like it one bit.

"Okay, why don't you two just go in different directions," I say, pushing Apollo toward the five girls in the back, who were all gawking at him and chuckling to themselves at the sight of his thick muscles.

"Why? You don't wanna hang with me tonight? Heath ..." He pretends a fake knife stabs him as he slowly walks backward into the girls. "You wound me."

"Don't hurt my brother like that, Heath," Orion says, throwing his arm around Apollo.

I snort. "You act like he ain't my brother too." I make a heart with my hands, and Apollo winks and turns around to head to the ladies.

"Jesus Christ, I can't believe you're all related," Silas says.

"Don't offend me. I'm nothing like him." Orion takes a sip of his wine and licks his lips. "He wishes he could be me."

I roll my eyes. "You wish."

"You three are fucking weird," Silas says.

I raise a brow. "Unlike you?" I laugh. "*All* our fucking families are weird, Silas."

Silas shrugs and strolls off. "Whatever. I'm going to throw out my hook. See if the fish take the bait."

"Fish?" Orion frowns. "What kind of nasty girls is he into?"

I snort. "Metaphorically."

"Oh …" Orion's voice suddenly gets all dainty as he runs his fingers through his wavy dark-blond locks. "So he's not into girls at all?"

"Oh, he is. But mostly for other kinky stuff," I reply, clearing my throat. "It's not my business."

I'm not about to tell the fucking world what it is we like to do.

Orion chuckles and puts his wine down. "Well, I don't blame him. So much pleasure in this world, yet we all hunger for more." He sighs out loud, like he's languishing in these bright strobe lights that flash through the dark rooms. "Man, these lights are giving me a headache. I'm going to find a private room to rest. See you later."

"Bye," I say, and he walks off, rubbing his forehead.

But my eyes immediately fall on the figure walking through the hallways with a giant bouquet, his brown, side-swept hair peeking out from the mask. My eyes narrow. That looks like …

Max.

***

IVY

I take off this damn mask, chuck it aside, and sink to my knees in front of the mini vault in this bedroom.

Jackpot.

I slowly begin to roll the buttons around to find the combination. I don't care how long it's going to take me; I am going to open this thing and get ahold of the money.

Sweat rolls down my forehead, and I pray no one will come inside. The party downstairs provides so much background noise that it's hard to focus on the task, but I refuse to give up.

This is my life.

Not just my livelihood.

My actual fucking *life* is at stake. And not just mine, but Cora's too.

I *have* to get this money, no matter the cost.

I wipe away the sweat and keep turning the buttons.

However, a sudden squeak in the back of the room makes me turn my ears like a goddamn cat, and I shimmy away to the desk, rolling underneath it before whoever it is sees me.

"Ivy? I know you're in here."

That sounded like …

Frowning, I crawl out from underneath the desk. "Max?"

Like all the other guests, he's wearing an eerie-looking white mask that belongs to the Phantom Society house, which covers only half his face. But it doesn't suit him at all.

He shuts the door behind him. "What are you doing here?"

It's only after I said the words that my eyes slide down his body, and I notice the giant bouquet in his hand.

Oh God.

THIRTY-THREE

IVY

"I was looking for you, but then your neighbor said you were here, and—"

"You went to my house?" I interrupt.

He approaches. "I wanted to tell you—"

I raise a finger to interrupt him. "Please ... don't."

"Ivy ..."

My eyes tear up. "No. Get out."

He raises a hand, the hurt on his face palpable. Visceral. Deadly to my own damn heart.

"I know what you're doing here."

"You only think you know," I scoff.

"Please. You have to stop this," he says, still getting closer and closer. "Before you get caught."

"No." My fists ball. "I need this money. You don't understand how much I've already sacrificed."

"Then tell me," he says, still clutching that damn bouquet. "Please, let me help you."

"Why would I trust you? Silas and Heath are your buddies. You made your choice," I scoff. "You let them use you to trick me with marked money and force you to your knees to tell me you love me to fool me? So that you could fuck me too? What a cruel joke."

"It's not a joke," he says, holding up the flowers in front of my face. "I have fallen in love with you. And I came to find you because I wanted to give these to you because I wanted to apologize." He swallows, and it feels like my lungs cannot drag in the air I so desperately need. "I'm sorry," he says. "I'm sorry for not telling you sooner. I'm sorry for betraying you. I'm sorry for taking part in their games. For making you confused, for—"

I slap him.

It only registers with me the moment a red mark appears on his face.

But then he leans in and pecks me on the top lip so gently it melts my heart. "Being obsessed. For making you feel something you don't want to feel. For falling deeply, madly in love with you."

More tears well up in my eyes, but it's the gentle, soul-crushing smile on his face that kills me.

And I throw my arms around him and kiss him so hard we nearly fall, but he catches himself on the desk, dropping the bouquet on the floor.

Still, I don't stop kissing him, pouring out all of my frustrations and needs into this one single kiss of desperation ... desperation to feel like I'm not alone, like my desires matter. To feel loved. And here he is, offering it on a silver platter like he's never wanted anything else than to please me.

How could I resist?

I'm still angry, still burning with fury over being used like a toy and seeing the one guy who made me think he cared to take part in it. But this boy has done something to my heart that neither of us can deny. And I'm done playing games, done feeling like I owe anyone an explanation for my wants and needs.

I kiss him with everything I have left in me despite my brain telling me I shouldn't and my whole goddamn life being on the line. I kiss him because if I don't, I will never remember how to breathe.

"Oh fuck ..." he murmurs beneath that mask, still kissing me. "Ivy, please, you have to stop."

"Why?" I ask.

He opens his eyes while kissing me. "Because I want you so badly, I can't even fucking breathe."

I smile against his lips. "I know that feeling. Don't hold back," I whisper.

His hands slide across my waist and cup my ass, and the groan that follows makes my body heat lightning fast.

How is it that he's so easily wound me around his finger?

Suddenly, he spins me around, shoving me against the desk before kissing me all over my neck, my clavicles, my chest, and every inch of skin his lips roam across, as though he's worshipping the mere presence of my body in his hands. And something about that is so damn sexy that I return the kisses with equal amounts of yearning, kissing and licking at his top lip until he shivers in my arms.

"I want you. I want you. I want you. I want you, I want you, God, I want *you.*" He says it so many times it almost feels like he's reciting a mantra. "Can I have you? Please, can you be mine?" He's whispering between kisses and touches filled with devotion, and even though I shouldn't, I desperately want to believe him.

My hands move down his chest as he pushes my legs apart with his body, curling up the fabric of my dress. I slide my hands inside his pants until he gasps and moans at the same time when I grasp his cock. He's already hard in my hands, and something about that makes me feel so damn good that I start jerking him off.

His lips claim mine with a ferocity he's not yet shown before as he plops me down on the desk and fumbles at my dress in an attempt to get the zipper on my back down. When the zipper is finally released, he tears down my dress in one go and pulls off my panties, all while never taking his lips off mine.

His tongue rolls around mine as his fingers slip between my legs and coax out the wetness by rubbing my pussy. He moans into my mouth when I rub him just as feverishly.

"You gotta stop me," he murmurs between kissing me. "I can't hold back."

"You want me, don't you?" I ask.

He nods, licking my top lip. "More than anything."

His breath falters in his throat when I squeeze his shaft and then release him. "Then fuck me."

He immediately grips my thighs, lifts my legs, and rips down his pants, ready to go.

CLAP! CLAP! CLAP!

Max abruptly stops, and we both turn our heads toward the sound, which came from what I thought was a bathroom door. But it turns out it opens into another bedroom instead, and the door just got slammed into the wood. A guy with a white mask on his face leans against the door opening, the tattoos and those familiar black tunnels in his earlobes immediately giving away who it is.

Heath Preston.

"Beautiful. Just fucking perfect." Heath's voice booms through the room.

"Heath?" Max mutters, swiftly pulling away from me.

"I'm impressed you managed to stop her from robbing them," Heath says, still leaning against the doorjamb. "Or maybe she's just distracting you so she can continue after she's tied you up."

"What?" Max says. "No. Of course not."

I feel exposed and embarrassed because Heath's eyes glide over my body like he's savoring a meal he's yet to consume.

"That's not—What are you doing here?" I sneer, trying to compose myself as I get off the desk and pull my dress back up into place even though it won't stay and keeps falling off my shoulders.

Heath tilts his head, his thumb brushing across his lip. "Oh, don't stop because of me."

"What do you want?" I ask. "Or did you just come here to humiliate me further?"

"No," he responds, dark eyes darting to Max. "I saw *him* and wanted to confirm my suspicions."

My eyes narrow. "Of what?"

"You, sneaking around to steal ..." I swallow. "Him, still trying to profess his love to you after everything we've done." He makes a tsk sound and shakes his head. "I'm disappointed in you, Max."

Max pulls his pants back up, but they barely fit over his hard-on.

Heath pushes himself off the wood and casually walks to the couch to the right of us, flopping down with his legs spread open wide.

"Well, go on then ... continue whatever you were starting there," he says.

I frown. "Have you gone insane?"

A wicked smile spreads on his lips, and he chuckles. "Maybe I have ... finally."

I roll my eyes and push Max away. "I can't do this."

But the second I head for the door, a certain clicking noise stops me in my tracks.

"Don't even think about it."

"Heath, no!" Max yells, anger distorting his face.

My eyes connect with the barrel of a gun.

"You want to shoot me?" I seethe.

But instead of pointing it at me, Heath points it at Max. "Do you want me to shoot him instead?"

I immediately step in front of Max to protect him. "Fucking try, I dare you."

Heath snorts. "So courageous, defending your boyfriend. It's cute."

"He's not my boyf—"

"Then what is he if not the boy you just kissed like you were madly in love and wanted to fuck his brains out?" He pauses before adding, "You *love* him."

A blush creeps onto my cheeks.

"You ... do?" Max mutters behind me.

Heath snorts, contempt dancing in his eyes. "It's obvious, and I feel so stupid not to have noticed it sooner that he wasn't the only one falling."

Max's fingers find mine in the dark, and I swallow back the nerves.

"Why do you even care?" I ask.

He frowns and places the gun down on the couch armrest. "Why do I care?" he repeats, leaning forward while gripping the armrests. "Because you stole something from me that wasn't yours to take."

My teeth grind together. "I'm already paying for that dearly."

"No," he says through gritted teeth.

What is he talking about? I already gave them my body in exchange for the money I stole. What more could he want?

"You two want each other so badly? Then have at it." He looks Max dead in the eyes. "Kiss. Her."

Max swallows and steps out beside me. "Why?"

"Prove it to me. Show me you're not lying. Show me ... what it looks like," Heath says, licking his lips.

Max tentatively nods at me while all I can do is glare at the gun on the couch.

"Relax, I won't shoot ..." Heath says, tilting his head. "But I can't promise the guys out there won't if they find out you were about to steal from them."

Of course, another veiled threat. What else did I expect?

I sigh and look at Max, searching for answers, but he's as much bound to them as I am. They use him like they use me. And I don't want to see him hurt either.

Max grips my face and makes me look at him. "Don't look at him. Look at me."

His lips slowly collide with mine, pulling me away from the dangerous eyes watching me from the couch. His lips push mine apart as his tongue laps me up, licking and suckling at my lips to pry out my tongue, so I join him in this dance of sexual tension. And the more he kisses me, the harder it is to resist.

"Kiss me," he whispers into my lips. "And I'll make you forget about him just like I have."

Just like I have? What does he mean?

Still, I kiss him back just as eagerly, roaming around his mouth with my tongue like my life depends on it. His moans suffocate whatever resistance I had left as his hands slip down my chest, fingers grazing past my nipples until they're taut and desperate for him to touch.

I moan into his mouth, and he hardens against me once more, his kisses becoming more brazen while he grips my breast and squeezes.

His lips disappear down my neckline, and I tug at his waistband to lower his pants.

"Yes, that's it," Heath groans. "Make him want you. Desperately. To the point he can't stand the thought of not being inside you right. Fucking. Now."

I pull out Max's cock and jerk him off because I must. Because I'm forced. Because ... I want to.

I shudder against him, my lips trembling as I pause.

"Don't think. Just fuck me," Max whispers. "Wherever you want, however you want, I'm yours."

I kiss him so hard I nearly forget Heath is even here. Suddenly, Max lifts me in his arms, cradling my ass, tearing down my dress again until nothing's left to the imagination. And when he lowers me onto his shaft, I mewl with delight.

My legs curl around his body, and my feet hook together as he begins to move me up and down while holding me by my waist. His kisses are so soft and gentle, almost like a caress, and they twist me into knots that are impossible to unfurl.

His cock feels so good inside me as he whimpers with each thrust, almost like he can't believe I'm in his arms and that he's allowed to take me like this. And something about that makes me so fucking feral that I grab his hair, tilt his head back, and force my lips onto his like a crazed animal.

Suddenly, two hands slide up my back and around my waist as a set of lips land near the base of my neck, dragging a line up toward my ear. "That's it, little thief ... let yourself go."

Heath's tongue drags along my skin, coaxing out more moans while Max buries himself inside me deep.

"You take him so well," Heath whispers, placing delectable kisses underneath my ear. "It almost makes me ... jealous."

Jealous? After everything he already took from me? What more could he want?

"Kiss him hard," he whispers, his hands slowly sliding up to my breasts, squeezing them. "Let me see your fucking undoing."

The moment Max's mouth lands on mine, I bite his lip in shock ... As another hard cock enters my pussy.

THIRTY-FOUR

MAX

Her dark eyes fill with stars the second he penetrates her, and my God, I nearly lose myself in them. His cock rubs up against mine as he slowly forces his way inside. She bites my lip again, the sting of the pain making blood rush from my cock to my mouth and back again. I tear away and look at her just as much in shock that Heath would do this.

"Kiss me."

She's actually begging ... *me*?

I swallow away the lump in my throat and slam my lips onto hers, fervently kissing her until her breath falters, swallowing down all of her moans.

"You're begging for kisses even with two cocks inside you?" Heath murmurs, planting his lips onto her shoulders. "That desperate for more..."

"Fuck," Ivy groans, nails digging into my back.

I know she wants to curse him, but it wouldn't help her case, nor mine. So I fuck her like our lives quite literally depend on it, holding her up by sheer will.

In the heat of the moment, Heath's eyes suddenly dart to me as his tongue dips out and licks her neckline all the way up to her jaw. But all I can focus on is the tip of his tongue inching across her skin. "She is such a delicious little thing, isn't she?"

I nod a few times, but Ivy grips my face and forces me to look at her.

"This isn't for him. It's for us," she says.

"Is it?" Heath thrusts in so hard her mouth forms an o-shape, and the moan that leaves her mouth is almost too depraved, even for his ears.

"Oh God," she moans.

"You're so damn tight when we fuck you like this," Heath groans.

From behind, his hands coil around her body and grip her breasts, squeezing her nipples with each thrust. She's as wet as can be, dripping all over our cocks, and it doesn't take long before she's also moving along with our rhythm, completely consumed with lust just like me.

"Fuck, I can't hold it much longer," I groan. "It feels so good. Your pussy is to die for."

"You'd die for her?" Heath's eyes find mine in the dark, and I swallow away the lump in my throat.

Because I most definitely would.

And I can almost feel the darts shooting from his eyes straight into my head.

"Please," Ivy moans.

"Pleading already?" Heath plants more kisses on her shoulders, his vicious eyes homing in on me. "For me? Or for him?"

She doesn't respond as she bounces on my lap, her nails scratching me to the point where I know I'm bleeding. But her longing kisses make up for it as I struggle to contain my emotions and greed for more of her.

"Fuck," she groans as we alternate our thrusts.

"You like this, admit it," Heath groans.

"I can't..." she murmurs, but she can't finish her sentence, and I'm not sure if it's because she truly can't or because she doesn't want to.

I keep kissing her as her mind slips into the nether along with us. With every kiss, Heath's languishing eyes home in on mine like a beacon in the dark. And I can't look away, no matter how hard I try, even though my lips and my tongue are still hooked to Ivy. I'm torn in two, twisted and coiled, and my malleable heart is being stretched to the limit.

He wants her, I know that. But I want her too, and I refuse to choose.

My tongue draws a line down her neck as her head tilts back and rests on Heath's shoulder.

Suddenly, he grabs her chin and pulls her face sideways, smashing his lips onto hers right in front of me.

And fuck me ... there isn't anything I've ever been turned on by more than watching them kiss.

My hard-on throbs inside her, and I can feel his shaft hardening against mine with equal bursts as his tongue lashes around hers, claiming her mouth... All while his eyes are locked on mine.

But it doesn't matter what he does. As long as I can have her, as long as she'll be mine, I can handle it all. If that means I have to share, then so be it. She gave them her body, but she gave me her damaged heart, and I'll give her the world if she'll treasure my broken heart too.

***

HEATH

I claim her mouth like it always belonged to me, stealing the love she gave to him. I don't fucking care it's wrong, I need her just as much as he needs her. I need this; I need it so badly I can't take it anymore. I throw out all my rage, all my anger into each thrust, coaxing out more wetness, more moans, more, more, more.

I need it all.

It's not fucking enough.

God, she looks fucking delectable in this small, glossy yellow dress, like a goddamn forbidden fruit.

I rip my mouth off hers only to run my tongue all along her neck and back, marking her with my saliva while my fingers slip down her chest until I find that one spot that makes her quiver.

"You want him so badly? Then mewl for him. Show me what it looks like when you give him your fucking lust," I whisper into her ear as I roll my fingers around her wetness.

She moans out loud while growing wetter and wetter, and the feel of her on my cock is beyond this world.

But I can feel him too, thrusting in and out against my shaft, sending shocks all through my body. And fuck me, if someone came in and killed me now for trespassing, I'd die without regrets.

"Look at him," I murmur. "Look at him while my cock and fingers give you so much fucking pleasure you can't help but moan for me."

There is nothing quite like watching him suffer over the fact that her pleasure belongs to me as I flick her clit and see her face scrunch up. Max bites his lip and leans in, planting kisses all over her clavicles and neck, desperate to be close. But my hand remains firmly between her legs as I claim that one part of her she doesn't want to give to me.

"Give it to me," I whisper. "Give me your fucking orgasm."

"Someone could hear us," she murmurs.

"I don't fucking care. Let them hear. If they try to intervene, I'll kill them all."

Her eyes widen, but I cover her mouth with mine before she can say another word. Her lips taste like sweet sin and everything I always wanted, but a hint of Max's kisses lingers on her lips, and it makes me bite down on her lip and tug until she bleeds.

She groans into my mouth, and I suck up the blood right off her lip, probing her mouth with my tongue as deeply as my cock pokes at her insides. I want her to feel me everywhere, I want to invade her body, consume it, devour it whole and leave nothing left for her to give to him.

Between kisses, my eyes find his as a proud smirk spreads on my face.

"Look at me, fucking the girl you love," I say. "She loves the feel of both our cocks inside her."

He swallows as his dick begins to throb inside her, and his eyes briefly flicker down to my fingers playing with her most sensitive areas.

"Please, Heath ..."

"You want her to come so badly?"

"I can't take it anymore," Max groans.

"Hold it," I growl, flicking her like a madman.

Her moans grow louder and louder as I fuck her hard together with Max while his fingers dig into her thighs, trying to hold her up. But I'm so damn focused I can't even look anywhere else but at him as I slowly bring her to a climax.

Once she reaches that pinnacle, I'm going to kiss her so hard she'll forget she even thought of needing him.

"Go on, then ..." I whisper into her ear. "Come."

She parts her lips, a soft whimper exiting her mouth before the loud moan arrives along with a pool of wetness, and so many contractions in her pussy that it makes my dick throb.

"Oh fuck, I can feel her coming. Fuck, she's so slick," Max groans, and a whimper follows before I can feel his warm cum roll down my shaft, his submissive eyes connecting with mine in a flurry of lust.

I thrust once more, but I can't stop the orgasm from overwhelming me, and a loud roar bursts out of me as I come deep inside that velvety fucking pussy, coating her with my thick cum.

But in my greed and delirium, I don't claim Ivy's delicious lips as planned.

Instead, I grip Max's face and smash my lips on his.

THIRTY-FIVE

MAX

One blink—that's all it took before the kiss was sealed.

My lips unlatch from his in absolute shock. But just that one blink was enough to tilt my fucking world on its axis.

Heath ... kissed me?

It takes a few seconds to register, almost as if my mind is still playing catch-up with my mouth.

His eyes roam my face, bewilderment slowly taking over his as he pulls out of her and backs away, his hard-on still dripping.

"Heath?" I mutter, utterly confused.

"Did you two ... just kiss?" Ivy asks as I place her back down on the floor.

But Heath keeps backtracking, and he pulls his cock back into his pants and zips up, almost as if to hide the evidence. But I remember. I vividly remember his lips slamming on mine instead.

Was it a mistake?

But before I can even ask him, he waltzes out the door and slams it shut behind him.

What the hell?

***

IVY

Max stares at the door, his eyes widening as if he had just seen a bomb go off, and he doesn't know what to do.

I place my hand on his face and gently caress him. "Are you okay?"

His tongue dips out, and he briefly bites his lip. Suddenly, he grips my face with both hands and smashes his lips on mine so hard I nearly fall over.

"I love you," he whispers against my mouth. "Nothing will ever change that."

I nod against his lips, smiling. His eyes immediately travel to the gun lying on the couch, and he goes to grab it, tucking it into his pocket before he zips back up again.

Suddenly, the door opens, and I pull my panties and dress back in place, hiding the evidence of whatever the hell that was. I don't know if I could call it a revenge fuck, or a jealousy fuck, or a complicated emotions fuck. But fuck, did it feel so fucking good.

I just took two dicks at once from two masked men.

And now I still feel ... insatiable.

"Max. Ivy." Silas's voice instantly makes my skin heat again. His eyes find Max first before they home in on me, and he narrows them. "What the fuck were you doing in here? I just saw Heath rushing down the stairs."

"Heath," Max mutters, and he briefly glances at me before rushing off, pushing past Silas. "I have to go."

He's gone before I can even say another word.

"Tell me what just happened," Silas continues.

"Nothing," I say.

I'm not about to give him more ammo.

Silas closes the door behind him and walks to the middle of the room. "You're lying to me." He crosses his arms.

I swallow back the nerves while he gazes around until he finds the mini vault.

"You were going to steal from the Phantoms, weren't you?"

I'm incensed he'd say it out loud. Even if it's true, it's none of his business.

"You just couldn't help yourself," Silas says.

"Fuck you, I'm out of here," I say, and I waltz past him, but he grips my arm and forces me to stay.

"You keep saying that word like you haven't already been fucked plenty." He eyes me up and down, briefly pausing near my thighs, and I can feel the wet cum creating a trail. "Is your pussy still throbbing from the aftermath of two dicks?"

I furrow my brows at him. "You just love to humiliate me, don't you?"

He smirks. "Very much … I'm fueled by the way you react."

"Fuel yourself on this," I say, sticking up my middle finger before marching out the door and slamming it shut behind me.

My plan got foiled. Completely ruined because Max found me, and then Heath too … and when Silas stepped into the room, I knew it was over.

There's no way I'm going to get that money out of the vault now. Silas would probably report me to the Phantom Society leadership, and I'd end up in jail. Or worse, somewhere dead in a ditch.

That money is gone, along with my hopes of keeping Cora and me safe.

Tears well up in my eyes, but I push them away.

The last thing I'm going to give those guys are my precious fucking tears.

"Ivy! I was looking for you." Océane's voice stops me in my tracks in the middle of the foyer. "Where were you?"

"I had to … take a long bathroom break," I lie.

I'm not going to divulge what I just did with two Skull and Serpent Society guys. I have enough to worry about as it is. I don't need reputation damage on top of it.

"Wait. Where's your mask." She places a hand on my arm. "Are you okay? Did something happen?"

I shake my head. "Think I'm going to head home. I don't feel good."

"Do you need someone to drive you? I can ask Talon."

"Ah, no thanks," I say. "I'll manage."

"You sure? You have a bike, right? The car would be much quicker."

How do I say I'd much prefer to be alone right now while I'm on the verge of breaking down?

"It's fine. It's not that far," I reply with a smile. "Thanks for the offer."

She smiles back. "Let me know if there's anything I can do when you get home."

"I will, thanks." I give her a fake smile and head through the masked crowd as swiftly as possible to get away from here.

I grab my bike, jump on, then race through the gates of Spine Ridge University.

The night that should've ended with happiness now ends in a giant blunder.

And with no money in sight.

Shit. Shit. Shit!

What am I going to do now?

***

SILAS

I walk down the stairs and look around, but I don't see Heath, Max, or Ivy anywhere.

Where the hell did they all run off to so quickly?

This has got to do with that fucking money she tried to steal again, and I want to know why.

On the way down, I spot Aspen dancing on her own near a pillar right next to the door to the dance floor. I waltz over to her and grab her arm so she'll stop moving and look at me.

"Have you seen Ivy?"

"What the—Silas?" she mutters, confused.

"I need to know where she is."

She frowns. "No."

"I know you're friends with her. I need to find her," I say, looking her directly in the eye. "Now."

"I don't fucking know, okay?" She jerks free of my grip. "Stop it. We're at a fucking party."

I grumble and turn around. "Fine."

I'll go look for her myself.

I don't care if I have to race around the entire fucking city. I will find her.

"Let her go, Silas," she yells across the hallway. "Whatever debt she has, she doesn't deserve your hate."

So she's told Aspen about the debt ... but does she even know why?

I throw her a glance over my shoulder. "You think this is hate?" A smug grin spreads on my face. "Do you even know what kind of deal she made with me?"

Her face droops, and her eyes slowly widen.

I guess she didn't.

"Enjoy the fucking party," I add, waving before I head out the door.

I check my phone and the tracker I swiftly installed on her bike the moment I saw it parked outside this damn Phantom Society. *Got her.*

I jog across the street, but instead of taking my car, I grab my motorcycle. After putting my helmet on, I jump on to rev the engine and race off.

***

IVY

I bike home as fast as I can, sweat dripping down my back as I make my way through downtown Crescent Vale City. The more energy I expend, the more anger I'm able to let loose. Those boys have been nothing but a problem to me from day one.

Dammit.

I have no time to waste. I need to get to Cora and get her out of there before that anonymous fucker turns on me.

I know he's waiting, waiting for me to admit I can't do it anymore. And I'd rather die than admit that.

Breathing wildly, I shift left and right across the lanes, passing the cars that are waiting at the red lights, risking my own life in the process. But I have no choice. I have to get to her as quickly as I can. Before it's too late. Before—

A sudden buzz in my pocket has me nearly falling over the front of the bike as I abruptly hit the brakes. I grab it and press the unlock button to check who sent what.

Anonymous: Time's up. Five grand or you're done.

I type back as quickly as I can.

Me: I need more time. Please. I will have it for you tomorrow night. I swear.

Anonymous: You can swear that to Stefano when I bring you to him.

My eyes widen as panic rises to the surface.

No.

No. No. No!

Cora!

THIRTY-SIX

IVY

I jump back on my bike and race off as fast as I possibly can, ignoring all the stop signs. I nearly get hit but manage to avoid a car by a hair. The driver hangs his head out the window to yell at me, but I ignore him.

There's no more time.

I have to get to her before it's too late.

Please, please, please, let Cora be okay.

Goddammit, I shouldn't have asked Mrs. Schwartz to watch her in my apartment. I should've just let her bring Cora to her place. At least then those fuckers might not find her.

I fish my phone from my pocket while driving and call Mrs. Schwartz's number three times, but she doesn't pick up.

"Goddammit!" I yell across the street, ignoring everyone who looks at me like I've lost my mind, racing around like this in a tiny yellow dress, but I don't care.

I stuff my phone back, so I can focus on biking as quickly as possible. Adrenaline drives me forward while sweat now cakes my entire skin as the heat rushes through my body, but I keep going. I refuse to give up. Not now. Not ever. I will fight tooth and nail until my last dying breath because that's what I should've done to begin with.

I will fucking make it.

I'm coming for you, Cora.

I race through the streets, my lungs nearly collapsing from the amount of oxygen they have to process, but when I finally reach my area, my eyes light up. There's no one here. Maybe I made it in time.

But the closer I get to my building, the more I'm feeling anxious. Weird. Like someone followed me here.

Still, I jump off my bike, park it in the usual spot, and turn around. Only to be pummeled in the chest.

I'm knocked to the ground, headfirst. I groan, sucking in a sharp breath, but my lungs sting. Suddenly, someone crawls on top of me as two hands snake around my throat, squeezing tightly.

I can't breathe.

What's happening?

"You thought you could escape?"

In front of me is a black mask ... with an emblem of Bones.

My eyes widen.

Oh God.

I fight back underneath the man, slamming my fist into his face, but it doesn't even seem to faze him.

"You think that'll stop us?" His fingers slowly unravel from my neck.

"Us?" I choke out, coughing.

More of those masked men come out of all the nooks and crannies in this street, even one from behind the building I live in.

"We know where you've been hiding, Ivy."

My pupils dilate.

I kick around, thrashing, hitting everything in my path, but some other fucker holds down my feet while another drags me away from underneath the guy.

"Tie her up and take her to the van."

"NO!" I yell. "Let go of me!"

I fish my knife from my pocket and slash at them as hard as I can, cutting through one of their arms. One of them howls in pain, but the knife is knocked from my hand with ease.

"Fuck, she cut me!"

WHACK!

A hard slap to the face makes my head spin.

"You're a spicy one, aren't you?" The guy laughs as he chokes me out. "This dress is far too fancy to spoil with blood. Maybe I'll take you to the boss in a few hours instead of right away. Have some fun with you while you beg for your life."

The sound of a motorcycle echoes through the streets, and the bright light blinds me. I shriek as it's headed straight toward me, but right before it hits, it swerves and knocks down the guy holding my arms.

The biker then drives right over him, breaking bone after bone in his body.

The guy gargles out a screaming moan.

Finally, I can breathe again.

Until some other fucker clamps down on my ankles and refuses to let go.

"Get off me!" I shriek, kicking.

Motorcycle guy has turned his bike around again, but I'm far too busy shaking this fucker off my legs because he won't let me go.

"Fuck off!" I scream, kicking him like my life depends on it.

After I roll around on the asphalt, he finally loses his grip, and I crawl backward away from him. The asshole still follows me, attempting to grasp my ankles again, so I swiftly get to my feet and attempt to brawl with him.

They wanna take me? Fine. I won't go quietly.

Motorcycle guy jumps off his bike as five more goons appear from the sidelines, all sporting butcher knives.

"You messed with the wrong fucking guys."

Motorcycle guy doesn't say a word as he casually unzips his coat and pulls out two sizable knives while I avoid a knockout blow to the face.

I throw a left fist and punch the fucker who tried to take me by the legs in the gut.

He groans in pain but swiftly regains his composure and grips my second fist midair, knocking me back into a wall.

"Whoever the fuck you summoned isn't going to fucking save you," he grits. "You're outnumbered."

"Says who?" I grit, trying to lie my way through this.

A fist comes at my face, but I lean sideways and narrowly avoid it. However, a second hit of his knee in my stomach makes me buck and heave.

The guy grabs me by the hair. "Not so confident now, are we?"

He kicks me in the shins from the side, and I'm knocked to the ground.

Suddenly, a knife comes flying right at us and hits the guy in the back.

He groans and falls over on top of me.

Motorcycle guy grabs him by the shoulders and hauls him off me, shoving him aside. He stares me down for a second, but I can't see his eyes behind that dark visor, and I shudder in place.

When the guy comes up to a crawl, another knife is thrown at him... straight in the back of his skull. Blood explodes everywhere—on the asphalt, on my clothes, my skin, on his helmet.

Who is this guy?

In shock, I stare, still on the ground, as Motorcycle guy waltzes off and slams his fist into another one of those fuckers who came for me, pummeling him to the ground before piercing his eye, pricking it to his knife like a goddamn marshmallow he wants to roast.

The guy screams in pain. "What the fuck?!"

Motorcycle guy grips his mouth and cracks open his jaw, shoving the eye inside.

What the fuck—

Two hands grip my ankles, dragging me across the pavement, and I shriek. "NO!"

I grab the knife stuck in the dude's head and rip it out, ramming it into the asphalt in an effort to save myself from being hauled away.

Motorcycle guy chucks one of his bloodied knives right at the fucker who's grabbed me, and it punctures his neck near the base of the skull, severing the connection to his own brain.

He collapses on the ground while I crawl away to a safer spot.

"What the fuck do you want?!" one of the other guys yells at Motorcycle guy.

All I can do is gape at the massacre in front of me.

Motorcycle guy straightens his back, muscles clearly rippling through his outfit. "Touch her, and it'll be the last fucking thing your fingers touch on this goddamn earth before I wipe you off it."

Wait a minute ... I recognize that voice.

He swings his knife around like it's a toy. "Now ... who's ready to die?"

"You motherfucker, you'll pay for this!" one of the men yells at Motorcycle guy.

Two, three, four guys all come at the stranger at once, but he dodges their attacks like he's done this a million times before. He shoves a knife into the first guy's temple, then pulls it out to slice the second one's face from ear to ear.

But a third one approaches him from behind, and I scream, "Watch out!"

I snatch the knife from the ground and attempt to chuck it at the third guy.

Too late.

The guy cuts him with a butcher's knife from the back, jamming the knife straight through his visor, shattering it to pieces.

I squeal in response, worried he's hurt, but in a millisecond while he turns to face the fucker, his green eyes find mine in the dark while red streaks of blood roll down his sharp nose. Those black-and-white hairs fluttering around his forehead make me hold my breath.

Is that...?!

He rips the butcher's knife out of his visor and jabs the guy straight in the heart.

"Fuck..." the guy groans before collapsing.

The fourth one's neck is sliced open, and blood sprays everywhere.

All of them fall to the ground while Motorcycle guy is covered in their blood from head to toe.

The road in front of me is littered with bodies, and I barely believe what I just saw with my own damn eyes.

An absolute slaughter.

My heart is going a million miles an hour.

But what surprises me the most is the thrill in my heart at the sight of vengeance over the people who tried to take me.

Motorcycle guy walks up to me, and I take a few deep breaths as he towers over me.

"Silas?" I mutter in disbelief.

He squats in front of me, the knife still firmly clutched in his hand, as he finally removes the helmet. "Nice to see you too, twig."

I'm too stunned to say a word.

Silas Rivera came to save me?

My eyes scan his face and flutter to the knife in an attempt to decipher the meaning of this.

He grips my face and turns it left and right, glancing at the red marks. But then his fingers curl underneath my shirt and tug it up, exposing the bruise on my stomach.

I immediately grasp his wrist. "I'm fine."

His gaze intensifies. "I'll be the judge of that."

My jaw slowly drops as my brain finally kicks back into gear.

"How did you find me?" I frown as he glances at my bike, and I realize what's going on. "You put a tracker on my bike."

"You think I'd let my property out of my sight?"

"*Property?*" I parrot. The insolence. "I'm no one's prop—"

He grips my chin and leans in, pointing the sharp end of the knife at my lips, and I shudder in place as it slowly slides down my neck all the way to my chest. "Did you forget the deal you made with me that night, thief?"

His knife circles my heart.

"I let my friends play with you because I love to see you squirm, but don't mistake my interest in sharing for leniency. Everything you are belongs to me. This body. This brain. This heart." He inches so close I can feel his hot, bloodied breath on my skin. "These lips and every inch of your skin is my belonging. My property. *Mine*." A diabolical grin forms on his face. "And *no one* touches what I deem mine."

My eyes travel across his face in an attempt to decipher why it feels like it's being suffocated.

Like I can't look anywhere else but at his face and those droplets of blood rolling down his cheeks, a testament to his power as a soulless killer.

He maims with ease.

He could end my life in an instant.

Yet he chooses to defend me instead.

With his bloodied knife, he draws a heart on my chest.

I try to breathe.

Honestly.

I swear on my life.

But my lungs are in dissent.

And my body, God, does it hurt ... and ache ... and long for more.

Fuck.

"I killed them all to protect you. Now, are you finally going to tell me why you need all that money, and if that's the reason they were after you?" He tilts his head while sporting a smirk. "Or do I have to fuck it out of you?"

THIRTY-SEVEN

SILAS

If I hadn't arrived in time, she would've been taken. Gone. Dead. Or worse.

Fuck.

My fist tightens around the knife as I slowly lower it along with my eyes, wondering how badly injured she is.

Suddenly, a car comes swerving in from the street to our left while another motorcycle heads our way from the same direction as I just raced through.

More enemies?

"Stay back," I growl as I get up and chuck my broken helmet aside, ready for the second wave.

But as they come closer, I recognize that motorcycle ... and that fucking car. "Wait a minute..."

Ivy crawls up from the ground. "Silas, there's more!" she screams.

Two more of those guys who were after her jump out of an alley near the building and point a gun at us.

The car races at us through the streets.

BANG! BANG!

A gun goes off right at the same time as the car drives over the guy.

The bullet scrapes my forehead and lodges into the wall behind us.

"Motherfucker," I say through gritted teeth, blood running down my face.

The one leftover guy bolts off, screaming like his head was cut off. But the other motorcycle enters the scene from the right side, and the driver raises a gun.

BANG.

A single shot is enough to kill him.

The screams abruptly stop.

The car parks near the bodies, and a guy wearing an LED mask steps out to kick one of them. "He's definitely dead, all right."

"Heath?" I say, recognizing his voice. "What are you doing here?"

Heath snorts as he tucks his gun into his pocket. "Protecting her."

The motorcycle stops between Heath's car and me.

The guy tucks his gun into his pocket removes his helmet, and Ivy smiles as she runs to him. "Max!" She hugs him tightly.

"Oh, hehe," Max murmurs, blushing. "Hi to you too."

"Wait, I didn't know you could shoot," Ivy says, eyeing the gun.

"Mom made all of us learn how," he explains. "I prefer not being seen by the people I kill, though. Unlike them." He nods at me and Heath.

But I can't stop fucking glaring at Ivy, wondering how much longer she's going to hug him and shower him with affection when I'm the one who saved her ass.

And I guess I'm not the only one, judging by Heath's stare.

She finally takes her hands off Max and blushes hard.

I clear my throat. "So. We all just casually decided to follow her?"

"I guess so." Heath shrugs.

"I followed him," Max says, briefly glancing at Heath, who doesn't even look at him. "But I knew we were all going to go find her."

What's up with those two?

Max hops off his motorcycle and grabs her hand. "Are you okay?"

God-fucking-dammit, the way she looks at him makes me antsy for my knife.

She nods. "A little bruised and beaten up ... but I'm alive."

The way she smiles back when he smiles at her, fuck, it makes me want to gouge out more eyes.

What is wrong with me?

"We gotta do something about these bodies, though," Heath says, approaching too.

"After we get her to safety," I say, and I grab her arm to drag her away from the scene of the crime. "C'mon."

She tears herself away from me. "No. I'm not leaving here without my stuff and—"

She chokes on her words like she's afraid she'll say something she shouldn't.

My eyes narrow. "*And* what?"

A blush forms on her cheeks while Max and Heath seem amused.

"Oh ..." Heath mutters.

"What? What am I missing?" I growl. "We don't have time for fucking games here. Whatever. We'll come back later for your clothes." I grasp her wrist again. "Let's go."

"No," she growls, jerking free. Before I can grasp her again, she's already bolted off toward the building on the other end of the street where she parked her bike.

"Why didn't you stop her?" I growl at Heath.

"Trust me when I say there's nothing that would stop her from going up there," he replies.

"Heath ..." Max mutters.

But Heath refuses to look him in the eyes.

"I'm going with her," Max says.

"Fine, then I'm coming too," Heath growls back, removing his mask.

"Okay, don't fucking wait on me," I retort as we all follow her into the building. It's grimy and completely worn down, with stairs that are barely kept together by broken wood and rusty metal. Everywhere I look, there are stains—on the walls, the floor, even the fucking ceiling—along with a ton of cobwebs and dust.

But by the time we get to her floor and see her struggling to even put the key into the lock, I pause.

This place ... is her home?

I look around at all the dust and grime. Why would she live here out of all fucking places? Is this why she needs that money so badly, to move out of here? There's no way anyone would break into a goddamn vault at the Phantom Society house, filled with fuckers who would kill you on sight if they'd only do it for the fun of it.

She finally manages to unlock the door but keeps it closed, breathing out loud like she's preparing for something.

What is going on?

"C'mon, open the door. We don't have time. There could be more of them coming out of the fucking woodwork any time now."

Max places a hand on her shoulder. "Don't feel rushed."

"You're one to talk. You weren't even here in time. I was," I growl back.

Max ignores me. "You can trust us."

With what?!

She pushes the door open and steps inside with Max, but Heath stays put in the doorway, his stance uncomfortable, muscles clenched.

I push him aside to see what she's been hiding, only to come to an abrupt halt in the door opening while I clutch the frame as a little girl merely the size of my fucking legs sits on the couch in the living room.

And I have never, *ever* been so fucking dazed as I am now.

This is what she was hiding?

A child?

I can't stop staring at the little girl who's sucking her thumb as she stares us up and down as if she's judging the weight of our value with her eyes alone. And for some reason, I feel like the entire fucking floor has just caved in underneath me, which is an unfamiliar feeling to me. This body was made to kill, and it doesn't fucking respond to any of my commands. That's what scares the living shit out of me.

I take a good look around the apartment. It's a shoddy mess, with patches of paint coming off the walls, a dirty carpet, and too many stains on the wall. This can't be fucking healthy. Especially for a child.

"Thank fuck you're finally here." An old lady gets up from the couch and turns off the TV. "I thought you'd never show up."

"Thanks for watching her, Mrs. Schwartz," Ivy says, her hands diving into her pockets to fish out some change and a couple of bills. "I'm sorry, this is all I have tonight. I swear, I'll repay you tomorrow."

Wait a fucking minute ...

Max steps forward and plucks a wad of cash from his pocket, stuffing it into Mrs. Schwartz's hands. "Consider the debt paid."

Ivy looks up at him. "You don't have to—"

"I want to," Max replies, smiling.

She blushes, and my nails dig into the fucking walls of her apartment.

"Thanks, sonny," Mrs. Schwartz waddles off in her slippers and pushes past us without even granting us a single look. "Oh, and feed that fucking cat, will you? He keeps nagging me, and I'm allergic."

A cat?

I look up at the windowsill where a black cat with vicious yellow eyes home in on mine, sharpening its claws to prepare for an attack. And I nearly fucking turn around and waltz off.

"Hey, Bagel," Max says as he pets that demon spawn on its head.

"Wait a fucking minute ... you're acquainted?" My eyes narrow as Max looks up at me, and then it finally clicks. "You've been here before."

He throws his hand behind his head and grins stupidly. "I was just looking out for her."

"Looking out for that fucking pussy, yeah," I grit, pulling up my sleeves.

Heath laughs, and I turn to glare up at him. "You knew?"

"Oh, he didn't just know." Max rolls his eyes.

My fingers dig into my palm so deeply they begin to bleed. "You both knew she lived here, and you kept it from me."

"I did what you told me to do," Max says.

"I never said you could lie to me."

"I didn't lie. I just ... omitted the truth." Max chuckles awkwardly. "Can you blame me?"

He glances at her with a crazy amount of love in his eyes, and for some reason, it makes me boil over with rage.

But that kid ... that kid is staring at me from the couch like she'll haunt me for the rest of my life if I don't stay. And I can't look away either because in her tiny hands is that red flower of mine.

"Cora, come here. It's okay," Ivy says, and the little girl runs into her arms to hug her tight.

Cora.

I try to swallow, but something's in the way.

"Wait, Cora?" Heath mutters, gazing at Max. "You said her neighbor's name was Cora."

Max begins to flush heavily. "Um ..."

"You lied." Heath forms a fist.

"Sorry," Max mutters.

"They're scaring me," the little girl whispers, huddling closer to Ivy, who throws me the sternest look I've ever seen. They radiate even more violently than my mother's eyes, which is an impressive feat.

"They won't hurt you," Ivy says. "Right, guys?"

Max smiles and approaches the kid, patting her on the head. "Of course not."

Ivy looks at Heath, who shakes his head. "I couldn't hurt a kid. Not ever."

Her eyes land on me at last, the look in her eyes deadly as can be. Maybe even more murderous than mine, and it silences the angered voices in my head.

"Silas. Promise me."

So ... *this* is the reason.

This is why she fought so hard, defied me so many times, stole from me without a conscience, and gave up her body to feed my wicked desires.

This girl.

I feel frozen to the floor as I stare at them both while an unfamiliar sense of caution overwhelms me. Like my body is being torn to shreds from the inside out. My hand instinctively rises to grasp my heart, as if it knows somewhere deep down something about it has irrevocably been changed.

But that doesn't make any sense. My heart doesn't beat for anyone else but me and my deranged desires to rip everything in my vicinity to shreds and watch it bleed to death. It beats for blood to rush through my veins so my muscles can keep on killing anything and everything that walks like the monster I truly am.

But this heart is beating violently as if it's been stabbed by the very same knife I carved her skin with.

Fuck.

What is happening?

"Promise me you won't let her get hurt," Ivy reiterates.

My lips have gone dry. "I swear."

She breathes out a short sigh of relief.

"Well, that was tense." Max laughs.

But I'm still not fully here. It's as though my mind has wandered off somewhere else.

Heath clears his throat as he looks at me like I've gone crazy. "Silas?"

Something warm rolls down my nose, and when my fingers swipe along, I can clearly see the blood, but it doesn't register with me at all.

Suddenly, a hand wraps around my arm and drags me away from the living room and into the bathroom. The door is shut, and I'm pushed down onto the toilet.

"Sit."

Ivy's blocking the door with her arms folded.

What the fuck?

She stares me down for a moment, then sighs out loud, turns around, and rummages through a tiny medicine cabinet above her askew sink. My eyes follow the curve of her small body, the thin waist and bones sticking out of her yellow dress, along with the high-inched heels she's wearing underneath. Those knees are barely thick enough to hold up that body.

Does she even eat enough?

And how the fuck does she go to school when she has a kid?

I swallow as she turns around and looks right at me, her alluring dark eyes catching me off guard. In her hands is a small box that she opens as she approaches me. But the moment she goes to her knees in front of me, that heart I thought beat only for violence suddenly beats out of sync.

"What are you doing?"

She pulls out a few cotton balls and pours some alcohol on them. "You're bleeding."

She holds it up to my face, and I flinch, which makes her pause.

This isn't how it was supposed to go.

This wasn't—

"It'll sting a little," she says, interrupting my train of thought.

Before I know it, she's dabbed the cotton against my skin, but the pain doesn't faze me at all. Blood drives me like adrenaline, even if it is my own I'm tasting. She doesn't fucking know pain is the only thing that makes me feel like I'm alive. Like I can feel anything at all.

Because I've never felt anything other than anger and the need to kill.

Nothing.

Just like she said, I'm a psychopath.

I don't have emotions.

Nothing.

Yet...

Her hand rises to dab the bloodied wound on my face, but I grasp her wrist midway there and force her to stop.

Stop this. Whatever it is, stop.

But the moment those eyes of hers find mine, I can't even say the words I thought I wanted to speak.

What the fuck is happening to me?

"I need to clean it, or it might get infected," she says, tilting her head. "Silas. Please."

Please.

That fucking word.

She's said it so many times before, yet it never, ever sounded so ... satisfying.

I let out a breath and release her.

She composes herself and starts working on my wound again, but something about all of this annoys the living shit out of me.

"I wouldn't have gotten this wound if you hadn't fled the fucking party."

She pauses, her nose twitching briefly. "I wouldn't have fled if you hadn't busted into the room to catch me in the act."

I raise a brow. "I wouldn't have caught you if you weren't being so obvious with your attempt to steal."

"And I wouldn't have to steal if I had money to survive. Money you hoard for fun."

"I don't hoard," I growl.

"Do you need three phones and fifteen parties per month in your lavish mansion?" she asks.

My nostrils flare, and when I don't respond, she keeps on dabbing my wound harder and harder like she's trying to make me bleed even more.

"I didn't fucking choose to be rich," I say.

That's your comeback? Jesus fucking Christ, Silas.

She throws me a damning look. "You think I chose to be poor?"

Fine. She wins.

My eyes travel across her face and those soft cheeks and lips that are in stark contrast to her bony, twig-like body. She got beaten up pretty badly, yet here she's taking care of me instead.

What the fuck have I turned into? Max fucking Fletcher?

Suddenly, she sighs. "I just ... wanted to thank you for helping me."

My brows furrow.

She's thanking me for killing now?

"You saved me."

"All right. That's enough." I snatch the little cotton ball out of her hand and chuck it into the bin behind her. "I'm fine."

But that raised fucking brow is still judging me like I'm a kid in need of a time-out.

"You really don't ever let anyone help you, do you?"

"No one can help me," I grit back.

Her lips slowly part, but not a single word falls off her tongue, and now I realize I may have said too much.

But no matter how hard I try, I can't look away from those damn downturned lips that are so luscious they make me want to lick them and mark them as mine.

What has this thief done to me?

"You'd be surprised by how much people are willing to do for someone," she says, getting up and packing up the items she used. "If you'd just show a little bit of appreciation."

Fuck it.

I grasp her throat, fingers digging into her skin as I pull her face toward me and smash my lips onto hers.

THIRTY-EIGHT

IVY

My mind instantly turns to mush the moment his lips make contact with mine. His mouth shatters my resistance as he claims me like he's never had anything sweeter than the taste of my lips. One devastatingly possessive kiss and I've already dropped everything I was holding.

I can't breathe.

His fingers tighten like a noose around my neck.

I can't breathe.

It doesn't register with me until it's too late.

My eyes nearly roll into the back of my head.

Knock. Knock.

Suddenly, he pulls back and looks at me. He unfurls his fingers from my veins, and my lungs suck in the oxygen.

Fuck.

Another knock on the door follows.

"Silas? Ivy? Are you okay in there?"

Max.

Silas and I look at each other. I can still feel his hot lips on mine, my tongue tracing his taste.

Another knock.

"We're fine," I reply, my eyes still fixated on his.

"We should go. We're sitting ducks here," Heath adds.

I swallow as Silas finally averts his eyes, and I put the box back into the cabinet along with whatever just happened, then open the door.

"I just had to clean up his wound. That's all. Finished."

"But ... he's still bleeding," Max points at Silas who waltzes out too.

"I'm fine," Silas says.

"You two keep saying that, but I don't think it means what you think it means."

"Max," Silas grits, shutting him up.

I immediately search for Cora to make sure she's safe. She's standing on a stool in the kitchen, grabbing three glasses. "Cora? What are you doing?"

I hurry to help her.

"I wanted to give them something to drink. Mrs. Schwartz always asks me." She pours water into the glasses.

"We don't have to—"

"I'm thirsty as hell," Max says, grabbing one of the half-filled glasses out of her little hand, and he chugs it down in one go, making Cora giggle.

I roll my eyes at how easily he's won her over already.

"You said hell," she says, giggling even more. "That's a bad word."

"Oops." Max covers his mouth with his hand. "Did I say that?" She giggles again as he pokes at her. "I bet you've never said a bad word in your life."

"Poop!" she screams at the top of her lungs.

"Oh fuck me," Silas groans.

"You said a bad word too!" Cora points at him.

Mrrrp.

Silas's eyes dart down between his legs, where Bagel curls his tail around his calf.

Silas's eyes grow big, and he takes two steps away to get Bagel to leave, but he keeps sticking to him. "No. No. Get away. Someone, do something."

Max laughs at him.

"What the fuck are you laughing at?" Silas growls.

"You," he retorts.

Silas's eyes narrow. "I'll kill you."

"C'mon, you two have been laughing at me for ages because I'm a simp. You can take one for the team." Max winks.

"Silas …" I mutter, staring at him as he keeps the cat at bay by making weird movements I've never seen him make before. "Are you afraid of cats?"

"What?" He stops and stares at me with vicious eyes. "Me? Afraid?" He snorts and pokes at Bagel before picking him up. "Do I fucking look afraid?"

He's holding Bagel really far away from him even though he's making air biscuits.

Meow. Silas glares at Bagel like his meow summoned a malicious god intent on wreaking havoc on earth.

"Have you ever even touched a cat before?" Heath asks Silas, laughing at him too.

"What am I supposed to do with it?" Silas asks.

I cross my arms. "*It*? Really?"

"You pet it," Heath answers.

"Fuck no." He holds Bagel even farther away like the cat's cuteness might be contagious.

"You'd better not hurt him," I warn him.

Silas seems even less amused.

"Let's just fucking go. More of those fuckers are out there, and I don't intend to sit around and wait until they come swarming in." Silas drops Bagel on the floor only to grab me instead.

"Wait—no. Where do you even want to go?"

Where did this sudden need to protect me come from?

"The Skull and Serpent Society," he grits.

"What?" I jerk free a second time. "No way."

"You are coming with me," he says. "I can't protect you out here."

"I'm not leaving Cora," I reply.

His eyes narrow, and his nostrils flare, but I'm not changing my stance. I know they're coming for us. They made that very clear when they decided to attack me out on the street.

But I would rather die than leave Cora.

"Fine," he says, licking his lips. "Bring her with you."

My jaw drops. "What?"

"You heard me." He grabs Cora's arm. "Let's go."

Cora pulls away from him and runs to me. "No, I don't wanna go. What about Bagel?"

"Wait a minute," Heath interjects. "The Skull and Serpent Society is no place for a child."

"He's right," Max says.

"You have a better idea?" Silas quips. "Go ahead, I'm waiting." He checks the clock. "While you're thinking about it, whoever was after her isn't calling back up at all."

The sarcasm is strong.

"But what if your dad finds out there's a kid on campus?"

"I'll deal with him." His eyes home in on me. "You can't stay here. I won't allow it."

Wow.

I've never seen him this determined.

I swallow away the lump in my throat. "Fine." I pick up Bagel and stuff him into Silas's hands. "But Bagel's coming too."

Silas stares at him like he's never seen anything more treacherous, and Max laughs under the palm of his hand.

"What the hell do I do with this?" Silas growls.

I grab the kitty box I have for vet visits and hold it out to him. "Here."

I reach for Cora's hand. "Let's go."

***

HEATH

Ivy doesn't want to leave Cora in my car by herself, so Max and Silas go ahead on their bikes while I drive in the car behind them.

I just fucking hope no one saw us even though I had my face covered with a mask and Max and Silas had their helmets. We'll have to exchange license plates quickly to avoid any involvement.

But first, we need to secure Ivy and Cora.

The slow ride up to Spine Ridge University is nerve-wracking. She keeps throwing me looks through the rearview mirror while clutching Cora like she'd take a knife for her, and I don't doubt she will. But I won't be the one throwing it her way.

She's got me all wrong, and I know it's my fault. I made her believe she should fear me like she should fear Silas. All I was interested in was using her for all my devious needs and to watch her fall apart just because I could, because it felt good to be the one to give her what she wanted instead of Max. But the more I played with her, the more the lines started to blur. And now I don't even know what I want anymore.

I sigh as we drive up the mountain, and I look out the window to take my mind off things.

But even in the trees, a shadow of her memory dances, irresistibly poisoning my mind with sweet agony. I can still feel her body close to mine, still taste that delicious skin ... still feel his lips on mine.

I touch my mouth, and for a moment, I wonder if I truly have lost my mind.

There's no way back.

I ruined everything.

Why couldn't I just be content with sharing her instead?

"I want you to know that just because I'm coming with you doesn't mean I trust you," Ivy suddenly says, breaking my train of thought.

"I never said you should," I reply. "But I do know one thing; Silas was right. The Skull and Serpent Society is about the safest place you can be right now."

She snorts. "I doubt that."

"You're surrounded by killers." I make eye contact with her through the mirror. "Killers who just swore to protect you and Cora."

Cora's hand entwines through Ivy's, her little body trembling. "Killers?"

"He's joking," Ivy says, throwing me darts with her eyes. "Right?"

"Yeah. Totally." I add a smile for good measure.

I'm not used to hanging around kids, and I have no fucking clue how to behave around them. But we'll make it work.

I'm not going to let anyone harm the one girl who's been out here wrapping us all around her finger.

When we're at the house again, I happily shut off the engine, but my eyes still find the little bottle of pills lying on the passenger's seat. Sighing, I grab it and take a pill, swallowing it down without any water.

"What's that?" Cora asks, and I nearly choke.

"Nothing," I reply.

"Pills," Ivy replies.

"For what?" the little girl asks.

"People take pills if they're sick," Ivy says.

Sick.

Maybe I am.

"But if he doesn't wanna tell, he doesn't have to," she adds, glaring at me through the mirror.

I nod, glad she's not prying. "Thanks."

I step out, close the door, and open hers instead.

"I can manage."

"Just because you can doesn't mean I shouldn't," I reply, smirking.

She rolls her eyes, but a tiny smile still quirks up her top lip, if only briefly.

"Cora, let's go," Ivy says, and she grabs her hand and helps her out.

I close the door behind them and follow them toward the door. Silas and Max have already pulled up to the house, and Silas is still wearing his broken helmet when he walks up to us.

"Why not throw that thing away?" I ask.

"And get shot in the head while driving?" Silas replies. "No, thanks."

"Wait, someone followed us?" Max asks, the panic clearly visible in his eyes.

"No, I checked," I reply, but he still won't look at me, and it fucking hurts.

My fist balls, and I move on ahead. "Whatever."

"Wha—" Max mutters, but I ignore him.

Ivy and Cora are already up ahead, and I'm more concerned with them right now. Ivy is being targeted by someone or something big, and I want to know why. Is it because she stole money from them too? Or is there something else at play?

Cora's eyes nearly start to dazzle. "We get to live here?"

Ivy grabs her and pulls her closer. "Don't get too excited. It's only for a little while."

"Aw ..." Cora pouts.

"For as long as you need it," I say, adding a smile.

Suddenly, she runs up to me and hugs my legs, and I don't know what to do with it other than stare. "Thank you!"

I just look at Ivy and back at Cora as a kind of warmth I've never felt before floods my entire body.

What ... is happening?

"Hey, why does he get all the thanks?" Silas says as he strolls inside. "It was my idea."

Cora swiftly releases me.

Ivy folds her arms. "She's right. This is a castle compared to where we live."

Maybe she's right. We are fucking rich, after all, and we've never experienced any kind of poverty, let alone having to take care of a kid too. It must've taken a toll on her.

"Can we go up to our room?" Cora asks.

"Of course, you can," Max says as he walks in too. "I'll show you where it is."

Dammit. I really didn't think this through.

Cora grabs Max's hand and drags him up the stairs, making me feel some kind of way I can't describe as I follow everyone.

"Fine, I'll come too," Silas grumbles, rolling his eyes, almost as if the mere idea of being nice annoys him.

Or maybe he's just not used to feeling ... something. Whatever it is.

Because I clearly noticed a shift in his behavior since he discovered she has a kid. And he's not the only one.

I breathe out a sigh and head toward the guest room with everyone. The moment Max opens the door, Cora begins to squeal at the small four-poster queen bed with fluffy blankets. She immediately runs to it and belly flops onto it with a giggle, rubbing the mattress.

"It's so soft!"

Ivy giggles as she enters the room and looks around. "This is ... spacious."

"There's a bathroom to the left with a tub," Max says, opening all the doors. "And here's your closet."

"Wow," Ivy says, her lips still parted as she gawks at all the stuff in the guest room. "This is ... almost too much."

"No, it's not!" Cora yells, making us all laugh. "I love it!"

"I'm glad you're happy," Ivy says.

"Aren't you going to test out your bed?" Max coaxes her.

"Um ..." Ivy blushes.

"Go ahead, it's yours now. You can stay as long as needed."

"I just ... kind of miss my things," Ivy responds, tucking her hair behind her ear.

"You've got more than enough stuff here," Silas says.

"Yeah, but not my clothes," she says.

"We'll take care of it," I reply.

A smile lifts her face, and my heart beats faster at the sight. "Really?"

"Tomorrow," Silas grumbles.

"Thanks," she says. "For everything."

I lower my eyes. "We just did what comes natural to us."

She folds her arms. "What, protecting people?"

Silas smirks. "Murder."

All the blood drains from her face, so I slap Silas on the back. "Time for us to go to our own beds."

"What, with all this blood still caking my skin?" Silas says, tugging at his shirt.

"Go wash up," I tell him.

"Don't tell me what to do, bitch," he spits back.

"Silas!" Ivy hisses, eyeing Cora. "There's a kid."

Silas just throws around an awkward look and sticks his hands in his pockets. He really doesn't know what to do with this, and I have never seen him so uncomfortably weird as he is now.

"Right, good night."

"Sleep well," Max says.

"Doubt it," Silas replies, waltzing off.

"What's his problem?" Max asks Ivy.

She shrugs. "I don't know. It started when ..." She gulps and withholds the words she was going to speak. "Never mind. It's not important."

She stretches and yawns.

"I think it's time for us to leave her to do her thing," I say.

Still, Max won't look at me, even when he says, "Yeah." He grins at Cora. "You gonna sleep through the night all by yourself?"

"Yes!" Cora exclaims. "I'm a big girl now."

Ivy's laughter fills the room, and it makes my heart swell once more, and I physically have to grab my own damn body to keep me from swaying closer.

"Thank you, Max. Heath." The looks she gives both of us makes me feel like there are so many words left unspoken, but I don't have a clue where to start. "Good night."

Max approaches Ivy and grabs her hand, squeezing tightly. "Sleep tight. We'll talk again tomorrow, okay?"

She nods and leans up to grab his face to peck him on the cheek, and it turns him into a beet. Goddammit.

"Thank you for helping," she says. "I mean it."

"Anything for you," he replies.

Anything for her ...
Of course.

My fingers dig into the palm of my hand, and I turn around and waltz off before I combust.

THIRTY-NINE

IVY

I roll around and look at Cora's little sleep-drunk face as the morning sunlight trickles in from the window in the back. She slept well in her own little bed. I'm surprised. She normally hates to fall asleep without me. But maybe this slight change in surroundings has done her good.

I mean, she loved splashing in the bath last night. Not to mention these beds. God, they feel so nice compared to our own. And I bet that's part of the reason she slept like a log.

Sweet girl. I just hope being here won't destroy her. She's far too young to witness the things those boys do in the name of ...

What, exactly?

Why did they save me?

I mull it over for a second. They already got everything they wanted out of me, and now my secret's out in the open too. I always assumed they'd laugh the moment they found out about Cora, but the dead-serious looks on their faces caught me off guard.

Even Silas and Heath were adamant about bringing me here despite the fact they've been the ones trying to punish me the most.

And then there's that kiss Silas gave me in my bathroom, the one that completely stole my breath away ... and made me yearn for more.

I swallow and turn on my back to stare at the ceiling, trying to decipher my own feelings, but it's only growing muddier inside my mind.

Suddenly, my phone buzzes, and I pick it up from the cabinet beside the bed.

Psycho: Come downstairs.

How chivalrous. Maybe I really did read too much into that kiss after all.

Me: Good morning to you too.
Psycho: No.
Me: Didn't sleep well?
Psycho: I didn't. At all.

Oh wow. No sleep for the wicked, eh?

Me: That's bad.
Psycho: It's time for breakfast.
Me: And?
Psycho: Come here. Now.
Me: Ask. Nicely.
Psycho: Do you want me to come and drag you out of there? Because I will, and I will definitely use your nipples as handles.

I snort at the insolence, yet my pussy just thrummed at the mere thought blinking in and out of my head.

Me: Just one day, and you're already treating me as your servant.
Psycho: If I wanted a servant, I'd beckon any girl on campus and they'd come. Willingly.

My eyes twitch at the thought.

Me: Don't even try.
Psycho: Getting jealous now?

My jaw drops at Silas's arrogance.

Me: You wish.
Psycho: If you wanted me to yourself, all you had to do was ask.
Me: Stfu
Psycho: Ask. Nicely.

My fingers nearly break the phone.

Me: Just because we have a deal does not mean you get to tell me what to do and where to go.
Psycho: You didn't just give me your body, thief, you gave me your soul for as long as I fucking want it in exchange for that money, and I intend to take fucking good care of it. Now come.

I groan and roll my eyes.
Silas fucking Rivera, taking care of my soul? That's rich.
Still, I get up and walk up to Cora. She's still sleeping, and I don't want to be the one to wake her up. I grab my phone again.

Me: Cora's still sleeping.
Psycho: Let her sleep, then.
Me: What if she's hungry?
Psycho: The kitchen doesn't close after an hour, twig. Come downstairs. Now. I won't say it again.

Jesus, why is he so adamant?
I open the closet and grab whatever is in there. A white T-shirt and a pair of leggings that fit surprisingly well, along with some slippers. Perfect.

I head downstairs and look around, letting my nose guide me to breakfast. My mouth is already watering at the smell, but the second I find all the food out on the table in the back of the dining room, I'm frozen to the floor. There's so much of it. The entire table is covered with fresh bread, fruits, cured meats, milk, expensive cereals, crispy bacon and eggs, rich coffee, all types of cheeses, and delicious-looking pancakes stacked up high with that amazing maple syrup on top.

Holy shit.

Silas is at the head of the table, staring me down.

"Sit."

I grab one of the chairs and sit opposite of him.

"Did you sleep well?" he asks.

I nod. "It's a ... soft bed."

"I'm happy."

I frown. "Are you?"

He clenches the chair. "Why wouldn't I be?"

"Do you even know what it feels like to be happy?"

He tilts his head, smirking. "I'm learning quickly." His eyes scatter across the table. "Grab some food."

I cross my arms. "I'm not hungry."

His eyes narrow. "I didn't ask. Grab. The. Food."

I narrow my eyes too now.

Is this some kind of game to him? Trying to make me bow just for saving me?

"I don't know what you're trying to do here, but if you think you can just command me around because you saved me, you're wrong."

"What I'm trying to do here is make you eat." He flicks his fingers, and some actual goddamn servants come forward and place a few different drinks in front of me—fresh orange juice, water, and coffee.

"Where is everyone?" I ask.

"I told them to leave."

I gulp.

"To give you and ... Cora some time to adjust," he adds.

The pause before Cora's name almost makes me think he has trouble remembering her name. That ... or it really hit him hard that I wasn't alone like he thought I'd be.

"Go ahead, try the food. You'll like it."

Why is he so fixated on this?

"I told you, I'm not hungry."

My growling stomach immediately reveals my lie.

And the smirk slowly growing on his face makes my whole body burn with heat.

"I heard that."

In my embarrassment, I grab a bunch of pancakes off the stack, cut off too much, and shove it into my mouth hole so I can give him a snooty look. Instead, the taste of the pancakes has me pausing mid-bite as I'm overwhelmed with the sensations.

God, I don't think I've ever had anything tastier than this.

I swallow it and take a sip of the freshly squeezed orange juice, which is equally delicious.

"I told you, you'd like it," he says, smugly leaning on the table with his elbow.

My nostrils flare, but I can barely stomach another swallow without tears welling up in my eyes. I put down my fork and turn away from him.

"Are you crying?" he asks.

I swiftly wipe them away. "Don't make fun of me."

"I'm not." He chuckles. "Though, having a girl cry over the taste of my food instead of the size of my cock is a new one for me."

Oh my God.

"You think it's all a joke, but it's not. You don't know what I've had to do to get food, and it never tasted this good," I growl.

I take another bite of the food before he decides to take it all away again. But the sudden change on his face catches me off guard. It's almost as if his gaze has ... softened.

"You don't have to gobble it down. It's not going anywhere," he says. "Not until you're full."

By the time I've eaten half the stack, it finally dawns on me that all of this could just as well be another way to manipulate me into compliance. Make me his plaything. That's all he wants, right?

And if Cora ever gets a taste of this ... she might never want to leave.

I scoot back my chair. "I'm done."

He frowns. "Already? You haven't even tried the rest."

"Why are you doing this?" I ask, running my tongue along my teeth.

He tilts his head. "Why are you being hunted down, and what did those men want from you?"

My eye twitches. I still refuse to answer.

"Fine. Another question. What was that red flower doing in Cora's hand?"

I frown. "What fl—"

My pupils dilate, and I interrupt my own words.

Is he talking about that plastic flower from his little box under the bed?

"I ... gave it to her. It seemed cheap. Meaningless."

"It wasn't," he scoffs. "Yet you told me you gave it to a random girl."

"Why is it so important to you?"

"So many questions we both refuse to answer," he says.

Shit. He got me there.

Suddenly, Heath enters the room, and I don't get the answer to the question burning in the back of my mind. He stops in the middle of the dining room when he sees Silas's burning gaze.

"Uhh ... am I interrupting something?"

"Didn't get the message?" Silas grits.

"No, I don't check my messages in the morning." Heath yawns. "Not before breakfast."

Silas rolls his eyes. "Figures."

Guess we're not alone after all.

"What? I'm hungry." He sits down on the chair beside me. "Jesus, that is one order you placed, Silas."

"I didn't want our guests to go hungry," Silas replies.

"We should have guests more often," Heath jokes, putting a bunch of bacon and eggs on his plate as well as some fruit. "This all looks delish." His eyes suddenly find mine after he's checked my plate. "Aren't you going to eat that?"

My cheeks flush. "I've had a bite."

"You need some more to fill up those bony cheeks, twig," Silas says.

Bony cheeks?!

I make a face at him, but he just stares back like he doesn't even care.

"And I don't mean your smile," he adds with a grin.

Just before I flip him off, Max enters the room, breaking my train of thought with his happy, "Morning, everyone!"

He looks at me, then at Silas, and briefly at Heath before sitting down on the other end of the table, far away from Heath.

"What is this, a grand buffet on a cruise?" Max says. "This looks amazing!"

"Silas went all out," Heath replies.

But Max won't look at him and keeps readjusting his cutlery and the plates like he doesn't know where to look until he finds me. "Sleep well?"

"Amazing, thanks," I reply. "You?"

"Never slept better." He stretches. "Though, I'm a bit worried about all those bodies we left in the street."

"I have it covered. I called one of my mom's men. He owes me one," Silas says.

"One?" Heath pauses with shoveling down the bacon. "You think one guy is gonna fix all of this?"

"I know my mom's men. They know how to get a job done discreetly."

"Your mom?" I mutter. "Penelope?"

"What about her?" he asks.

"She has men to clean up *bodies*?"

"His grandpa is an underground Mafia hunter. Takes money from the rich and gives back to people in need. A notorious hater of everything criminal," Heath explains. "She inherited his *business*." He makes quotation marks with his fingers.

"Wow." I lean back in my seat. "No wonder you're like this."

Silas narrows his eyes at me like I caught him red-handed.

"You said that out loud," Max whispers into my ear.

"I know," I say, unafraid.

"Those men were after you for a reason," Silas says, putting his elbows on the table as he leans his chin on both hands. "So what was it?"

"Do we have to do this now?" Max asks.

"Yes," Silas replies. "Now."

I grind my teeth. I'm not about to tell them my entire life's story when they could use it against me.

"I owed them ..."

"What?"

"Money."

He snorts. "Money for what?"

He won't stop prying until he's satisfied, will he?

"Why do you care?"

"I care because there's no way those violent fuckers would come after a girl like you without an ulterior motive. What kind of money could you have borrowed? What amount would warrant a murder in the middle of the streets?"

"I never said I *borrowed* money."

"Then why did you need to pay them back with the money you stole from us?"

"I was being blackmailed," I sneer. "The same way you're blackmailing me."

"The only difference here is that I'm offering you protection," he says.

"By locking me up in this gilded prison?"

His eyes flicker with contempt, as though he hates the very idea of this house being a prison, but we both know it's the goddamn truth.

"I don't need protection if it comes at a price I'm not willing to pay." I scoot back my chair and march off.

"Wait, but you haven't even finished eating!" Max yells, but I ignore him.

I'm not going to just sit there and be interrogated in exchange for some food. I'm better than that. Even if Max is the nicest of them all, he's still on their side. Can I even trust him to keep me safe from the others? No, Silas and Heath run the show here. This is their domain, and I'm just a passenger. A welcome guest ... until I'm not. And I brought Cora right into the wolf's den.

Fuck.

I head up the stairs, but when I get to the room, she's still sleeping soundly, with a little bubble of snot blowing out of one of her nostrils, and it makes me grin.

Sweet girl doesn't even know what's going on. She just wants a safe home.

I sigh and open the closet to see if I can find anything we can take with us, but there's only two sets of clothes, one of which I'm wearing right now. None of this will ever be enough to keep us warm, let alone the fact we don't have a home to return to.

At least not for the foreseeable future. Those fuckers who tried to take me are probably waiting right by my door to strike again if I ever show my face.

It's not safe.

A sudden hand on my shoulder makes me jolt up and down, and I peer over my shoulder.

"You can't go back to your home," Heath says.

It's like he can peer into my mind.

"Why do you care what I do?"

"Silas wants to protect you. I know he's an asshole, but he won't let anyone harm you. Trust me."

"Why should I trust you?" I jerk free of his grip. "You literally tried to shoot me the last time we saw each other."

His face darkens. "They were blanks," he says.

"The gun was empty?" I scoff

"I was never going to shoot you. I couldn't. Not ever."

I snort. "Yeah, that's rich after you already threatened me."

When I try to leave, he places a flat hand on the door, stopping me in my tracks. "I needed to know how far you would go for him." He grabs my chin. "How hard ... you'd fallen for him."

So that's it? Jealousy?

That's why he tried to shoot?

"We're killers. No one here would be better at protecting you and Cora."

"The police, for one," I reply.

"You think they wouldn't throw you in jail after discovering your involvement with all those dead bodies they probably already found by now? Your fingerprints were all over that crime scene."

I gulp. He's right. They'd immediately lock me up if they got their hands on me even though I'm innocent. Who will vouch for me? I'm just a lowly thief, and the guy who sent those fuckers to get me will surely testify on their behalf.

Shit.

"You're safer here than anywhere else," Heath adds. "I swear on my fucking life."

"Why? Why would I be safe here when I have nothing of my own and no one I can trust?" I ask. "I don't have any of my stuff, I don't even have clothes. All I have is this room, Cora, and you guys."

I tilt my head back so I can look him in the eyes and determine if he really is truthful with wanting to protect me.

"Because ..."

His thumb brushes over my lips as his eyes home in on them, almost as if he's studying the very shape of my face.

"I ..."

Suddenly, Cora turns around in her bed, and we both gaze at her while holding our breaths. Luckily, she falls right back to sleep again. It must've been a rough night for her.

Bagel jumps off my bed and curls around my legs instead, meowing.

"I didn't even bring kitty food ..." I pick Bagel up to hug him. "I'm sorry, Bagel."

"You know what? C'mon." Heath grabs my arm.

"Wait, what about Cora?"

"Max will watch her and feed her when she wakes up. Don't worry."

I only barely manage to release Bagel before I'm dragged down the stairs.

"Where are we going?" I ask.

The grin on his face predicts trouble. "Shopping."

FORTY

HEATH

Our first stop is the pet store to get food, toys, and a litter box for Bagel. The moment we walk out of the store with a whole bag worth of groceries seems to ease Ivy's mind a little, and I can visibly see the weight slowly dropping off her shoulders.

"All done?" she asks as we hop inside the car.

"Not yet," I reply, driving off.

"What else is there?"

"I've gotta stop by a car dealer," I reply, racing through the streets. She holds the car door. "Not so fast."

"Sorry, can't help it. Learned from the best." I wink.

"Who?" she asks.

"My dad," I reply, though I'm definitely not eager to see him.

When we finally get to his car dealership, I get out and open Ivy's door for her just like before.

"Were you always this chivalrous, or is this your way of apologizing for your behavior?" she says.

I close the door and snort. "Please Me? Apologizing?" I laugh. "Don't be delusional."

She rolls her eyes. "Figured."

"I'm not opposed to begging for forgiveness, though," I add while on the way to the shop.

She stops abruptly like she just couldn't believe her ears.

But I meant every word.

"Are you coming?"

She clears her throat but doesn't ask me anything. Instead, she follows me inside the shop, where it smells like expensive leather and untouchable metal. Like, for real, if anyone touches these cars, they're dead. At least, if my dad catches them in the act.

"Heath, that's a surprise, seeing you here."

My dad walks out from behind his desk in his fancy suit. He doesn't have to work here because he's got a ton of companies under his name, but he still prefers to be hands-on at his favorite job, which is working directly with the cars.

"To what do I owe the pleasure?" Dad asks.

"Save it. I just want my old license plate back. Do you still have it?"

He frowns. "Why?"

"Does it matter?"

"Yes," he replies, leaning on the desk as he casually swoops his dirty blond hair aside. "If you're going to do stupid shit, I'd like to know about it."

With a smug smile, I reply, "Too late."

His face drops. "Tell me what you did."

"I'd rather eat shit," I reply.

"Heath ..." He groans, rubbing his forehead. "Listen, you can't just come here and rope me into whatever."

"You're the last one to lecture me, Dad," I grit. "It's not like you and your friends were such Goody Two-shoes in school."

His pierced brow rises. "That was different."

"You were young," I retort. "Now you're not."

"Wow." He makes a fist and stomps his own heart. "Right in the chest."

Ivy snorts behind me but quickly uses her hand to hide her laughter.

"Who's this fine young lady?"

"No one you have to know about," I reply.

"Well, you're here in my car dealership, trying to get your old license plate back. I think you're not in a great position to bargain," he quips, with a nasty grin that reminds me way too much of what I look like in the mirror.

Dammit.

"So, who's this lovely lady?" my dad asks, looking at Ivy.

Ivy steps forward. "Hi. My name's Ivy."

He shakes her hand. "Caleb Preston. Nice to meet you. Are you his girlfriend?"

I nearly choke on my own spit. "Jesus Christ, Dad, no!" Ivy looks mortified, so I shove my old license plate in his hands to change the conversation. "You've met her now, can I please have the old one back?"

"Fine, since you asked nicely this time." He winks, embarrassing me all over.

Goddammit.

He goes to the back of the shop where the supplies are kept.

"So, that's your dad, huh?" she mutters.

"Yup."

"You two sure are alike."

"Fuck no," I growl, folding my arms.

She chuckles right when he comes back.

"What's so funny?" Dad asks.

"Nothing," I reply.

"I'm just impressed at how much you injected your genes into him," Ivy muses.

"I know, I'm proud of my best work," he says, patting me on the shoulder. "If only he didn't get himself into so much trouble."

I swat his hand away and snatch the license plate from his fingers.

"Would it kill you to hate me less?" he asks.

"Yes. It would," I retort, and I promptly turn around and wave. "See you later."

"Stop by the house some time, Heath. Mom misses you," Dad calls as we make our way outside.

"She'll be fine," I yell back.

"Why do you talk to him like that?" Ivy asks.

"We're not on the best of terms right now," I reply.

"Why?"

I pause. "Do you have to pry like that?"

She puts her hands against her hips. "Like you're prying into my life?"

Touche.

I open the car door, but she refuses to get inside until I finally speak up. I sigh out loud and run my fingers through my long hair. "He and my mom decided to ship my sister off to a boarding school and didn't tell me until it was too late to say goodbye."

The look on her face softens. "I didn't know you had a sister."

"Now you do. Well, I had one, because she hasn't contacted me ever since."

She steps inside and I shut the door before fixing the plate on the back of the car. Then I hop behind the wheel. It's quiet for some time as I start up the engine, but after I've driven off, she starts chewing her lip.

"I'm sorry."

"About what?"

"It must be tough for you."

Is she ... pitying me?

"I'm fine," I reply, grinding my teeth.

I don't need pity, especially not from her.

"You obviously love your sister a lot," she says, eyeing the bottle of pills still lying on my dashboard.

I swiftly snatch them off and tuck them into my pocket.

Still, she can't look away. "You only have one family, Heath. Please, be kind to them."

"Don't concern yourself with mine when you've got your own shit to deal with," I retort.

"I don't have any," she replies.

I frown, glancing her way between driving. "What do you mean?"

She averts her eyes. "I'm alone with Cora. I haven't seen my mother in a long time. I can't even remember the last time I saw her happy." She sighs.

"What about your dad?"

"He's dead," she answers abruptly.

Oh. Fuck.

I did not see that one coming.

I swallow back the lump in my throat. "I'm sorry."

She nods. "I'm just saying, don't take the family you have for granted."

Maybe she has a point.

And now I feel stupid for lashing out at her instead.

She's done nothing to draw my ire. Nothing that involves my family, anyway. I grab her hand, squeezing it softly.

She briefly glances up at me, and a small smile tips up her lips before it immediately disappears again, and she pulls her hand away from mine, her cheeks flushing with heat.

"What size of clothes does Cora have?" I ask.

"Huh? Why do you ask?"

"I think it's about time we put this baby to use." I slap the steering wheel. "Now tell me where to drive, and I'll take you there."

***

After we've finished shopping for Cora, I put everything in the trunk of the car, then take Ivy to one of the high-end boutiques in Crescent Vale City.

Nothing is more satisfying than watching her put on twenty or more outfits to see if they fit. Her figure really shines in these gorgeous Chanel dresses, and I can't keep my eyes off her.

Every time she exits the changing room, she looks like a completely different person, chic, daring, provocative, luxurious, all of it combined. And even though she has no clue how to wear the dresses, the dresses fit her to a T.

"What do you think?" I ask.

"They look lovely, but …" She turns around in the mirror and finds the tag, her face losing all its color. "That price tag, my God."

I tap my fingers impatiently. "What about it?"

"It's too high. I can't pay for this," she says.

My brow lifts. "How high?"

"Ten."

"Million?"

Her pupils dilate. "God, no. Thousand."

I snort. "I thought it'd be more."

Now her mouth widens too, southward. "You've gotta be kidding me. I can't take this."

She immediately goes back into the dressing room, and I sigh, rubbing my eyes.

When will this girl accept there is no saying no to us?

"Heath, can you help me?" she asks after a while.

I get up and approach the curtain she's hiding behind.

"The zipper is stuck."

I push open the curtain and find her half-dressed, with the golden dress drooping over her shoulders, the curve of her breasts clearly visible through the fabric, barely hiding the nipples.

And my God, does it make my mouth water.

I pull the curtain closed behind me and bring my hands up to her dress, slowly zipping it down. Wherever my fingers go, goose bumps follow in their tracks as my eyes connect with hers through the mirror.

"You look gorgeous in this dress," I mutter.

She blushes. "Thank you."

I pause near the crevice in her back while she clutches the dress close to her body, almost as if she's afraid of revealing what's underneath even though I've already seen every inch of her delicious body.

But I want more.

So much fucking more.

This girl who has taken ahold of Max's heart is fiery and brave, and I want nothing more than to steal her heart away before she gives it to him.

But is it already too late?

I brush along the sides of her arms, barely grazing her skin, and all the tiny little hairs on her skin come to life under the palm of my hand despite it being the smallest of touches.

"What did you mean when you said I stole something from you that wasn't mine to take?" she asks, still looking at me through the mirror.

She looks so fucking beautiful in this dress.

More beautiful than anything I could've ever imagined.

And all I want to do is tear it all off and take her right here, right now.

I lean in to whisper into her ear, "You stole something precious from me... something I kept to myself..."

I place a soft kiss underneath her ear and watch her reaction in the mirror as I slowly draw a line down her neck all the way to her shoulder. She tilts her head sideways.

She sucks in a breath, clearly struggling with being so close to me. "Is this because of ... Max?"

My eyes bore into hers.

No.

Not now.

Not him.

Me.

I have her now. She's mine. And if he wants her so badly, then I'll make *her* want *me* instead.

So I grip her face and force her to turn as I slam my lips onto hers.

FORTY-ONE

IVY

I don't even know what's happening.

One moment, I'm overwhelmed by the mere touch of his fingers sliding down my spine ... and then the next his lips are ravaging mine.

My God, the way he kisses me is beyond any kind of kiss Max has ever given me. They're sultry and greedy, wild and deepening with every stroke as his tongue forces apart the seam of my lips and invades my mouth. Still, I don't stop him.

He groans against my lips as he sucks on them, rolling his tongue around mine as if he's been fighting the desire to claim me for his own all along. As if something, or someone, has been holding him back.

But not anymore.

His grip on my face lowers to my neck, fingers tightening around my throat as he pushes me up against the mirror in the back of the booth and kisses me senseless, breathless, completely out of my mind, overpowered by desire.

And still, I don't stop him.

Instead, I kiss him back just as feverishly, struggling to maintain balance as his package prods into my belly, and a hungry groan emanates from deep within his chest, turning me on like nothing else.

What's wrong with me?

When he finally releases my throat, I murmur, "Wait—"

I pull away despite wanting it so badly.

"No. I've waited long enough to have you for myself," he groans, still nibbling at my lips. "I need you. Now."

Fuck, this deal I have with them sure is trouble.

"But we're in a shop," I murmur.

"I don't fucking care." He grips my waist and lifts me with ease, using his muscular arms. "Let them listen to you moan. They'll never experience the kind of pleasure I can offer you."

He kisses my neck and drags a line down toward my clavicles, stopping only to rip my dress away with his teeth so he can suck on my nipple instead. And fuck me, my entire body comes to life under his touch.

"More than anything Max will ever be able to give," he grits, kissing me senseless.

I breathe a hampered breath as he lavishes my nipples with dirty licks. "You're jealous of him?"

"I'm jealous of what you two have," he replies. "Of what you give to him. Of what he gives to you."

The kiss they shared instantly invades my mind, but the image dissipates the second Heath's strong hands grip my ass and wedge me against the mirror. "Wrap your legs around me."

Even though it's wrong, I still do what he says.

Not just because of the deal we have ... but because my body is yearning for his touch.

The way he made me shiver was no accident.

I want him, just as I want Max and Silas, but I can't say it out loud.

So I just let them use me and tell myself it's for the best, that they'll protect me, and I will come out of this unscathed.

Even though we all know my soul has already been lost to these devilish monsters.

"Higher," he says, lifting me even farther until my legs are clasped around his shoulders and his face is right between my legs. "I want to taste you just like the first time."

"The first time? When—" I can't even finish my sentence before his tongue has already speared my pussy, and fuck me, I nearly let out a squeal they'd be able to hear out on the streets.

His mouth expertly swirls around, spreading my wetness all over, lapping me up like he hasn't had a meal in days. But it's the feel of his tongue pressed up against my slit that feels familiar. Invasive. Like something I've definitely felt before.

But how? Heath hasn't licked me. Right?

"That's it, spread those legs for me," he groans.

I shudder against the mirror as his fingers dig into my thighs, tongue circling my clit like a madman.

"You taste so damn good when you're all mine," he says. "You make me want to do this every fucking day."

"I don't understand." I clutch his head for support, but also because it feels so damn good, I just want to shove him in farther.

"What don't you understand? That I want you more than anything? Or that this is not the first time I've made your pussy wet for my tongue?"

My eyes widen. "What?" I mutter.

He smirks against my slit, gazing up at me with those daring eyes of his. "You remember me, don't you?" He swipes his tongue around my pussy. "Right. Here." He presses down on my clit, and I nearly fall apart right then and there, but he pulls away, glancing up at me with darkened eyes, almost as if he wants me to suffer just a little longer. "You remember the feel of my tongue on this needy little clit as I made it come for me."

So it is true.

"When?" I say between ragged breaths.

"That night you fucked Max ..." he whispers into my thighs. "I watched."

I suck in a breath and can't for the life of me push it out as he keeps on licking me, all while gazing at me from underneath those lashes.

"How?"

"I came in through the window after you fell asleep." He grins against my skin. "And that key you thought he took was mine."

"You stole it," I say.

"Just like you stole from us," he replies.

Before I can say anything else, he kisses my pussy and nibbles at my clit, a warning not to overstep.

"It was you. You left that cum on my body," I whisper.

His fingers dig into my ass. "That's right, Ivy. I wanted you, so I took you. Even in your fucking sleep."

Goose bumps scatter on my skin, and my legs clench together behind his neck. I want to hate him for invading my house, for using me, even in my sleep ... but my God, he does it too well for me to even become mad.

I can't. It's no use.

His tongue is far too good at this to make me want to stop.

"And you know what? I loved how powerless you were to stop me from ravaging you in your sleep. The moment I first tasted you I knew I needed more," he groans. "So much fucking more."

The tip of his tongue drives into me, lapping me up from the inside, coaxing out more delicious moans.

"I needed to feel you come, over and over again," he says. "Until you got so sick of it you'll only want *my* fucking tongue and no one else's."

"But you were there when I made that deal with Silas," I reply.

"I don't fucking care about that deal. I can't stop Silas from taking you ... but he can't stop me from claiming what I want either." He circles around so expertly I tilt my head back and let him do what he wants despite my brain telling me to put a stop to it.

"I want you, Ivy. I fucking want you just as badly as I want—"

He chokes on his own words and briefly glances up at me.

"What?"

Suddenly, his hand slides from my ass all the way to my pussy, and he drives it inside, fucking me so fast and wild I moan out loud. "Oh fuck!"

"That's it. All I want to hear from you are your moans," he growls. "Moan for me, Ivy. Show me how much of a good little slut you are for me. And maybe I won't be so fucking obsessed with having you for myself."

Every time he thrusts in, my moans become louder than the ones that came before. Behind the curtain, people begin to whisper, but none of it matters because of this tongue that's driving me insane.

"Come for me," he groans, licking me with fervor. "Moan my name and drown me with your fucking wetness."

His filthy words send me over the edge, and my clit begins to thump uncontrollably as I clench my legs tightly around his neck. "Heath! Fuck!"

His tongue doesn't relent as he eats me up, fingers still thrusting into me as the wetness begins to drip out.

"Damn, you taste so fucking good when you come all over my face," he groans, ripping down his zipper. "Such an obedient little slut." He lowers me. "Now coat my cock with that wetness."

I gasp as he impales me on his cock, no-holds-barred. Not a single inch is spared as he thrusts in, burying himself inside me to the hilt, piercings coaxing out that squeaky moan from my throat. His fingers dig into my ass as he pulls out only to thrust right back in again, plowing through me like he's been dying to have me. Like it would kill him if he didn't fuck me right now. And those eyes of his brimming with desire tell me it's not just a figment of my imagination.

"God, you feel so goddamn good," he says.

And he's right.

It does.

It feels too good, and I don't want to stop even though I should.

"A perfect little pussy desperate to be torn to shreds by my thick cock." He thrusts and thrusts and thrusts until my entire body begins to quake, and my pussy contracts around his shaft again.

Oh no, not already. Not this quickly.

"You're gonna come all over my cock," he growls.

"No, wait, I can't. They'll hear us," I say.

"It wasn't a question, Ivy," he says. "Let me fucking see you fall apart."

"Why? Why do you want it so badly?"

"Because I fucking adore the way you look when you do," he replies, setting my entire body on fire. "Now come for me."

I mewl with delight as he impales me, driving in so deep I'm seeing stars. And right when the orgasm happens, he plunders my mouth with his tongue, driving inside so deeply I lose my breath, too.

His cock begins to throb, and hot cum fills me to the brim as he falls apart with me.

"Fuck, I need more. So much more. It's never going to be enough, is it?" he groans, almost as if he's mad at himself for letting things get this far.

But we're in too deep now. There's no going back. Not from this.

Not from a public fucking in the middle of a shop, just because he touched me.

Because I dared to look at him when he kissed my skin.

Fuck.

He might not be the only one addicted to the thrill.

***

HEATH

I'm still hard, still brimming with desire as I pull out of her. My cum drips down onto the floor while I set her on the small bench right in front of the mirror and spin her around. "On your knees for me."

She eagerly complies and kneels on the bench with her ass out, completely drunk on the lust I've injected straight into her veins.

But I don't care if this becomes her undoing.

I need this more than I need her to keep her sanity.

More than anything in life itself.

So this is what he felt when she kissed him.

What they both felt when they took her.

I want it. All of it.

And I fucking want her to want me too.

I curl her hair around my fist and slide my cock all over her ass. "You ready for me, little slut?"

"What?"

I tilt her head back until her eyes connect with mine through the mirror. "Look at me. Look at the man who will make you beg for mercy."

Her lips form an o-shape as I thrust into her ass instead, and she lets out an incredibly loud moan.

"That's it, make those sounds. Let them all know who you belong to."

"Fuck, you didn't warn me," she growls.

"This fucking ass needs a warning." I slap her cheeks. "For how fucking good it feels."

She clutches the bench, nails digging into the wood as I thrust in and out of her ass. Her ample wetness was all the lube I needed to enter her, and my God, does her ass feel good.

No wonder Silas couldn't hold himself back.

"This ass was made to take our cocks," I groan. "Now take it. Take it deep like a good girl."

I twist her hair and pull her head back, forcing her to keep her gaze fixated on me while I plow into her.

"I'm not gonna stop. Not before you give me two more orgasms."

"What?!"

She tightens but still accepts me as I bury myself to the hilt inside that tight little hole of hers.

"That's it. Yield. Give me your fucking soul like you so easily handed it on a silver platter to him," I say.

Her eyes glimmer in the light, but she won't say a single word.

But I don't need her words to know exactly what she's thinking right now.

I can feel her body zinging with pleasure, her pussy still dripping wet.

She wants this just as much as I do.

If only she could admit it.

"Say it. Say you want this hard cock up your ass," I growl, tilting her head back even farther.

She looks me in the eyes as she murmurs, "I want it."

"Louder," I growl.

"But they'll—"

"Let the fucking world hear it." I thrust in deep.

"I want your cock," she cries out, her ass contracting from the sheer amount of fucking I'm doing.

"Good. You take my thickness so well. It'd be a shame not to admit that." I grab her face and keep her centered. "Look at yourself. Look at how well you take me."

I plow in deep and bring my hand between her legs, flicking her clit until her juices roll down her thighs, and I swipe my fingers along.

"Look at how wet you are for me."

I bring my fingers to her lips, coating them.

"Doesn't it feel good?"

I dip my fingers into her mouth and spread her juices all over her tongue.

"Yes," she moans. "Please ..."

"Please what?"

"Please ... make me come."

A devilish smile forms on my face as I fuck her mouth just as hard as I fuck her ass.

"Good girl."

Right when she gags, I pull out and spread her saliva all over her clit before circling it just the way she likes it. And within seconds, she falls apart, toes curling, nails digging into the wood, her eyes nearly rolling into the back of her head.

Still, I don't stop fucking her ass through all of it, and I wipe her juices all over her ass for more lube. I pull out, spit, and thrust back in again, coaxing out more ragged moans.

"You'll come from my cock in your ass alone, won't you?"

She moans. "Oh fuck, I can't."

"Yes you can, little slut. I'll fuck you from one orgasm into the next. I won't fucking stop until you give me what I want."

"What more could you want?"

"Isn't it fucking obvious? I want *you*," I groan. "Give me your fucking heart like you've given it to him."

Her eyes flicker in the mirror, but she doesn't say a word as I thrust in and out of her. She shakes her head again and again.

"Yes. Come. Give it to me. Now."

She has no control.

Right here, right now, her body belongs to me, and I will *make* it come.

I slap her ass. Once. Twice. Thrice. And with the fourth slap, I bury myself so deep that I can feel her contract.

"Fuck me, Heath! Don't stop, please!"

There it is.

That's the fucking bullet I needed.

Straight to the fucking heart.

I hold her thigh as I bury in deep and release a jet of seed. While I'm still inside her, I tilt her head back and slam my lips onto hers, sealing all of my need, all of the pent-up frustration and desire for something that didn't want to be mine into this one fucking unruly kiss.

Even if just for a moment, it's enough.

Enough to fill that tepid void inside my heart, languishing, begging for a warmth it will never feel.

All because of a mistake I made.

Two hearts collided because I orchestrated it ... not realizing my own was already tethered to them both.

I relish the moment, savor her taste on my tongue before I release her from my grip. But those eyes, God, those fucking eyes undo me.

I pull out, and a strangled moan leaves her mouth.

Right then, the curtain is shoved aside, and her bare pussy and ass, and my half-hard cock are on full display in front of the old shop owner.

Oh fuck.

FORTY-TWO

HEATH

"Enough!" the shop owner screeches.

Ivy grabs the dress and pulls it back up, her face growing redder by the second. "Oh God. I'm so sorry."

"Get out!" the lady yells.

I step into her aura, and she backs away. "No. Not before I've bought these dresses."

The old lady's eyes widen. "What?"

"You heard me." I glare at her while she cowers underneath me. "I want to buy these. Go to the cash register." When she doesn't move fast enough, I clap my hands in front of her face, and she dashes off.

I grab the outfits off the rack in the booth and tear the tag off the one Ivy's wearing now.

"What are you doing?" she asks.

"Turn around."

After she's done what I asked, I zip her back up.

"Gorgeous."

The blush that follows is all I need before I march toward the cash register and put down all the outfits she's had on. Then I slam my card down in front of the old lady, who just stares at me with a blank face.

"Which one?" she asks.

"*All* of them." A smug smile spreads on my face. "Including the one she has on."

"Oh no, please, I can't pay for this," Ivy mutters as she comes up behind me with her old clothes.

"That's fine because I won't allow it," I say as I swipe my card.

The old lady starts packing up the outfits one by one, glaring at us both with disdain.

"But I can't pay you back. Not for any of this," Ivy says.

I turn my head to look at those beautiful eyes that have managed to mesmerize me so. "I don't expect you to. It's a gift." I snatch the bag off the counter and push it into Ivy's hand. "No strings attached."

She swallows as I grab her other hand and take her out of the store with me, back to the car. I open the passenger's side door and wait until she's inside before I run over to the driver's side and jump in too.

But the moment I start the car, she gazes off into the distance, distracted by whatever thoughts are swirling through her head.

"I recognize that look," I say.

"What look?" she retorts.

"The one where you wistfully stare off into the distance instead of saying what you really think."

She narrows her eyes.

"I do it all the time," I add with a lopsided smile.

"It just ... feels wrong to take these." She glances down at the bag.

"Why? They're my gift to you."

She looks my way, concern contorting her face. "Because I don't normally wear any of these. Each one costs more than a month of rent." She takes in a deep breath. "We fucked, and I go back to the Skull and Serpent Society with this."

I grasp her chin to make her look at me. "I didn't pay you to have sex with me, Ivy. You did that out of your own volition."

She makes a face and turns away from me.

I hit the gas in response, frustrated that I can't get through to her because I can't find the goddamn words I need.

Why does this have to be so complicated?

"Fuck the deal," I grit.

"But—"

"No. You're not a whore. Even if we treat you like one. Even if we love making you feel like our whore. That doesn't make you one because whores sell their body, and I wouldn't fucking let anyone else touch you, ever. If anyone even so much as tried, I'd chop off their hands."

Her eyes widen, and she immediately tucks her hair behind her ear like she was shocked she got caught listening.

"Yes. Tuck that hair behind that ear because I need you to hear me out." My cock twitches from the mere idea of reminding her who she belongs to once more even though I just had my way with her. "No one else fucking touches you. We own you. You are our whore when we want you to be, but we will fucking treat you like a princess if you let us." I slide my hand up her neck and caress her cheek. "So take the goddamn gift, Ivy. Let me spoil you."

A hint of a smile forms on her lips before she turns away again.

But I saw it. And I'll definitely remember it.

***

IVY

The moment we get home, I jump out of the vehicle and shut the door before he has a chance to do it himself.

Because my God, I couldn't take my eyes off those muscular arms and those hands as they wrapped around the steering wheel, controlling the car just like he'd controlled me in that changing room.

My heart is racing, but I had to get out of there as fast as possible.

That man did something to me in that booth that should be illegal. It felt straight-up raunchy and so freaking good, I was nearly ready to beg for more.

I clutch the bag close and glance down at the expensive outfits he just bought especially for me because I told him I didn't have anything to wear, and for some reason, it makes me blush.

Goddammit. What have these guys done to me?

His car door slams shut, and I push back the thoughts.

"You didn't wait for me," he says.

"I needed some fresh air."

"Could've told me. I would've put on the AC," he replies, grabbing the cat supplies from the trunk. "You feeling okay?"

"I'm fine, thanks," I say, pushing myself off the car.

"No need to thank me. I'm just doing what I'm supposed to," he says as we both walk up toward the Skull and Serpent Society.

"Which is what, exactly?" I ask. "Making Max jealous?"

He flinches briefly, but I noticed.

I have to remember who these boys are and their purpose: To use me as a toy, a plaything to be discarded the moment they're done with me.

And who will protect Cora and me then?

I swallow back the lump in my throat at the thought of being out there by ourselves again without a safe landing spot.

I can't rely on anyone but me.

I head inside the house, but the moment I try to place down my bag filled with clothes, a hand wraps around my wrist. Silas drags me closer to him. "Where were you?"

"Out. With me," Heath growls back.

"To do what exactly?" Silas's eyes travel down my body, and he checks me out thoroughly. "Shop?"

I drop the bag on the floor. "Heath got me clothes because I didn't have any."

Heath plops the cat supplies on the table. "And food for Bagel."

Silas does not seem amused at all, and his eyes are visibly twitching. "Do you know how fucking dangerous that is?"

Heath frowns. "It was just a few shops."

"Those fuckers are out there looking for her, and you chose to drive off without any fucking protection?" Silas growls. "She could've died."

My eyes widen.

Fuck. He's right.

I could've died at any point, and then Cora wouldn't have anyone left to take care of her.

"She didn't," Heath retorts. "She's here, in the flesh, as I'm sure you can see."

Max approaches from the kitchen. "What's going on here?" He's still eating a sandwich but stops immediately when he spots the furious look on Silas's face. And Heath.

"Heath took Ivy on a little shopping trip."

"Sounds nice, what'd you get?" Max asks before his eyes finally land on my dress.

And the sandwich nearly drops from his mouth. "Wow."

"A couple of outfits and dresses as you can see." Heath holds up the bags, but Max still won't look at him and eyes me up and down instead.

"Where's Cora?" I ask in a hurry.

"Taking a nap in her own bed. I wore her out with games," Max replies, smiling. "Don't worry, she's as safe as can be."

Silas steps in. "Heath, flaunting your goddamn money doesn't warrant going out there in broad daylight without a fucking weapon," he grits. "And she is *not* prepared."

"What do you mean?" I ask.

Silas grabs my arm and drags me across the floor to the stairs.

"Where are you taking me?"

"Fine, I'll bring some weapons next time if that will ease your conscience," Heath yells, but Silas ignores him as he hauls me all the way upstairs and through the corridors.

"Silas!" I grit, but he still refuses to tell me, so I jerk free of his grip right as we enter a room.

A whole goddamn room filled with weapons.

My eyes bulge as I turn and look around at the multitude of knives, guns, clubs, whips, and all the sharp tools one could need for a job called murder.

Jesus Christ.

"What is this place?"

"Our weaponry."

"That sounds medieval," I jest even though I know this is no fucking joke.

"As medieval as the torture that's dished out by the people we kill," he says, ripping a big-ass knife off the shelves. "I kill for sport, but most of my victims ... they're the worst kind of criminals who don't deserve to see the daylight." He turns toward me, pointing the knife at me. "And those are the kind of fuckers after you right now."

I gulp.

He flips the knife over and holds the handle out to me. "Take it."

"And then what?"

A devilish smirk forms on his face. "We train."

* * *

MAX

The moment the door to the weaponry closes, I turn around and walk back into the kitchen, determined to finish that goddamn sandwich. They might've eaten breakfast already, but man was I busy entertaining Cora while they went off to shop. She is one goddamn tornado.

I wore her out with some much-needed races up and down the stairs by pretending to be a crook while she played the cop before she finally collapsed in her bed again. The little munchkin really didn't get enough sleep yesterday. Or maybe she just likes taking naps to get her energy back up. Who knows.

"I don't care what Silas says, I spoiled Ivy, and I'm damn proud of it."

Heath's voice behind me makes me stop chewing my sandwich immediately.

"She needed the escape, and I needed the release."

The release?

My throat feels clamped shut as my heart sinks into my shoes. "You fucked her?"

I ask the question before I even dare to look at him. But the smug smile on his face confirms my thoughts.

"Her pussy was so goddamn wet for me ..." he growls as he steps closer and closer, removing the space between us. "And when she came all over my goddamn cock, she screamed *my* name. Not yours. *Mine.*" He taps my chest so hard I flinch.

"I ..." I swallow. "If she wanted it, who am I to stop you?"

His brows furrow even more. "What?"

"You two made that deal with her," I say. "I can't stop you. I won't." I push back the tears. "But if you're trying to make me jealous, job well done."

I waltz off and head into the game room where the bar is, and I grab myself the scotch I never go for and pour one out, downing it in one go. I cough and heave, but the burn is not enough to quench the fire raging in my chest.

The giant TV in the back crackles from the fake fire being displayed on it while I just try to breathe.

Breathe, Max. Breathe.

FORTY-THREE

IVY

I chuck the knife at the board in the back of the room but miss, and the knife clatters to the floor.

Silas picks it up with a smug smile. "Again."

"How many more?" I ask.

His brow rises. "Until you hit the center."

"Why? I already know how to hit a fucker with a knife. I'm not afraid to hurt people," I reply.

"Hurt, yes. Kill?" He makes a face as he hands it back to me. "Doubt it. Now try again."

Sighing, I accept the knife from him, but the moment our fingers touch sends electrical currents up and down my spine. I brush them off and focus on the board in the back, the center feeling more like an eye staring right back at me.

He comes to stand behind me and suddenly grips my arm, lifting it. "Higher."

I try to focus, but it's hard with him breathing down my neck.

"Center yourself." He kicks my legs open. "Spread them."

Jesus.

Why did that make my stomach flutter?

"Even if I aim correctly and make the hit, it's just one knife," I say.

"Just that one knife could make the difference ..." he murmurs, standing so closely to my side I can barely even breathe. He pushes my hand up to exactly where he wants it to be, as his other hand slowly snakes up my body, pulling me closer to him until I'm turned sideways.

"Between life …"

I throw.

"And death."

And hit.

My God.

Is it the room that's hot, or is it me?

"Knew you could do it," he murmurs, grinning against my skin. "Well done, thief."

I swallow down the lump in my throat as his hand slowly lowers from my waist, and he steps away to pull the knife out of the board.

"Why are you doing this?"

The words roll off my tongue before I realize it.

His brows draw together. "What? Teaching you how to throw a knife?" He casually tosses it in the air like it's a plaything to him. "Because I can teach you a whole lot more if you're into it."

I don't doubt he could, but that's not what I want to know. "Why are you trying to help me?"

He pauses, his green eyes flickering with interest as if he hadn't considered my question's answer before I said it out loud.

Slowly, he walks toward me, and with each step, I take one back, afraid of what might happen if I let a guy like him get close.

Because he's no longer just that unhinged bully, that crazed killer.

Not since he saved me.

But the wall and I meet at an untimely moment, and I hold my breath as he plants a hand beside my head.

"Am I not allowed to help the girl who gave her body to me?"

He leans in, hovering dangerously close to my face.

"Am I not allowed to protect what's mine?"

A shiver runs up and down my spine from the way he breathes close to my skin.

"You call me a monster, but far worse monsters are beyond those walls, and I think you know that."

My teeth begin to clatter as he reaches for my arm and tucks the knife into the palm of my hand, curling my fingers around it.

"Take the knife. Wield it. Own it. So that when I'm not around ..." He breathes out a sigh. "This body will still be safe." He taps my chest, then turns around and nonchalantly walks to the middle of the room ... right in front of the board.

"Now show me what you can do, twig."

I grind my teeth. "Stop calling me that."

"Or what?" He tilts his head, a mischievous smile forming on his face. "You gonna hit me, twig?"

My nostrils flare as I tighten my grip around the knife.

"Stop," I grit.

"Just like you stopped depriving yourself of food when I told you to eat, twig?"

He doesn't even have the slightest clue why, and it pisses me off.

"Go on, then. Throw it. Hit me. I know you want to."

He's just taunting me. The annoying part is that it's seriously working.

"Aim here." He points at his own heart. "If you can actually find it, you can keep it."

I raise the knife and chuck it right at him. No hesitation. But the moment it leaves my fingertips, a pang of regret instantly hits me sharper than the tip of that knife as it flies toward him.

He catches the knife midair, inches away from his chest, not by the handle, but by the blade.

Droplets of blood slowly roll down the palm of his hand.

"A twig that breaks easily under pressure ..." The deadly smirk on his face could make any girl's heart stop. "Turns into the sharpest weapon."

Including mine.

"Beginner's luck," I retort.

"No. That's what determination looks like," he says, squashing the knife even farther in his hand, speeding the bleeding. "You actually thought for a moment you could kill me." The killer smile on his face only widens. "You *wanted* to kill me."

After everything he's done ... maybe I did.

For a moment.

But that moment passed as quickly as the knife flew through the air.

"I'm not a murderer any more than you're a savior," I murmur.

We are who we were born to be.

And he ... he's just what he said, a monster.

He deserves it.

But then why didn't I actually want him dead?

Is it pity?

"I thought the same thing, twig ..." He brings his hand up to his mouth and actually licks the blood off his skin. "So then tell me why I need to kill everyone who even thinks of putting their hands on you?"

I can't stop staring at those lips caked with blood as he steps closer and closer while my heart beats faster and faster.

"Why I want to give you the skills to defend yourself, even against someone like me?" He points the knife at my belly, right where he created the scar.

"Why I can't stop thinking about having you, over and over again, until I'm so sick of it that I don't even *want* to kill anymore?"

My heart skips a beat.

The tip of the blade pushes aside the slit in my dress until my skin is exposed, along with the word he carved into me.

"You're a thief ..." he mutters, bringing the knife up to my heart. "Through and through."

My downturned lips curl. "A thief ... who needed it more than you did."

His eyes narrow as the knife slides up toward my lips, but I stay put, unafraid.

Even as the knife pushes my lip down and slowly slips inside my mouth until it's sideways between my teeth.

I can taste the tinge of blood on my tongue, but it's the hungered look in those piercing green eyes of his that haunts me the most.

"Do you, now?" He bites his lip. "All you had to do was ask."

Suddenly, he grabs my throat, drags me toward him, and smashes his lips onto mine, kissing the knife as harshly as he kisses me. The blade cuts into both our lips the deeper his kiss becomes, mingling our blood together, but the sharp pain doesn't even compare to the throbbing heart in my chest as he licks each droplet of blood right off my lips, groaning into my mouth.

His tongue wraps around the blade, stealing it from my lips, before he chucks it aside and growls, "Fuck it," slamming his lips back onto mine.

I'm stunned. Too dazed to even think straight as his all-consuming kisses devour any meaningful thoughts I had left, replacing them with debauchery and a kind of greed I've never felt before, but my God is it a rush.

So much so that I actually start kissing him back.

And fuck me, his grin I can feel forming against my lips is nothing short of infuriatingly hot.

"My needy little thief ... take it then if you want it so much."

His tongue drives into my mouth, claiming every inch of space, every sliver of blood as he nearly kisses the soul of my body.

If he wanted it so badly ... all he had to do was ask.

I pull away in abjection at the thought that just flashed through my mind. My fingers instinctively reach up to touch the blood on my lips while simultaneously staring at those darkened eyes filled with lust, desire ... betrayal.

I knock his arm away from my throat as I backtrack to the door, eyes flashing to the knife while I consider if I'm going to stab him for making me want to kiss him back ... or myself.

But my brain finally kicks into gear, and I knock open the door and exit swiftly.

***

MAX

Ten minutes ago

The door to the game room opens, and I can feel a dark cloud literally swoop in from the accompanying wind.

"So this is it?"

At the sound of Heath's voice, I close my eyes while he shuts the door behind him.

"This is how it's going to be from now on?" he grits.

I clench the glass in the palm of my hand, wishing I knew what to do, but he's made it impossible to even think straight.

"You're going to ignore me."

"No, I ..." I mutter, swirling the scotch around.

"You can't even look at me while you're standing there thinking about her. You don't even fucking drink scotch. Ever. And now you're just going to chug it down instead of talking to me?"

He's right, but I don't know how to handle this situation.

"LOOK AT ME!"

His pained voice instantly makes me look up like a beacon in the dark of my mind. And my God, the contortion on his face is too much to bear.

"Please, Heath ..."

"Tell me you fucking love her," he says. "Say it. Say it out loud."

"I love her," I reply.

His lip quivers. "Did it hurt when I took her with me? When you learned I fucked her under your goddamn nose?"

Grinding my teeth, I nod.

"Good," he snarls, stabbing me right in the heart.

"I'm ..."

"Say what you need to say, Max," he grits. "Or I swear to God, I will fucking ruin her right in front of you."

I put the glass down. "I did exactly what you told me to do."

"I told you to fucking seduce her, not fall for her!"

I don't even know how to respond.

"Is that why you're doing this?"

He grinds his teeth. "Maybe."

"Why are you so obsessed with making me jealous? Isn't it enough already?" I stare him down, clenching my jaw. "You had Mavis, and you cast her aside so you could go after Ivy instead, just to hurt me."

"Don't you understand? I *used* Mavis as a distraction, just like I fucking used Ivy as a distraction."

My eyes widen.

He averts his eyes. "But along the way I started feeling things I didn't expect."

"You ... you're in love with Ivy too?" I ask, confused.

He balls his hand into a fist. "I *want* her. Badly. But I fucking wanted *you* first."

FORTY-FOUR

MAX

What?

My lips part, but the oxygen refuses to exit my lungs.

He wants *me?*

He points at my chest. "That heart of yours should've been *mine.*"

Oh God.

"But you only wanted girls," he says, the suffering on his face clear as day. "And it fucking killed me." He shakes his head and snorts. "All these fucking years, I never once thought of any of them as more than a distraction, a way to fill the void, while I yearned for someone who wouldn't even look at me that way. What a joke."

He fishes the bottle of pills from his pants and pops it open.

Ketamine.

The pills he's been downing every time he looked depressed.

And I could never figure out why until today.

All this time.

He wasn't jealous of me because I had *her.*

He was jealous of her ... because she had *me.*

I march over to him and slap the pills from his hand, the bottle flying halfway across the room. I grab his face with both hands and smash my lips onto his, kissing him the way I've dreamed about more than a million times. And God, they taste like blissful sin.

But his lips immediately rip away from mine, the confused look in his eyes anything but comforting.

"I don't want a pity kiss," he growls.

"You kissed me first," I retort. "And then you walked away."

"Because I was terrified!" he yells, tears staining his eyes.

My eyes hover over his face as I mutter, "Of ruining us before we even happened."

His top lip curls. "But you ignored me."

"Because I was terrified ..." I parrot. "Terrified that it was only a mistake and would never happen again."

His eyes flicker with shock.

I grab his face with both hands to try to stop us from overthinking all of this. "Kiss me."

He searches my face for the answers he's been looking for all this damn time, but I am right here, and I will wait. Forever if I have to.

But within a single second, he's already smashed his lips onto mine.

***

HEATH

God, the moment those lips touch mine, I lose every bit of self-control I have, and I claim them like no one ever has before. I don't care anymore what anyone thinks. I'm fucking taking what I want, and what I want is him, right here, right now.

I grip his throat and push him back through the room until his back hits the bar, never taking my lips off his.

He wants me to kiss him? Fine, I'll fucking devour him and leave nothing left.

With my fingers digging into his neck, I pry open his lips and force my tongue inside, rolling around in his mouth like I goddamn own the place and made it my fucking home.

All this fucking time, he's been flaunting his love for her in my face, and I'm tired of not having a slice.

So I take and take, kissing him until he nearly passes out, then finally release my grip on his throat to allow him a single breath.

But the moan that follows ... God, it riles me up almost as much as listening to her moans.

"You ...want this?" I mutter, still hot and heady.

He nods, out of breath.

"Since when? The kiss?"

He shakes his head, and it makes even my breath falter.

"Years," he murmurs, his cheeks flushing with heat.

"But you were always looking at girls," I growl, cornering him against the bar. "You like girls, or you like boys, which is it?"

"Both. I just didn't understand what I felt ... until you kissed me," he says, looking up at me with those puppy-dog eyes that make me want to raw-dog him against this goddamn fucking bar.

"Why didn't you tell me?"

"Because I thought you'd hate me and laugh at me."

My nostrils flare. "Why the fuck would I?"

"I don't know ... I was confused, and I just thought you weren't into guys at all."

"I wasn't into anyone but you for a long goddamn time," I growl, inching closer and closer. "And you didn't even fucking notice when it was right. In. Your. Face."

He averts his eyes. "I'm sorry. I just thought ... I was imagining things. I honest to God thought it'd be better if I didn't tell anyone what I felt and just did what was expected of me. I didn't want to get hurt."

Fuck.

All this time he kept his true feelings hidden just so he wouldn't get hurt?

I grip his chin and force him to look at me. "Don't *ever* fucking lie to me again."

He gulps.

"Do you understand?"

He blushes intensely, then nods.

"Use your fucking words."

"Yes, Sir."

My dick throbs from his groveling voice.

"Good boy." I move my fingers down from his chin to his throat. "But you've been such a fucking sore to my heart, clinging to the girl we both share. You couldn't help but flaunt your love for her right in front of me..." I squeeze tighter and tighter. "You wanted me to be jealous of what you two had." I grab his package, and his eyes flash with surprise. "I am *fucking* jealous. Of both you *and* her."

"Please ..." he squeaks, nearly moaning when I begin to rub him right through the fabric of his pants.

"Please ... what?" I release the pressure just a little to allow him to talk, but not enough to let him get comfortable.

"I'm yours," he says. "Use me. Do what you want with me, please, I'll take anything. I need you. Desperately."

"How desperately?" A grin forms on my face as I lean in, amused by his beggary while I slowly rub him into submission.

I could listen to this all day and still not have enough after what he put me through.

"Whimper for me like you did for her," I growl.

And the whimper that follows, my God, now that gets me rock hard.

I immediately grab his shoulders, twist him around, and bend him over across the bar.

RIP!

I tear off his pants in one go, not giving a shit that the button is still closed.

All this fucking time, this is what's been between us, and I'm tired of denying myself the pleasure of his body.

I grab a bottle of olive oil from the cabinet above the bar and pour it all over his ass.

"You want me?" I ask, and I zip down and take out my hard-on. "Then fucking take me all the way, like a good fucking boy."

"Wha—"

His words are interrupted by an ungodly moan as I thrust into his ass, filling him up within seconds.

"Oh fuck!" he moans, bracing against the bar, nails scratching across the top. "You're huge!"

"That's it, show me how badly you've yearned for this fucking cock." I slam into him with everything I have. I grab him by the hair and tilt his head up. "Let me hear those moans you've been giving to her instead."

Every thrust is another moan scratched off my to-do list, but it'll never be enough.

All this fucking time we've been pretending we don't feel anything, while we've been secretly longing to have each other, and I'm tired of it. I'm tired of this dance of avoidance, this game we've been playing.

"Enough," I grit. "Tell me. Tell me you fucking love me like you love her."

"I love you," he whimpers. "I've never not loved you."

"Fuck. Yes."

I thrust into his ass so deep his eyes nearly roll into the back of his head, and I grip his throat and force him to keep the moan inside. "No. This one's for me and me alone."

I smash my lips onto his, forcing him to let it all out into my mouth so I'm the only one in this house who can hear him. Even if he isn't mine forever, he's mine for now, and I will make it last an eternity if I must.

"God, you taste so fucking good when you're taking my cock like a good boy," I groan against his lips.

His entire body shivers. "Yes ... more. Please. I need more."

Smiling against his lips, I bring my hand down his stomach and grip his cock. He flinches, startled as I squeeze and start jerking him off. "So fucking sensitive," I whisper. "How many strokes do you think it'll take? One?" I jerk him off just once. "Two?" Another stroke and he's actually quaking. "Three?"

He whimpers, "Oh fuck me."

"Oh, my fucking pleasure." I grip his dick and pull back until his tip glistens with pre-cum, then thrust into him so hard I can feel his balls tighten underneath the palm of my hand.

"I can't hold it," he moans.

I pause inside him and stop jerking him off, and his cock bounces up and down in the air. "You didn't ask permission."

"Please ... can I come?"

"Go on," I whisper.

"Please, Sir, I want to come so badly. I'm begging you."

His whimpering makes even my cock throb inside him.

"Do it, then. Paint the fucking floor."

I pull him away from the bar and force him to stand facing the middle of the room, and I lock his arms behind his back. "No touching. You did it for her. Now, do it for me."

"What?" he mutters.

I thrust into his ass instead of answering his question and let him find out on his own. An unhinged moan leaves his mouth as his cum shoots out in ropes, his entire body trembling as I fuck him hard and fast, groaning along with him until I come too, filling up his ass.

Suddenly, the door cracks open and in runs Ivy.

She abruptly stops the second she spots us.

And so does my orgasm.

Fuck.

FORTY-FIVE

HEATH

"What the ...?" Her words are cut off by her own jaw dropping while her pupils begin to dilate.

I pull out of Max's ass, and my cum drips down his thighs.

"Oh God," Max mutters, his whole body turning red this time. "It's not what it looks like."

"Damn right, it is," I growl.

I pluck a cleaning towel off the bar to wipe off my dick before I waltz over to Ivy with my erection on full display.

"Ignore me. I'll just leave you two to it and pretend I didn't see," she mutters as she turns around.

Before she can make a beeline, I slam the door shut, planting my hand on the wood. "You're not going anywhere."

"Wait, Ivy? What are you doing here?" Max mutters, swiftly pulling up his pants as if that'll hide the evidence of what we did in here.

She tucks her hair behind her ear. "I could ask you the same thing."

Max's face begins to glow. "I thought you were training with Silas," he stutters.

"She obviously got tired of him," I say, smirking.

"Whatever." She tries to move away from me, but I plant another hand against the door, trapping her inside. "Why won't you let me leave?"

"You think I can let you go after what you just witnessed?"

"Is this supposed to scare me?" she asks, folding her arms. "What do I even gain from spilling your dirty secrets when I'm already practically your fuck doll?"

I run my tongue along my lip. "Tell everyone. I don't care."

She frowns. "Then why are you stopping me?" She briefly glances at Max, who's still hiding in the corner. "You're obviously busy."

A smirk forms on my face. "Are you jealous?"

Her jaw drops, and she makes a choking sound, but no actual words come out of her mouth, and that tells me enough.

"You are," I say.

"I just got caught off guard," she mutters.

"For what? Running away?" I tilt my head. "You can't escape any of us. Not Silas, not me, not Max." She swallows as I inch closer. "I thought we made that very clear."

"I guess all that stuff you said back in the shop was a lie, then," she says.

"What did you tell her?" Max asks.

"He said he wanted me to give him my heart," she says, eyeing Max. "And you told me you loved me."

"I do. I do love you," Max says, stepping closer.

A part of me wants to rip her to shreds for earning his love ... but another part of me wants to lick her until she screams my name. Fuck. I've never felt so torn between two people in my life.

"But I just caught you two having sex. Do you want me, or do you want him?" she asks Max and me. "Which is it?"

She may have stolen his heart like a true thief, but she will fucking learn to share, and it starts now.

I grab her throat and shove her against the door while her eyes widen. "Both."

I smash my lips onto hers, claiming her just like I did in the changing room, right in front of Max. And fuck me, does it feel good to kiss both of them right after each other.

I pry open her lips and make her yield with my tongue alone, probing inside. She moans and squirms underneath my hand, but she's helpless against the onslaught of lust already coursing through her veins just from my kiss.

With my other hand, I splay her legs and push up her dress until my fingers reach her pussy, and I start rubbing it again.

God, she looks so fucking good in that dress I bought her.

Suddenly, she bites my lip, and I withdraw, tasting my own blood.

"You bit me," I mutter.

"You kissed me," she retorts.

I turn around when I notice Max hovering so close I can barely contain my raging boner from plowing through him once again. I'm still hard as fuck and not nearly finished with either of them.

Something's got to give.

These walls are coming down.

I grab Max's hair and kiss him just as hard, right in front of her, licking the roof of his mouth, twisting and turning my tongue around his until his breathless moans fill the room. All while I'm still fondling her. From the corner of my eye, I watch her reaction, the goose bumps growing on her skin, the lip that's tugged by her teeth, and fuck me, I don't think there's ever been anything hotter than this.

Maybe this is what I've been craving all along.

Not just her or him ... but us.

Together.

"Please," Max murmurs, pulling away to look at Ivy, who leans back against the door, all flustered. "I love you, Ivy. But I love him too, and I don't want to choose."

She sucks in a breath, hesitant but so very fucking sexy. I can't get enough.

I push Max closer. "Kiss her."

He leans in to plant a kiss on her neck, sucking on her skin like it's nobody's business. I lean in too and suck on her earlobe, slowly drawing a line all the way down to her clavicles where I meet him, and I kiss him between kissing her neck as we slowly make our way back up to her face.

And the second he plants one single, soft kiss on her lips, I add a hungered one of my own, biting and tugging at her lip until she can't distinguish either of us or the conflicting needs coursing through her veins.

"Do you hate me so much for kissing you? For wanting something more from you than just a fuck?" I ask, swirling my fingers around her most sensitive areas. "I told you, it's not enough for me."

"I thought you only did it to make him jealous," she whispers between our delectable kisses.

"Making him jealous ... felt so damn good, I'd do it all over again." I grin. "So let me make him fucking jealous and enjoy the fireworks," I muse, biting her lip before I drive my tongue into his mouth.

Max moans against me, his cock already hard again just from the idea of having two of us to play with.

"Fuck," she murmurs.

I keep rubbing her faster and faster. "You thought I only craved him? You belong to all of us," I say as I draw a line across her lip with my tongue. "We share you ... you share us."

Her eyes close as I inch closer and closer ... and kiss her full on the lips together with Max, tasting the most hedonistic pleasures known to humankind.

***

IVY

I tried to resist, I honestly did, but the moment both their lips landed on mine, I lost my sense of self-control. Their kisses are hypnotizing, to the point where I can't tell the two apart, and I want nothing more than their lips on my skin, everywhere, anywhere, all the fucking time.

I don't understand how I've so easily succumbed to their greed, yet I don't want it to stop.

Not just one but two boys are in love with me ... and each other.

This intoxicating mix of all three of us will be the death of me. Yet I let them walk me right down to the gateways of hell.

Heath pulls me away from the door, pushing me up against his muscular chest, while Max kisses the back of my neck and sucks on my ear. He zips down my dress while Heath pushes it off my shoulders, both working in sync to get what they want—me.

And fuck me ... I can't say no anymore.

"You're our toy, our little plaything, now let us fucking use you," Heath groans into my mouth before dragging me all the way back to the pool table, kissing both me and Max between every step as my dress drops to the floor, all of us absolutely consumed by lust.

How did they so easily persuade me to participate?

And why is my pussy throbbing so goddamn much?

Heath's lips cover mine again, and I shut my brain off to stop myself from feeling guilty.

Guilty for the lust taking over my entire being.

Guilty for the promise I made myself that I would never fall for any of these boys.

God.

It's too late.

It's entirely too late.

My fingers curl underneath Heath's shirt, equally as desperate to touch him too after he so deliberately played with me. He pulls his shirt over his head in one go, exposing his muscular body riddled with tattoos and piercings on each nipple.

Before I can even process what I just did, he slams his lips back on mine, fingers splaying on the back of my head as they thread through my hair, his breath ragged, unhinged.

"Please ... let us have you," Max moans behind me, kissing my back as his hands curl around my body to fondle my breasts. "Fuck, you're so pretty. I can't stop touching you."

"I'm not just a toy," I mutter between their kisses, desperately trying to cling to my self-worth, which is quickly dropping to the floor along with Max's shirt and pants.

"No. You're *our* toy. No one else is allowed to touch you," Heath groans.

I tug at his waistband, tearing down what little self-respect I had left as his pierced cock springs free.

"Fuck, I want to be inside you. Now." Heath hops onto the pool table and drags me along with him, grasping my legs as he props me up on top of him.

Within seconds, I'm lowered on top of his cock, and my stifled moan is swallowed up by Max's hungry kisses. His mouth covers mine as Heath fucks me hard and fast, wasting no time to claim me.

"Come here," he barks at Max. "Fuck her wet little pussy, just like last time. Together."

Max gleefully obliges, spreading my legs even farther as he positions himself between my legs and pushes the tip inside.

"Oh fuck, I can feel every ridge," I say as he slowly enters me.

It's so full but so fulfilling too.

"Don't stop," Heath growls. "Fuck her like you mean it. I know you want to."

Heath eggs him on until he finally loses control, and I gasp as Max thrusts in to the base, burying himself inside me to the hilt together with Heath.

"Fuck!" I groan.

"Oh shit, I can feel your piercings," Max moans against my ear.

Heath leans forward and slams his lips onto Max while I'm sandwiched between them, like a literal fuck doll.

And I don't even despise myself anymore for loving it.

Fuck, I need this. Whatever it is, I need more of it. So much fucking more.

"Please ..." I whimper as they pull out, only to thrust back in together.

"God, I love it when you beg," Heath groans as he sucks on my earlobe. "Show her how much you love her, Max. Let me see the fucking devotion."

Max smashes his lips on mine, and I moan into his mouth as he brings his fingers to my slit and starts rubbing me.

"That's it, make her fucking come while she's being railed by the two of us," Heath groans. "Make her fucking want it."

Max flicks my clit like he knows exactly how to make me squirm, his eyes fully homed in on me as though he enjoys watching me fall apart on Heath's cock.

"Come all over our fucking cocks, slut," Heath groans.

"I can feel her orgasm. Oh God," Max moans, his fingers fluttering back and forth until I reach that peak of no return. And when I finally fall, I slam my lips onto Heath's, burying my tongue inside his mouth to let go of all the pent-up need.

Suddenly, Heath picks me up and lifts me off both their hard-ons, spins me around, and lays me flat on the pool table.

"What are you doing?" I ask.

"You thought we were done with you?" He snorts as he nudges my legs, forcing them apart. "I haven't even fucking begun enjoying the taste of all your body has to offer ..." The mischievous glint in his eyes as he focuses on Max makes me question my decisions. And morals. "And I can't wait to fucking share it with him."

****

MAX

All this time I felt so bad for yearning Ivy while Heath was right there, but I always assumed he was straight and wouldn't ever want me like that ... until that kiss.

It shocked me so much I couldn't even look at him, and I felt so bad for hurting him.

But now all I can think of is all the devious games he intends to play with me. With us. And it makes me want to submit.

"Tell me what you want me to do," I say.

All I wanna do is make it up in whatever way I possibly can.

"I'll grovel, I'll beg, I'll kiss every inch of your skin if you'll let me, but I don't ever want you to doubt I want you just as badly as I want her ever again," I say, swallowing when both of them glance at me.

"I know I talk a lot, but I just wanted you to know the truth. I love you. Both of you, and I'd pretty much do anything either of you'd tell me to," I add, out of breath from my own damn rambling.

This man and this woman are all I've ever wanted, and finally I get to have both of them without feeling guilty. It's like a dream come true.

"Max," Heath says, smirking. "Shut up."

I gulp.

"On your knees." Heath points at the floor right in front of his feet. "Crawl here. Now."

God, I don't think I've ever heard anything more attractive than Heath finally asserting his domination over me. And fuck me, I'm already dripping from the tip of my cock at the thought.

I immediately drop down and crawl to him, sitting on my knees in front of him.

"Good boy. Now put that fucking mouth to good use."

I do what he says, but he bends over Ivy instead.

"You like to boss him around just like you boss me around," Ivy says, chuckling.

"How could I not when both of you are such fucking whores for me?"

Her gasp makes him laugh.

"Now let me eat this fucking pussy while I choke him with my cock," Heath groans.

"Wha—"

I can't even finish my words as he immediately thrusts into my throat, filling me up and then some. He's huge and thick and all things unholy, and I can't even cope with how badly I've wanted this that I whimper with delight.

"That's it, take it deep into your throat," Heath groans. "Both of you are whimpering for *me*."

Ivy's legs quake on the pool table above me, her body shivering from the licks he gives her.

"God, you're so fucking wet," Heath moans.

Her wetness is dripping down onto me, but I can taste her in my mouth from Heath's cock alone, and it's sending me to heaven and back.

"Fuck," I say, gargling when he pulls out. "You're so thick."

"Wait until you taste how thick my cum is," he groans, thrusting right back, leaving not a second for me to breathe.

I'm drooling all over him and myself, and my dick still bounces up and down despite the fact I already came. But I've never been so turned on in my entire life.

"Yes, just like that," Heath growls. "Wrap your tongue around it and suck the cum out of me like a good fucking boy."

"Oh God, this is so hot," I say, sucking him off like my life depends on it.

And to hear her moan and squeal while he pleasures her and licks her off is the icing on the cake.

But the door suddenly cracking open silences all of us immediately as Silas steps inside and slams the door shut behind him. Heath's lips are still all over Ivy's pussy, and my lips are still wrapped around his delicious cock.

Oops.

FORTY-SIX

SILAS

Three fucking liars all fucking on the pool table in the dorm room.

Well, if that isn't the start of a joke, I don't know what is.

"I can explain," Max mutters as he takes his lips off Heath's dick.

"And here I was thinking you were only into girls." I cross my arms. "Well, this explains everything."

If he'd simp for Ivy, of course he'd simp for Heath too.

"Wait, it does?" Max mutters.

Heath leans up too. "I thought—"

"What? That I wouldn't notice you two fighting in silence?" I snort. "You were too obvious. But I see you finally got it sorted out."

Max's entire face turns red, his lips still hovering close to Heath's dick.

"Oh, don't fucking stop on my account," I tell them.

I don't fucking care what they do with each other as long as they leave me out of it. I'm far too busy obsessing about the girl they're both trying to fuck.

Heath smirks and starts rubbing Ivy's pussy, shoving a finger or two inside to make her squirm on the table.

I approach Ivy, who covers her breasts with her hands like I haven't already seen every inch of her delectable skin.

"You couldn't help yourself, could you," I say as I come to stand behind her.

"I don't remember promising myself *only* to you," she quips.

"No, but *you* just ran away from *me*," I respond, narrowing my eyes. I push my fingers underneath my shirt and pull it over my head. Her eyes immediately flutter up to look at every ridge of my trained abs along with the many tattoos riddling my skin all the way up to my neck. She bites her bottom lip, before pretending she never did. But I saw. "*After* I kissed you and you liked it."

She tries to lift her head, but I grasp her arms and pin them down above her head.

"Oh no, you're not going anywhere," I say. "Unless you want me to chase you through the dark again."

"You already did that," she retorts.

"And I'll gladly do it again. This time without turning on the lights," I say with a grin. "Especially after you decided to go and seduce *them* instead."

The lust still swirls through her eyes, despite her rebuttal. "I didn't do anything, they cornered me."

"*We* cornered *you*?" Heath muses, leaning over her to look her in the eyes. "I seem to recall you interrupting us mid-fuck. But maybe I need to jog your memory from the inside out."

He thrusts three fingers in total into her pussy, and we both watch her writhe on the pool table before he bends over to lick her needy little clit again, and her face scrunches from the pleasure.

"Oh, you're loving this," I say.

"Fuck …" she mewls, clearly unable to control the lust building inside her.

"You've only given me one orgasm so far," Heath murmurs against her pussy lips. "You think I'd settle for less than five?"

"Five?!" she squeals. "But I already came a bunch of times in the changing room too!"

"Sounds like you've been quite the slut," I say, leaning over to see the scowl on her face appear after being confronted with the truth. "A slut more than willing to please three boys hungering for her."

"It's just a deal," she mutters, out of breath from the way Heath licks her.

"Fine, then," I grit. "Have it your way."

And I grasp her face and pin it down on the table before I zip down and ram right into her throat, no-holds-barred.

She'll have to learn the hard way she can't say no to us. Not just because we won't let her but because she won't be able to resist. Because despite my cock being inches deep inside her throat, bulging against her neck, her pussy is still dripping wet, and her tongue still wraps around my shaft, just like a good, obedient little slut's tongue would.

"You want to be used just like you were told? Then fucking open that pretty little mouth wide and take it deep."

I grip her throat and sink in even deeper, listening to her gargles and groans as she struggles to take me all the way. But I won't fucking settle for less.

"More, twig. Give me more," I grit, thrusting hard. "You handed it to them on a silver platter, and now it's my fucking turn to enjoy the spoils of my raid on your body."

Every inch I go deeper, I squeeze her throat just a little tighter until the light slowly starts to go out in her eyes. I only pull back just one second to allow her a single breath before I plow right back in again.

"Max, stop," Heath growls. "Before I fucking come down your throat too."

"Please, I want it," Max moans.

"No. You don't deserve it. Fucking earn it first," he grits, pulling out underneath the pool table.

When Max rises, Heath grips his throat, all while still licking Ivy.

"Look at her. Look at how she's writhing on this fucking table from my tongue alone," Heath says. "You want her, don't you?"

With a drool-covered face, Max nods as he hovers closer and closer.

"Then watch like a good fucking boy while I make her come," Heath groans, rolling his tongue around that sweet, wet pussy.

"Oh, please ..." Max mutters as he starts stroking himself.

But I'm far too busy with her throat to mind whatever they're doing. The minute she denied me that fucking kiss, I knew I needed to remind her who this fucking mouth belonged to.

I bury myself to the hilt and wait, throbbing deeply inside her while she struggles with her leftover oxygen.

"Can you feel me here?" I ask, pointing at her neck. "Nod."

She does what I say, her eyes widening with every missed breath.

"This cock belongs here for as long as I call you mine. You might deny me a kiss, but everything you are, this body, every inch, every breath, every scar, every lick, every drop of blood, every bead of sweat, and every fucking drip of your saliva belongs to me now," I growl before pulling out. "Now say it. Who do you belong to?"

"You," she says, coughing.

I pinch her cheeks and lean over to look her in the eyes. "Now you're starting to get what it means to be mine. Now give me a kiss." She frowns but still perks her lips, and I smash my lips onto hers, boring my tongue into her mouth to roll it around hers before I bite on her bottom lip to make her bleed so I can savor the taste. "That's my good girl."

A faint blush appears on her cheeks as I grin with satisfaction, and I arch my back and grip her face again to slam right back into that perfect little mouth I intend to use so many fucking times until she'll want nothing but my cum for breakfast, dinner, and dessert.

"Oh fuck, I'm coming," Ivy moans when I pull out.

Her whole body begins to shake, but Heath refuses to relent, his tongue swiping along her slit to lick the juices off.

"Please ... let me have a taste of her," Max begs, distracting me.

"She will come on my tongue again, and you will wait like a good fucking boy," Heath growls. "Go play with her nipples to drive her mad."

"Yes, sir," Max responds, climbing onto the table to fondle her tits.

She moans from all the sensations overloading her, and the sound only turns me on even more. My cock throbs deep inside her as I thrust and thrust, coating my shaft with her saliva while I hold her head in place.

I don't care that I'm face fucking her because she fucking adores it.

I can fucking feel it from her tongue wrapping all around my shaft.

I can fucking hear it from the amount of moans she's letting out.

And I can fucking see it from the literal goose bumps scattering all over her skin.

She likes to be dominated, to be used, to be controlled ... to be subjugated and forced into submission.

And no toy in the world could offer me more pleasure than a fucking prey who likes to fight back.

"You ran away from my tongue penetrating your mouth ..." I groan. "So now I'll claim it with my goddamn cock instead."

She's the perfect girl for all my fucked-up wicked desires, and the more I fuck with this girl, the harder it becomes to stop.

And judging from the way Heath and Max are toying with her like they would kill to hear her moan, I'm not the only one who's become obsessed.

"Fuck, she's gushing," Heath groans, lapping her up like he hasn't had a meal like that in years.

Max lavishly kisses her nipples. "They're so perky, so damn perfect."

I pull out to allow her a few breaths. "You ready, little thief?"

"I can't breathe," she mutters.

"You don't have to. All you need to do is swallow and say thank you."

"What?!"

I pinch her nose and force my way past her lips again until my piercings scrape across the back of her tongue and past her uvula.

"Now come," Heath growls at her.

She squeezes her thighs together as his tongue circles around her most sensitive spot while I thrust and thrust until she can't breathe any longer as I choke her on my length. I roar out loud and finish inside her.

But as she shakes her head, I grip her throat and keep my cock in place.

"Swallow. Swallow it all like the good fucking slut you are for me."

"Fuck, I could feel her coming all over my fingers," Heath groans against her pussy, driving his tongue into her.

"Good," I growl, "Because you've had more than your fucking fair share of her. Now give her to me."

I pull out of her throat, and the sound of her heaves as she swallows down even more saliva mixed with cum is like music to my ears.

"What do you mean? You just had me," she says, leaning up.

I laugh as I walk around the table, drawing a line with my fingers across the pool table, waiting for Heath to step aside as I reach the edge where her feet are planted. "You thought I was done with you?" I draw her legs apart and drag her to me. "I will never be satisfied with just one part of you." My fingers slide up her thighs, digging into her skin. "Not today. Not tomorrow. Not ever."

"But the deal ends when I've paid off my debt," she mutters.

I lean in and plant sultry kisses all over her thighs, watching her toes slowly begin to curl. "Your debt ends when I've been satiated, and I am fucking insatiable for you. No amount of sex can fill the void in my body, and I am so goddamn fucking hungry." I drag her closer. "So let me eat *my* fucking pussy and devour it whole."

FORTY-SEVEN

IVY

I'm lost in sensations.

Lost in submission.

Lost in the insane desire taking over my body.

I'm so lost, and I don't want to find my way back.

These boys have wrecked me.

Destroyed every inch of my self-preservation, and now there's nothing left but the feral need to embrace their sweet madness.

Falling into the pits of hell shouldn't feel this good, but it does. God, it fucking does, and I can't get enough.

My hands find Max's hair, and I squeeze it tightly, forcing him down onto my nipples.

"Please, more," I beg.

"Max, come here and lick this pussy too. It's crying literal tears for more attention."

"Oh fuck off," I groan.

SLAP!

I squeal from the sudden spanking to my pussy.

"No back talk, twig," Silas warns.

"How about we spice things up?" Heath says, grabbing a small box that he places on the table.

"What is that?" I ask.

Silas's smirk predicts trouble as he opens the box. "Balls."

"What kind of balls?"

He holds them up, showing four small balls, one with the number five on it and the rest the number zero, all half the size of his hand.

"Mini cue balls," Heath muses.

Silas grins. "Just the perfect fucking size for a needy little pussy."

My eyes widen. "What?"

He licks off one of them. "Don't be so afraid ..." He pushes my knees up to my chest. "*You* wanted to play with *us*, remember? So let me teach you a thing or two about the games we enjoy."

He shoves the first ball up my pussy, and I gasp in shock at how cold it feels inside me. And full.

He sucks on the next ball, swiping his tongue across like he wants me to shudder in preparation of what's to come.

"That'll never fit," I mutter.

"Yes, it will," he replies, shoving in the next one. "You'll make them fit."

I gasp as the two of them connect inside me, while he pulls his fingers out, only to plunge right back into the box to take out the next zero.

"You're doing great, slut," Heath says, slapping my inner thigh, and the shock reverberates through my entire body, my pussy throbbing so badly I nearly come again.

What is this?

"Never used Ben Wa balls, I see," Heath muses.

"Who has?" Max mutters.

"I have," Silas says, running his tongue along the third. "It's quite the fucking show."

Then he shoves Max's face into my slit. "Who said you could stop? Keep fucking licking."

"I'll make sure he does his job," Heath groans, and he approaches the table from behind, where Max kneels on the green tarp and shoves two fingers into his ass.

"Fuck," Max moans into my slit, making me needy, possessed with having more.

I've already had so many orgasms today. I couldn't possibly handle more.

"Another one," Silas says, pushing the next ball inside.

"Oh fuck! It's so full," I moan.

"You think this is full? Wait until you feel three cocks all at once," Silas says, spreading my legs even farther apart. "Now take them all."

"I can't do three—"

I moan wildly when Silas adds the last one, pushing all four balls up against each other inside me.

"Now tell me what's inside you," Silas says.

"Mini cue balls," I reply.

THWACK!

The pain of another spank to my pussy turns into pleasure almost immediately, and I can feel it rippling all through my body. Max's tongue swiping across my clit only adds more to the sensations until I can't tell whether I'm willing to beg them to stop or willing to beg them for more.

"What are the numbers?"

I frown, trying to think. "Five. Zero. Zero. Zero."

Max's tongue is making it so hard to focus.

THWACK!

"Five grand!"

"That's it. Knew you'd figure it out," Silas muses. "Now bring me the fucking cue."

"What, why?" I mutter, leaning up.

"Max, keep fucking licking her," Heath growls, shoving his fingers into Max, making Max mewl. "Yes, Sir," he says, immediately amping up the speed of his tongue movements.

There's a squirting sound, and suddenly, something cold is pushed against my ass. "Oh God."

"I'm going to enjoy this."

Silas actually inserts the back end of the cue stick into my ass, pushing it farther and farther until I can feel it against the curve of each ball.

Plop. Plop. Plop.

I moan with each movement, growing wetter and wetter as he enters me despite the shame.

"Fuck!"

"That's it. Moan for me, moan like the fucking slut you are," Silas groans.

Heath steps up onto the pool table, but it barely registers with me as Silas begins thrusting the cue stick in and out, past the balls, over and over, until I'm crying out in bliss.

"Fuck, please!" I mewl, unable to stop myself.

"You want me to fuck you more with this cue?" he asks.

"Please ..." I mutter, wishing he wouldn't make me say it out loud.

Heath grabs my face and parts my lips with his thumb. "Say that word again."

"Please."

"Fuck." He smashes his lips onto mine, stealing a kiss along with my breath.

"Beg for it, then. Beg like a good little slut, and I might let you come," Silas groans, fucking me with that cue stick as though he's enjoying the sight of me writhing on this goddamn table like the sadistic fucker he is.

But my God ... is he good at what he does.

"Please ... give it to me," I whimper.

"Open your mouth," Heath says, and I do what he says.

Not because I want to but because my body and all the lust dancing through my veins forces me to.

And he dribbles spit onto my tongue. "Taste how hot you are for us. Swallow."

He pushes my lips shut, forcing me to gulp down my own pussy juices as I struggle to fight the next orgasm.

But it's too late. They've contorted me into a being I don't recognize, a vixen consumed with the next hit. A hit of them.

"You gonna come like the slut you are?" Silas asks, pausing mid-stroke.

"Yes, yes, please, let me come," I moan.

As he deepens his stroke, he suddenly lets go and says, "Flip her over."

Heath pulls me up with ease and lies down underneath me, pushing Max out of the way while he sets me down on top of him at the edge of the pool table with the cue stick still inside my ass. The balls begin to shift, and I mewl with delight. He tugs me down by my nipples, then grabs Max by the throat to pull him in for a savage kiss.

Out of nowhere, Silas pulls out the cue stick. "Fucking gush."

He drags it out in one go, and one by one, the balls plop out of me like heavenly domino, followed by the most intense orgasm I have ever fucking felt in my entire goddamn life, as the wetness literally squirts out of me and onto the pool table.

Heath moans. "She actually squirted, didn't she? Oh fuck, I wanna feel it."

Before I know it, Heath's pushed me down onto his dick, his wide girth entering me with ease because I've turned into a sloppy mess.

"Fuck yes." Silas pushes his fingers inside too, filling me up, and it floods my body with more endorphins. He smacks my ass, making me yelp. "Needy little slut. Come here."

He forces me even farther down onto Heath, then pulls me up by my arms until I'm riding Heath's cock.

"That's it, ride me like you own this fucking cock, thief," Heath moans, biting his lip, before he pulls Max closer to steal another kiss. "Fuck, I need both of you together."

"No. This pussy is mine now," Silas growls, and he grabs my hips like they're handles and positions his tip against my entrance, forcing his way inside right beside Heath.

"Fuck!" I cry out as he thrusts in completely.

Two giant cocks inside me, and all it does is make me want to beg for a third.

Fuck, Silas was right.

I've turned into their willing slut without so much as a single inch of resistance left inside these feeble bones.

I am truly lost.

Lost to their depravity.

Lost in the wicked hearts of these boys.

And I'm done fighting to find my way back to heaven because this hell they've created ignites my body in ways I could only dream of.

"That's it, little thief," Silas whispers into my ear. "Break for me."

That's it.

I'm done.

"Please ..." I whimper. "Give me more."

Silas grins against my cheek. "Good girl."

***

MAX

The boys alternate strokes, stretching her to the limit, and fuck, it looks so goddamn appetizing I just want to lean in to take a lick of her delicious pussy while it's being plowed.

Suddenly, Heath grabs my waist and forces me on top of his chest.

"What are you doing?" I ask.

"Fucking sit. Sit on me."

"I am," I say, not sure what he wants.

"No, fucking sit on my face and let me taste your fucking cock like you tasted me," he growls, gripping my thighs to drag me closer to his face.

"What?" I gasp in shock.

But before I can even process what's happening, he's already taken my cock into his mouth like we're going to do position sixty-nine and swallows my dick like a hungered beast. The untethered moan escaping my throat is nothing short of animalistic. "Oh fuck ..."

He pushes my back forward so my face is closer to Ivy. "Kiss her while I suck you off."

He doesn't have to tell me twice. I'd pretty much kiss her any chance I'd get.

Leaning on my hands, I smash my lips onto hers, kissing her like my life depends on it, her mouth tasting as divine as his tongue feels around my shaft. I moan into her mouth as Heath begins to suck. He spreads his saliva all over, and I can feel him swallowing me down even farther. Fuck, it feels so damn good. I could come again just from how deep he takes me.

THWACK!

Ivy bites my lip from the spanking Silas gave her ass.

"Ride us," Silas tells her. "Don't fucking stop."

He spanks her again and again until her whole face scrunches up from both pain and pleasure, so I smash my lips back onto hers to kiss the confusion away.

"Fuck ..." she murmurs against my lips while the two boys thrust into her pussy. "Please ..."

"You want more?" Silas groans, pulling in and out just to hear her writhe.

When she doesn't respond, he slaps her again. "Yes!" she cries out before crashing her lips back onto mine.

"Then take my cock up your ass like a good fucking slut," Silas growls before thrusting into her other hole.

She mewls with delight, and I smother her with more kisses, desperate to siphon her pleasure off her like an addict. She is my fucking drug, and I'm the whore willing to beg for a hit.

My heart belongs to her *and* him. I need them both so badly I can't stop, and I don't want to stop.

Suddenly, two fingers are shoved inside me, and I bite her lip too as I cry out.

"You thought she was the only one getting railed in both ends?" Heath chuckles. "I like hearing you both moan, so fucking moan for me, sluts."

He thrusts his fingers in and out of me while licking my shaft, and the combined sensations remind me of him fucking me in the ass. It was my first time ever, and it felt so fantastic that I can't stop wanting it again and again, and the mere memory makes me want to ride his face like a goddamn cowboy.

"Oh fuck, kiss me now," I moan before my lips land right back onto Ivy again, and I smother her with my arousal while my tongue rolls around hers.

"Good girl, bounce that ass up and down, soak our fucking cocks," Silas groans, and I can hear the sloshing sounds.

"She's so goddamn wet, dripping all over my cock," Heath says. "You can taste the desire on her tongue, can't you, Max?"

"Yes, fuck yes," I moan into her mouth, kissing every inch of her mouth and chin. "Fuck, don't stop. Please, don't stop."

Heath takes my cock out of his mouth, and it bobs up and down against his chin as he taps several licks against it to see me shudder on top of him. "You gonna come for me, slut?" Heath adds another finger into my ass, going farther and farther each time, twisting and turning it until I nearly lose it. "Do it, then."

Just the tip of his tongue is all he gives me, but it's enough for me to explode all over him while whimpering. He licks and sucks at the tip, drinking my cum like he loves the taste, and I slam my lips onto Ivy, boring my tongue into her out of sheer lust.

"Fuck, I'm gonna fill her up," Heath moans, and he thrusts a few more times before roaring out loud.

I can see the cum dripping out of her as she keeps riding him, up and down, up and down, up and down, the sloshing sounds too appetizing, too tempting. And as Silas grasps her hair and tilts her head back, I bend over and lick her pussy, sucking Heath's cum right off her.

"Fuck!" she mewls.

"Yes, come all over his fucking dick," Silas growls at her, slamming into her from behind.

Her nipples peak, and she begins to shiver all over, her skin flushing red hot from another orgasm.

A loud roar fills the room as Silas drives into her ass, filling her up to the brim. When he pulls out, she collapses on top of me, dripping from head to toe.

Heath shoves me aside and leans up, grabbing a fistful of Ivy's hair, pouring my cum into her mouth from the top before kissing her right on the lips. Then he grabs me by the throat and slams his lips onto mine, kissing both of us so fucking good I nearly melt into a puddle.

Silas steals her away from Heath's grasp, turning her head around to claim her for a kiss too.

THWACK!

We all sit up and look around.

"Does no one respect our goddamn privacy in this hou—" Heath abruptly interrupts his own words because the door just slammed open, the wood nearly cracking under the pressure as Dean Felix Rivera stomps inside.

Oh shit.

FORTY-EIGHT

IVY

I sit up straight and scramble off Heath, trying to cover myself up with my hands, but honestly, nothing is left to the imagination.

"What the..." The dean stops in the middle of the room and stares us all down.

Mortified, I swiftly grasp my dress off the floor and put it back on haphazardly even though the straps won't hold without the zipper being pulled up. My entire skin is flushed red, and I feel so goddamn hot. I wish I could step under a shower made of pure ice. I'd probably settle for a fridge right about now. Not just to cool down in but also to hide in.

"Silas," the dean grits, his sanpaku, hollowed-out eyes looking ghostly. "Fuck, I should've known."

"What? That I'm just as fucking freaky as you are?" Silas steps away from the pool table, nonchalantly zipping up like he wasn't just caught red-handed, while Heath and Max both silently slither off the table and put their pants back on.

"In the fucking game room?" The dean points at the table. "I just had that reupholstered!"

"Relax, it's just a fucking pool table," Silas replies.

The dean's eye begins to twitch as he looks at me. "Who is this?" The dean's eyes narrow. "Is this what I think it is?"

Silas places a hand on my shoulder and pulls me behind him. "So what if it is? It's none of your business."

"It is when you decided to involve your mom's men," he retorts. "What the hell were you thinking? Calling them to clean up some bodies in the middle of the street?"

My eyes widen.

Oh God, he knows about the killings.

"What? It's not like they don't do that on a monthly basis for her," he replies.

"Undercover!" The dean points his finger at Silas's naked chest. "I warned you not to overstep, and you went out there and murdered a dozen people in broad daylight."

"Actually, it was in the middle of the night," Max mutters, but after a stern glance from the dean, he immediately raises his hands. "Semantics. Never mind."

"I told you to control your urges," the dean hisses at Silas. "You broke our agreement."

Silas swats his finger away. "I did what I had to. Those men were after her."

"Then you should've called *me*," the dean says with a low tone that brings goose bumps to my skin.

"It's solved, isn't it? The bodies are gone. No one noticed." Silas shrugs.

The dean runs his fingers through his short, dark-brown hair. "Tell that to the lady who lives in the building across the street."

"Mrs. Schwartz?" I mutter. "She wouldn't tell a soul."

His eyes nearly bore a hole into my forehead. "If you want to stay alive, stay away from him."

Silas's face contorts. "I might be a fucking psychopath, but I would *never* let anyone lay a fucking hand on her."

I glance his way, my throat suddenly feeling clamped up.

"He's telling the truth," Heath says.

"Yet you can't stop leaving bodies everywhere you go," the dean says. "Why?"

"To protect *her*." Silas's green eyes flash with obsession, and I suddenly find it hard to swallow.

The dean crosses eyes with me before refocusing on his son. "Do you even know what you've gotten yourself into? Those men were part of the Bones Brotherhood."

Bones Brotherhood.

My skin begins to crawl.

"If your mother hears you've been messing with them, you're done for. Over," Dean Felix growls, and he grabs Silas by the back of the neck and goes head-to-head with him. "Do you hear me? You. Won't. Survive."

I swallow.

Jesus Christ. What kind of a woman is his mother?

"I can handle myself," Silas growls back.

"Yeah? You think you can protect her too?" He points at me now. "Whatever you three are doing, it stops right fucking now."

"I'm sorry," Max squeaks, but Heath puts his finger against his lips to shush him.

The dean turns around after another drawn-out stare toward everyone.

"And clean up this fucking mess. Undergrads are coming to the open day next week, and I don't want them to be discouraged from joining the Skull and Serpent Society because it smells like wet pussy." He frowns as his nostrils flare. "This is *my* fucking Society, after all."

He slams the door shut behind him, leaving the paintings on the wall quaking.

"Jesus," Max says, sitting on the chair in the corner.

"Tell me about it," Heath says, chuckling at Silas. "I see where you get your temper now."

"Shut up," Silas growls.

"What was your dad talking about?" I ask. "With the whole under-cover stuff. I thought her business was stealing from the Mafia?"

Silas narrows his eyes at me. "You want me to tell you all about my family business while telling me nothing about yours?"

I slam my lips shut. "Fine."

Silas rolls his eyes and sighs. "My mom's the head of an organization that infiltrates and destroys underground trafficking rings. There. Now you know."

I frown. "That's more than just the Mafia stuff you told me about earlier."

"Your turn," Silas says. "Care to tell me why literal Bones Brotherhood men were after you? The same men my mom's been hunting for years?"

I tilt my head. "They want something I have."

Silas makes a face. "What? Money? You?"

I swallow. I don't trust him enough to divulge the truth.

Heath snorts. "Wake up, Silas. She's not going to tell you."

"I told you the truth," Silas grits.

"I didn't force you to," I reply.

His fist balls. "Playing games again, thief?"

"Guys, guys, calm down. There's no point arguing when clearly she doesn't wanna tell for good reasons. Why else would she still keep it a secret?" Max says, getting between us.

"She still doesn't trust us," Heath says.

"She just needs a little bit more time," Max interjects, grabbing Heath's arm. "Please. You promised me we were done fighting over her."

He sighs and rubs his forehead. "Fine."

"Silas?" Max asks gently.

"How am I supposed to protect you when I don't even know from what?" he grits.

"Then don't. I never asked," I respond.

Silas scoffs, "And then what? Let you get dragged away by those fuckers? Is that what you want?"

I stare him down, fiercely holding my ground. "I'm done owing anyone anything."

The room grows quiet. So quiet it becomes awkward.

"So ... what do we do now?" Max asks.

"What do you mean, what now?" Heath frowns. "The dean was pretty clear. Let's go clean up the pool table. And the floor." He eyes his pants, which have a stain on them. "And ourselves."

Max snorts and hides his laughter with a smile.

I sigh and walk to the bar, grasping a bucket from underneath so I can fill it with water and a bit of dish soap.

"What are you doing?" Silas asks as he approaches me.

"What does it look like?" I reply, grabbing a sponge too. "You wanted me to clean, right? So get out of my way."

He pulls the bucket right out of my hand. "No."

He snatches the sponge away too and chucks it back into the sink. "I had a debt. You told me to clean, so I'm cleaning to clear that debt, and now you don't want me to clean. So which is it?"

"We have maids for that," he says.

He has got to be shitting me. "You say that now?"

"Yes. But you knew that already." He grabs a loose strand of my hair, playing with it like he's thinking about something, but I can't tell what. "You knew I liked watching you get filthy for me and clean up after me ... and you also know you enjoyed every second of your submission to me." He tucks my hair behind my ear. "Admit it."

I swat his hand away. "This is all transactional, that's it."

He grabs my wrist midair. "Is it? Or are you just too afraid of what else it might be?"

Panic flashes through my body.

I can't, it isn't safe. Cora needs me.

"Run from me again, and I *will* chase you," he says.

I frown. "Duly noted. Now let me go." I jerk free and pass by him.

Bagel enters through the door and zigzags through my legs, headed straight for Silas right when he was about to grab me again.

"Goddammit," Silas growls, trying to shake him off.

A short snigger escapes my mouth, but I stop it immediately when they all look at me. "He needs someone to play with him."

"And?"

I shrug. "You've got enough makeshift toys lying around here. Good luck."

"Wait, where are you going?" Max asks.

"To check on Cora by myself. Or do I need to be supervised within the house too?" I quip.

Max pouts. "But I still wanted to ... talk. About this." He circles his finger around the room, insinuating all four of us.

But I really, really don't want to talk, and especially *not* about this. Because whatever *this* is ... it's not good.

It felt good—it felt *too* good.

Their greedy kisses, their possessive touches, all the tongues everywhere, and God, those fucking dicks inside me made my entire body zing. Fucking them ... was like everything suddenly didn't matter anymore.

And that scares me.

"Not now ..." I say, opening the door while adding, "Please."

Max licks his lips. "I love you."

And I can tell from the way he says it that he truly means it. I feel it too, deep down in my heart, but the problem is that I'm not sure he's the only one, and that's what I'm not ready to face.

"I ..." I mutter.

"You don't have to say it if you're not ready yet," he adds.

Thankful for the grace he extends me, I smile back, then close the door behind me and head up the stairs.

***

SILAS

"What the hell am I supposed to do with this *thing*?" I growl, looking down at that cat prancing between my legs.

"What she told you," Max says, casually chugging down some water. "You play with it."

"Whatever," I say, rolling my eyes. "I don't have time for this." I open the door. "I want to know why the fuck the Bones Brotherhood was targeting her."

"Obviously, she has a beef with them," Heath replies, folding his arms. "How much you wanna bet she owed them money too?"

My eyes narrow. "That can't be it. There's a reason she was stealing from us. No thief would pay one debt by creating another."

"Except a thief who's desperate," Max mutters.

Desperate ... for what?

"Meow."

That demon is between my legs again, dancing around on its toes, rubbing its tail against my calf, and it's beginning to annoy the shit out of me. "What do you want from me?"

"He obviously likes you," Max says.

"Wrong person," I growl, and Max laughs at me. "C'mere then, you deal with this."

"You've been chosen by the Bagel." He shrugs. "I don't make the rules."

Max walks right past me.

"Hey!" I try to catch up, but this cat keeps following me everywhere, nearly making me trip. "You can't leave me with this *thing*."

"His name's Bagel!" Max calls back as he walks off.

"What am I supposed to give it? A dead mouse?" I grit, annoyed at myself that I'm even entertaining the idea of playing with this cat.

Heath grabs the curtain near the window and rips off the tassel. "How about this?" He throws it at me, and as I catch it, that cat leans up to claw at it.

"Jesus, it just tried to fucking claw out my eyes," I say.

"Oh, stop exaggerating." Heath laughs as he walks past me. "Good luck!"

"Hey, wait a second—You can't just leave me with this *Bagelthing*."

"I sure can. Try not to kill that *Bagelthing*," Heath replies, winking. "Unless you want to give *her* an actual reason to kill you."

FORTY-NINE

HEATH

The next day

Thwack. Thwack. Thwack.

"Can you please stop throwing that ball against the wall?" Max asks.

"No," I reply.

Thwack.

"I'm trying to read."

Thwack.

"I'm trying to think."

"About what?"

"Things," I reply.

Lots of things actually. I'm worried. Ivy hasn't attempted to talk to us at all about our situationship and retreats into the guest room after each meal. I don't know if she just wants to think or if she's just trying to ignore us until it's safe again to leave the Skull and Serpent Society and let us simmer in our own fucking stew.

Meanwhile, Max hasn't put down his book since yesterday, and I feel like I'm the only one worrying about this.

"What are you reading?" I ask.

"*Things,*" he says.

"Ha. Touché." I stop throwing my stress ball. "You don't wanna tell me."

He lowers the book and looks at me. "You wouldn't enjoy it. It's non-fic."

"Why do you assume so much about me?" I reply. "Haven't I already proven it's all wrong?"

His cheeks turn fiery red. "I just ..." He tucks it underneath his ass. "You and Mavis mostly read occult books and fantasy fiction, right? This is a self-help book."

"So?" I shrug. "Doesn't mean I can't also enjoy something else for a change." I sigh. "Besides, I haven't actually met up with Mavis in a while."

"Because of me?" he asks.

I take a deep breath. "Both of you."

He sits up straight. "I don't want you to stop seeing your friends just for our sake. You deserve friends that make you happy, and she does."

I stop throwing the ball. "You're too nice. Has anyone ever told you that?" He blushes even more now, and I get up to wrap my arms around his shoulders. "Too nice for your own damn good." I plant a succulent kiss right below his ear, and his entire skin erupts into goose bumps. "Too sweet ... and delicious ..."

His giggles make me grin. "We just had sex."

"So? We have to make up for all the missed fucking months," I reply.

"Have you always been this affectionate?" he asks.

"I hovered over you every single day. Is this the first time you've noticed?"

He laughs when I begin to caress his nipples. "Stop, that tickles."

"In a good way or a bad way?"

"Good ..." he moans when I draw a line with my tongue all the way from his ear to his neck. "But we really shouldn't be doing this here."

"Why? Scared someone will come in and see us?"

"I mean ... no one knows about us. Except Silas and Ivy," he replies.

I lean back. "Are you afraid people might assume you're gay?"

"I love you. But I love her too," he says.

"So what, you're bi." I tilt my head to look at him. "I am too."

He frowns. "Are you?"

"I am fucking drowning in need from wanting both you and her at the same time. Do you fucking think I'm anything but bi?"

He laughs, and the sound makes my heart swell.

"Case closed," I add. "And you know what?"

I wait until he looks at me. "What?"

I grab his chin and slam my lips onto his, claiming that mouth just like I claimed hers. "I don't care who knows as long as I get to kiss these fucking lips."

He smiles against my mouth. "That sounds like something I could get used to."

"Well, well, this is interesting."

Elliot's voice has Max darting up from the couch. "Oh, shit."

Elliot laughs. "Relax. Relax. It's fine. Carry on whatever you were doing."

"Wait, you're not shocked?" Max asks.

"Why would I be?" Elliot says with an affected accent. "Hello, it runs in the family."

I snort. "Like dad, like son, you mean?"

"*And* brother." He winks. "So ... happy coming out day, I guess."

"Thanks." Max licks his lips. "Please, don't tell Mom. Not yet. I'll do it when I'm ready."

Elliot puts his fingers to his lips and makes a key in a lock sign. "My lips are sealed."

"Why your mom in particular?" I ask.

"Because she's friends with *your* mom. They might not like you two fucking around, you know?" Elliot shrugs.

"They'll just have to fucking deal with it," I say.

Elliot grins. "That's the spirit." He clears his throat. "Hey, weird question ... why is there a kid in the Skull and Serpent Society?"

My face goes white. "Uh..."

Well, shit, I never thought I'd be the one to have to explain this.

"It's Cora. Ivy's kid," Max tells him.

"Both of them are staying," I say. "And I don't want anyone messing with the two of them. Make sure everyone in the house understands."

"Aye aye, captain," Elliot says, saluting me.

I roll my eyes. "Stop the theatrics."

"Why? I'm having the time of my life. Sue me," Elliot says, laughing before he grabs the handle again and slowly closes the door. "Enjoy your casual canoodling on the couch. Bye."

"Casual canoodling …" I parrot through gritted teeth, while Max is apparently dying from laughter so much he's holding his breath.

Someone shuffles into the room backward, half huddled over while making weird *pssss* sounds. And when I look up, my jaw drops. Silas is actually luring Ivy's cat into the room.

"C'mon, Donut."

"*Donut?*" Max sits up straight, and we both watch in shock as Bagel waltzes inside and eats up the kibbles … right out of Silas's hand.

He guides him all the way to the table and places a kibble down then says, "Up."

Bagel actually listens to him, and I am too flabbergasted to even know what to say. He's eating that shit up right out of his hand.

"Good boy." Silas pats him on the head and then says, "Paw."

Bagel offers his little toe-beans to him, and they shake on it before Silas offers another treat.

"What the fuck …" I mutter.

"Oh, you're here too?" Silas says, mildly amused.

"What are you doing?" Max asks.

"What does it look like I'm doing?" he replies. "I'm training the cat."

"Jesus Christ, that's a quick U-turn you did there," I say, tilting my head as Bagel literally cuddles up against him.

"This Donut here is a better listener than you two."

"Hey!" Max sputters. "That's not fair. He's a cat. Of course he listens. He gets food and pets."

"You want kibbles?" Silas holds up a treat, then chucks it at Max. "Say woof."

"Fuck off," Max barks back.

"Oh, nice bite," Silas says, laughing.

"Wait, you're training him for what?" I ask.

Silas shrugs. "Do tricks. Pick up stuff. Steal things. Maybe attack someone."

I stare at him for a moment before I burst out into laughter. "Bro thinks the cat is a goddamn pit bull. Oh my God, I'm dying."

He throws a kibble at my face so hard it leaves an indent. "You're laughing now, but I will make it happen. Just fucking watch me."

"Sure," I retort, chucking the kibble right back at him.

"For your information, the name is Bagel," Max says.

"Nice to fucking meet you, Bagel," Silas says, throwing Max a dirty look.

"Ha, ha, you're so funny," Max retorts, making the same ugly face back.

A knock on the door has us all looking up.

"Excuse me." It's the cleaning lady holding something in her hand. "I found this yesterday on the floor in the game room."

My ketamine.

I immediately walk to her and take them from her. "Thanks."

"Of course, Sir. If there's anything else you need, please let me know."

I nod, and she walks off again, but my eyes settle on the pills that Max knocked out of my hand the second I attempted to take a couple again.

These pills are all that have kept me standing for a long time. My mind has been one jumbled mess, and ever since my sister left too, I've struggled to maintain my calm without them.

But now ...

I breathe out a sigh. "You know, speaking of Mavis, I think I'm going to go see her."

"Really? But isn't that awkward?" Max mutters.

I tug at my piercing, trying to settle the nerves before I look his way and smile. "I need to make it right."

He smiles back. "Of course."

"I'm not planning on doing anything with her," I say.

"I know," he answers casually before picking up his book again.

I'm not used to us being so calm and ... out.

It's refreshing.

I head out the door and walk across campus to Mavis's sorority, where I knock on the door and wait for the ensuing giggles from the girls perched at the windows. I don't have to wait long for the door to open.

"Hi, Heath," some random girl I've never seen before says. "You here for Mavis?"

Do they all know? Probably.

I snort. "Is she here?"

"She's upstairs," the girl says, "I'll call her for you."

"Thanks," I say, and she closes the door.

I hear some footsteps running up and some muffled laughs. I peek at the window again, and all the girls duck for cover. I guess my good looks have all of them fumbling like schoolgirls. And I have to admit, it was definitely fun for a while. Especially to get some ass while Max wouldn't look my way. But now I have him and Ivy... and I no longer feel the need to fuck everything I see.

The door opens up again to Mavis tilting her head at me. "Heath. Nice of you to show your face again."

"Hi," I say awkwardly. "Can we talk?"

She folds her arms. "Sure. Go ahead."

"I wanted to apologize for ghosting you," I say, narrowing my eyes when the girls all start to giggle again. "I didn't mean to but my emotions got the better of me."

"Emotions?" She frowns. "For who?"

I take in a deep breath. "Ivy and—"

"Wait ... Ivy, as in that thief?"

I avert my eyes. "Things got ... complicated."

"Sounds like it," she says. "But wait, you said 'and' ... what else?"

I lean in and whisper, "Max."

Her eyes widen, and she looks at me with her lips shut even though I can see her actual jaw drop. She's basically gawking at me without actually wanting to show it.

"I told you, it's complicated."

"He's your best friend," she whispers.

"Yeah ..." I rub the back of my neck. "We still are. It's just that, now we're more. Together with Ivy."

Now her lips finally part as the shock begins to ripple through her entire body. "You're in a threesome?"

I shrug. "Four if you count Silas."

"WHAT?!" She steps out and shuts the door behind her. "You've got to be kidding me. Silas?!"

"Ha, yeah, it does sound like a good joke, but no," I reply. "We're all ... fucking with Ivy." I make a loop with my finger and shove the other index finger inside for added context.

But her godawful stare tells me that was a big mistake.

"Oh. Wow." Her face scrunches up. "No wonder you've been acting all odd lately."

"I'm sorry, I didn't mean to put you on the side-burner," I say.

She holds up a hand. "It's okay. You don't have to apologize."

I frown. "I don't?"

"You always asked me to hang out, not the other way around. So when you stopped, I kinda figured something important must've been going on." She swallows. "Though, I always thought you were just hanging out with me to get into my pants."

I rub my lips together. "I ..."

She takes in a deep breath. "It's fine."

"It's not. And I was a fucking asshole for trying."

She nods. "Yeah, you were. Lucky for you, I was pretty much the only girl who wasn't ever remotely interested in you that way."

"True, but I'm not just interested in sex, okay?" I grab her hand. "I want to be your friend. Please."

She smiles and narrows her eyes as she looks up at me. "You mean that?"

"Who else is going to curse these fucking teachers with me?"

The grin that spreads on her face makes all my worries disappear. "It's about time they got a taste of their own medicine."

I grasp her shoulders and pull her to me, hugging her tightly. "Goddammit, I missed you, Mave."

"Mave?" She pushes me away. "Nuh-uh, no way. That's what my brother calls me." She shivers violently. "The thought of hearing that from your mouth makes me want to puke."

I snort. "Oh, c'mon, you love him. Admit it."

"Only because I have to or my mother will kill me," she retorts. "Also, I doubt this will go well with Mom either if she finds out."

"Don't tell her I told you. Not yet," I say, lowering my gaze. "She'll kill him. Or all of us. And then Silas will torment me in the afterlife for telling you in the first place."

She sniggers. "Fine. I'll keep your dirty little secret, but you owe me."

I raise a brow. "What do I have to do?"

She pulls open the door with a mischievous look on her face. "Time to walk that fucking talk and get to work. I just got a séance board, and I'm ready to put that bitch to good use."

My jaw drops. "A séance board!?" The grin on my face grows even wider as I step inside and slam the door shut behind me. "Count me the fuck in."

***

SILAS

That night

From the corner of the street, I watch two fuckers enter the grimy building and head up the stairs. I lift my visor and take a picture of their faces before they're out of sight.

I hop off my bike and park it far away from the building before I head across the street, which has apparently been thoroughly cleaned since the last time I was here. Not a speck of blood is left from my rampage. I'm impressed. Mom's men really do their job diligently.

I tap each bell until finally someone answers. "Yes?"

"Delivery," I reply.

The door opens, and I swiftly step inside.

There is no delivery except death for whoever gets in my way, and they won't know until it's too late.

I sneak up the stairs, careful not to make a noise. Once I finally get to the floor they're on, I hide behind a pillar near the elevator and peek around the corner to watch two men as they break in the door to Ivy's apartment.

Of course, they'd come here.

The men who were sent to get her were lackeys after all, and there are plenty more waiting to be told what to do by their boss. And I intend to find out whoever the fuck it is.

I don't need her to tell me who's after her. I'll just make them tell me instead.

I sneak closer and hide behind the next pillar so I can listen in to their conversation.

"They're not fucking here," one of them says.

"I told you that!"

"Don't blame me. The boss told us to go look again. See if she came back."

"What the fuck are we even doing here?" one of them complains. "It's not like the others already came in here a million times. They're not here, and none of this is worth anything."

"Doesn't matter, the boss doesn't even want any of this shit."

"I thought he was a money-hungry wolf."

One of them snorts. "You think she has a lot of cash? Living like this? I doubt it."

They both laugh.

So the guy who orchestrated all this definitely isn't after the money ... but after her.

"You think the girl will come back?"

"Maybe. Looks like she left in a hurry."

And I'm fucking glad she did because these fuckers would've found her by now.

"Let's leave a note just in case."

"Why?"

"Ivan said she'll definitely have more up her sleeve, and he wants to force her to give up."

Ivan? Who the fuck is Ivan?

Is that the guy who's after her?

I approach the door, listening carefully as they plant some kind of paper on the kitchen table.

"Let's go."

That's my cue.

I fish my knives out of my pockets and move away from the hiding spot, slowly coming into view as those fuckers exit the door and freeze while the grin on my face spreads from ear to ear.

"Who the fuck are you?" the guy on the left asks.

"Why the fuck is he smiling like that?" the one on the right whispers, but I heard.

I flick both knives in my hands. "Do you think the devil cried or laughed when he took unsuspecting souls back to hell?" The angered looks on their faces makes the thought of slicing them open from top to bottom even more enticing. "Now who's first?"

FIFTY

IVY

Tonight is the night.

I wait until everyone is sleeping. Then I sneak from room to room, hall to hall, until I find what I'm looking for: A bed and a little girl still deep in her slumber while hugging her cat. I drag her out of bed and shake her to wake her up quickly, but nothing feels real, not even the way she looks at me. Her tiny hand sits snugly in mine as I bolt off with her and the cat through the endless hallways.

But the walls feel like they're caving in on me, and the doors feel endless.

I pause and shush her silently while we wait for a guard to pass the stairs so we can sneak past.

"Let's go," I whisper, but my voice sounds muffled in the void.

I pull her along while holding the cat tightly, and we head through the corridor and down the stairs into the garage.

"Ivy!"

A loud voice echoes through the hallways, and the light fixtures flicker.

Over and over again, the voice booms from ear to ear as it gets closer and closer while sweat begins to drip down my neck.

I hold the girl closer as I run toward the only bike in the garage, put her on the seat together with the cat, and jump on.

Get out, get out, get out.

If I get caught ... I'll die.

I sit up straight in bed, breathing wildly as the sweat tumbles down my forehead. I immediately look to my right, where Cora is still happily snoring away, and I smile at her content little face.

I wrap the warm blanket tightly around her little body and get up. Every time I wake up in this house, the unfamiliar feeling tightening like a noose around my neck strengthens.

It's not safe.

But where else am I supposed to go?

A knock on the door pulls me from my thoughts. "Ivy, Cora, are you awake?"

It's Max. "Come in."

He opens the door softly and peeks inside, but when he sees her, he melts. "Aw ..."

I put my finger to my lips. "Don't wake her, please."

"It's been tough on her moving here, huh?"

I suck in a breath. "It's not the first time she's had to do it."

He frowns. "Oh?"

Shit. Maybe I shouldn't have said that.

I avert my eyes and clear my throat.

"So, uh, school," I mutter.

He rubs the back of his neck. "Right, I almost forgot about that after this weekend."

But I'm far too concerned about Cora to worry about what happened between us four. "What am I supposed to do about Cora? I can't bring Mrs. Schwartz here."

He steps inside. "You don't want to take a break from your classes?"

I shake my head. "Not a chance. Going to this university means too much. I can't waste this opportunity."

He nods a few times. "I understand."

"You do?"

"Yeah, you don't want to jeopardize your future, and this college feels like the only way out. Did I get that right?"

My cheeks heat. "I ..."

"You know what? I'll ring my own au pair, Mrs. Davey."

"Your what?"

"Au pair. A live-in-nanny," he says, like it's the most normal thing ever. "Mom hired one to take care of me and my siblings while she was at work. Mrs. Davey is such a sweetheart. She adores kids. I swear, you'll love her."

"Can I trust her?"

He pulls his phone from his pocket. "Absolutely. I'll PM her right away. See if she can come today."

I'm surprised he still knows her phone number after all these years. He taps away on the phone lightning-fast until he tucks it back into his pocket and says, "Done."

My jaw drops. "Wait, what? You got her to agree to babysit Cora for me? That's quick."

He smirks. "Yup."

I hold up my hands. "But that bill—"

"Taken care of."

Wow. The confidence he says that with makes my spine tingle in such a good way I nearly want to do a little jiggle to get rid of it.

"I told you I want to help," he says, tilting his head in such a sweet way that it melts my heart. "And if I can do anything to ease the load on the heart of the girl I love, then I will do it." He winks. "Now, let's get to class."

***

"You didn't tell me I was going to be turned into a bodyguard." Heath takes a drag of his cig before he chucks it onto the gravel below his feet and stomps on it. "People will talk."

"So?" Max shrugs. "I don't see the issue, honestly."

"What's going on?" I ask.

Heath throws his arm over my shoulder, pulls me close, and points at Max. "That guy over there is using me."

"Like you haven't used me too," Max retorts.

Heath narrows his eyes. "That was different."

"You wanted me to seduce her, I want you to protect her while we get to class. We get to be obsessed. Any problem?"

"I never said I had a problem with that part," Heath jests. "But the three of us together will definitely raise eyebrows."

"Four," Max says, wriggling his brows. "But who's counting?"

Heath sighs and raises his brow at him. "You're awfully content with yourself, aren't you?"

The smirk on Max's face is too cute. "I take pride in being as annoying as possible."

"Good." Heath releases me and rubs his fist through Max's hair until it's all messed up. "Keep it that way."

"Goddammit," Max growls, making me laugh.

"But where the fuck is Silas?" Heath asks, checking his watch. "He's supposed to be here for his classes. They're about to start."

I pull my bag closer to my shoulder. "I haven't see him in a while, actually."

"I think he needs some time to think too," Max says.

"About what? Murder?" Heath scoffs, snorting.

"Wait, he hasn't talked to you guys either?" I ask, looking at them both.

They shrug in unison.

I frown. "And it doesn't bother you?"

"That's just how he is," Heath says.

"Sometimes he just vanishes off the face of the earth for a couple of hours. Sometimes days." Max looks around to see if anyone's listening. "Maybe to get rid of his 'urges.'" He makes quotation marks with his fingers.

"Whatever, it's not our problem, and if he doesn't ask, I'm not helping," Heath says, throwing his bag over his shoulder. "You have class soon. You coming, or what?"

"Who told you about my schedule?" I say as I walk behind him.

He glances at Max over his shoulder and winks.

Max just grins awkwardly, making me laugh.

"He's an obsessed little twink," Heath says.

"Heath!" I stop in my tracks. "Oh my God, you did not just say that."

Heath shrugs again.

Max chuckles. "Twink? Hmm. It does have a ring to it."

"Really?" I mutter.

"Fine then, little twink, guard our little thief," Heath says, adding another wink while he comes to walk beside me. "If those fuckers came to attack her out on the street, they're definitely not afraid to try it here."

"C'mon, guys, I'm fine," I say.

"Let me do this, please," Max says, grabbing my hand. "Just for now."

"And me," Heath says, grabbing my other hand. "I don't fucking care how long, as long as you're safe."

Before I know it, they've pulled me inside against my will.

"But wait, what if someone sees us like this?"

"You're mine, and I don't care who sees," Heath says.

"Ours," Max corrects.

"Fine. But *you're* mine too," Heath growls, making Max blush too.

"Wow ..." The unimpressed mumblings from a partially green-haired bombshell known as Sunny Reed standing in the corner make me swallow away the lump in my throat. "Two guys, huh?"

"It's none of your business, Sunny," Heath retorts.

"Uh, did you forget he's my brother?" she retorts, pushing herself off the wall to get in their way. "Anything he does, I make it my business."

"Whatever. Just don't get in our way," Heath says.

Sunny grabs Max's arm, stopping us all. "Are you okay, lil' bro? Just say the magic word."

"Magic word?" I mumble.

She looks me up and down, slightly less unimpressed but with an obvious smirk on her face. "I guess you'll do."

Wow. I don't know if that was a compliment or an insult. Maybe both.

"I'm proud of you, lil' bro," she says, slapping him on the chest a couple of times. "But she's got her other hand locked with Heath-Emo-Ledger over here, and I don't know if you intended to share?"

"*Ledger*?!" Heath growls. "My name is Heath fucking Preston."

"Relax, wrinkle-dick, I wasn't talking to you," Sunny says, lowering her eyes at him.

Heath's hand squeezes mine. "You fuckin—"

"She's my sister, Heath. Please keep it civil," Max says, putting his hand against Heath's chest right before he's about to barge over to her.

"Civil?!" Heath growls. "You heard what she called me!"

Sunny laughs. "Be glad. I rarely give anyone a compliment like that."

Heath pulls up his sleeves. "Okay, that's it."

"We're together. All of us," I blurt out just to stop the fight that's about to start.

And it wasn't just Sunny who heard me say it. The entire hallway did, and everyone, literally everyone, is staring at us.

Oh God.

I slam my hand in front of my mouth.

"What ...?" Sunny says with a low tone, her face completely gone off the rails stone-cold. "You're together, as in, the three of you?"

"Four, actually, if you count Silas," Max says, with an obvious blush on his face. "But he's only with her."

"Silas ..." she mutters. "*Silas* has a girlfriend?" Then she bursts out into laughter. "Oh my God, this is too funny." She wipes away a tear, and her smile disappears almost instantly as she focuses her gaze onto Heath. "If it wasn't for the fact that you're fucking *him*."

Max butts in and comes to stand between them. "Don't start a fight on my behalf now, Sunny. It's not worth it."

"Fuck me ..." Heath grunts, wiping his face.

"Sorry," I say.

"It's fine. I'm not worried about what anyone thinks," Max says, shrugging it off. "And Sunny doesn't get a say in who I date."

"Whatever," she says, shrugging too. "I'm not gonna protect you from Mom, though."

"Then don't tell her," Max says.

"Like I have time," she retorts. "Good luck with keeping this from her, though." She puts her fingers to her lips and gives him an air kiss. "See ya later, lover boys."

"Bye," Heath growls at her. "Good riddance."

Max slaps him on the chest. "C'mon. She's not that bad."

"She's worse than that," he says.

"She's protective of me. That's a good quality," Max says.

"*I'm* protective," Heath says, pointing at his own chest. "She's nosy. There's a big difference."

"Nosy or curious?" I say, winking to lighten the mood.

"Doubt it. She has boys literally lining up to fall over themselves to let her stomp all over their hearts. This whole foursome thing is nothing unfamiliar."

"Noted," I reply.

"But you already knew that," Max says, checking his phone. "Anyway, let's get to class. We're late."

"Shit," I mutter to myself before running off.

Max and I walk into the room that we're supposed to be in and swiftly wave goodbye to Heath, who has to attend a different class.

"Late again, Miss Clark?" The teacher, Mr. Alec Caruso, places his book down on the table and throws me a stern look. "And you, Mr. Fletcher. Out of all people, I'd expect to be on time." He raises a brow at Max.

"I apologize, honestly," Max says. "It won't happen again."

"It'd better not. Same goes for you, Miss Clark."

"Yes, sir," I reply, taking a deep breath.

"Take a seat," Mr. Caruso says, still carrying that emotionless face.

Max and I walk up to some empty benches in the back and sit down, ignoring annoyed looks from other students.

I put down my books and wait until Mr. Caruso continues his lecture before I whisper to Max. "Doesn't Silas also have this class?"

He nods. "His dad's the dean. Silas's attendance doesn't matter. Only money does."

Well shit. If only I had someone to fix my life with the snap of a finger.

"Lucky him," I say.

"You wouldn't say that if you'd met his mom," he says.

"She's really that bad, huh?" I ask.

"Not bad. More like ... terrifying."

I laugh. "Well, I can't wait to meet her, then."

***

HEATH

Hours later

After my classes are over and the sun's about to set, I head outside for a much-needed cigarette break before it's time to grab some dinner with the boys. But when I pull the packet of cigs from my pocket, the bottle of Ketamine spills out too.

I pick them up from the ground and stare at the bottle for a moment.

Do I continue as usual? Do I slowly taper them off? Do I quit in one go?

Would I be able to live without them?

My phone buzzes, pulling me out of my thoughts. I fish it out of my other pocket to see who it is. My dealer is calling me. Odd. I'm normally the one to call him first.

"One sec, let me get somewhere safe first," I say as I pick up.

"Sure ... I got time," he replies.

I walk across the path and go behind the second university building, where people only go to smoke and fuck in secret. "What's up?"

"You still need more pills?" he asks. "You haven't bought any for a while now."

"No. I'm ... slowing down." I clear my throat.

It's not an easy decision, but I owe it to Max. To Ivy. To myself.

"You sure? Because I have this crazy deal right now where you get a bottle of whatever you normally want, plus an additional bag of coke. How does that sound?"

I frown and run my fingers through my hair. "I don't know, man."

"Come to the gate," he says.

I push myself off the wall and walk across campus some more until I get closer to the gate. My dealer is right there, waiting in his car.

That's ballsy.

"Hey," he says, and I lower my phone.

I look around to make sure no one saw me come here before I head out the gate and approach the car. His arm is hanging out of his window, and he's not wearing any protective gear to hide the obvious gnarly-looking scar on his face. "What the fuck are you doing here?"

"I was just ... looking around."

"It's dangerous here," I say, leaning over. "You know that."

"Trying to spot more customers," he adds. "You know how the business goes." He grins. "Hey, you wouldn't happen to have seen this girl, have you?" He holds up a paper with a poorly printed photo on it, but the moment those downturned lips and those striking eyes appear, it feels like the world is caving in on my fucking feet.

"She stole something that wasn't hers to take."

Fuck.

"What did she steal?" I ask.

His lip curls up. "A girl."

Fuck no.

It couldn't be ...

Cora?

FIFTY-ONE

HEATH

I try to take a breath, but my throat feels constricted.

"No, I haven't seen her," I lie.

She couldn't have ... stolen Cora from someone, could she?

"Yeah, good luck with that, Ivan," I say, tapping the car before I walk back to the gates.

"I'll find her," he yells after me, and I stop in my tracks. "I know she's here."

His car swerves around, and he races back down the mountain.

While the bottle of pills in the palm of my hand cracks.

Ivy didn't just steal money ... She stole a human being.

No wonder she didn't want to tell us anything.

She's not just a thief but a liar too.

And a good one at that.

She almost had me fooled.

My phone buzzes, and I check who it is. Silas.

A smile forms on my face when I read his message.

Silas: I know who's after her.

Good. The truth beneath the lies will always surface ... Time's up.

***

IVY

In the middle of my last class for the day, my phone suddenly buzzes. I fish it out of my pocket at the same time Max does, but it doesn't register properly with me as I'm too busy focusing on the message appearing on my screen.

Psycho: Come to The Shack. One hour.

I frown, staring at the screen, confused as fuck.

Me: Why would I do that?
Psycho: I want to show you something. A gift.

Okay. Ominous.
Max looks up from his phone, mortified.
"What?"
He holds up his phone, showing me the exact same message about a gift meant for me. And my blood begins to run cold.
Fuck.
I look at the clock, but the seconds feel like hours as they slowly pass while I chew on my lip and flip my pencil back and forth. I hate that I have my last class so late in the afternoon that the sun's already setting because my stomach is rumbling, and I'm hoping for dinnertime soon. A dinner I doubt will happen because of my impending meetup with Silas and whatever the hell he wants to gift me.

I'm barely listening to the teacher anymore while I try not to succumb to the adrenaline slowly taking over my entire body. Every so often, I glance at Max who stares at me with equal worry marring his face. I wonder what he's thinking. If he'd even say it out loud.

I swallow away the lump in my throat as the final minutes begin to pass. I still manage to catch some final words from my teacher before he tells us our assignments for next week.

I grasp my bag, stuff everything inside, and bolt off.

Max catches up behind me. "You thinking what I'm thinking?"

"Shack," I say. "ASAP."

He chucks his bag over his shoulder. "What do you think Silas wants to show us?"

"I don't know, but it can't be anything good," I reply, waltzing toward the exit.

"Wait, we gotta call Heath," Max says, and he pulls out his phone and calls him. But no matter how many times it rings, he won't pick up. "C'mon, dude. Don't flake on me now," Max mutters.

"Maybe he's still in class?"

Max shakes his head. "It ended ten minutes ago." He puts his phone back into his pocket. "Let's just go without him. I'm sure Silas messaged him too. He'll catch up with us later."

"Sure," I say, walking across campus.

He grabs my arm and drags me toward the Skull and Serpent Society house. "We'll take my bike."

"Oh God, why?"

"It'll be much quicker," he says, holding out a second helmet. "I promise, you'll be safe with me."

I take in a deep breath. "Okay, fine. You convinced me. Let's go." I put on the helmet and jump on behind him.

"Thank you for trusting me," he says before he knocks down his visor and revs the engine. "Hold on tight."

Max hits the gas and we race across campus, destroying a bit of grass and gravel in the process. He carefully manages to avoid people walking on the roads as we exit through the gates and head out onto the long winding road down the mountain. The wind blows through the forests around us and brushes through my hair, causing wisps to cover my helmet. I hold Max's lanky body tightly as we zoom down the narrow paths right beside the steep mountain with loose rocks lying around everywhere, but he expertly zigzags around them all.

Finally, we get to The Shack, and as he comes to a stop, I jump off and throw my helmet on the grassy ground.

"Wait, don't we need to prepare or something?" Max asks, following me inside.

"How? How could you ever prepare for Silas fucking Rivera?" I reply.

His mouth opens but quickly shuts again as he raises a finger. "Good point."

"Let's go." I push open the door and look around the pitch-black house. "Hello?"

A loud, muffled scream from upstairs fills the house, and goose bumps scatter my skin.

"Up here."

That was definitely ... Heath.

A tiny sliver of light is peeking through the door to a room upstairs.

Clutching the railing, I walk up the familiar stairs that still haunt me. The last time my feet touched these steps, I was running for my life away from them ... and now I'm slowly walking into their trap. Willingly.

All because of that one word.

Gift.

Something about it draws me in like a moth to a flame.

A promise of a life-altering moment ... worth the risk of death.

Because what is it that he wants to give me so badly it would make him miss out on his own classes?

I swallow the lump in my throat as I approach the bedroom door. The same bedroom where I hid from them the first time they came to find me.

But now, both Heath and Silas are hovering over the bed like they already found their prey. And it's not me they're after this time.

Because on that bed, strapped to each post, are two guys, back-to-back, with their mouths stuffed, and all of their nails pulled out.

All the blood in my veins runs cold.

Not only because of what he's done to them ...

But because I know these two.

Silas glances at me over his shoulder and grins, in his hands a set of pliers still dripping with blood. "So glad you're finally here. Isn't it nice to see old friends?"

FIFTY-TWO

SILAS

She stares at them like she's seeing two ghosts, and my, oh my, that fucking fear riddling her face is a sight to behold. God, it really gets me going.

I pull the stuffed rag from one of those fucker's mouths. "Go on, tell them what you told me."

The guy keeps his bloodshot eyes locked on her. "Please, help me."

Her lip begins to quiver. "Why? Why are they here?"

"I found them snooping around your home ... looking for money ... and you." I tilt my head and watch her reaction, then grab my bat and smack it into the fucker's knees.

He cries out in pain.

"Stop! Fuck, it hurts!" he shrieks.

I laugh. "You think this hurts? I could cut off all your fingers and your dick and make you eat them."

"Please, no." Sweat runs down his forehead. "Have mercy."

"Why were you in her apartment?" Max asks.

I point my bat at the guy's face. "Tell her who sent you."

Ivy shakes her head.

"Stefano sent me."

The mere mention of his name makes her pupils dilate and fill with rage.

There it is. That's what I was looking for.

"Shut up," she hisses.

"Why? Is he reminding you of something you don't want to remember?" Heath asks, looking at her with a stone-cold face.

"Who's Stefano?" Max asks.

"No one," she hisses. "No one you ever need to know about."

"But that's just it, little thief … I do. I want to know." I approach her slowly, sliding my fingers across the headboard. "I want to know more than anything." I bring my bloodied fingers to her forehead. "What makes you tick." And I tap. Once. Twice.

She swats away my hand when I attempt it for a third time, and it brings a wicked smile to my face.

"I told you, it's none of your fucking business."

"Is it? Or is it just because you don't want to admit to whatever you did that made you piss off these fuckers?" Heath asks, his face still emotionless and deadly like he's lost all will to care.

I smirk. "You stole from them, didn't you?"

She lifts her fist, but I grab it just in time. "You're taking your anger out on the wrong dude."

I force the palm of her hand open and shove the bat inside.

"You hate them, don't you?"

She seems confused, then apprehensive, at first, as I step aside and point at the guys.

"Go on … give it your best shot."

She clutches the bat tighter, and the determination suddenly flickering in her eyes makes me so goddamn hard I nearly come right there and then.

"I told you I had a gift for you …" I whisper into her ear as she hovers closer and closer to the two guys I have strapped to the bed. "So take it."

"Ivy, you don't have to do this if you don't want to," Max says, but she's not even listening anymore. I can tell from the way her eyes have glossed over.

"Wait! You can't do this to me. I'm—"

She lifts the bat and swings …

Right into the fucker's face.

His jaw dislodges and knocks sideways, teeth flinging left and right. Blood spatters everywhere, and I'm on the verge of pronouncing my fucking undying devotion to this fucking girl. This girl who is every bit as fucked up as I am.

"You fucking thought you could come to my house and take Cora?!" she screams, and she hits him again, this time straight in the nuts, blood splattering onto the bed, and the other guy, his screeches fill the room like a crescendo of madness.

I made her a monster.

My own vicious little monster.

And I am so fucking proud.

She drops the bat on the floor and steps back to witness the on-slaught she just created like a dazed animal headed straight for the lights. But I grab her face with bloodied hands and make her focus on me.

"This is what you needed. This is what you deserved. Revenge." I plant my forehead against hers, smearing the blood all over us both. "You're such a fucking good girl for me, aren't you? Now help me take care of the other one."

"No, no, no, please!" the guy begs.

I look up, grinning at how badly he's already soiled his pants from the thought of being callously murdered by the girl they thought they could chase.

But she is all mine.

Mine to hunt.

Mine to catch, taint, and devour.

My delicious little prey.

And I will cheer her on while she wreaks havoc on these fuckers like it's a blood rain day from hell.

"Please, Ivy, it's too late. Ivan already gave the order."

She stops in her tracks even though she was about ready to swing.

"The dealer," Heath mutters to himself.

Ivy's eyes twitch as she looks up at him. "You know Ivan?"

Heath lowers his gaze and starts to disengage emotionally. "I know more than you think."

Well, this is getting interesting.

Ivy suddenly grabs the guy on the bed by the throat. "What order?"

The guy's eyes flicker between all of us, settling for a few seconds on Heath before he circles back to Ivy ... and laughs. "There's no more time left. This is all your fault. You can blame anyone you want, but this is on you. You should've paid him, kid."

My eye begins to twitch.

Is that what she's been doing?

Paying off a debt to some guy with our money?

She raises the bat again.

"Fuck! Please, it's not my fault," the guy cries. "I was just doing what I was told. Please, have mercy."

"Like you had on us?" she barks. "You know your fucking friends came for me."

"We were doing what we were told."

"You know damn well why you were told to do it!" she yells back. "You deserve the same pain I had to endure."

She lifts the bat high.

The man begins to laugh. "Killing me won't help you now. It's too late for you and your little Cora."

She pauses midair. "What?"

"Check my phone if you don't believe me. Ivan already told him everything he needs to know ... Stefano is coming."

Her whole face turns white as snow.

THWACK!

She hits him right in the head, knocking him out.

THWACK!

THWACK!

Blood oozes from his ears, but she keeps hitting him over and over until nothing is left except her anger slowly flooding out of her like the blood leaving her victims.

Her breathing comes out in ragged breaths when she stops, her clothes completely soaked through with blood as she chucks the bat aside.

Fuck.

Yes.

This is the one.

The one thing that can make my dead heart tick.

**

IVY

Two people, gone within an instant.

Wiped off this planet with the strength of my own two hands.

I stare at their mangled bodies and the onslaught I left behind.

I swore I would do anything to protect her, and I did.

Honest to the devil ... a murderer of his making.

My darkened eyes find Silas's lethal eyes from across the room, the red hue of annihilation flickering behind them, finally feeling familiar.

So this is what it's like to become a monster.

I wipe the blood off my face with the back of my hand. "Happy now?"

A proud fire rages in his eyes. "Well done."

"Is this what you wanted? To turn her into a fucking killer?" Max grits, as he barges at Silas and grabs his shirt. "You had no right."

Silas jerks free from his grip with ease. "She wanted this."

Maybe I did.

But could I ever say it out loud like he so proudly does?

"Bullshit," Max growls. "You did this for you."

Silas laughs in his face. "So what if I did? I do what I want, when I want. No one controls me."

Max shoves Silas forward, clearly upset he put me in this position.

But Max doesn't understand the visceral brutality hiding beneath these layers of endurance I've been forced to wear.

Max doesn't feel the need to blow up and destroy, but Silas does.

"Max is right," Heath says, stepping in. "What was the point of all this? You could've just killed them yourself."

"No. This was what she needed," Silas says, tilting his head at me like he's waiting for me to admit it.

But all I can do is stare at the two bodies like I'm waiting for them to come back to life just so I can kill them again.

He's right. I did need this.

Desperately.

More than any one of these guys could ever understand.

"She was being chased by a debt, and I took care of it," Silas adds.

But that's just it.

Killing these two didn't change anything.

The second they stopped me from looting the Phantom House, it was already over.

These fuckers know we were hiding at the Skull and Serpent Society.

Ivan knew ... because of *them*.

"No," I mutter, and everyone looks at me. "It only made it worse." I throw a damning glance at Heath. "You ... you know Ivan. You told him about my location."

"I did not," Heath growls back. "But you didn't tell us the fucking truth about Cora."

What?

My eyes flicker with unseen rage while I glare at Heath, the tension like crackling lightning.

Heath picks up the bloodied bat, gazing at it with intent before his eyes fixate on mine. "She's not yours, is she?"

Fuck.

That's it.

That's the one thing I told myself that would make me want to pull the trigger and blow up the whole thing.

For the first time since I met him, Silas genuinely looks shocked.

"W-What?" Max stutters. "You aren't her mom?"

"She's not going to give you the answer, Max," Heath says.

A kind of darkness that makes me shiver has fallen over Silas's face. "Once a liar, always a liar."

Fine.

He wanted me to break?

Force me to reveal the truth?

They can have it ... after they pry it from my cold, dead hands.

A deadly but disappointed smile forms on my face before I turn around and run.

FIFTY-THREE

MAX

The girl ... isn't hers? She's not Cora's mother?

No, that can't be right. This has to be a mistake. She wouldn't steal ... a child?

Heath nearly breaks the bat in two with just his fist.

Suddenly, she turns around and runs off down the stairs.

"Ivy, stop!" I yell, but she ignores me completely.

I bolt down the stairs and follow her out of The Shack. But she's already jumped on my bike, and my hands immediately fly to tear out my own hair. "Wait, that's my bike!"

She turns the handle to speed up, and the wheels skid in the grass, spraying mud everywhere.

Silas bolts out the door, yelling, "Do you even fucking know how to drive?"

"You don't understand what you've done!" she yells back, racing off.

"Oh fuck no." I fall to my knees. "No, my beautiful bike. What if she crashes it?"

Heath runs out the door too, growling, "Where is she?"

"Gone," I lament.

Heath throws the bat to the ground, incensed. "Fuck!"

"Where's she gonna go?" I mutter. "Everyone will see her covered in blood."

Silas fishes a cigarette from his pocket and lights it up. "Cora."

Heath's eyes flash. "You don't think she's gonna ..."

"She's gonna run," I mutter as I stumble to my feet. "Oh God, we gotta stop her."

"We can't," Silas says.

"We have to," I say, grabbing Silas by the shirt so he knows I'm serious. "If anyone sees her like that, they're gonna ask questions, and she'll definitely implicate us."

"Never mind that," Heath says. "What are we gonna do with those bodies up there? Penelope's men will definitely snitch. She'll kill you for real this time."

"I don't fucking care. It was worth it." Silas fishes his phone from his pocket. "I'll make one last phone call to my mom's men... and then we chase her."

***

IVY

I race up the mountain as fast as I can.

C'mon, c'mon, c'mon, you stupid bike, go faster!

I pull the handle harder, trying to zigzag past each rock on the street, just like Max did, but he made it look so effortless while it's so damn hard that I nearly lose control of the bike. With the sun quickly setting, it's becoming harder and harder to see. But I have to keep it together. I have to get to her before Stefano does.

Ivan was the anonymous phone number demanding money from me.

I knew it from the start because he's the one who caught me when I took Cora.

Ivan ... Stefano's most trusted personal guard.

The same fucking Ivan Heath bought those damn pills from.

Fuck!

I should've known he would rat me out.

I should never have trusted those devils from the Skull and Serpent Society.

Now it's going to cost me my life.

And Cora.

Fuck no. I'm not going to let them take her. Over my dead fucking body.

I race up the mountains and through the gate, all the way back to the Skull and Serpent Society, where I jump off and rush inside. There are a ton of guys now, all chatting about their day-to-day life, but they ignore me as I head up the stairs. Someone must've told them Cora and I were here and to act normal.

But it's not safe to stay here anymore.

I rush to Cora's room and quickly wipe down my face with my shirt before I open the door.

She's playing with a giant dollhouse that's filled to the brim with furniture and dolls. "Ivy!" She runs into my arms and hugs me tight, but then looks up at me in horror. "What's that ... on your face?"

I wipe away some more. "Paint." I look at the dollhouse, confused as hell. "That wasn't here before," I mutter.

"Heath gave it to me," she says.

I frown. "When?"

"This morning. He said it was a gift and that I could play with it as long as I'd like. Can I keep it, please?"

My heart aches for her.

"Oh, sweetie ..." I go to my knees. "I'm sorry."

"Can we stay here, please?"

Her begging will be my undoing.

"We can't, I'm sorry," I say.

She pouts. "But I like it here."

"I know you do," I say, hugging her again. "But this is a school. It's not a house."

"But plenty of other people live here. Everyone has their own room. That's a house, isn't it?"

She's got a point there.

"Yes, and no. Look, this was only supposed to be a temporary solution."

"But where are we going to go?" she asks, grabbing her little red flower lying on her bed and clutching it tightly.

Every answer I have to give her breaks my heart a little bit more.

"I don't know, sweetie ..." I blow out a deep breath. "We'll figure it out. I promise." I rub her little cheeks before I tuck her little red flower into her small pocket. "C'mon. Grab your things. It's time to leave."

I grab a bag from the closet and stuff it with clothes and shoes, then grab all of our belongings and her little hand and bolt off into the next room, Silas's room, to search for that same little box of money that I found the first night I came into this godforsaken house. I rip open all of his drawers until I find it hidden underneath his desk.

Gotcha.

I stuff it in the bag too. I'll worry about how to open it later. Even if only a couple of bills are inside, anything is better than nothing.

I rush through the Skull and Serpent Society house and haul everything downstairs.

"Why do we have to run so much?" Cora says, breathing wildly. "I can't, my feet hurt."

"Yes, you can. You must." I grip her hand tighter so I can focus on getting us to safety first.

BAM!

The moment my foot touches the last step, I'm blasted backward into the stairs as a loud explosion fills the room, and my head knocks back into the wood. The bag is flung out of my hands. I'm disoriented from the blast, and my ears are ringing and my eyesight has gone hazy. But I can definitely see four masked men barging into the house, guns pointed right at the other students.

Bang! Bang! Bang!

Gunshots fill the room with smoke and death, blood splattering everywhere. The screeching of students brings me back to the here and now, and I cover Cora with my own body to shield her from the rain of bullets.

Left and right, students go down instantly, unprepared for the sudden assault, but to my surprise, none of the bullets even so much as grazes my skin. I breathe in and hold it as hard as I try to hold my courage to keep Cora from feeling the fear taking hold of my heart.

Until hands wrap around my arms and drag me away from her.

"No, no, no!" I shriek, trying to maintain balance despite being hit in the head by what feels like a sledgehammer.

"Keep quiet, bitch," the guy who holds me says.

And I have to watch in abject horror as they drag me farther away from her ... while she screams my name.

"Ivy!"

Another guy picks her up and throws her over his shoulder. "Move!"

Even though I'm bleeding from the back of my head, I still knock myself back right into the guy's forehead.

"Fuck!" he yells.

And I kick back into his nuts and bite down on his arm, leaving a bloodied indent.

"Let me fucking go!" I scream.

But the more I kick and shove, the harder he clamps down on my body.

"This bitch bit me!" the guy yells at the others.

"Fucking handle it!" another one yells back. "We gotta get back to the van. Now!"

They march out the door with both of us, but the moment we're outside, we're split up.

"Cora!" I yell while I drag my feet on the ground to slow them down as we head farther and farther away from the Skull and Serpent Society, the only safety net I still have left. Down, down, down, into a dark void I'm shoved, and the only light I have is destroyed by two doors slamming shut.

But I don't care about any of that. I don't care if I have to rot in here for all of eternity as long as I know one fucking thing.

"Where's Cora?!" I yell. "Where is she?!"

FIFTY-FOUR

MAX

I've never seen Heath drive this fast up the mountain. He's so fixated on the road that I can't even get through to him.

"Hello, earth to Heath?" I say.

"Let him drive," Silas barks.

"Well, he wouldn't have had to if she hadn't taken my bike because
you scared her off," I retort, narrowing my eyes.

Even if Silas and Heath believe Ivy stole Cora, I know deep down
she did it for the right reasons.

Silas crosses his arms. "You're looking at the wrong guy."

"I didn't do shit," Heath growls back.

"She ran off because you said you knew Ivan," Silas says. "He's the
dude you got your pills from, right?"

"Yes, but how was I supposed to know he's been blackmailing her?"
Heath retorts, jerking on the steering wheel. "He told me she stole
Cora."

I hold my chair tightly, but the buzzing in my pants catches me off
guard. I fish out my phone and check, but message upon message of
screaming all caps has me on edge again.

"Oh no."

"What?" Heath growls.

I hold up my phone. "The Skull and Serpent Society is under attack."

Heath's eyes widen, and he immediately hits the gas even harder.
"Fuck!"

"It's those fucking Bones Brotherhood fuckers. I just know it," Silas grits. "They came for her, just like that guy at The Shack said they would. Fuck!"

Silas chucks his phone to the floorboard.

Heath swerves around the corner, nearly crashing into the gate as we get on campus. People jump aside to avoid getting hit by the car because Heath is focused on getting to the building as fast as possible.

My nerves get the best of me, and I gaze around in the dark to see what's going on, but there doesn't appear to be any cars or trucks or men left at the scene. My eyes widen at the sight of the blasted-in door and the drag trail across the grass, accompanied by obvious car or van tire marks.

Shit. Shit. Shit!

Once the car comes to a stop, I immediately jump out to bolt inside. "Cora? Ivy? Cora? Please, anyone!"

On the floor are dozens of students, all riddled with bullets. Including my own brother.

"Fuck, Elliot!" I go to my knees in front of him. He's been hit in the thigh.

"It hurts, it hurts so much!" He grips his leg in pain.

"Fuck, fuck, fuck." I rip off a piece of my shirt to wrap it around his leg. "I'm sorry."

"They're gone," one of the other guys says, spluttering up blood. "They only came ... to take the girls."

"Silas, Heath!" I scream over my shoulder. "I need help over here!"

Heath and Silas rush in behind me, but their faces grow cold at the sight of all the bodies littering the halls.

"Oh fuck," Heath mutters.

"Call an ambulance!" I yell.

Silas puts his phone to his ear. "Dad, the Skull and Serpent Society has been hit. I need help. Now."

Heath runs to another student and pushes down on the open wound in the belly created by a bullet. "I don't know what to do."

"Keep pressing on the wounds," I say. "Call more help."

"On it." Silas runs outside, where more people have finally gathered to see what's going on.

But even as dozens of my fellow society mates have been injured in what is undoubtedly the most heinous attack on campus grounds, and I am doing my best to split my attention between all of them to keep them from dying on me, my mind still wanders off to Ivy and Cora, and how fucking hard it hurts that I couldn't be here in time to save them.

**

IVY

I throw my body into the van's doors, again and again, like a crazed bull ready to fight off those matadors in a ring. My shoulder is bruised, and my arm feels like it's about to dislodge, but I don't care about the pain or my ringing ears.

I have to get out of this van.

I have to get out and find Cora.

Because if I don't ... everything we've been through, everything we've had to endure, everything I've had to sacrifice will have been for nothing.

"Let. Me. Fucking. Out!" I say through gritted teeth, still hammering the doors. "Let me out!"

The doors open right when I was about to charge into them, and I fall onto the muddy ground instead, my face hitting the asphalt first. Blood rivulets down my forehead, and I groan from the pain of falling on my head twice in a single day.

"Get her up."

Two strong hands drag me up by my arms, but the moment I lock eyes with Ivan, I completely forget any and all pain I felt before.

"You ..." I hiss.

He throws me a disgusted look. "I told you, you can't win this. You think I wanted to do this? You forced my hand."

"I didn't do shit. Where the fuck is Cora?"

He laughs. "Wouldn't you like to know..."

"Tell me!" I screech, kicking and biting with every inch of energy I have left.

"Not a chance," he replies, turning around.

"You promised! You swore you wouldn't fucking rat us out!"

He shrugs and glances at me over his shoulder, winking. "Guess you shouldn't trust just any man."

That fucking ... asshole!

"Fuck you, Ivan!" I yell, cursing the ground he walks on.

I look around and try to shake off the guards holding me back from jumping him and twisting his neck, but there are many more of them than there are of me.

"Bring her to the boss," Ivan says.

Panic bubbles to the surface. "No."

"Let's go," the guy behind me says, shoving me forward and dragging me along by my elbow.

"Tell me where Cora is," I growl at the guy behind me, but of course he doesn't reply.

That's just how these men are. Exactly how I remember them to be. Ignorant, mindless drones who only listen to one man.

Dread fills my bones at the thought, so instead, I focus on looking for a way out. There must be something I can do. Anything.

I swallow away the lump in my throat as we approach the big mansion. The one I swore I would never come back to.

Fuck.

I dig my heels into the gravel, but it's no use against this fucker's strength.

"Keep walking," he growls.

"If you hurt Cora, I will kill you," I say out loud, hoping Ivan hears too.

I can hear Ivan's laughter from inside the house. "You think you're the one we should fear?"

Shit. This is getting serious now.

If I step foot inside that house, my death is as good as certain.

So I make one last ditch effort by shoving both feet into the door-jamb and then knocking my head against my captor, butting him out of the way. Finally, he loses his grip, and I bolt off back across the path.

I have no choice. I have to run. If he finds me, he'll kill me.

I'll come back for Cora.

Suddenly, two hands wrap around my ankles, and I'm tipped over.

No, no, no!

"You think you can run from this?" Ivan yells from the house.

"Fuck you, you know he'll kill us both!" I scream.

"No ... I think he'll just kill you, and I will happily watch as he drains the blood from your body."

The guy who caught me drags me by my feet all the way back to where we started. When I kick and thrash, another one joins, each one hauling me by the ankles back into the house and across the threshold. The moment the door closes, panic takes hold of my heart.

"Hello, Ivy."

My blood runs cold.

Stefano.

"Leave us."

As the men drop me, I take a few breaths to pull out the residual courage from deep within. Then I grab the small table to my left and fling it toward Stefano, but he sidesteps to avoid it hitting him, and it crashes into the wall instead.

"Is that how you greet the man who welcomed you into his house?"

"You're not a man. You're a fucking monster!" I yell back.

He snorts. "The only monster here is you."

"Where is Cora?!" I scream at him.

"Inside. Safe," he says, going to his knees in front of me. The thick bristles of his mustache don't hide the wicked smile on his face. "Away from you."

My nostrils flare, and I spit in his face.

He wipes it off, then grasps me by the neck.

SLAP!

His flat hand hits me so hard my nose begins to bleed too.

"She's. Not. Yours," he growls, squeezing my throat so tightly I can't breathe.

Then he shoves me away.

"You will never see her again," he says.

I shake my head, rasping, "No."

"Yes." He throws me a devilish glance. "In fact, I think it's about time you learned what it means to steal from a man like me." He snaps his fingers, and the guys drag me farther into the hallway and into a room with just a bed and some machines bleeping away. Tubes are attached to the machine and lead all the way to a woman lying motionless in a bed.

And I hold my breath.

Perhaps forever.

As the tears I've been holding for so long finally begin to cascade down my cheeks.

"All this running, fighting, hiding, trying to escape my men, and for what?" he whispers into my ear.

And I whisper back, "Nothing."

"That's right." He places a hand on my shoulder. "You did this."

I shake my head, tears still marking my face with all the emotions I've kept bottled up for her sake. Cora always said I was strong, stronger than anyone she ever knew.

But this is where my greatest weakness lies.

The one thing that could shatter me into tiny little pieces.

Knowing that, after everything I did, it still wasn't enough to keep everyone I love safe.

I whisper, "I'm sorry."

Stefano wickedly sniggers behind me. "Sorry won't save you now."

FIFTY-FIVE

HEATH

When the ambulances have finally arrived to help take care of the wounded and bring them to a hospital, I head upstairs to see where Silas has run off to. There's ruckus in the weaponry, and when I peek inside, he's throwing all the knives and guns into two big bags.

"What are you doing?" I ask, clutching the doorjamb.

"What the fuck does it look like?" Silas replies. "I'm gonna fucking rescue Ivy."

"What about Cora?" I ask. "Does she even need to be saved? Whoever has her must've taken her back to her real parents. That's why they came for her."

He pauses and looks at me like I'm the one being weird.

"Ivy stole her from that Stefano guy," I add.

"I don't fucking care what she did." He stands up and looks me dead in the eyes. "Ivy belongs to me. Not him. And I'm taking back what's mine, with or without anyone's help. End of story."

I frown. "But what are you gonna do with Cora? Leave her there?"

"I'll figure that out when I get there." He grabs his bags.

"Wait."

"Why? So you can try to convince me to stay?"

"No, I—"

He pushes me aside. "Then get out of my way."

I follow him down the stairs, unsure of what to do. I'm torn since I found out she stole Cora away from another family. Was she ever even truthful to begin with, or was everything, including us, a lie to keep them safe?

The medics downstairs are busy tending to the wounded, with Max aiding them as best as he can. Silas's father has arrived along with a bunch of cops, keeping the scene free from curious onlookers, as well as marking down the scene of the crime.

"That's a lot of people who got injured on your watch, Rivera," a cop says.

"Trust me when I say it won't fucking happen again," the dean growls back. "I'll run by each and every one of my guards to see where the weak point is." He cracks his knuckles. "These fuckers slipped through the cracks." He focuses his gaze on the cop. "I'd appreciate it if you'd let me solve this, Foley."

Agent Foley scoffs, "Not a chance." He opens his notebook. "This is going on the record. All of it."

The dean seems pissed, but I'm far too busy figuring out what I need to do now to be worried about some cops flooding the Skull and Serpent Society. Dean Rivera will no doubt handle it well.

I walk out the front door, where Elliot Fletcher is being lifted into a van so they can cart him off to the hospital.

"Don't worry about me, I'm okay," Elliot says. "Besides, Mom's going to be there."

Max nods as he follows the cart out. "Are you sure?"

"Take care of the others," he says. "And find her."

Max nods.

Find her.

His words reverberate in my ears until I get so sick of it, I punch my own fucking head to get rid of it.

"What's wrong?" Max asks me.

"What are we gonna do?" I mutter.

"I know what the fuck I'm gonna do," Silas growls as he waltzes past us.

But his own dad stops him and grabs the bag. The long-drawn-out sound of metal cling-clanging against each other as he shakes the contents makes everyone pause.

"Where the fuck do you think you're going with that?"

"To get Ivy. Don't even fucking try to stop me."

His father furrows his brows, the pause before he speaks as deadly as the look in his eyes. "Those fuckers you left for dead on the street came to get payback. This is on you."

Silas grinds his teeth. "Get out of my way."

"Or what? You're gonna kill me too?"

"Jesus," one of the other students mutters.

"Family feuds," I say, shrugging at the guy to defuse the tension.

"Who is Ivy?" his father asks.

Silas lowers his gaze intently. "*That* girl."

His father's eyes twitch, and his nostrils flare. Then he closes his eyes and says, "Do you need my help?"

"I can handle it," Silas says, walking right past him.

I'm amazed at his brazen courage against the only man who could quite literally make him stop with just one finger. Or maybe he just needs her so much it negates any and all reason.

My eyes widen.

That's it.

I bolt past his father too and follow Silas outside to steal the bag.

He snarls, "You'd better have a good reason to—"

"I'm coming with you," I interject.

He stops and looks me up and down. "Why? I thought you didn't trust her anymore?"

I shrug, smirking. "I changed my mind."

A cocky smile spreads on his face. "And here I was thinking you got too butt hurt by her betrayal to your sappy little heart." He opens the car door. "Fine then, let's fucking go."

"Wait for me!"

We both turn around to look as Max runs out of the Skull and Serpent Society, breathing wildly.

"I'm coming too," he says.

"Thought you were busy in there taking care of the wounded," Silas says.

"The medics are here now. There's not much I can do anymore, and I wanna help."

"You wanna help?" Silas pulls something out of the bag before he throws it at him. "Carry this for me while I figure out how we're gonna get inside."

"Inside? You know where they've taken her?" Max asks as we all hop into the car, me behind the wheel, Silas in the front, and Max in the back between all the weapons, which he cuddles like they're his kids.

"Not yet." Silas grins as he puts on the red purge mask, and then hands me and Max one too. "But we know a fucker who does. And Heath knows just where to find him."

***

IVY

Her body is a mangled mess, full of scars and bruises, as she lies in the bed like a porcelain doll, surrounded by bleeping machines. She's dancing the balance between life and death, but nothing about her feels alive.

He left me alone with her so I could bear witness to the power he holds and feel small. Unimportant. Insignificant.

Just like anyone else who gets in his way.

The last laugh he gave me before he waltzed out and sealed me in here with her sealed my fate.

Beep.

Beep.

Beep.

And something in me snaps.

I walk to the machines and rip out the wires one by one until nothing is left, and the beeping fades into a never-ending one.

Just like the hatred in my soul.

Tick. Tock.

The clock moves on.

And so will she.

Tears run down my face for minutes before it's finally over.

The door is slammed open.

"What have you done?!" Stefano barges inside and shoves me away from the machines.

"Too late," I mutter.

He grabs the wires and tries to reattach them, but it's no use. She'll never return to him.

A smile forms on my face.

THWACK!

The first punch lands the hardest, and I'm knocked back onto the floor.

"How fucking dare you?!"

His voice booms through the room.

THWACK! THWACK!

Still, I can't stop laughing.

He grabs me by the throat. "You kill her, and you're laughing?"

"She's free." I smile. "And I will be too soon."

"I will fucking kill you," he spits.

"Go ahead," I murmur.

"You think I won't do it?" he growls.

"Do it. Before they're here," I whisper.

"Who?"

I grin. "The boys hunting me."

For a moment, he stares at me in disbelief.

And all I can do is laugh.

"Fine, you want to play rough? I'll play along," Stefano growls, and he rummages around in a drawer until he finds what he's looking for, fishing out a dangerous-looking handmade device. "I knew you'd try to rope others into your little scheme, so I came prepared."

My eyes widen as he pulls out a rope too.

But before I can crawl away, he kneels on top of me, punching me so hard I nearly lose consciousness.

He rips the earpieces from my ears, leaving me in silence.

Each punch fades into the other as I lie woozy on the floor.

Everything is spinning.

I'm not sure I care.

My vision is blurry, and I've lost track of time.

All I know is that this ends with me.

**

SILAS

The moment Ivan spots us as we approach his usual spot where he sells his drugs, he tries to run back to his car, but I swiftly chuck one of my knives at him. It lodges into his back, and he cries out in pain as he tumbles over his own feet and falls to the ground.

He attempts to crawl away, but I grasp him by the shirt. "You think you can get away with what you did?" I growl as we haul him off the ground and shove him against the wall.

"Not so tough now, are you?" Heath growls.

"Heath, we're buddies, aren't we?" Ivan says, trying to butter him up. "I sell you my best stuff."

"You're just in it for the money, and I'm not your buddy, you fucking rat," Heath growls.

Heath smashes his face into the wall.

"Fine, I blackmailed her. So what?" the guy growls. "I helped her escape, and in turn, she helped me. Big deal."

"Bullshit! You didn't fucking help her, you used her!" Heath growls.

"Stefano has her now. It's no use anyway trying to hurt me. It won't get her back," he says.

I lean in and growl, "I will fucking rip each and every one of your fucking fingers out of your fucking hands and shove them up your own fucking ass if you don't tell me where she is right now."

"You think you can save her?" Ivan laughs.

Heath grabs his hand and pushes it to his back, side-eyeing me, so I tug at the guy's index finger and cut it off cleanly.

He cries out in agony, immediately pissing his pants when I hold the finger up in front of his face.

"I gave you an opportunity to tell me right off the bat, but you chose the hard way instead," I say. "I'm gonna enjoy listening to you cry for death instead of ten of these going up your ass in one go without lube."

Heath rips down his pants.

"No, no, no, please! I'll tell you," he begs, shivering from sheer terror.

"Speak up," I say, contorting his wrist the wrong way so he's in misery.

"She's at Stefano's house ..." he whimpers. "Please, don't do this, let me go. I swear, I won't blackmail her anymore. Or anyone else. I'll stop. I swear."

My nostrils flare. "Give me the address."

"It's in my phone," he says, sweating profusely as he eyes his own back pocket. "In there."

Heath plucks his phone from his pants. "How do we unlock this fucker?"

I grab his thumb and cut it off. His yelps are like music to my ears.

I throw the thumb to Heath. "Try this."

"Why'd you have to cut it off?!" Ivan cries out. "I would've opened it!"

"Because you need to learn a lesson or two about what it means to steal my girl from me," I reply, grinning against his ear. "We have a special trophy case to display our enemies' limbs."

His pupils dilate. "What?"

I cut off his pinky for good measure, and the wail that follows is so goddamn satisfying.

"Got it," Heath says, holding up the phone to show me the address.

"Perfect. Let's tie him up and stuff him in the trunk."

Heath grabs the rope and wraps it around his wrists and abdomen, sealing him in.

"Why? Please, let me go. You don't need me," Ivan begs.

"No, you're right, we don't," I reply, watching Heath do what he does best.

When he's secured, I slap Ivan on the cheeks. "But I know someone who does."

"Who?" he asks.

"Let's deliver Stefano a nice little package."

"No, no, no, please!" Ivan begs as Heath drags him all the way back to the car, and we each grab one end of him and throw him in the trunk, then seal him shut before he can whine some more.

"What the fuck was that?" Max asks as he lowers his window. "Did you just put Ivan in the trunk?"

I put my finger to my lips. "Just pretend you didn't see."

"But I can hear him," he replies.

"Then ignore the screams. Simple," I reply.

Max looks disgusted. "There's blood all over your hands. It'll get on the car."

I shrug. "Risk of the trade."

"I'll turn this baby inside out and clean the fuck out of it after we're done," Heath says.

I slap the top of the car. "Let's go."

"Did you get the address?" Max asks.

Heath hops inside and turns to grin at him. "Yup. And I think it's time we paid Stefano a little visit."

"Wait, you mean ... actually going to a drug lord's house to ambush him?"

I smile too. "Sounds about right. You in?"

"Will Ivy and Cora be safe?"

I tilt my head. "You think I'll let anyone touch her and live to tell the tale?"

Slowly, a smile spreads on Max's lips before he fishes a gun from the bag and loads it like he's a goddamn expert despite the fact that I've not seen him hold a gun since I met him. "I guess it's time for me to dust off the skill set my mom taught me a few years back and finally put it to good use."

FIFTY-SIX

HEATH

We park the car outside the gate and look around.

Several guards are stationed out front, and who knows how many more will be inside the mansion. I'm sure a drug lord like him doesn't go anywhere without proper security. But we came prepared.

"You ready?" Silas asks.

I nod, and Max throws us the bags. "Ready."

"Meow. Mrrp."

We all turn our heads to see Bagel casually washing his ass on the shelf in the back behind the passenger's seats.

"What the fuck?" I mutter. "Why is Bagel here?"

"Shit," Silas says, sighing out loud. "I forgot he was in here."

"Why the hell did you bring a cat to a shoot-out?" I groan.

"Because I was trying to train him to hiss at people trying to break into the car, okay?" Silas explains. "And then I forgot."

"Wow, you forgot about her cat? This isn't going to end well for you," I joke.

"How long has he been in here?" Max asks.

Silas shrugs. "A few hours, maybe."

"Well shit, what are we gonna do with him?" I ask.

"Just leave him here. He'll be fine," Silas opens the compartment in front of him and takes out some kibbles.

"You're keeping cat kibbles in my car?" I growl.

"What else do you want me to use? Wet food?" Silas responds, like it's not at all fucking weird he did this. He throws some of the kibbles to Bagel, who happily chomps on them.

Max scratches his little head. "Who's a good kitty?"

"All right, stop. Enough with the cat. Can we focus on our task?" I say.

"He'll be fine. We'll take care of business. In and out. Done and over." Silas grabs a couple of smaller, quicker blades from the bag, along with some guns. "Let's go get them."

"Fine, but if that cat pisses all over my car, you pay for it," I growl, and I grab a couple of thick blades as well as a few guns.

Max takes back the bag and throws it over his shoulder. "Yell if you need more."

"Got it."

We get out, and Max whispers at Bagel before closing the door, "You stay and watch the car like a good boy."

Some of the guards near the gate approach us.

"You think we can convince them to let us in quietly?" I ask.

They're already clutching their weapons.

Silas tilts his head. "Not a chance."

I casually pull a screaming Ivan out of the trunk and hold him up as bait. "Surprise! I brought your lil' friend back."

They raise their guns, and so do we.

BANG! BANG! BANG!

I use his body as a shield, and he flops around a few times before dying on me.

Three shots, two down. One of them hides in the bushes and aims.

BANG! BANG!

Silas and I duck for cover just in time.

A voice-over can be heard coming from the bushes.

"Incoming. Front gate. I need backup!"

THWACK!

Silas knocks the walkie-talkie from his hands with a knife and then chucks another one right at his throat, and blood squirts everywhere.

I march up to the gate and flop Ivan's body down in front of it to use him as a step-up. Then I prop up my hands so Silas can use it as a step to jump over. He holds out his hand to pull Max up too. I go last as I'm the biggest, with Max and Silas both grabbing my wrists to drag me over the gate.

More guards pour out from the front door, but we came prepared. I aim and shoot, but suddenly, Max sets down a sniper rifle on the ground and goes to town.

BANG! BANG! BANG! BANG!

One by one, they go down like flies.

"Wow, I'm impressed," I mutter.

He winks at me. "You thought I didn't know how to shoot?"

"You should do it more often," Silas says. "Let's go."

"I'll give you guys cover." Max aims at the door and waits for more to come out.

Silas and I run to the mansion. The garage door opens, and a driver steps out from behind several expensive-looking vehicles with an automatic rifle, but Max shoots him down from a distance before he's able to even take one shot, so I stick up my thumbs in thanks.

We can use two windows on each side of the mansion for a surprise attack. I throw Silas a glance and say, "You seeing what I'm seeing?"

He nods. "You take the left. I'll take the right. Meet up in the hallway."

Behind us, Max approaches steadfast, pausing every other second to take aim.

"Max, front door! We'll flank," I yell.

Silas disappears from view as we each go to our side of the mansion, and I start searching for the way in. There's a half-open window on the second floor that I can reach by climbing up the vines. No fucking problem.

I grasp the ledge and swing myself up, taking hold on the vines with my feet to keep myself steady as I pull myself up on the balcony. I drop down, pull out my knives, and kick in the window, jumping inside.

There's no one here, it seems, but the moment I step one foot inside, the door slams open, and three dudes with guns open fire.

BANG! BANG! BANG!

I roll to the side and hide behind a bed, waiting for them to waste their ammo before I chuck one of the knives at the first fucker, piercing his skull.

The two others reload, and I throw another knife at the right guy's chest, knocking him backward. He tumbles down on the floor, bleeding profusely, right when the third one finishes.

I swiftly pull out my gun, and we fire at the same time.

BANG, BANG!

The guy drops to the floor, and I move ahead. In the hallway, Silas is fighting with two guards. One of them has him in a dead-lock, while the other attempts to cut his throat, so I aim and shoot.

BANG!

The knife falls out of his hand before he drops like a sack of potatoes, and Silas elbows the guy holding him in the stomach. The fucker releases him, and Silas rams his knife straight into his eye, twisting and turning until the guard flops down, dead.

"Thanks," Silas says, pulling his knife from the guard's skull.

"Don't mention it."

BANG!

More gunshots downstairs draw our attention as the front door is slammed open by two bodies dropping down to the floor. Max steps inside and waves. "I'm here!"

I lean over the banister and yell down, "Max, have you seen Ivy yet?"

He shrugs, but then something is thrown at him and explodes.

"MAX!" I scream and jump down the stairs to get to him.

He's coughing wildly, and I pull him out of the smoke.

"Do I have my fingers? Please, Heath, you gotta tell me. Do I have all my toes? I can't feel them," he says, but when I look him up and down, he seems perfectly okay.

"You're fine," I reply.

He breathes out a sigh of relief. "Phew. Anxiety got the best of me there."

I roll my eyes. What a drama queen.

BANG!

Max drops from my arms and immediately reaches for my knife in my pocket, then chucks it at the guy who shot at me.

"Nice throw, twink," I muse.

He blushes. "I learned from the best."

"Who, me?" Silas says smugly as he rushes down the stairs only to jump on a guard I didn't even notice hiding out in a crevice beside the stairs. Silas climbs on top of his shoulders and slits his throat from the top. The body drops to the floor while Silas is still on top of him, and he uses it as a stair to get off.

"No, my mother," Max replies. "But thanks for the save."

"Where the fuck is Ivy?" Silas growls.

"If you're looking for us ... we're in here."

We all look up at the sound of that ominous, low voice.

That came from the kitchen.

Silas immediately raises his knives at eye level, so I do the same with my gun, while Max clutches his sniper rifle close as we home in on the room.

Only two entryways lead into the kitchen, at least from this hall-way, and no more guards appear to be blocking our way through either door. But it feels like a trap. Still, we move forward, determined to save Ivy and Cora.

Even if she is a liar and a thief.

Even if she felt betrayed because I knew Ivan.

Even if the girl is not her kid.

I want them to be safe ... no matter the cost.

***

SILAS

We head inside the kitchen, where Ivy lies passed out on the floor near the gas stove with bruises all over her skin and some blinking object tightly strapped to her chest. Rage takes hold of my savage heart.

"Ivy!" Max yells with pain in his voice as he steps forward.

I hold him back from getting closer because we're definitely not alone.

A man steps out from the kitchen, casually chewing on half a piece of apple while holding a pocket knife. The other half he holds between his fingers, and he hands it to someone out of sight behind a wall.

Cora.

"What have you done with them? Why is she out cold?" I grit. "Tell me, right now." I clutch my knife so tightly I can feel it etch into my skin. "Did you fucking hurt her?"

"After the stunt she pulled, she should be happy she still lives," he replies, swallowing down the apple in the most aggressive way I've ever seen.

That's it. I'll fucking kill him.

Suddenly, Heath grips my shoulder right as I was about to move.

"Not so fast," Stefano says, holding up a phone with a button on the screen. "If you so much as touch me, her life will be forfeited."

I glance at Ivy and the object tied to her chest.

A bomb.

"You strapped a fucking bomb to her chest?!" I say through gritted teeth.

"I knew you lot would be coming, so I made sure to prepare."

"She doesn't deserve this," Max says.

Stefano approaches. "She is a thief who needed to be taught a lesson, so I gave her one. And you don't have the slightest idea what you've gotten yourself into."

When he gets too close, I point a knife right at his skull. "Take one more step and I will flay your fucking skin off your living body."

The man merely smiles like he's enjoying this.

Groaning in the back makes me instantly look up and lose sight of the man in front of me.

She's awake.

"You know, I think we may have gotten off on the wrong foot," Stefano says, stepping back a little to avoid the pointy end of my blade.

"I doubt that," I reply. "You fucking destroyed our house."

"That was an unfortunate necessity," he says, still twirling that damn knife of his. "After I finally learned where Ivy was keeping ..." His eyes darken. "*My* daughter."

FIFTY-SEVEN

MAX

So it is true. Cora isn't hers.

Ivy's eyes crack open, and I glance her way.

"So you see, this was all a misunderstanding."

"Misunderstanding, my ass," Heath growls back. "There has to be a reason she stole your daughter."

Ivy whimpers.

"Ivy," I mutter, wishing I could take her pain away.

"You won't get her back. She stole my daughter after all, so it is my job to punish her as I see fit," Stefano says.

"Punish her?" I ask, shaking my head. "You don't know how well she took care of Cora. It's all a big mistake, I'm sure."

"A mistake?" Stefano raises his brows and lifts a finger. "Oh no. She planned this for months."

I glance at Ivy, who eyes me with despair, hoping it isn't true.

But when she opens her mouth to try to speak, only gibberish comes out.

"What is she trying to say?" Silas mutters at Heath.

"I don't know."

"Don't bother. She'll only try to lie some more to spin a web around you like a goddamn spider," Stefano says.

"Daddy? I'm scared. Can I go to my room?" Cora asks.

Fuck, hearing her panicked little voice makes me want to grab her and take her with me right now. But Stefano's hell-bent on keeping them both here at all costs.

"Soon, honey," Stefano replies. "Daddy has to take care of some guests first."

"You mean Silas, Heath, and Max?" Cora mutters.

His eyes narrow. "Yes. I believe they stormed into my house uninvited. How many men did you take down? Five?"

"Twenty. At least," Silas retorts.

He snorts arrogantly. "You think that's a lot?" Roaring laughter follows. "How many men do you think I have, kid? Just a couple hundred?" Suddenly, his laughter stops. "I am one of the lieutenants of the Bones Brotherhood, and you are in way over your head."

Silas's face darkens. "Send me a thousand, I don't care. I will kill them all to get to her."

A smile tugs at Stefano's lips. "Brave. I like that. So what do you want, boy? Money?"

Silas lifts his knife higher. "You think I need money?" He laughs menacingly. "I have more money than I could ever fucking dream of."

"Then what do you want? The girl?" Stefano snorts. "You can have her after I'm done with her."

"Over my dead body," Heath growls.

I'm glad he feels the same way.

Stefano chortles. "That can be arranged, no problem."

"I don't think you understand us," Silas says. "We're not leaving here without her."

"What about Cora?" I ask.

"Cora stays here. With me," Stefano growls.

"Daddy, I'm scared."

"I know, honey," he says.

"Don't be scared, Cora. We'll take care of everything," I tell her.

"You think you're the good guys?" Stefano growls. "When you harbored the thief who stole my child out of my own damn home?" He points at Ivy. "My wife is *dead* because of her."

I gasp. "What?"

And it's hard to believe for me as well.

"She destroyed our family. And you gave her a pass."

My gaze fixates on Ivy, who desperately tries to speak, but her throat seems to have been clamped shut by all the pain she's had to endure from whatever this fucker did to her.

I home in on her face to try to decipher what she wants, but then I realize her earpieces are missing.

Fuck.

***

IVY

I've only just woken up after being flung headfirst into the oven, and I don't know how much time has passed since the lights went out in my head.

But my God … It hurts. It hurts so fucking much that I can't even move without feeling pain all over my body.

He did this.

Stefano hurt me as retribution for taking Cora away from him. And this is only the beginning of all the cruel punishments he still plans to inflict on me.

This is what he does best. What makes him feel powerful. Superior. Like a walking god on this goddamn forsaken earth.

"Please …" I squeak, but my voice box is completely broken from the amount of pressure he put on my throat.

I can't speak. I can't hear.

All I see are body parts and lips moving, but with hazy sight, I can barely make out what they're trying to say. Lip-reading is hard when you've just gotten your consciousness back.

My head throbs, and I try to make out what they're trying to say, but I only catch a couple of words.

Cora. Thief. Killer.

***

SILAS

"See? She is not who she's made herself out to be," Stefano says, ignoring Ivy. He takes in a breath, his finger still hovering over the button on his phone like a threat.

And I contemplate shooting him right there and then, but if I do ... his fucking thumb might still hit that button, and then it'll all have been for nothing.

"Come with me. I'll show you the proof if you don't believe me," Stefano says, walking out the second door in the kitchen.

"Proof of what?" Heath asks.

The only reason we follow him at all is because of that phone in his hand.

"Wait, you guys," Max says. "I think Ivy was trying to tell us s—"

He abruptly stops speaking. In the bedroom across the hallway, an extremely pale woman lies in a bed, along with the machines next to her body, which are deadly silent.

"Ivy unplugged my wife from this machine that kept her alive after she stole my child."

Heath shakes his head like he can't believe what he's hearing.

"It's true," Stefano says. "This is the proof."

"Why would I believe you?" I growl.

"Why would I kill my own wife?" he says, grabbing her hand to kiss it. "I loved her."

I turn to look at Ivy again, who continues mouthing words without saying them out loud as if her voice box has stopped functioning.

I don't fucking know what she's trying to say, and it pisses me off.

Pushing herself up from the floor, she brings her hands together, making some strange movements with her fingers that I can't decipher or comprehend.

But Max's eyes widen, and he sucks in a breath as his eyes skitter between us and her.

What did he see?

Suddenly, he bolts to her, distracting me for a moment.

Just one fucking second looking away.

OOMPF.

A knife is flung at me, and it hits me straight in the thigh.

"Stupid fucking boy, you think you can take my child and not pay a price?" Stefano yells as I go down to the floor in agony.

"Silas!" Heath pulls me back and aims for Stefano's head.

BANG!

A smoke bomb goes off, swiftly filling the entire room and hallway with smoke.

"You cut the wrong guy, motherfucker!" I yell at Stefano as I rip the knife out of my bleeding leg, but he's already bolted out of the room.

BOOM!

Panic seizes control of my heart, and I sit up straight.

Did the bomb just go off?

Ivy!

FIFTY-EIGHT

IVY

Max's eyes connect with mine as he drops to his knees in front of me.

He brings his fingers up to eye level ...

And signs.

Close your eyes.

But I'm too flabbergasted for a moment.

He knows how to sign?

Something goes off in the hallway, filling the hallways and the kitchen with smoke. Then a knife is pushed against my chest, and I swallow away the lump in my throat.

Even if I'm scared, I have no other option but to trust Max right now.

I gulp in a breath and close my eyes, then wait.

He cuts through the straps with ease, and the bomb falls off. He catches it and chucks it into the hallway.

A bright flash fills the area, and the floor beneath me shakes.

Cora's panicked face frightens me. I can see her scream even though I can't hear it.

Can you walk?

Max signs to me again.

I nod.

He helps me up and signs once more.

I believe you.

Tears make my vision cloudy, but from the corner of my eye, I spot the barrel of a gun coming from the hallway. I try to scream.

Too late.

It happens so fast.

One flash and Max is on the kitchen floor, bleeding from a gunshot wound in the back.

I grab his face.

Max, please! Get up.

He leans up to sign.

Can't. Take Cora. Run.

I sign back to him.

You're hurt. Can't leave you.

So he signs back.

You should. I love you. Stay safe.

Tears roll down my cheeks, but I still get up, grab Cora, and run like hell. Through the smoke, through my tears, through the pain in my legs, through all the horrors I've endured in my lifetime, I run, and no matter how far I have to go to keep her safe, I will get there, no matter the cost.

Her little hands hold me tightly. Despite everything we've been through, she still trusts me enough to take her to safety, so I will.

I jump over the bodies littering the hallways and bolt outside into the fresh air, where I heave and cough to get the smoke out of my lungs. Still, I keep running across the grass and the pavement, all the way to the locked gate.

Behind me, Stefano is catching up.

"Shit!" I hiss.

I put Cora down and grab a gun from one of the dead guards, then shoot off the lock.

I kick open the gate, grab Cora's hand, and pull her with me toward Heath's car. I tug at the door, and surprisingly, it opens. The key is still inside, probably so they could make a quick escape.

I jump in and put Cora on the passenger's seat, then close the door, and hit the gas.

Right as that fucker Stefano runs up to the gates.

More flashes go off, and I can feel the car vibrate from the gunshots going into the metal as we drive off.

My heart is racing as fast as the car as I try to bring us to safety, but where the fuck do I go?

In a blind panic, I drive toward the only place I once deemed safe; my home.

I swerve through the streets, trying to get to my apartment building. We're so close, I can almost taste the freedom. But every once in a while, I glance at Cora to make sure she's still here with me because it all feels like a fever dream. She's crying and shaking, traumatized by what happened, and I'm sorry that I don't know what I could possibly do to fix this.

Suddenly, something jumps on my shoulder, and I freak out, nearly driving into someone crossing the street.

A familiar set of paws taps my cheek.

Bagel?

He jumps off me and onto Cora's lap, where he settles, and she begins to pet him.

Why is he here?

A smile forms on Cora's face. Even though I have no clue why Bagel is in Heath's car, at least he brings Cora a little bit of happiness.

BAM!

Another car drives into my back end, and I scream as the car begins to swerve across the road.

I throw a glance in the rearview mirror. Stefano's behind the wheel, menacingly glaring at me like he intends on driving us straight into hell.

This man won't rest.

Not until we're all dead and buried.

Grinding my teeth, I grab the steering wheel and hold on tight to regain control, but the car is being pushed forward by his.

Fuck. At this rate, we might crash.

He's completely lost it.

He'd rather kill his own kid than let us escape?!

I jerk the wheel sideways to keep us from crashing straight into the wall of my apartment building. I brace for impact, shielding Cora with my body as the back of the trunk hits the corner of the wall and spins around.

Finally, we come to a stop against a fire hydrant, which bursts, water cascading all over the car's roof.

I blink a couple of times. My head hurts, and my bruises sting, but I'm still alive ... and so is Cora.

But when I look up into the rearview mirror, there he is again, slamming his car door shut as he waltzes over to our car.

I grasp Cora, who holds Bagel tightly, and kick open the door.

A blinding light radiates off the hood as a bullet skitters past us. I duck behind the wall and slip past, holding Cora tightly as we run into the building.

My heart is racing in my throat as I run up the stairs, dragging her along, while she barely manages to hold Bagel. We go all the way up to our floor, but my house is no longer safe. He knows where I live, so the only option I have left is...

I knock on Mrs. Schwartz's door, and the second she opens up, I shove her aside and burst into her home uninvited.

I can see her yelling at me with a frying pan in her hand.

What ... you ... doing? I'm ... cook!

I try to lip-read, but it's hard when she's mad.

I close the door and put my finger to my lips. "Please," I mouth. "Help us."

She makes a weird face. *What ... saying? Can't ... understand you.*

Grunting, I grab a piece of paper, steal her lipstick, and write down the words: *Hide us. Or we die.*

Her eyes widen, and she immediately puts down her pan, grabs me, and ushers me into her bedroom. She points at the closet, so we get in and hide underneath her clothes.

Cora huddles closer to hug both Bagel and me, squishing us both, and I pat her back to make her feel better. I know she's scared. She doesn't deserve any of this fear, but how do I take it away?

I can feel Bagel purring against my belly, but all I can think of is how many people have had to die for us to be safe. How many people got shot and wounded because of me?

Max.

My heart aches at the thought of him lying there in a pool of his own blood.

God, Max ... please, let Max be okay.

***

HEATH

Minutes ago

When I finally make my way through the smoke in the hallways while carrying Silas, I find Max lying on the floor, blood staining his shirt.

"Max!" I scream, and I put Silas down so I can run to him.

I get on my knees and pick him up. "Max, please, stay with me!"

He groans. "Ugh, my shoulder hurts."

Tears stain my eyes. "You're alive."

"Pffft, you think I'd die after only kissing you twice?" he jokes.

"Fuck, c'mere, you little twink." I grab his face and smash my lips onto his. "Don't you go dying on me now."

"I won't, promise," he groans. "It's just a gunshot wound to the shoulder blade. No big deal."

He's joking now, but I know he's just hiding the pain from me.

"What happened?" I ask.

"Stefano shot me after I pulled the bomb off Ivy's chest," Max says.

"Where the fuck is she?" Silas growls. "I can't find her, and I can't see shit."

"I told her to run," Max says. "Cora is with her."

"Fuck," Silas grits, getting up. "We gotta go after her."

"Stefano's gone too," Max says. "He ran after her. I saw it."

"Okay, time to go." I grab Max by the waist and throw him over my shoulder.

"Wait!" Max yelps, pointing at something on the floor near the kitchen door. "Her hearing aids."

I bend over to grab them and shove them into his pockets.

"Jesus Christ, everything hurts."

"Stop bitching, we gotta go save Ivy and Cora, remember?" I tell him as I help Silas out the door too.

I'm the only one left standing, and I'm not about to let my best friend and lover die on me.

But the moment I step outside and gaze across the yard, my car is nowhere to be found.

"Where the fuck is my car?" I yell.

"Shit, Ivy must've taken it," Silas responds.

"There!" Max points at one of the expensive cars in the garage next to the mansion. "We can take that one."

"Fine. He stole our girl, so we'll steal his car," Silas says, hobbling over to the garage.

Stefano's personal driver lies on the asphalt, dead as can be, and Silas fishes the key from his pocket. "I'll take that."

Skid marks are all over the grass leading to the garage. Someone hastily drove a car away from here.

"Shit, Stefano must've taken the other car that was here," I say as I set Max down in the back seat. "We gotta hurry."

"I'm coming!" Silas snaps, jumping into the passenger's seat while I get behind the wheel and put it in reverse.

"Let's go get our girls."

***

IVY

Sweat drops roll down my back as I keep Cora and Bagel close to me, praying he won't find us. The door slams shut, and I know it's too late.

He's here.

I grab Cora's face and make her look at me so she understands what I say. "Stay."

She nods, and I swiftly exit the closet so I can grab a knife from the kitchen before he finds us. It won't do much against a gun, but I'm not gonna sit around in there and wait until he finds us and drags us all the way back to that hellhole.

Fuck no.

I won't go down without a fight.

If he wants to take her, he'll have to go through me.

I take the biggest knife I can find and hold it out in front of me as I step out into the living room. He's got Mrs. Schwartz in a chokehold, and the frying pan she was using to cook her bacon in drops to the floor.

I clear my throat and try to form the words as best I can despite not knowing how they sound. "Let. Her. Go."

A wicked smile forms on his face, and he shoves her toward the couch, where she hits her head on the table. She's passed out and bleeding from the head.

Fuck.

Sweat drops roll down my back as he steps closer and closer, taunting me, trying to get me to flee. But I am done running from this monster.

Clutching the knife tightly, I jump at him, cutting into him with everything I have. I manage to hit him in the arms before he grabs my wrist and locks it behind my back, knocking it out of my hand. I fight against his grip and kick him in the balls, and he briefly buckles, allowing me to break free.

I ram my knee into his face, and he stumbles backward, bleeding from the nose.

"That's it."

I can read the words from his lips, and they strike fear into my heart.

I punch him in the gut, but he swiftly pulls back, grabs my hand, and twists it around until I'm squealing in pain. His other hand wraps around my neck, twisting tighter and tighter until it becomes impossible to breathe. I claw at his fingers, to no avail.

No. Please. I don't want to die.

But it doesn't matter what I try to say.

My throat has already clamped shut, and my voice stopped working the second he got his hands on me. Slowly, I can feel myself slipping away.

Something thuds beneath me, and when I blink, two tiny hands are smashing against Stefano's knees, and it's enough to bring tears to my eyes.

Cora, no!

I open my mouth to speak, but the words refuse to come out.

Please, Cora, run!

Despite the fact that I'm fighting him off as hard as I can, my muscles are slowly losing their strength, my grip on his hand waning.

This is it.

This is the end.

I'm sorry, Cora. I tried. I tried so hard, and still, it wasn't enough.

Suddenly, a knife flies out from the hallways and hits Stefano in the shoulder, and his fingers finally unravel from my throat. I suck in a breath as he releases me, and I drop to the floor, dragging the oxygen into my lungs like a fish on land.

I look up to see Heath standing in the hallway, with Max and Silas behind him, supporting themselves on the wooden beams next to the doors just to stay standing.

Max is alive, thank God.

Max huddles closer to the door and chucks something my way: My hearing aids.

He nods with a gentle smile, and I swiftly put them in.

"You motherf—" Stefano growls as he gets up, and he reaches for a gun in his pocket.

No, I won't allow this to keep on happening.

He can't keep hurting the people I love.

I rip the knife Heath threw at him from his back and ram it straight into his thigh. He howls in pain and sinks to his knees.

"I am done running from you. This is the last time, you hear me?! The last time you ever fucking hurt us!" I scream at him with a squeaky voice from all the damage he did to my windpipe.

"You fucking brats, you all just couldn't stay out of my business," Stefano growls at Heath. "You want to aid a fucking murderer? She stole my child and killed my wife!"

"He's a liar," Max says through gritted teeth, repeating the words I told him in sign language. "That woman in the bed was Ivy's mother."

FIFTY-NINE

HEATH

It feels like the floor has been ripped out from underneath my feet.

That dead woman was her mother?

She wouldn't kill her own mom. No way.

"Wait, is that true?" I mutter in disbelief.

Ivy nods. "He hurt her." The tears began to roll. "Over and over. Every single day. She only stayed with him because of Cora." She bites her lip. "I couldn't take it anymore, so I took Cora and ran." Cora suddenly runs up to her and clutches her thigh. "Away from my own mother just to keep us both safe."

Stefano laughs even though he's wounded. "That woman was *my* wife."

"No. I know the truth. Ivy signed it at me. *You* killed her," Max says.

"No, she pulled the wires out of the machine that kept her alive!" Stefano growls.

"To save her from you!" Ivy screams, silencing everyone. "You wouldn't even let her die in peace!"

"When I left, she wasn't in that bed. She was still walking, still able to talk," she says, her voice fluctuating. "He dragged me back in there and locked me up with her brain-dead body kept alive by machines. Just to punish me."

"What the f—what kind of a deranged fucker would do that?!" Silas yells, incensed, and it's impressive, knowing even a psycho like him thinks that is going too far.

My hand balls into a fist as we get closer to him, keeping Silas from falling by supporting him with my shoulder. But I have to get closer.

I have to fucking put a wedge between Stefano and Ivy so he doesn't kill her too. I would rather die than let that happen.

Stefano raises his gun. "That's close enough."

Still, I move in, unafraid of the gun's barrel pointing in our direction.

All this time, I thought she stole someone's child, but it turned out, she was protecting Cora from *him*. Even after all the torture she endured, she still stands tall, and I feel so fucking bad for ever doubting her.

God, if only I would've trusted her.

I'm sorry.

***

SILAS

For a long time, I thought I had no conscience, no emotions, no heart.

But seeing how much this fucker has hurt her, not just physically but mentally too, has awakened a deep-seated hatred inside me that I didn't even fucking know existed until now.

My jaw is clenched together, words escaping my grasp as I would love nothing more than to chew my way through his neck and tear out his arteries and rip him to shreds with my bare fucking teeth.

But only one fucking thing stops me.

Her.

Because if I do something now that only ends up hurting her more, I wouldn't be able to fucking live with myself.

"Are you her fucking father?" I growl at him.

He laughs diabolically. "Fuck no, I wouldn't dream of being the father to a sewer rat like that."

I raise my gun right back at him. "Good. I'm so fucking glad you're not her fucking father, so I don't have to feel bad for her when I take your fucking life. Because now I get to tear your fucking head off for calling her that."

Stefano laughs at me. "So what, are you going to kill me in front of my kid?"

Cora hides behind Ivy, and I don't know why, but it stops me from pulling that trigger.

Fuck.

"You're a lying piece of shit," Heath growls. "You never wanted your kid back. You just wanted to punish Ivy for trying to take her away from you."

"She had no right," Stefano grits.

"I had every right to keep her safe and away from you!" Ivy's voice croaks through the room.

Stefano glances at her over his shoulder. "You know, there is only one thing I regret. That after knocking some sense into your goddamn mother, I spared you."

The pain in her eyes is immeasurable, and it's like a fucking knife straight to the heart. A heart I didn't know was beating until I laid eyes on her.

"Fuck you," Ivy grits. "You don't deserve my mother or Cora."

Stefano roars, "She is *my* child, and you took her from me!"

"Oh my f—my head ..." The lady who owns this house is slowly recovering, and she squeals the second she sees the gun in Stefano's hand.

"Shut the fuck up," he hisses at her.

Suddenly, he turns around and grabs Ivy, pushing her in front of him, then placing the barrel of the gun to her head.

"You want her so badly, then you'll get her back in a body bag!" he yells at us.

"Put the fucking gun down," Heath growls, keeping his gun pointed at him. "You're not going to get away."

"Let her go, Daddy!" Cora begs, wrapping her little hands around his leg.

He kicks her aside, and she falls to the floor, crying her eyes out.

Something snaps in Ivy.

She grabs the knife stuck in his thigh, rips it out, and thrusts it back into his crotch. The scream that leaves his throat is nothing short of pure satisfaction.

She stumbles away from him, directly into Heath's arms, right as Stefano aims his gun at her. "You bitch!"

Heath moves in front of her, shielding her body with his. "Fucking shoot, then, because I'll take a million fucking bullets to keep her from harm."

Shock riddles Stefano's face, but then he reaches for Cora and holds her in front of him, putting the gun to her little head instead.

"No, don't!" Ivy screams.

"Move, and I put a bullet in her," Stefano grits.

"That's your own fucking daughter," I grit.

"Let her go, you fucking monster!"

"You think I'll let you kill me? Fuck no," he spits back.

Ivy's face is like lightning in a bottle, and she reaches for my pocket, takes out a knife, and aims, just like I taught her.

A twig, when broken, turns into the sharpest weapon.

THWACK!

Before he can even fire the weapon, the knife lodges itself between both his eyes. They roll back into his head as he sinks down onto the couch, squirting blood from his forehead.

WHAM!

The lady lying on the floor slams a frying pan against his head so hard it puts a dent in his skull. Permanently.

"Would you fucking shut up already?" Mrs. Schwartz says. "Jesus fucking Christ."

"Amen," Max mutters while little Cora immediately runs to Ivy.

"You sure have interesting friends, Ivy." Heath snorts.

Max sinks against the wall and breathes a sigh of relief. "Thank fuck that's over."

Ivy's breathing wildly as she wipes his blood off her hands. I stumble inside, ignoring the pain in my thigh because right now, all I care about is making sure the only fear I've ever felt in my life is instantly quelled.

"Are you okay?" I ask, tilting my head.

She sucks in a sharp breath, swallows the rest of her tears, and nods briefly. Then she turns around and goes to her knees in front of Cora. "Are you alright? Are you hurt?"

But all I can think of is how she chose to run, fight, and steal just to stay safe, knowing full well that fucker would come after her.

This fucking girl.

I clutch my chest as the same tightness I felt before takes hold.

She smiles at Cora like everything will be okay.

Just one fucking smile...

And it finally all clicks into place.

***

IVY

Heath helps Mrs. Schwartz up from the floor. She groans but abruptly stops the second she spots all his muscles. "Oooh. Now, who are you, Mr. Handsome?"

Heath laughs. "Maybe we need to get that head wound checked out."

"Oh no, I'm fine. Perfectly fine," Mrs. Schwartz replies. "But if you want to check me out, I have a bathroom to the left and plenty of fun stuff in there."

"I take it back. No amen for you," Max mutters, making us all laugh.

Cora hugs me tight, and the tears roll down our cheeks, not from fear but from happiness of finally being free.

"I'm sorry," I mutter to her.

"Is it over?" she asks.

I nod. "Your dad ... he's ..."

I can't bring myself to say the words out loud.

"I don't want him to be my daddy. He hurt Mom," she says, hiccupping. "And he hurt you."

I hug her tighter. "I'm sorry. I'm so sorry, Cora. I wish I could make it all disappear from your memories."

We cry a little more, and after a while, she breathes out a sigh and says, "I love you. You're my big sister."

"I love you too, sweetie. And I promise I will never, *ever* let anyone hurt you again. No matter what happens, I will always be there for you." She hugs me so tightly that it hurts, but the pain is worth it.

"This is too beautiful," Max mutters, coughing before wiping away a tear.

"Are you getting all emotional on us now?" Heath snorts before he slaps Max on the thigh. "Enough crying for today."

"I got shot. Twice. I think I deserve a few tears," Max retorts.

"No, Heath's right," I say, standing up. "Stefano's drained enough happiness from our lives as is. We've given him enough."

"True," Max says, eyeing the body. "Is he even dead?"

While we're all still staring at Stefano's body, waiting for him to spring back to life to try to attack us again, Bagel casually prances out of the cluttered bedroom and hops onto the couch to sniff at him.

Then he sprays him ...

Literally sprays him with piss.

And Stefano still doesn't react.

"Guess he's as dead as a Dodo," Max says.

Heath checks his pulse. "Yup. Dead."

Mr. Squiggles, her wiener dog, prances out of the bedroom like it's no one's business but stops when he sees the cat. Mrs. Schwartz picks him up and hugs him tight. "Ivy, why the fuck did you bring this stinky cat into my house?!" Mrs. Schwartz says, wafting her hand in front of her wrinkly nose. "Even Mr. Squiggles is scared of him."

I laugh so loudly that the whole building could probably hear, but I don't care.

I haven't laughed so freely in a long time, and the feeling overwhelms me with joy.

"Good job, Donut," Silas says, clapping his hands before cringing from the pain in his bullet wound.

I abruptly stop laughing and glare at him with a raised brow. "*Donut*? His name is *Bagel*."

Silas awkwardly stares back with a stupid grin on his face. "Not anymore."

"Uh-oh," Max mutters while Heath begins to snigger.

My brows furrow suspiciously when *Bagel* jumps down onto the floor and begins to curl his tail against Silas. "What have I missed?"

SIXTY

SILAS

"This should be tighter," Mom says, tugging at my bandage.

"Ow!" I yelp, swatting her hand aside. "Stop."

"I wouldn't have to do this if you didn't get knifed in the first place, Silas," my mom growls.

"It's just a flesh wound," I retort.

"Stay still." She retapes the bandage onto my skin. "There. Better."

"You really think you can do it better than the nurses?" Dad asks, leaning back in the plastic chair in the corner of my room.

"Yes." Mom folds her arms. "They do a piss-poor job here compared to a real hospital."

"A *real* hospital. Where they will be asking questions about why our son was shot," my dad grits.

Mom rolls her eyes and throws her purple hair over her shoulder.

"It's fine," I say, leaning back in the bed. "It'll heal."

"My heart won't," she says. "Do you know how worried I was when you called your dad? You should've told me you were going to go on a goddamn hunt for the Bones Brotherhood Mafia."

"She's right. When you're out of here, you're in a fuck ton of trouble," Dad hisses. "Do you even fucking know what the Bones Brotherhood is?"

"Whatever," I reply. "The guy was a piece of shit who sent his men to drag a girl off the streets. He hurt his wife and her kid, and almost killed her. He deserved it."

"I can't believe you went out there on your own," Mom rages. "Why?"

But I'm not sure I'm ready to say the words out loud yet, so I let the silence speak for itself.

"Twenty corpses, Silas. Twenty. Maybe more. That's how many my men had to clean up. Do you know how much blood there was left?"

"Mom ..." I sigh.

"No, don't Mom me." She grabs my chin, forcing me to look at her. "I know what it was like to be young, okay? I was there."

"She's right. She killed a ton of people," my dad says nonchalantly while staring at the wall ahead.

"Many more violent than the ones you encountered," she adds.

"And?"

Her grip grows softer as she begins to caress my cheek. "I need you to be more careful. I know murder runs in your blood. But I don't want to lose you to it."

She suddenly hugs me so tightly that it catches me off guard.

"I was so goddamn worried about you," she murmurs. "Promise me you will tell me next time you wanna plan another murder spree."

"Mo—"

"Promise me."

I roll my eyes and smash my lips together. "Fine, I promise."

"Thank you." She smiles while grabbing my shoulders. "And just so you know ... I won't stop asking why you did this until you tell me the truth."

I snort. "Good luck with that."

***

MAX

Being shot twice definitely wasn't on my bucket list of things to do, but I am so damn glad the doctors were able to take out the bullet while keeping my ability to walk and ride my motorcycle intact. God, do I miss riding ... and other things.

I groan as I get out of the hospital bed to go to the bathroom, but the second I open the door, Ivy jumps into my arms, hugging me so tightly I instantly forget all about my mild pain.

"Wow, where'd you come from?" I mutter, confused about how she got here so suddenly.

"The doctor told me you're finally getting out of here, so I asked Océane to drop me off. I've been staying in her sorority," she mutters. "Anyway, it doesn't matter. I'm so happy you're okay."

"How are you doing?" I ask, worried about the wounds she sustained.

"I'm okay. The doctor said I just got bruised ribs, a broken nose, and a concussion from the wound on my head, which they fixed. As long as I don't hit my head and don't get hit in the face again, I'll be fine," she replies. "What about you?"

"Much better now that the bullet has left the building. And my body," I say, making her laugh. "But God, these hospitals are boring. And Elliot's already been discharged, so I can't go bother him either."

"Lucky him," she jests.

I smile and go in for another hug. "It feels so good to hug you while standing up."

"Me too. I wouldn't have been able to forgive myself if you'd have died."

I push her back. "Hey now, don't say that. I'm still here, in the flesh." We both gaze down at my hospital gown. "Maybe a little too literal."

She laughs. "Are you even wearing underwear?"

"No, that's not allowed." I frown suspiciously. "Is it?"

She snorts again, and it immediately makes me blush and cover up. "Is it airy in here or what?" I stammer.

She grabs my face and kisses me so gently I completely melt in her arms.

Yep, that's the one thing that can get me to shut up.

"You always talk too much," she whispers.

"I just have too much to say, honestly," I reply. "I mean, you don't know how hard it's been staring at a white wall all day, all night. I have plenty of imaginary friends I can talk to now, though."

She smiles and kisses me again. "Thank you."

My cheeks heat. "For what?"

"You saved me," she says.

Well fuck, now I'm really blushing.

"I just did what anyone would have," I say.

"No." Heath's voice makes me look up as he saunters into the hallway with all that swagger he usually carries, putting a big smile on my face. "You knew what she was signing. How?"

I shrug. "I just taught myself."

His eyes narrow as a slow but hot smirk builds on his face. "It's that book. I knew it." He claps his hands. "I fucking knew it."

"What book?" Ivy asks.

I shush him, but it's too late.

Heath crosses his arms behind his head. "He learned sign language just for you."

Her jaw slowly drops, and the sight of them both in awe makes me want to turn this hospital gown inside out just so I can hide.

"You learned it ... *for me?*" she mutters.

"I wanted to be able to understand you, even if you weren't able to communicate with words. I wanted to be able to meet your needs, so I could be there for you when you needed me to."

She suddenly wraps her arms around me and hugs me so tightly I can't breathe.

"Thank you," she whispers.

"Don't thank me. I only did what was necessary. I can't really do it well either, but—"

She plants a finger on my lips. "Stop questioning yourself. You are more than I could ever ask for."

She grabs my face and kisses me so hard I lose my breath as well as all of the thoughts swirling through my head about how I should've done better. All the doubts and worries instantly evaporate when she kisses me.

God, this woman.

She fought so goddamn hard to save herself and her little sister. She sacrificed her body and all the money in the world just to provide that girl with a little bit of safety, and I am in awe of her strength.

I would die for her, and I almost did ... And still, it wouldn't be enough to describe the depths of what I'm willing to sacrifice to walk beside her in this world.

Besides *them*.

***

IVY

When our lips unravel, Max glances at Heath, waiting for me to turn around too so he can say what he needs to say. But I'm scared of the consequences, scared that when I do, I won't ever be able to look away from them again.

But Max's eyes reflect the longing in Heath's eyes and all the terrible regrets.

Finally, I turn to look at him, and the agony in his eyes is almost too much to take. "Heath ..."

He instantly drops to his knees. "I'm sorry." His nails dig into his knees. "I'm sorry for ever doubting you, for buying drugs from Ivan, for trusting him instead of you, for not believing you when I should have, for punishing you by taking your body, and for not giving you all the money you needed to save Cora and yourself. I don't fucking deserve your forgiveness ... but I will beg for the rest of my life that you do. Because I cannot live without you. Either of you."

Fuck.

I go to my knees in front of him, interrupting his train of thought by getting on his level.

"You didn't know," I say, grabbing his face. "It's not your fault."

I wish I could've told them straight off the bat, but I didn't trust them enough with the truth ... and it nearly makes me want to tear up because these boys literally killed to get to me.

"If I had trusted you, you wouldn't have gotten captured by Stefano, and Max wouldn't have been shot," he continues. "And your mother would still be alive."

Max sinks to the floor too, despite the half-healed wounds on his back, and he wraps his arms around Heath. "Stop. This is not your fault. Stefano caused all of this. Stop letting the guilt eat you alive."

"He's right," I say.

"This is why you needed those ketamine pills, didn't you?" Max asks him.

Heath nods, but he can't even look us in the eyes. "They gave me a means to escape my own emotions, because it was easier to deny them than to feel like the world was caving in on me," he says. "To feel like I was being crushed by the weight of my own fucking love for the people close to me. And I failed you both."

Those pills allowed him to hide, to exist without feelings, to lull the dull ache living in the corners of his heart. He wanted to be loved so badly, and no one ever noticed.

I hug him even tighter, feeling overwhelmed by how much he's kept buried.

"It's okay," I say. "You made a mistake, and you fixed it."

"I didn't fix shit. Max did. He gave you an escape," he says through gritted teeth.

I grab his face to make him look at me. "And you came back for me. Even when you were the only one left standing, you came to my aid. You protected me with your life."

He lets my words sink in for a moment. I can see it in his eyes.

"I wanted to save you and Cora. No matter if it cost me my life. I needed you to be safe," he says. "I needed you ..." He doesn't finish his sentence.

Doesn't finish the thought because that's just it.

This is the end of it.

This is what he's been wanting to say to both of us.

"I love you," he murmurs.

"What?" I mutter, leaning back.

He stares into my eyes, almost as if he wants to drown in them. "Even if you don't want me anymore. I will fight for you."

Part of me wants to push back, pull away, and run.

But another part of me desperately wants to return to whatever it was that we had when we were together. All four of us.

And I don't want to lose that either.

Sudden clapping has us all looking up. "Wow, what a sappy love story."

We all get up off the floor now that he's here to judge us.

"Silas," Max says with an annoyed look on his face. "Glad to see you're back up and running."

"Who said anything about running?" Silas retorts, limping closer. "That'll take a few more days."

"You sound like you're back to your old snarky self." Heath clears his throat. "I almost missed it."

"Almost?" A filthy smirk forms on his face. "Aw, you wanted me dead instead?"

"Of course not," Heath retorts.

"You were knifed in the leg, not the heart. Don't exaggerate," Max says.

"Well, something hit him in the heart, that's for sure," Heath jests.

"What did?" I mutter. Max and Heath stay awfully quiet, and it pisses me off. "What aren't you telling me?"

"Nothing," Silas swiftly says, clearing his throat. "So how have you been doing?"

Fine. If he doesn't want me to know, then he can keep the info.

"Good," I reply, folding my arms.

"You found a place? Or is that lady with the frying pan still terrorizing you?"

"I've been staying at Océane's sorority, Alpha Psi," I explain. "The girls were quite welcoming. Even to Bagel."

He nods a few times. "It's safe?"

Even now, he still wants to know if I'm safe despite the fact that he was the one who used to make me want to feel the fear in my bones.

What's changed?

Have I? Or did he?

"As safe as can be, with Talon watching over her shoulder like a bulldog," I say.

Heath snorts. "Sounds about right. I've seen him train. That guy could probably take down a dozen guys with just one fist."

"Well, I'm glad your friends were there to help when you needed them," Max says, smiling.

"Yeah, I'm grateful," I say, taking a deep breath. "I'm just glad we got to put this whole thing with my stepdad behind me. I can finally start off with a clean slate and not feel like I'm being chased." I eye Silas. "At least for now."

Silas's eyes narrow.

"I mean, the debt never ends, does it?" I mutter. "Now that you also helped me get rid of him."

His jaw tenses as he swallows.

Still, he doesn't say a word.

Why should I expect anything else? After all, he's still the same guy—still a psychopathic serial killer, still ... heartless.

I take in a deep breath. "Anyway, I have to go," I say. "I have something I need to take care of."

Max raises a finger. "Wait, but..."

I glance at all three. "Yes?"

"What will you do after? You know, when you can't stay at the sorority any longer?" Max asks.

I shrug. "I'll figure it out. I'll make it work as long as I have Cora and we don't have to run. Somehow." I turn around and walk.

"Will you come back to us?" Max asks.

I pause. "That depends..."

"On what?" Heath asks. "I'll do anything."

"Anything?" I quip.

Even Silas's eyes sparkle with excitement. "Anything ... and *every-thing*."

I remember those words all too well, and they still make me shiver, still make me crave.

I bite my lip and glance at them one last time. "Forgiveness only happens when it's earned. So earn it."

Slowly but surely, that same wicked smile that still haunts my soul to this very day forms on his face. "Deal."

SIXTY-ONE

HEATH

Weeks later

Through the bushes, I watch Ivy scatter her mother's ashes on the cemetery grounds. She grabs Cora's hand tightly when the girl starts weeping, and it makes it so hard for me not to come and hug them tight.

The trees whistle in the wind while they stay put to watch the dust settle on the grass.

I know I should stay away.

I know I should let her deal with this in peace.

But a gnawing part of me just can't let go.

Even if I have Max now, it feels like I'm missing a part of me without her.

Max was right. We've gotten addicted. Addicted to the rush of having a girl like her at our beck and call. And then we fucking wasted it all because we thought she was a liar.

Prejudice is the killer of love.

Now we have to watch her from the sidelines, wondering if she's doing okay.

Silas warned me not to overstep, so I won't, even though I wasn't the one who said "deal."

But if I made a move now, it would only establish what we already know to be true; the Skull and Serpent Society men take what they want with no regard to anyone else.

So I stay put and watch her from a distance.

For a second, she turns around, wiping away a small tear, her eyes briefly connecting with mine before I disappear into the trees.

Even if she doesn't want us close right now, I will always keep watch over her and Cora.

That is the promise I made to myself the moment she walked out of that hospital on her own despite every bit of adversity thrown her way.

A deal I made with myself when I swore I would never touch those fucking pills again.

And I intend to keep that promise until the day I die.

***

IVY

"Why can't I take Bagel to school?" Cora whines.

"Because cats aren't allowed in there." I laugh. "Besides, the teacher would probably get holes in her clothes from the number of times he'd want to jump on her lap for cuddles."

"Aw ... but he's so cute." She cuddles him thoroughly, entirely against his wishes as he moans in cat language to *please let him go.* I don't speak cat, but I consider myself a connoisseur in Bagel-ese, and I know what it sounds like when he's annoyed.

"But he'll be so alone, all by himself," she says, then she starts singing the lyrics to that song, making me laugh again.

"He's surrounded by plenty of sorority girls more than willing to pet him," I reply. "I'm sure he'll be all right."

"Ivy's right; that cat has more game than the boys from the Skull and Serpent Society, and that says a lot," Océane says as she leans against the doorjamb of the guest room I'm staying in. "We have alternating classes here, so I doubt he'll be alone."

"Exactly what she said." I wink. "Now, let's go. We're almost late." I grab her bag and drag her along.

"You need a ride?" Océane asks. "Talon can drive."

"It's only a short ride down the mountain. Max offered to bring her."

"That's awfully chivalrous of him. You two dating or what?" she asks.

I blush. "Maybe. I don't know. It's complicated."

"Hey, you do you," she says. "Good luck at school today, Cora!"

Cora waves as we exit the house, where Max waits on his bike for us.

When he takes off his helmet, Cora immediately runs to him to hug his leg. "Hey, kid, long time no see."

I cross my arms. "It hasn't been that long."

"Too long," Max replies. "You ready for a ride?"

Cora has a beaming smile on her little face. "I'm going on a motorcycle? That's so cool!"

She almost jumps up and down out of sheer excitement.

I chuckle. "You just made her first new school day extra special."

"Gotta earn those bonus points somehow." Max winks.

"This is so freaking awesome," Cora says as Max grabs her and puts her on.

"Safety first," I mutter.

Max swiftly pulls out a small helmet and plops it on her head, tightening the straps. "You didn't think I was going to drive away without this, right?"

I narrow my eyes at his coy smile. "You've gotten bold ..."

"And?" he asks, raising a brow. "You like it?"

I playfully slap his shoulder. "You keep talking like that, and I will make you regret it."

He makes a filthy moan-ish sound. "Don't threaten me like that. It only makes me want it more."

"Want what?" Cora asks.

"Nothing," Max and I both say, and when he glances at me over his shoulder, we both burst out into laughter.

After we've dropped Cora off at school, Max brings me back to Spine Ridge University, and I peck him on the cheeks before he drives off again to take his bike for a spin. Our classes don't start until late this afternoon, and he probably doesn't want to encroach on my need to distance myself for a while.

And he was right ... I did want to be left alone for some time so I could properly grieve our mother's passing together with Cora.

So I could navigate my way through a world without parents.

Without a solid base.

Without a house to call home.

But we'll get there someday.

I breathe out a sigh as I walk up the stairs in the Alpha Psi sorority house and head into the guest room where we've been staying all this time. Bagel greets me with a purr and a tail rub against my leg, and I pet him a little to feel grounded again.

Little Bagel and I have been through so much together. He was my mother's first pet and her only companion through the abuse my step-father flung at her. Sometimes I still can't believe I was able to steal him away too while I ran with Cora in one hand and Bagel in the other.

I pick him up and settle down on the bed so I can give him some much-deserved chin rubs. However, he's really not feeling it and jumps out of my arms to strut all over my desk, making a mess every-where he goes.

"Bagel!" I scold him as the letters fly through the room.

Letters I don't remember putting there.

I go to my knees to pick them up from the floor. They're all notices from a bank, banks I never contacted, and my name is clearly printed on the label, but it was sent to this sorority house.

How?

I open the envelope and read the letters, but the longer it goes on, the more it feels like the flooring has been ripped away from underneath my feet, and I'm falling. I'm falling so hard I can't breathe.

Money.

Millions and millions of dollars have been put in a bank account ... in my name.

So many letters are here that dizziness takes over, and I collapse on the bed while gaping at the bank account clearly in my name, along with all those zeros.

I didn't steal.

I didn't even try.

There is only one possible answer.

Stefano.

But how? He'd never give me this money willingly. In fact, I'm pretty sure he wrote a will outlining all the ways I would never get my hands on a single dime. He'd rather go to the grave with all of his money than gift it to the one girl he hated more than anyone in the whole damn world.

"Sorry, I should've told you. A bunch of mail came in for you, so I put all of it on your desk." Océane's words interrupt my train of thought. She clutches the door, furrowing her brows at me. "Are you okay?"

I nod, still in shock. "More than okay."

She smiles. "Good. Let me know if you need anything. I'm here all day. I don't have classes today."

"Wait, I wanted to give you this," I say, handing her the cash I borrowed from her. "I promised I'd give it back."

"Thanks. I appreciate it."

When she's about to walk away, I add, "Can I ask you something?"

She pauses. "Sure."

"When you got together with Talon ... how did you know he was the one?"

She stares at me for a moment, completely befuddled. "I ... I just knew. When I thought of him, I could feel him. Physically. Inside." She points at her heart. "I don't know, I can't explain it. But if I had to put a finger on it, I'd picture what it'd feel like if he wasn't mine, and that eviscerated me. So that's when I knew I wanted to be with him."

That sounds awfully familiar.

I swallow. "I see."

"You still not sure about Max?" she asks.

"No, this isn't about him. It's ... more than just him."

Her eyes widen. "Oh wow. Really? Multiple guys?"

"I'm trying to figure that out." I look at all the letters.

"If those came from your multiple guys, then you've got your answer." She snorts. "Think about it. Whatever it is, you'll figure it out." She winks and closes the door while I'm left staring at my letters.

Because what if she's right?

I open more of them, searching through each one of them until I finally find my answer inside a small box that Océane also brought to my room.

I sit down on the bed and open it up on my lap.

Inside is a knife, covered in blood.

Fresh blood.

I swallow away the lump in my throat as I pick it up and inspect it.

This is ... this is Silas's knife.

The knife drops from my hand and clatters to the floor, spilling droplets of blood everywhere.

But something at the bottom of the box draws my attention the most. A letter stained in blood.

***

SILAS

Ten years ago

I suck on my straw, sipping my coke, while watching my mother pierce through balloons with a few darts at the fair.

Of course, I'm not allowed to do this particular stand. I can hit some clowns with a few balls, but the second I go near any sort of sharp object, no one ever trusts me not to try and hit the guys behind the stands instead.

And I suppose they're right. It is fun watching them squeal their heads off as I 'accidentally' pierce their thighs with a dart.

Grinning at the thought, I take another sip of my coke.

"Yes!" Mom high-fives Mavis and Aspen after she's knocked out all the balloons in one go.

"Knew you could do it," my dad says, winking.

The guy in the stand laughs. "Well done. You win. Pick whatever you want."

Mom points at a plastic flower in the back of the stand, and the guy brings it to her.

"There you go."

"A flower?" I mutter to myself. Mom turns to look at me, and I shrug. "Whatever."

She holds the flower in front of me. "For you."

I scowl. "For me?"

This doesn't make any sense. Aspen likes flowers, not me.

"Yeah, because I love you, silly." She attempts to kiss me on the forehead.

"Gross," I say, wiping it off immediately.

She chuckles. "Don't be so scared of a little bit of love, Silas."

"He doesn't know what to do with it," Aspen says, sticking out her tongue at me.

"Shut up!" I yell back.

"Silas ..." Mom grabs my shoulders. "Just ignore it."

"It's getting on my nerves."

"I know."

I grind my teeth. "I wanted to throw those darts too."

"I know that too, but we also know what you like to do with sharp objects."

I lower my eyes.

"You're just a little ... different. And that's okay."

Is it?

Or are they just saying that because they don't know what it's like to feel nothing but the instinct to kill?

Mom presses the flower into my chest. "Hold onto it. One day, you will feel what it means. And then you can give it to a girl and make her happy."

She smiles, but it doesn't make me smile.

Neither does the plastic flower I'm forced to hold onto for the rest of our time at the fair, wondering if she just picked it so she could give it to me.

To try and get me to feel something.

Anything.

When we're finally home, I sit on my bed and stare at the box on the floor. The one Mom once gave me to store away memories I want to keep forever.

The plastic flower in my hands feels so goddamn meaningless.

So goddamn worthless.

Love.

Like I will ever understand what it means.

I throw the flower into the box and lock it, then shove it under my bed, groaning impatiently as I cross my arms.

Fuck love.

I don't know what it is, and I will never, *ever* need it. Especially not from some girl.

That flower will stay in its prison, rotting away for eternity.

***

IVY

Present

I pick up the letter and read the words.

I was right. You are a thief.
But you were right too. You needed it more than I did.
So I've made sure that all the money Stefano kept in his bank that he tried to take to the grave was put in your name instead. Along with all the funds in my bank account.
All of it belongs to you now.
Every dollar. Every dime. Yours to spend as you see fit.

I try to read as fast as I can, but my heart is racing.

I once had a red flower.
A cheap, meaningless, plastic flower.
When I was young, my mom once gave it to me and told me to give it to a girl.
It would make her happy, she said.
I kept it in a box because I didn't want to make anyone happy.
Until you stole it.

My throat feels constricted.
That's why he wanted that plastic flower I gave to Cora back.
I stole the only way he knew how to show love.

It's yours now, so keep it.
I also want you to have the knife you killed him with.
I told you, I'd make you fucking love sharp things just as much as I do.
Now go on, little thief ...
Take what's left of my fucking soul.
Silas

PS: Did you know even serial killers have a heart? I didn't.

The letter shakes in my hand as tears begin to well up in my eyes.

He gave me and Cora ... *everything.*

Just like I once promised him.

I stare at the words, wondering what on earth they mean, when a teardrop rolls down and falls on top, mixing with the ink. Ink ... that turns red like blood.

And suddenly, it hits me.

I snatch the bloodied blade off the floor and rush out the door. I can't storm down the stairs fast enough as I bolt out the front door, ignoring everything the girls are saying to me while I run as fast as I can toward the Skull and Serpent Society.

Now, more than ever, do I wish I could run faster.

When I finally get to the door, I ram the door so hard I nearly break through the wood. "Let me in! Now!"

When the door finally opens, Heath stands there, sheepishly staring at me like he can't believe I'm here in the flesh.

"Move, now!" I yell.

He frowns. "What, why? What's going on?"

"Silas has given me all of his money and a knife with blood on it," I reply. "*His* blood."

His eyes widen, and he immediately pulls away and bolts up the stairs with me, where I bump into Max on the way up.

"Ivy? What's going on?" Max asks, still in his biker clothes.

But we both ignore him as we head straight for Silas's room. Heath breaks down his door, and we rush into his room.

"Stop!"

SIXTY-TWO

SILAS

I look at my blood-caked body in the mirror and the scar permanently etched into my skin. Pain. God, the pain feels so damn good, I don't think I can ever stop, and I don't fucking want to.

Inside me is a void I kept filling with unending violence like some kind of black hole sucking everything in, and it was never satisfied.

Never.

Until ...

Through the mirror, I stare at her over my shoulder and at the knife I gifted her. The knife she earned with just as much violence as I love to inflict.

In silence, she stares back at me through the mirror.

There's blood all over the palms of my hands and my naked, tattooed torso. In disbelief, her eyes hover on my heart, where fresh blood still glistens from the letters I carved into my own skin.

Liar.

"Silas, what are you doing?" Heath asks.

Ivy's whole body begins to shake. "Why did you do this?"

"I lied to myself. I truly thought I was a psychopath, just like you said." My lip tips up into a half smile. "But you stole something from me that I didn't even know existed."

She looks shocked by what I've done and the words coming from my mouth.

A wicked smile forms on my lips. "Don't you understand?" I point at my chest where my heart is. "My heart only beats when it's in your hands."

Her eyes are riddled with shock. Her lip quivers, but I need to say these fucking words, and she'd better fucking listen to me.

"I have never, ever felt anything … not for anyone," I say. "Until you came along. And no matter what I do, who I hurt, who I kill, I can't make it stop."

This heart of mine was never made for beating.

And it definitely wasn't made to be loved.

I smirk. "Like I said in my note, I was right. You really are a thief, through and through." Blood rivulets down my chest. "I've given you everything I have. Everything I am. Even my own flesh and blood. And it still isn't enough to stop me from wanting you so badly it makes me want to rip out my own heart and hand it to you on a silver platter." I tilt my head back. "This is the deal you made, little thief. Your heart will never beat for me, so at least let me have the privilege of gifting you mine because you already stole it from me."

Tears begin to form in her eyes. "You shouldn't have done this."

"I gave you that fucking scar," I say, pointing at her abdomen. "So now I gave myself one too." I swallow. "That's what you wanted, right? Justice."

I drop my knife on the floor.

Her face contorts at the sight of me, but I still step closer.

"Silas, don't do it," Heath warns, but I ignore him.

"Use the knife I gave you. C'mon, give it your best shot. I won't stop you this time." I open my arms. "Take my fucking heart … you need it more than I do."

Her eyes flicker with shock from those words.

I've said them before, but maybe she never understood what I meant until now.

"You fell in love with her," Max mutters from the door opening.

"You asshole," she says through gritted teeth.

Her knife clatters to the floor as she storms at me, grabs my face, and kisses me.

I'm stunned.

Fucking stunned beyond comprehension.

She's actually fucking kissing me.

And my fucking heart is beating faster than it ever has before.

I pull away and scan her face, her downturned, red lips, that quirky nose, and those deep-set eyes that haunt my fucking soul, along with every inch of her tan skin, taking it all in at once, like time has suddenly come to an abrupt halt, and all that's left is her and me.

"This little thief called Ivy ... and the lying psycho whose cruel heart she stole," I murmur. "What a story."

Her lips slowly part. "You've never called me by my name."

A filthy grin forms on my face. "How does it sound?"

She begins to smile too. "Odd. You've called me thief and twig so many times now, I've grown used to it."

"Wait a minute ... you actually like him?" Heath narrows his eyes.

"*Like* is a big word," Max jokes before I can even speak up. "More like hate-to-like."

"She's a thief who's an expert at hiding things," I say. "Aren't you?" I nip at her lips, biting, tugging until it bleeds so I can suck up the droplets. "I already knew you were a filthy one the moment I got my hands on you." I stare into her eyes, wanting to see the reaction unfold. "You were dying for someone to come and eviscerate the people who fucked you over." I drag my thumb across my scar and wipe the blood on her lip too, mixing us together. "Someone who could show you how to use your rage. Your fear. And all your diabolical needs." I push my thumb deep into her mouth, deeper than her fucking uvula, and she still doesn't gag.

And fuck me, that greedy look in her eyes does something to me.

"You'd better fucking pick up that knife and kill me now," I say. "I'll never be satisfied, Ivy. I'll chase you to the ends of this earth if I have to."

"No," she says, her tongue wrapping around my thumb.

"Last chance, twig."

"You'd better believe he means it," Heath says, sporting an equally excited grin.

Still, she kicks the knife farther away.

My heart twists into violent knots when I look at her, but not in the way it used to.

I don't want to hunt her for the thrill ... I want to hunt her to make her fucking mine.

A smirk forms on my face as I curl my fingers underneath her shirt. "Is that the way you're going to treat the beautiful knife that gave you this pretty scar?" I pull up the shirt and push down her pants, running my fingers along the ridges of her marked skin until her whole body erupts into goose bumps.

This body has been through so much. "You really need to eat more, twig. Put some meat on those bones."

"Meat ... like this?" Heath grabs his package, making us all laugh.

"You're ridiculous," she says, narrowing her eyes. "You want to love me? Then start by begging." She puts a flat hand on my chest to keep me at bay. "On your knees."

My eyes twitch, but I still do what she says, dropping to my knees in front of her because she asked so nicely.

"Max, tie him up."

Max points at himself like he can't believe she's trying to rope him into this, but with one stern look, he swiftly runs to my cabinet and takes out some rope.

"Smart, using him to learn where I keep the good stuff," I say, tilting my head.

She smiles. "I learned from the best."

Fuck, I love this mouthy side of hers.

Max grabs my wrists, puts them behind my back, and ties me up. "Sorry if I'm too harsh."

"Don't be a wimp," I tell him. "I can handle it."

Heath rubs his hands. "I love where this is going."

"Talk shit, and I'll cut you a new smile after I'm free," I growl.

Suddenly, she grabs my chin, forcing me to focus on her. "You want to be with me? Then show me how much you're willing to do for me."

She leans in to press a kiss to my lips, and I force them apart with greed, shoving my tongue into her mouth right when she pulls away again, leaving me with a growing appetite for more.

Fuck, she knows exactly what she does to me, and she's enjoying it.

"Max ... tie Heath up too next to him."

Heath's look immediately changes from amusement to confusion, but I don't fucking mind, and he still goes along with Max as he sets him down beside me.

"Not talking so high and mighty now, are you?" I jest.

"Shut the fuck up," Heath growls, making me laugh.

Suddenly, she scoots a chair right next to me and settles her boot down on top of it. "That mouth is doing an awful lot of talking. Put it to better use, Silas. Unzip me."

I'm almost inclined to just bite her and leave my marks all over her for her insolence, but I'll give her the benefit of the doubt ... for now. After all, this is her only chance to take from me what she wants before it's my turn.

I lean in and bite down on her zipper, slowly pulling it down.

"Max, come here."

She grabs Max's hand and shoves it down her pants, and he immediately begins to glow like it's the first time he's touching her. God, that fucking simp is so easy to please.

"You two are going to watch while he plays with me," she says.

"What?!" Heath rasps, nearly breaking out of the ties that keep him bound. "That's not fai—"

She holds up a finger in his face. "What's not fair is that you two have been having your way with me all this time all because of some money I stole"—she shifts her finger to me—"and then you had the audacity to transfer all of the millions you have to *me*. So what was it all for? Lust? Power?"

"Obsession," I answer, looking her directly in the eyes until I can see it do something to her.

She loses track for a moment and clears her throat. "You two need to be punished for your crimes, and you *will* do what I say."

"Fuck, that just got me hard," Heath groans, and I wish I could punch the shit out of him for saying that out loud, but I can't because of these fucking ropes.

Goddammit.

Max moans out loud from touching her.

"Go on, that's it," she eggs him on.

He's getting a hard-on too. Now, it's so obvious.

"Oh fuck, you're so wet," Max says. "God, I love touching you."

"Max has been nothing but supportive, willing, and nice," she says, eyeing both of us.

"I can be nice," Heath says.

I snort. "In your dreams."

Suddenly, she slams her lips onto Max's mouth right in front of us, distracting me from what I wanted to say. Fuck me, the way she sticks her tongue into his mouth nearly makes me jealous enough to want to break free and steal her mouth for myself.

She keeps kissing him, and he keeps fingering her until her pants finally drop. Her wet pussy is exposed, and my mouth begins to water to the point that I have to swallow.

"God, you know just how to play with me," she moans as Max circles his fingers around her pussy.

"Make me come," she moans, looking me dead in the eyes while he plays with her.

I didn't think anything on this planet could make me more violent, but I guess I was wrong because not being able to touch her while he gives her all the pleasure is turning me into the unhinged psycho she made me out to be.

"Christ, this is too hot," Heath moans, clearly affected as well.

Her pants slowly drop below her thighs as Max wriggles her panties down until she's fully exposed. His fingers go to town, and she moans louder and louder until finally, she begins to shiver, and all the little hairs on her body stand up straight. "Fuck, Max," she moans.

My cock strains in my pants from the sight of her falling apart in front of me, desperate to feel just how wet she's become.

Suddenly, she grabs my hair and tilts my head back. "Beg."

My teeth grind together as I hiss, "Please ..."

A dangerous smirk forms on her face. "Now beg for forgiveness from my pussy... with your tongue."

Well, fuck me, with that attitude, I might just let her do this.

She hovers over my face, and my tongue greedily sticks out to claim the sticky mess Max left behind. God, she tastes so fucking good, I might almost forget she's got me roped down on the floor.

"That's it. Work that tongue," she moans while I swirl around her wet little pussy and suck on her swollen clit until it throbs for me again.

"You like this a little too much, twig," I growl while eating her out.

"She's finally giving you a taste of your own medicine." Heath chuckles.

She glares at him. "You think you're being spared?"

His eyes widen, and he swallows.

Suddenly, she grabs Max's package, rips down his zipper, and pulls out his dick right in front of Heath.

***

MAX

"Play with yourself. Don't let him touch you," she tells me.

I was already hard as can be from just touching her. If I start touching myself now, I might explode too soon. "God, you're ordering everyone around today, aren't you?" I say, jerking myself off.

"You like that, don't you?" Heath grins.

"Is that a surprise?" I retort, spreading my pre-cum everywhere.

"No ..." Heath's eyes gorge on my cock and her pussy, like he's having the time of his life watching both of us. "I can't take this much longer."

"You will because you're a good boy, aren't you?" she says.

His eyes twitch. "What did you just call me?"

When he attempts to get up, she forcefully pushes him down. "Who said you could stand? Stay there and earn the forgiveness you begged me for."

He swallows and grinds his teeth at the same time.

"I guess we both don't mind being her toy for today," I add.

He smirks. "For as long as Silas can hold himself back, you mean."

"Shut up," Silas grits, still licking her like he hasn't had a meal so good in years. "So goddamn wet. Are you ready for another orgasm?" he murmurs.

She shoves his face in further. "More licking, less talking."

"Fuck, that's sexy," I moan, rubbing myself until my veins throb.

"Both of you," Ivy says, looking at Heath too now.

"What? Your pussy?" Heath raises a brow.

She shoves me forward until my dick hits his lips.

"Him." A sexy smile tips up her lips. "Go on, show me how good you can suck."

What?

In shock, I stare down, my cheeks reddening quickly as Heath's eyes shimmer with enthusiasm. And then he opens his mouth and sticks out his tongue.

"Oh fuck … is this really—"

He wraps his tongue around my cock and sucks so hard I lose the ability to speak.

"You're a sensitive little twink, aren't you?" he groans, swirling his tongue around. "I like that. I like how desperate you are for more of my tongue." He swivels his tongue across the head. "More of my lips." He wraps them around the edges. "More of my throat."

He sucks me in farther and farther, beyond his uvula, soaking me in his saliva as my toes begin to curl and a half-cut-off moan exits my mouth. "F-fuck."

"Take him deeper," Ivy says, eyeing Heath. "I want you to feel what I felt when you fucked my throat."

"Fuck, you're a raunchy one, little thief," Silas groans, lapping her up. "You're just begging to be punished again, aren't you? If I wasn't tied up—"

"You'd what?" she taunts, tilting up his head by his hair. "Spank me?"

"Worse," he says.

"Thrust something up my ass?"

"More ..." The evil smile on his face only gets her going.

"Good thing you're stuck on your knees, then," she retorts before shoving his face back into her pussy.

But it's so damn hard to focus because of what Heath's doing with his tongue. He sucks me off like he's never had a more delicious snack in his life, and my nails are literally digging into his shoulders as I try not to come.

I can't help but move along with his rhythm, slowly going in and out to coat every inch of my dick with his saliva as the pre-cum begins to pour out of me.

"Fuck, I need you," Heath groans between thrusts. "Faster."

I never imagined he'd be on his knees for me, licking me off. It's all thanks to her and because of her that I finally had the confidence to confront my feelings, both for her *and* him.

I look at Ivy as she rolls her hips above Silas's tongue, and my God, it's so fucking sexy I just want to bury myself inside Heath's throat just from watching her enjoy herself thoroughly. We're both being pleasured side by side, and I can't help but grab her face and lick off her cheek the way he's licking me. But then she turns her head and kisses me right on the mouth, and I can't for a second even think of denying her the privilege of my lips as they part and her tongue invades.

"This feels too good," I groan, rolling my tongue around hers as my cock begins to throb inside Heath's mouth. "Don't stop."

"Come inside his throat," she whispers between kisses.

And I am fucking done for.

Completely lost inside that amazing mouth of hers.

I come so hard inside his throat that I whimper against her lips while Heath begins to choke and cough from my cum. But none of it matters as she drives her tongue inside my mouth, drowning out my sounds with her own as she rubs her clit on Silas's face.

"Fuck, she's coming," he groans, thrusting his tongue into her.

Heath pulls away to swallow, but I'm far too busy kissing Ivy to care. She grabs my shoulders and pulls me away from him until we're out of reach from both of them.

"Hey ..." Silas growls.

But she ignores him as she's kissing me, and I don't mind one bit.

"Don't fucking leave us hanging like this," he growls.

"That wasn't nearly enough for me," Heath groans, my juices still dribbling from his mouth.

She taunts them to the limit with these kisses before finally glancing at them as she pulls away from my greedy lips.

"Are you hard? Throbbing?" She grins.

"Fuck, please ..." Heath's begging too now, and I have to admit, I love hearing how guttural he sounds when he does it.

"Too bad because you're not getting any. This is *your* punishment."

Silas's eyes flicker with sudden fury. "You'd better take your fucking lips off him right now and come here and take this rope off, or I swear to God, I will come and impale you on my cock where you stand."

Suddenly, she pulls away from me and drags her panties back up, zipping up her pants. Then she picks up the knife from the floor where she dropped it.

"What are you doing?" Silas grits.

She points the sharp end at her own skin near her hand.

"Don't even think about it, twig—"

The blade cracks her skin open, blood running down her fingertips onto the wooden floor.

And Silas is beside himself with madness and a frenzied lust.

"You want this?" She tilts her head. "Then come and get it."

She throws the knife near his knees.

Oh, no.

This won't end well for her.

Silas's grin is beyond this world. "Wrong move."

***

IVY

Within seconds, Silas takes the knife between his teeth and cuts through the rope on Heath's wrists, who breaks free only to rip Silas's binds with his bare hands.

THWACK!

The knife zooms past my head, and I instinctively turn to look as it lodges into the cabinet behind me.

What the—

One sharp breath and he's right in front of me with that same vicious smile that used to make me want to scream.

He leans in so close I can feel his breath on my skin. "God, you smell so good when you're scared, my pretty little fucking thief ..." he whispers into my ear. "Run."

SIXTY-THREE

IVY

I don't wait even one second before I bolt out the door.

I glance over my shoulder as Silas and Heath casually grab the red purge masks lying on the cabinet beside the mirror, the same masks they had on when they first chased me into the woods, and the elation that ripples through me is riveting.

Heath throws Max a mask too. "Your turn to fucking hunt her down with us."

A smile forms on my face before I bolt through the hallways. "Can't catch me!"

"Watch us." Heath's warning as he puts on the mask, leaving an eerie glow near Silas's door, gives me the chills.

Goddammit, I missed this.

It's messed up and insane, but the moment they run after me down the stairs is when I come alive.

God, I am just as demented as they are, but I don't care anymore. I need this. I need it as much as they do.

I run down the stairs as fast as I can, leaving blood drops everywhere as breadcrumbs. I bolt out the door and across campus, all the way to Prior Forest way beyond. The trees loom over me, blocking out part of the sun, with the occasional chirping of birds to break the silence.

Until a cold, unhinged laughter fills that void. And my pussy actually throbs at the sound.

"Didn't you hear? There's nowhere you can hide from me, little thief. I will always fucking find you."

I stop and clutch a tree, smearing my blood all over the trunk.

"That pussy is *mine*."

His voice only makes me run harder and faster until my legs start hurting and my lungs become deprived of oxygen. Even then, I keep running, not because of my fear but in spite of it. After all, no one could ever harm a girl with monsters chasing her into the abyss.

Freedom has never tasted so bittersweet because even though I am free of my burden, my past, and my debt, this heart has been torn asunder by these boys ... but I wouldn't dream of stitching it back together. All the dark fragments of my soul belong to them, and I just know they'd guard every fucking piece with their lives.

I keep running through the forest until I reach the same rocky alcove where I first hid from them, and I come to a stop to take a breath. Around me, birds flutter through the trees, and I turn to see where the sounds are coming from.

More laughter emanates from the forests behind me, so I swiftly turn on my heels, ready to bolt.

A set of bright eyes flicker in the dark.

"What are you going to do now?" Heath's dark voice breaks my calm.

I shiver, still taking ragged breaths, while three devils in red LED masks approach steadily from each corner of the forest. But the thrill of the chase hasn't created the fear I'd expected it would ... instead, all I feel is tempestuous excitement.

"Nowhere to run, little thief," Silas says as he steps out half-naked from between several high trees beyond, the scars on his chest clearly visible in the moonlight.

"Except right into our arms," Heath adds, walking out from the left while tucking his hair into a bun as if preparing to sprint.

"God, I can't fucking wait." I can hear Max's voice far behind me, gentle, soothing ... provocative.

I step backward, driven by those LED masks alone, but I bump into the rocks instead.

Suddenly, they run at me, and I try to flee by crawling on top of the rock, leaving bloodied imprints in my wake. Two hands wrap around my ankle and pull me back down while my nails scratch at the stone.

"Gotchya," Silas whispers, licking the rim of my ear.

"No, it's too quick!" I yelp.

"Should've run faster then, thief," Heath growls before he approaches with a whole bunch of ropes.

My eyes widen. "What are you going to do with that?"

"What do you think?" Heath grins.

"Oh God, this is going to be so damn good. I can't wait," Max says, salivating at the mouth as he approaches too.

"I don't take kindly to being denied the pussy I love so fucking much," Silas whispers into my ear. "So now you'll be tied and used like the good little slut you are for us."

Heath throws the ropes around my wrists and ties them together.

Silas grips my bloodied hand and leans in to take a whiff, groaning wildly. "Your blood is like an aphrodisiac to me." Suddenly, he puts a knife to my throat, making me whimper. "Go on, aren't you going to scream for me? You know how much I love the sound."

"Don't you know me by now? I need a little bit more than just this," I say with a grin.

"You greedy little thief ..." he hisses through his mask.

"Don't tempt him," Max warns me.

"Too late."

Suddenly, Silas puts the knife to my pants instead.

RIP!

I shriek as he tears through it in one go—all the way from my butt down to my legs, shredding my clothes. He plants a hand on my back to keep me from moving as the knife handle slides up and down my slit. "You think it's a smart idea to tease a serial killer like that?"

"You deserved it," I murmur, trying to keep my whole body from shivering just from the touch of his blade.

I used to hate this so much ... but now, when that cold metal hits my skin, it makes me want to moan.

"And you deserve everything you have coming for you," Heath says, grinning as he kicks my legs apart.

"I told you I would make you love this damn knife ..." Silas whispers through the mask, pressing his body up against me. "As much as you fell in love with me."

Oh fuck, I'm already as wet as can be as Silas slowly inserts the handle of the knife into my pussy.

"Tell me. Say it out loud. Say you belong to me."

"I'm yours," I murmur between moans.

He leans in to whisper, "Good, because you've stolen my tainted heart, little thief. And you'd better take good care of it while I love you with every inch of my obscene fucking soul." He grins against my skin. "Now stand there like a good slut and take every inch of this knife until I'm satisfied."

He thrusts it inside while pressing himself against me as if he wants me to feel him invade my space, and I moan wildly, completely unhinged with lust.

It feels so good. I don't want him to stop even though that same knife once created the scar on my abdomen. He's twisted my mind beyond comprehension and distorted my heart until all it wanted was the debilitating taste of freedom after the fall straight into hell.

Heath grabs my breasts as I'm splayed against the rock and squeezes so hard I mewl.

RIP!

He tears the fabric of my shirt apart until my breasts spill out.

"That's it, moan for us," Silas groans behind me, thrusting it in so hard, I can feel his balled fist against me, warmth spreading between my legs.

Max rips down his zipper and pulls out his cock again. "God, I'm already hard again."

"You had your turn, twink," Heath says, licking his lips. "She's ours now. You sit and fucking watch."

Max settles on the rock in front of me so he can look at me while rubbing himself, and it only makes me even wetter.

"You like being watched, don't you?" Silas spanks my ass. "Filthy little slut."

"Fuck," I groan as he keeps going, alternating slaps with thrusts until my breath becomes hot and heavy.

"She's not allowed to come yet," Heath growls, twisting my nipples until I scream.

THWACK!

Silas's laugh fills my soul with unending lust. "Scream, thief, scream!"

THWACK!

The next slap is so hard my legs squeeze together as the pain sizzles through my entire body.

"Don't move," Silas grits, releasing the knife. "Keep it there and feel the fucking throbbing of your pussy as it falls apart for me."

He's right. I'm a throbbing mess, ready to come again so easily it shocks even me.

"Fuck, it's so hot to watch you guys use her," Max groans. "I've dreamed of this so many times."

"You're not the only one," Heath says, twisting my nipples once more until I squeal with delight.

Silas brings the hand he used to fuck me with the knife to my face, and my eyes widen.

He's covered in blood.

"See what your greed does to me? See how far I'm willing to go to fuck you and satisfy that wicked craving inside you?" He rubs it all over my lips and pushes them apart, shoving his fingers inside. "Taste me. Taste how much I want to fucking bleed my soul out for you."

He sinks deeper and deeper as the knife is firmly lodged between my pussy lips, a forever reminder of what I've become. What a sloppy mess I've turned into ... willingly.

He groans when my tongue wraps around his fingers, and he bites down on my shoulder, drawing blood as well as a scream as I come right there and then from the knife lodged inside me.

"Fuck, I love you. Now let me fucking take you to purgatory."

When the orgasm slows, he pulls me away from the rock while Heath pulls the knife out of me.

"So fucking wet," Heath mutters, licking it off. "I can't wait to taste it ten more times."

"Ten?!" I huff.

Silas spins me around and lifts me against the rock, then rips down his zipper.

"You wanted to taunt us, twig. Now accept your fucking punishment while we nail you to the fucking shrine where we initiated you to our immoral ways."

One thrust and I'm already lost as he impales me on his rock-hard cock, driving me insane.

"Open your mouth," he growls.

My lips part instinctively, and he spits inside, rubbing my tongue with his fingers as if to spread his toxic love like venom, and there is nothing more I want than to become poisoned by their love.

"Mine."

He smashes his lips onto mine, ravaging them with his tongue before splitting them open and forcing his way inside, invading me in every possible way. I am lost to them, lost to the way these boys claim me and mark me as theirs.

When his lips tear away from mine, Silas left a bloodied mark from a bite I hadn't even noticed he'd given me. And the smirk on his face is like a drug to me as he licks it off his lips. "Delicious."

Max approaches out of nowhere and goes to his knees below the rock. "I can't take it anymore," he mutters as he throws off his mask.

He positions himself beneath us, between Silas's legs, just so he can reach up to lick me. Feeling his tongue along with Silas's length as it throbs inside me is almost too much to take. My head tilts back, right where Heath has crawled on top of the rock.

He grabs my neck, squeezing the life out of me as he forces me back right onto his cock so I'm impaled on both ends. The lack of oxygen makes me feel like I'm on cloud nine.

How these boys keep doing this, I don't understand, and I don't think I ever will. But I don't need to understand my own desires in order to own them and give in. This is what I truly need, what I could never get enough of. These boys have invaded every fiber of my being with their filthy madness, turning my mind and heart into a captive to their every desire.

And even though they hurt me, knowing everything these boys have done for me, every sacrifice they made in my name, I would still make the same choice over and over again.

Because these boys who hunted me ... are *my* insane monsters.

***

HEATH

I bury myself inside her throat and watch her struggle against the rock, her fingers tightening and releasing the deeper I go. I squeeze her throat with one hand and her nose with the other, stopping her from taking even a single breath.

"Don't you understand? Every inch of you belongs to us, along with every fucking breath you want to take," I groan, pulling out. "Now suck in that oxygen, little slut."

She coughs and heaves for one second because that's all I'll allow her before I dive back in.

"Wrap that pretty little tongue around my cock," I say, slapping her cheeks until she finally does it. "Good girl. I know you like being used like this."

"Fuck, she's so tight," Silas groans, burying himself inside her to the hilt. "Take my fucking cock deep."

"Fuck, she's drenched," Max moans.

"You lick that sweet little pussy, Max. Keep her on that edge, don't let her come again," I growl, thrusting into her mouth like it's a pussy.

"This throat is so goddamn good for fucking I'm going to blow my load."

She mewls and shakes her head, so I grab her wrists and put them on her belly. "You keep those hands there while I coat that tongue with cum."

"You're gonna take him all the way, thief," Silas says. "We're going to fucking fill you to the brim, and you're going to keep it all inside, aren't you?"

"Swallow me down," I groan as I thrust three more times before going balls deep.

My cock throbs deep inside, and my eyes nearly roll into the back of my head as I roar out loud while my seed spurts into her, coating her throat.

I slap her cheek and pinch her nose. "Now swallow. Swallow, or you won't get to breathe anymore."

Her eyes are red, and her lips are swollen, but she still does exactly what I say like the greedy little slut she is, and I can feel her tongue wrapping around my shaft to clean it all off. "Good girl."

"Oh please, can I taste it?" Max moans.

"Fine then," Silas growls as he pulls her down from the rock and bends her over. "Open your mouth, slut."

I grab Max by the neck and push him down, tilting his head up by his hair. "Open your mouth."

She dribbles what's left of my cum right into Max's mouth, who gobbles it up like a needy little twink. "Good boy."

Now this? This is what I would fucking die for.

He leans in and steals a kiss from her while I tear off my mask. So I do the same, stealing him away from her, before I kiss her too, tonguing the two of them at the same time until our moans turn into one.

Not one, but two of my favorite toys as my fucking lovers. Mine to use … mine to fucking cherish. Until the day we fucking perish.

***

SILAS

I rip Ivy away from their lips and throw her down onto the muddy ground where my knife lies. I straddle her and shove her legs up far above her waist, exposing that filthy little pussy for everyone to see. And I give it a good slap so that I can listen to her scream.

"That's my girl," I growl as I push the knife into her cheek. "I need more. I'll always fucking need more, little thief. The one thing you stole wasn't yours to take ... so now you'll have to endure a lifetime of beggary. Think you can do it?"

"Silas," Max says through gritted teeth like he's scared for her.

But Heath holds him back by grabbing his throat and kissing him instead, distracting him long enough so I can finally have some one-on-one time with her.

She whispers, "You won't kill me."

The edge of the blade punctures her skin. "Tell me why you think that a serial killer would be able to stop himself."

"You made a deal ..." Her eyes sparkle. "A new deal. One neither of us can ever run away from."

Forgiveness.

That's what she promised to deliver to my greedy fucking heart.

The one thing I will never be given freely ... unless I work for it every damn day of the rest of my life.

Grinning, I pull at my mask and tear it off, chucking it aside. "Then you truly are a master thief," I say, slowly sliding the knife down her body as I lean up to watch the fear slowly build in her eyes. "Stealing not just my heart ... but my freedom too."

I puncture her skin right above the scar I have already created to draw out a letter.

"You're chained to me, Ivy," I murmur as I pierce her skin again, finishing the first letter.

"And I need the entire world to know you belong to me in every sense of the word."

"God!" she yelps as I carve the second letter.

"God can't hear you in the depths of hell, little thief. But the devil can ... and he sure loves to hear you beg," I murmur.

Her blood pulsates with heat, and I bring some to my lips and suck it up gleefully before adding the third letter.

"You can do it."

She sucks in a breath through her teeth.

"Look at me."

Tears stain her eyes, but she keeps them fixated on me as I carve the fourth one deep into her skin.

"Good girl. Just one more."

I bring my thumb to her eyes to pick up the stray tear and lick it off. Then I etch the final word into her skin while her drawn-out moan fills the open air, and birds flock to the scene.

I throw the knife to the side. "Now, say the word I spelled out."

She bites her bottom lip. "Silas."

As blood rivulets down her skin, I admire my artwork, and my fingers trace the lines. "Silas's thief."

I bring my fingers to my lips and suck off her blood, the taste exhilarating and beyond this fucking world.

I lift her hips and watch her eyes follow me down as my tongue dips out to lick the blood straight off the letters on her skin. I shove two fingers into her and roll them around while I apply lavish licks to the wound I created until the agony on her face is replaced by bliss, and nothing is left but sheer wantonness for my deranged love.

And I keep thrusting them in and out of her, coaxing out more moans while watching her unravel right in front of me.

"Fuck, I'm coming," she mewls.

"Yes, come all over the blood on my hands," I say, rubbing her G-spot.

She moans out loud as her legs quake, and all the hairs on her skin come to life when suddenly, her pussy contracts around my fingers.

I grin with pride as I lower her down and bring my tip to her slit, hovering so close I can feel her whole body tighten. "Now beg."

"Please ..." she whimpers, lost to both the pain and the pleasure while I rip through her pussy with no-holds-barred.

My hand lodges around her throat as I bury myself deep inside her and lean over to smash my lips on hers. "My fucking thief. To have and to hold."

I fuck her so hard, her whole body begins to quake, and her bound hands search the air for something, anything to hold on to. I offer her my neck, smiling proudly as she digs her nails into my skin and squeezes my throat shut.

But I will never, ever stop fucking with her. She is mine now, and I am hers.

And with the taste of her blood running down my fucking tongue, I come harder than I ever have before. Inside *my* fucking thief.

The only girl who has ever managed to steal this fucking pitch-black heart.

SIXTY-FOUR

IVY

Suddenly, he lifts me and spins us around until he's beneath me, and I'm on top of him, where he keeps fucking me.

"You thought I was finished?" he says.

"Fuck, I can't take this any longer," Max says as he kneels behind Silas just to touch me.

"Use her then if you want her so badly," Heath says, approaching from the front, admiring the view of me riding Silas.

But I'm too lost in ecstasy, and the need for more of this fucked-up love has drowned out all the noise inside my head.

Silas suddenly picks up the knife and pushes it into my hands.

"Now it's your turn."

"What?" I mutter.

"Cut me."

I shudder in disbelief, but Silas grabs my wrists and forces me down on top of him. The sharp end of the knife pushes into his skin ... right where he marked himself.

"You know your name. Give it to me."

When I don't move, he forces me to, writing out the first letter.

"I."

When the letter finishes, his hard-on twitches deep inside me.

He likes this.

He likes to feel pain as much as he likes to dish it out.

My hand instinctively moves to the next letter without conscious thought. And when I carve it into him, he thrusts in deep, moaning out loud.

The sound gives me goose bumps.

"Don't stop," he growls.

"V."

His hand guides me across his chest to the final place for the letter, and I push the knife to break the skin.

"Y."

Right then, Max pushes up behind me and enters my pussy too, the pressure causing me to scratch out the last remaining letter until it deepens the scar already on Silas's chest. "Apostrophe S!"

"Fuck!" he grits before he grabs my throat and smashes his lips onto mine.

I can't help but let him in and consume me whole as his tongue rolls around mine, thrusting into my mouth as violently as these boys are fucking me.

"Fuck, that must've hurt." Heath bends over, as my lips tear away from Silas, only to land on his instead. Heath's lips slam into mine with desire, and he grabs ahold of both my nipples and twists them to his heart's content. Only a scream can manage to tear away my lips from his.

"Yes, that's it, little thief. Scream for us," Heath says.

"Fuck, she's so tight," Max says, burying himself inside me. "I want to come inside you. Please, can I? Please?"

His begging nearly sets me off. "Fuck, yes."

Silas snatches the knife from my hand and chucks it away. "Look at what you did, little thief. Read it. Tell me what I am."

"Ivy's liar," I reply.

"The liar who didn't believe his heart would ever be stolen, and the thief who fucking took it anyway belong together. Do you hear me?"

But I can barely hear his words.

All I can focus on are the two cocks thrusting into me and the hands that toy with my nipples, all three playing with my soul.

"I want you to be mine too," Max says.

"You belong to all of us," Heath says, gripping my throat to make me focus on him. "We are yours, and you are ours."

"Yes," I say between breathy moans.

"Now ride us, little thief," Silas says. "Like a good little slut ready to be fucked every day of the rest of her goddamn life."

"Mine." Heath squeezes my neck as he slams his lips onto me, sealing his promise with a kiss. "Forever and fucking always."

I kiss him back just as feverishly, completely overcome by passion.

"Is this a marriage proposal?" I joke.

"Shut the fuck up and take that dick deeper into that wet fucking pussy like a good little slut," Silas growls, stealing my lips from Heath to smother me with more devilish licks.

He thrusts along with Max, both dicks rubbing up against my insides, while Heath twists my nipples just to listen to me squeal.

"Oh fuck, I'm gonna come," Max mutters, and I can feel him explode before he's even finished his sentence. "F-fuck!"

Heath suddenly drags him away from me while he continues to spurt out cum. "Keep going."

"How?" Max mutters.

But Heath settles down behind him and directs his cock at my ass instead. "I'll make you."

Max is forced into my ass by Heath as he thrusts into Max, and I cry out in both pain and bliss as the two cocks inside me pulsate, one in my ass and one in my pussy.

"Greedy little thing ... you can't get enough, can you?" Silas says, pumping away.

"Fuck, you're so big," Max moans.

"Shut it, little twink. Take that dick like a good boy," Heath groans, and I can hear them going at it behind me. "Fuck her like you mean it."

Max's pace increases, and he grips my ass to plunge in deeper and deeper while I fight the urge to come again.

"Oh fuck, your ass feels so good," Max moans.

Silas grips my nipples, pulling me down with him just so he can lavish me with obsessive licks.

"Fucking come for us, then. Come all over our cocks."

And I do.

Not just from his words but from their dicks filling me up and then some.

"Oh no, I can't hold it," Max mewls. "You're hitting my—"

His words are replaced by a long-drawn-out whimper as his dick throbs inside my ass while Heath pounds into him. Warm cum fills me to the brim.

"Fuck!" Heath pulls out of Max and shoves him aside to thrust into my ass instead just one final time before exploding inside me too. And he leans forward against my back, kissing me softly before collapsing.

Max and Heath are wasted as they sink onto the grass, breathing out of control.

"You're so fucking filthy just for us," Silas says, swiftly switching from my pussy to my ass too. "Take my cum too, slut."

And he roars out loud as he plunges in deep, filling me to the brim a final time.

I slump down on top of him, all my energy completely spent.

My body was destroyed, but my mind ... invigorated.

All that's left are our soft breaths carried away by the wind.

His fingers softly grab a few loose strands of my hair from my forehead, the caress that follows so gentle it nearly makes me want to melt into his skin and stay there like the scar I just created.

"Did you mean it?" I mutter.

"What?" he asks.

"When you said you loved me."

His eyes flicker with interest as a smile tugs at his lips. "You tell me. Are the words of a liar reliable?"

I lean up, slapping him in the chest. "You did not just fucking say that after making me go through—"

"The most amazing sex you've ever had in your entire fucking life?" Heath interjects.

Max laughs. "Wow, arrogant."

"And you love it, admit it," Heath retorts.

Max chuckles. "True."

"The point is ... you made me put my name on your skin," I say, trailing my fingers around the bloody scar. "That means something."

"Something ..." He raises a brow as he grabs my fingers and brings them to his lips, licking off the blood. "Or *everything*?"

I shake my head and snort.

"I love you," Max says. "I'll say it every day. Every hour. Every minute."

"If you say second next, I will shut you up with a dick in your mouth, and that is not an empty threat," Heath warns him.

"Oooh ..." Max blushes. "That's a hard choice."

"Wait until I make it even harder by not letting you come for the rest of the week."

"What?!" Max sits up straight. "That's not fair."

I chuckle at their banter. "You two really were made for each other."

"How can you tell?" Heath jests back, but then he leans in to peck me on the cheeks. "But Max is not the only one who's fallen madly in love."

I blush. "Oh."

Silas grips my chin. "I was the first."

"You really do that name on your chest justice," Max says. "Liar."

"That's not for you to decide," Silas says, still gazing at me. "Do you believe me or not?"

"I don't know ... how can one ever believe a liar?" I say coyly.

"It's not like I don't have a fucking lifetime to prove it to you." He smirks. "Because none of us are going anywhere."

"Deal."

His eyes narrow like he can't believe his own ears. "Are you trying to make a new agreement with me, little thief?"

"I need to know for sure."

Suddenly, he puts both hands on my ears and rips out my hearing aids, chucking them aside.

"Hey!" I yell, but I'm not sure I said the right word because I can't hear.

He grabs my face with both hands, forcing me to focus on those piercing green eyes that haunt me.

And then he draws out words. In the air.

With sign language.

I love you.

The silence is overwhelming. Overpowering. All-consuming.

I swiftly draw some signs in the air.

You can sign?

That same vicious smile I used to hate now makes me fall.

He opens his mouth to say the words along with his signings because they're still choppy, like how a beginner would use them, and I read his lips to fill in the missing words.

I learned it because of you.

I want to be inside your mind even when you can't hear me.

Because you made me feel my heartbeat for the first time in my entire fucking life.

The tears roll down my cheeks right onto his lips, which he gleefully sucks in like it's nourishment to his soul.

"I. Love. You."

He says it out loud and in sign language.

But I heard.

Not with my ears but with the entirety of my soul.

I look up at Heath, who also signs to me while saying the words, trying his very best.

I learned it from Max's book, so I will never miss out on a vital piece that makes you who you are ever again. Because I love you too.

Max smiles.

I've always loved you, you know that, and there is nothing in this world you could ever do that could make me unlove you.

Their signings are rudimentary, but it matters. It matters to me because I feel seen in my needs.

And I realize now I'm not the only thief. I never was.

These boys have seized my soul ... And I never want them to give it back.

SIXTY-FIVE

SILAS

"Wow, you fixed up this place real quick," Ivy says, looking around the Skull and Serpent Society house, which is looking brand new after a quick fixer-upper and a lick of paint.

I casually saunter up the stairs. "You think no one will notice a bomb went off?"

She snorts while walking beside me. "The new wood on the walls makes it pretty obvious."

"Well, shit," Heath mutters as he follows us. "Guess Dean Rivera will be pissed."

"He'll be fine. He's trashed this house on multiple occasions himself," I reply.

"How do you know?" Heath asks.

I frown. "Because he told me. Duh."

"So why did you want me to come?" Ivy asks.

Max waits for us at the top of the stairs. "You ready?"

She looks awfully confused. "For what?"

"It'll all be clear the moment you see," Max says, and he hooks his arm around hers. "C'mon." He impatiently drags her to the guest room.

"You sure this was a good idea? What if she doesn't like it?" Heath grumbles.

"She will," I say, following them through the hallway.

Max puts his hands in front of her eyes. "Wait until I say you can look."

"Okay ... This is awkward," Ivy says. "What kind of secret is this?"

He opens the door and the curtains and turns on the lights. "Open your eyes."

She looks around and marvels at the newly painted walls, the decor, and all the new furniture inside the guest room.

"What ... what is this?"

"Your new room. On the weekends anyway," I say, smirking.

"You redid it all for me?" she says, tears in her eyes.

Heath opens the closet door and shows her the rows and rows of new clothes and shoes, and he holds up one of the size cards. "That's you, right?"

She touches the fabrics and nods like she's dreaming.

"And that's not all," Max says, opening the next door. It leads into our second guest room, which has been filled with all the toys a small girl like Cora could ever wish for. "She'll never be bored."

"I ... I don't know what to say," she says.

"You don't have to say anything," Heath states.

"We just want you two to be happy," Max declares.

"While you're our guest," I add, raising a brow. "Which will happen every weekend."

"Oh?" She grins. "You've made plans?"

"You made the deal, not me," I say, folding my arms. "And I thought I was being more than generous by allowing you the week off to catch your breath after we fuck you senseless."

"Though, I can't promise I won't visit your home every weekday too," Heath says, clearing his throat.

"Same," Max says, giggling as he comes to stand beside us. "I can't wait for her to see it."

She frowns. "See what?"

I throw her a key, and she catches it just before it hits her in the chest.

"Rosewood Street, 320. Downtown Crescent Vale City. A three-bedroom, two-story house with two bathrooms, a garage, and your own fenced yard. It's yours."

For a moment, she merely stares at me in disbelief.

"You didn't have a house anymore, right?" Heath says. "Now you do."

Suddenly, she runs up to us and wraps her arms around all three of us, squishing us together so tightly I can't even breathe.

"Thank you," she murmurs, and for the first time since I heard those words, I actually feel my heart squeeze like it's grateful or something. Weird fucking feeling I'm not used to yet.

"Anything for you," Max says.

"Don't be such a fucking simp. I'm doing this for me," I retort, pulling away.

She snorts. "Of course, you are."

I grab her throat and pull her close. "You need to be available to me, so I made it happen."

The excitement in her eyes tells me enough.

"Whew, it's getting hot in here already," Max says.

Suddenly, a loud bang downstairs makes us all look up.

"What was that?" Max mutters.

Heath pushes past us and barges out the door to check, so we follow him out.

"SILAS!"

"Oh God, run," Max mutters as we approach the stairs while Heath starts to bite his nails.

"Who is that?" Ivy asks as we look at the woman with the long black hair barging into the house. Lana Rivera.

Max squeaks. "Oh God, my mother."

"Silas, what the fuck did you do to my son now?" She steps closer until she's right in my fucking face. "You've been dragging him into your murder sprees?"

"That's my fault," Ivy says.

When Max's mom fixates on Ivy, I block her with my body. "It was my idea to go there in the first place. I take full responsibility."

"I went along with it on my own accord," Max says, quaking in his shoes. "I couldn't let her die."

"I'm sorry, I didn't mean to involve any of them in my mess," Ivy says.

"But we just wouldn't leave her alone," I say, smirking.

The door cracks open again, and now my mom and dad also barge in, breathing wildly.

"I tried to stop her," my mom says between breaths.

"She wouldn't fucking listen to me," my dad grits. "As usual."

"I needed to hear this with my own ears," Max's mom says.

She glares at Ivy, looking her up and down like she's inspecting her worth and the weight she carries in the world.

"She's the girl I told you about," my dad says. "The one they rescued."

Lana's eyes widen and narrow within a fraction of a second. "So ... this is her? This is the girl you three killed for?"

"Her name is Ivy," Max says.

"She needed our help, so we gave it to her," I say.

"It's not what you think," Max mutters.

"It is, and I'm not fucking hiding it anymore," I say. "We're in love with her."

Lana's jaw slowly drops. "We?"

"Oh God ..." Max hides his face in his hands.

"Don't be a pussy, Max," Heath says, slapping him on the shoulder.

"Shut up," Max's mom says, her black hair swaying over her shoulder.

"Wait ... You actually fell in love?" my mom asks like she's in shock.

I grind my teeth. "Is that so hard to believe?"

Lana tilts her head at Ivy. "Let me see you."

Ivy steps out from behind me despite me trying to hold her back from both moms' wrath.

"I apologize for all the damage he's done on my behalf," she says. "But I owe him my life."

"Really?" Mom throws her purple hair back, a smirk slowly appearing on her face. "I never imagined my son would actually kill for a reason other than self-gratification."

"Wait, what?" My dad's brows furrow. "You're actually okay with this?"

"If it's for the right reasons ..." Mom says.

"She had a child. Well, not hers, technically, but she was taking care of her. Her name's Cora, by the way. Her half sister. She's really sweet. Poor girl was thrown between father and her mother, who died because of him, by the way." Max just keeps going until Heath finally steps on his foot, and he whimpers in pain.

"Max, that's enough, thank you." Lana sighs.

"Wow. I'm so sorry, Ivy. That sounds horrible," Mom says.

"It was," Heath says. "Silas had good reason to go on a murder spree. You'll just have to forgive him."

"Do I now?" Mom raises a brow. "But all those murders still don't account for the missing money in Silas's bank account..."

She homes in on me, and I feel like I just got caught red-handed.

Fuck.

I didn't know Mom and Dad actually kept an eye on it.

Ivy rummages in her pocket. "Actually, I've been meaning to give this back."

"What?!" I grit, but she still hands it over to me.

"I don't want this. I have enough," she says, smiling. "I have enough when I have you guys."

I was almost ready to throw her over the railing and spank her ass right in front of everyone, but that smile ... God, that fucking smile makes my heart throb so goddamn hard I can't fucking say no.

Still, I push her hand back. "I want you to buy every goddamn food you could ever dream of, every damn day, for the rest of your life with this money. So keep it."

She smiles. "I don't need all that. Please, take it back. I don't want to be the reason y'all start a family feud," she says, pressing the transfer paper into my chest. "You've given me everything I'll ever need."

"Aw ..." Max's eyes tear up.

But it's the way she said "please" that makes me yield.

I grunt and snatch the paper, tucking it into my pocket. "Fine. But I will be buying you *and* Cora breakfast, lunch, and dinner every day of the fucking week."

"I'll hold you to that." She winks.

She thinks this is funny, but I'll punish her for this later.

"I'm impressed." Mom snorts. "It's not every day someone actually manages to bring Silas to his knees."

My eyes begin to twitch, and my mom just laughs, patting me on the shoulder. "You'll be fine. Your father got used to it too."

"Used to what? Having feelings?" Heath snorts.

"Wait, so you're just gonna forgive him?" my dad growls at her. "He gave all his money away, they killed a dozen or more in the streets, destroyed a fucking mansion, murdered twenty more, *and* damaged the Skull and Serpent Society house, Pen."

"And? My men took care of the bodies, erased their tracks, she just gave the money back, and the house has been fixed, hasn't it?" Mom shrugs. "I'd say they did a well enough job, considering they had the best intentions."

"*Best intentions*?!" my dad shouts.

Heath laughs, but quickly shuts his mouth when my dad throws him a look with those laser eyes of his.

Man, I understand now how people can instantly tell they're my parents.

"C'mon, Felix ... don't pretend you don't remember what it was like for us." Mom winks. "You know damn well you were the same. Give these boys a break. They did well."

Dad's jaw tenses, and he rolls his eyes. "Women ... Fine," he grumbles, and he walks over to me to give me an awkward, over-the-top, manly hug. "I'm proud of you."

"Thanks," I say. "But please don't ever hug me again. It's fucking weird."

Max laughs, and first, everyone looks at him like he's lost his mind, but then Heath, his mom, and my mom all begin to laugh, along with myself. And finally Ivy does too.

"Oh, cheer up, grump," Max's mom says, punching my dad in the shoulder.

"Your mom's not that bad, honestly," Ivy whispers into my ear.

"You should see her wrangle my extra dads," I reply.

"Wrangle who?" Uncle Dylan says as he walks in. "Sorry, I didn't catch that, care to repeat before I light your room on fire?"

"Oh, fuck no," Heath says, awkwardly turning away. "I'm going."

"Stay," I bark, dragging him back by his shirt.

"What? I just arrived. The party's only getting started when I'm here," Dylan says, flicking his lighter up and down. "What'd I miss? Who are we punishing? I'll bring the heat."

"Dylan..." my dad groans, rubbing his forehead. "This doesn't involve your kids. Stay out of it."

"It will involve them at some point. Guarantee it," he says. "They have a knack for getting themselves in big trouble. Especially when it comes to their unhinged half brother."

"Unhinged?" I parrot.

"Only mildly," Max mutters under his breath, so I throw him daggers with my eyes.

"I'm sure you'll be there to protect them all when the time comes," Alistair says as he throws his arm around Dylan's shoulder. "Right?"

"What are you guys even doing here?" I ask.

"Checking up on my nephew. Is that a crime?" Alistair asks. "Be glad we stayed outside until after Pen and Felix berated you all." He winks.

"They insisted on coming too," Mom explains.

"It was needed, after what I heard," Dylan says.

"Don't act like you didn't break down the entire Skull and Serpent Society with your dad," my mom tells him.

"Says the woman who lit Spine Ridge U on fire," Dylan retorts.

Ivy's eyes widen. "What? She set the building on fire for real?"

Now everyone begins to laugh, except Ivy, who doesn't have a clue what kind of family she's gotten herself into. But she'll learn soon enough. I'll make sure of that.

Alistair clears his throat. "So ... now that we're all together, who's up for a family dinner next weekend? Of course, Heath, Max, Elliot, and all the other kids are also invited."

"Wait a minute, you mean Kai, Nathan, Uncle Felix, and Dylan will be in the same room?" Max asks.

"You got a problem with that?" Lana asks him.

"No, no, not at all." Max laughs and puts his hands up like he's calling out a truce. "I just thought it was weird."

"Why?" Ivy asks curiously.

"Oh, Dylan and Kai, as well as Felix and Nathan have a very violent history," Max whispers into her ear.

"Nothing to concern yourself with," I add.

"The past is the past," Alistair says. "So are y'all coming or what? Atlas, Orion, and Apollo will also be there, Heath."

"What about Ivy? Is she welcome too?" Max asks.

"Of course, the more the merrier," Dylan says.

"You're awfully casual about inviting someone you don't know," Alistair says.

"Pfft. Of course, it's not my house." Dylan shrugs.

"Where is it, then?" Max asks.

"Torres Casino restaurant. We've got the whole floor."

"Holy shit, Kai and Ares's casino?" Max mutters.

"I don't know if I like this idea," Heath says, folding his arms.

"You should come," Ivy says, wrapping her arm around his. "I'd like to meet your families."

"Aw ... who can resist that cuteness?" Max rubs his lips together.

Heath rolls his eyes. "Fine, fine, we'll go."

Ivy smiles. "I'm glad you changed your mind."

"You won't say that after someone pulls out a knife just for being offended," I say.

"No. No, no." Alistair raises a finger. "No weapons. No knives, no guns, no machetes, and no baseball bats. Nothing. That's the rule at the family dinner table."

I grin. "Who said anything about needing a weapon to inflict pain?"

Mom makes a face. "Felix, remind me to make sure Kai and Ares bought those plastic forks."

"Your families sure are a violent bunch," Ivy whispers.

I whisper back, "You don't even know the half of it." I grin like the psycho I am. "Welcome to the asylum."

EPILOGUE

HEATH

I sigh and put my phone away. "Why did I even say yes to this?"

Ivy throws her arm around my waist and drags me along. "C'mon, you'll be fine. It's just a family dinner."

"You don't know our history," I say.

"My stepdad literally tried to kill me," she says.

I nod. "Okay, fine, you win in the shitty family category."

She winks. "Your family loves you. Even if you don't see it."

"I'll just sit it out." As we make our way to the restaurant, I keep tugging at my clothes. "Jesus, are these suits supposed to feel so tight?"

"No, your muscles are just that big," Max says, licking his lips like he wants to take a bite out of me even though we're all wearing the same thing. "You look handsome."

I grab his chin and make him look even more. "And you look appetizing. Might take a bite out of you later after dinner."

"Oh ..." He blushes. "I'll be your dessert."

"Don't go playing around without us," Silas says.

"Family time first, then playtime," Ivy says, winking.

"Playtime? Now you've got my attention," I say, raising a brow as I pull both of them close. "I have a closet full of toys back at home that I can't wait to use. On both of you. Maybe at the same time."

"Dude, we're in a casino. People can hear you," Silas grits.

"So? I don't care who sees," I say, squeezing them against my pecs. "I fucking love these two."

"Don't claim her all for yourself," Silas says, throwing me a look.

"Claim who?"

I come to a full stop from the sound of that voice, my whole body vibrating as though time has ceased to exist.

Cecelia stands in the doorway to the restaurant area, her arms casually folded, her blue-studded dress gleaming like the smile on her face.

"Cece," I mutter, completely overwhelmed.

"We'll let you two talk," Silas says, dragging Max and Ivy away from me.

"Hey, little brother," Cecelia says, tucking back her curly blond hair. "Missed me?"

"You're here." I'm still in disbelief. "How?"

"Mom and Dad begged me to come back. At least for a week or so."

"Wait … *begged*?" I frown. "I thought Mom and Dad sent you off to that boarding school."

She rubs her lips together, then sighs. "I'm sorry, Heath. They were lying to you."

My fist balls. "Why?"

She averts her eyes. "Because I wanted them to. I asked them not to tell you."

"What? But that doesn't make any sense. They shipped you off to that boarding school, right?"

She shakes her head. "No. I went there because I wanted to."

All this time, I was so angry with my parents for forcing her to go there and not telling me until it was too late. But it was all her idea, and I don't know how to feel about that.

My face contorts. "Why couldn't you just tell me?"

"Because I knew you'd never let me go there," she says. "It's Prodigium Academy."

Damn right, I wouldn't. That place is filled to the brim with pretentious and rich assholes.

She approaches me and grabs my hands. "I didn't tell you because I knew you'd try to stop me before I could even try." She squeezes them softly, looking up into my eyes. "It was a once-in-a-lifetime opportunity, and I didn't want to risk losing the chance."

"So you had Mom and Dad take the fall," I grit.

"They agreed to do it for me because they love you. Don't be mad at them, please," she says, her eyes tearing up. "Please, I don't want my decision to be the reason you hate them."

"I don't... hate them." I sigh and look away. "I'm angry that you thought you had to force them to lie to me just to get what you wanted."

"I'm sorry, Heath. I just know how you are. I know you only want to protect me," she says.

Screw it.

I wrap my arms around her and hug her so tightly she can barely breathe, but I don't care.

"I'm sorry," she mutters again.

"Stop apologizing."

"But I hurt you," she says, hugging me back.

"You did it because you thought I would take away your only opportunity at something you really wanted to do," I say. "And I'm sorry I made you feel like you had to lie."

We hug for a few more minutes as I soak in the fact that she's back.

"I missed you, Cece."

"I missed you too, lil' bro," she says, sniffling as she pulls back.

"So ... you're a Prodigy now, huh?" I say, and I mess up her hair. "My fucking sister is studying with the richest of the rich."

"Heath, stop it," she hisses. "I'm trying to look good for the rest of the family too."

"Maybe you should drop by more often so they'd see you more too," I say.

"Hmm ... maybe..."

I cross my arms. "I promise I won't force you to stay."

She narrows her eyes. "You swear you won't try to stop me from going back there?"

"On my life. And his," I say, pointing at Max over my shoulder because I know he's watching us.

I could feel his eyes beam into my back.

"Wait, what?" Max mumbles, making Cece laugh.

"I couldn't ever fucking hurt him, so my promise is solid, trust me on that," I say.

"Why?" She's got that smug smile on her face just like I remember. "Something I need to know, Heath?"

"Actually, we're dating," I say, stepping back to pull Max into the conversation.

Max splutters, "Wait, hold up—"

But I kiss him on the lips to shut him up and show the world I mean it.

"Wow, holy shit," Cece says.

My lips leave a stain on his, along with a giant blush turning his entire face red.

"I didn't know you were gay," Cece says.

"No."

Ivy's standing in the hallway, so I go and grab her and kiss her too, right in front of Cece.

"Bi," I add after I've taken my lips off hers. "And damn proud."

Cece's staring at us with wide-open eyes. "Wow ... two at the same time?"

"Well, uh, it's complicated," Max says, scratching the back of his head while laughing.

"Three, if you count Silas." Ivy shrugs.

"THREE?!" Cece screams. "Holy shit, girl, nicely done." She high-fives Ivy. "Also, Silas? I thought that dude didn't have a heart."

"I didn't think so either, but I guess we were all wrong," Silas interjects. "Mom asks if we're coming."

"Right, of course," Max says as Silas walks off again.

"Wait," my dad's voice makes me turn around.

Mom and Dad are standing in the hallway, staring at us so uncomfortable that the room feels like it got ten degrees colder.

"Yikes," Max mutters, grabbing Ivy's hand. "Let's go introduce you to the rest of the family."

He pulls her away from us, so I have some time alone with my family.

"Heath," Mom mutters, tears staining her eyes. "It really hurt."

I walk to them and grab my mom, hugging her tightly before she begins to cry. "I'm sorry, Mom. I'm so sorry."

But it's no use. We're both fucking crying, and I don't want to stop either.

"It's okay," she whispers, caressing my back.

"No, it's not," I say.

"You were angry," my dad says. "I get it."

"You love Cece, and you wanted to protect her. That's a good thing," Mom says, grabbing my face. "That's why we had to lie. For her sake as well as yours so you wouldn't go get her back. She needed the time alone."

"I understand now," I say. "And I'm sorry for fucking things up."

My dad pulls me in for a hug. "Come here."

Even Cece comes in for the hug.

"Group hug," she muses, making us all laugh.

"I'm glad you're back, sis," I say when we're all done squeezing each other to death. "You missed a shit ton of stuff."

She raises a brow. "Oh? Well, then, tell me all about it over dinner."

"There's just one more thing I have to do," I say, walking to the bathroom.

"Cool, I'll see you in there," Cece says, wrinkling her nose when she smiles.

I head to the nearest toilet and pull out my bottle of pills.

The one bottle I've been carrying with me all this time because I wondered if I would need them again. But that's just it. I don't think I do.

These feelings I've been numbing are allowed to exist, no matter how dark or sad or how incredibly overpowering they get. Nothing is too difficult to deal with that it will ever make me want to hide again.

Because I have them now.

Ivy and Max.

And the loneliness will never again take hold of my heart.

I open the lid of the toilet, pour out the bottle's contents, and stare at the pills for a few seconds before I flush them down.

And it feels like a giant weight has been lifted off my shoulders for the first time in a long while.

* * *

MAX

I pull out a seat for Ivy and let her sit down first before I sit beside her.

"So ... who's that lady over there?" Atlas asks, running his fingers through his wolf-cut hair.

"She's taken already," I say, putting my arm around her shoulders.

"Relax, I was just asking." He chuckles. "I have better things on my mind than girls."

"I haven't seen you before," Ivy says, holding out a hand. "Ivy Clark."

"Atlas Torres," he says, shaking her hand. "Pleasure to meet you."

"You aren't at Spine Ridge U yet, are you?" she asks him.

He shakes his head. "Not yet. I'm planning to go there next year. If it all works out."

"Wait, I'm confused. Are you Levi's brother?" Ivy asks Atlas.

"No, Apollo's," I explain. "I know, it's confusing. Levi is my half brother. Atlas and Apollo are Crystal and Ares's kids. He's the youngest of the two."

"Youngest, but not the dumbest," Atlas says, snorting.

"If you say so," I reply.

"Don't get all crummy on me, Max. That's not your style."

"Max has style?" Elliot Fletcher muses as he sits down beside me, and he punches me in the shoulder. "Good to see you finally got the girl."

"Hold on, he's sharing," Heath says as he sits down across from us together with Cecelia. "With me and Silas."

"Three boys from our family?" Sunny Reed suddenly comes to sit beside Ivy. "Damn, girl. I don't know anyone who'd have the stomach for that."

"Don't listen to her. She hates everyone in this room," Elliot whispers to Ivy.

Sunny chucks a piece of bread at him so hard it leaves an imprint on his forehead. "Shut it, lil' dicky."

"Little?!" Elliot scoffs. "I do not—"

"Prove it," Sunny says, leaning back in the chair. "Go on then, show the rest your teeny tiny dick. They're waiting."

"Sunny, we're at a family dinner, please."

My mother steps closer and clutches our chairs. Sunny immediately straightens herself in her seat.

"And you boys, behave around the new girl. For the love of God, we do not need to scare her away the first time she meets us," my mom tells Atlas and Elliot, and they immediately look away as if they're scared for their lives.

And something about that is so fucking funny, I burst out into laughter.

Mom leans over to stare at me with those killer eyes of hers. "Stop laughing."

I nearly shit my pants.

"Yes, Mom."

"Good."

She smiles. "Keep it civil. This is a family dinner, after all," she says before walking off.

"Holy shit, your mom's intimidating as hell," Ivy says.

"You should've seen her when she was in her twenties." I look up at one of my extra dads, Nathan, suddenly hovering over my chair.

"Jesus, where'd you come from?" I say, grabbing my heart. "I didn't even fucking see you approach."

"I'm a ghost." Nathan wriggles his fingers in the air.

"The ghost with nine fingers, how scary," Dylan says, wriggling his fingers in the air too.

And boy, I have never seen anyone more willing to grab a fork and stab Dylan's eyes out. Luckily, they're all made of plastic. Silas's mom knows how to prepare for the worst.

"Not again ..." My other extra dad Kai shakes his head from the corner of the room. "Can you guys not start another fight for once? We promised Penelope and Lana."

"Kai's right, don't offend the moms," my dad says, patting me on the shoulder. "I'm proud of you, Max. You did it."

"Thanks," I say.

"I love these family dinners," Blaine, Orion's dad says, as he leans back in his chair. "Reminds me of the good old days."

"You make it sound like we weren't fighting every other day," Ares, Atlas and Apollo's dad, says.

"Me? Fighting? With who?" Blaine raises his brows. "I was just reading my books in the corner, minding my own business, enjoying the view."

"The view of us knocking each other's heads off, yeah," Kai says, chuckling.

"That's just the Phantoms and Skull and Serpents being uncivilized," Blaine muses.

"*Uncivilized*?" Nathan rasps.

"Tartarus is a much better house, let's be honest," Ares says, stoking the flames.

"You want to prove that, brother?" Kai says, leaning his chin on his elbow.

"Jesus Christ, how much longer is the food going to take?" Silas interjects from a few seats down, breaking the icy mood. "I'm fucking famished."

Aspen is sitting beside him, and she shoves her elbow into his side.

"Silas!" Penelope warns him.

"Yeah, Silas. Chill," Mavis says from across the table. "Eat the fucking table if you're so damn hungry."

"I'll chomp off your fingers first," Silas retorts. "Tasty snack."

Melody, Silas's younger sister, giggles like it's funny even though it's not. "Silas, can you come and pose for me sometime? I really want to paint you when you're angry."

Silas sighs. "If I get the painting, sure, I don't see why the hell not."

"So, is that girl the little thief you were talking about, Silas?" Mavis glares at Ivy. "Do I still need to cast some spells?"

Silas makes a fist. "Don't you fucking dare hex her."

"Do those two even like each other?" Ivy asks.

I snort. "She's his sister. Of course he loves her."

"No, I said *like*."

"No one ever said you needed to *like* your siblings," Heath says.

"I don't, that's for sure," Atlas growls, sipping his drink.

"Thanks, bro," Apollo says as he pats Atlas's shoulder. "Remind me to kick your ass when we get home."

"See? He likes me," Atlas jokes.

"Guys, guys, where is the love?" Orion Navarro approaches with a glass of wine in his hand. He looks wasted already. "There's a new girl in our family and you guys can't even stop one day and just … smell the roses." He sucks in a breath through his nostrils. "C'mon, do it with me. Breathe in, and out."

Sunny just glares at him. "Shut the fuck up."

Orion stares at her, his eyes widening, then relaxing, before his entire body shivers.

"Orion, can you please stop drinking wine?" Crystal rubs her forehead. "You aren't even old enough yet, and you look drunk."

"Mom, please, not tonight," Orion says, making a face. "Can't you see this family is driving me to the edge?" He's so dramatic when he talks.

"Orion, I thought you cared about your skin?" his father, Blaine, asks as he takes a sip of his water. "Drinking will age it even quicker."

Orion's eyes widen, and he immediately puts the wine down.

"You have … an interesting family," Ivy tells Heath, smiling.

"You think?" Heath replies, snorting.

She sniggers behind her hand. "I'm sorry."

"Don't be. I feel the same way. But they're my family, and I love them," Heath says.

"Aw ..." Orion hugs Heath from behind. "Thank you, big bro."

Heath's mom, Crystal, claps her hands. "Everybody, find your seats!"

"Yeah, yeah," Levi Torres says, eyeing the seats left. He sits down at the far end of the table next to Mavis.

"So, I heard you three were together now. Is that true?" Levi asks me casually.

I blush. "Um, yeah. Pretty much. Ivy is with me, Heath, and Silas."

"Interesting ..." He taps his knuckles on the table as he looks at Ivy. "I've seen you around. You're Aspen's friend, aren't you?"

Ivy nods. "We met on campus. All of us, actually." She laughs awkwardly.

This must be so fucking weird for her.

It's normal to us, but our families aren't exactly the regular kind.

We tend to kill people if they do us wrong, and that's okay. Every family has its flaws.

"Anyway." Levi shrugs, turning to Mavis instead. "So, are you coming on the camping trip next week, or what?"

Okay, this conversation shifted out of nowhere.

"You know, I thought about it, and why not?" Mavis replies, leaning over the table on her elbows. "Are we just going hiking up the mountain, or are we going to go visit some spooky shit? I'm talking graveyards, abandoned houses, stuff like that."

"No, I was actually thinking of going far beyond Lake Verity," Levi says. "There's another ridge there that directly overlooks the sea. I think it'd be nice."

"Oh ..." Mavis sounds disappointed.

"Romantic," Apollo jests, winking at him. "With Silas' sister?"

"You'd better not say that out loud again if you value your life, Torres," Silas grits.

Apollo clasps the table as he stands up, those muscles looking all menacing. "I'd love to see you try to kill me."

"Apollo ..." his father's voice booms across the table, silencing everyone. "Sit. Down."

"Yeah, shut up." Mavis throws some bread at Apollo too.

Finally, he sits, the annoyance clearly showing on his face.

"Why is everyone throwing the bread around?!" Penelope growls, and half the table begins to chuckle.

Ivy frowns. "Wait a minute ... A camping trip?"

She looks over at Aspen, whose eyes have widened, and then she quickly turns to chat with her brother Xavier.

"Never mind." Ivy casually tucks her hair behind her ear.

Xavier throws his arm around Aspen. "We're coming too!"

She punches him in the shoulder.

Levi grins. "Perfect."

"I wish I could come to the camping thing ..." Melody mutters to herself, rolling a strand of her hair around her finger before sighing loudly.

"Camping sounds dreadful, not gonna lie," Orion says, shivering again. "All those bugs out there crawling across your skin."

"No, it's gonna be fabulous, and I, for one, can't wait," Elliot says. "I'll be there, along with Talon and Océane, and maybe some others, if we can convince them. Oh, and Cecelia's coming too!"

"Wait, what?" Heath furrows his brows. "Since when do you like camping?"

"Since I just came back from Prodigium Academy. I mean, why not?" Cecelia says. "You should come too."

Heath grimaces. "No, thanks."

"Party pooper," Cecelia says.

"More fun for us," Elliot says, leaning back in his seat.

Which only seems to piss off Heath even further.

"Don't worry, I'll take Heath's place. If *Sisi* is going, I'm going," Apollo says, winking.

Cecelia scowls. "Stop calling me that."

Apollo laughs, as though he enjoys pissing off his family.

"God, I hope you hired a good chef, Kai," Milo says, licking his lips. "Let's see if he can top me."

"Ego, much?" Blaine muses.

"Oh no, his sushi is the best there is, trust me," Kai says.

"FOOD'S HERE!" Mom's sudden shout makes everyone sit up in their seats.

"Fuck, Lana," Kai says, dragging her back down into her seat. "Be a little more ... subtle. Please."

"What?" Lana scoffs. "I'm hungry."

"You don't want to see how she eats when she gets mad, trust me," Silas's dad says.

And everyone begins to laugh.

***

IVY

1 week later

"You can open your eyes now."

Heath removes his hands from my face, and when I blink, my heart nearly jumps out of my chest. A brand-new, gleaming red Corvette is standing right in front of me with a giant pink ribbon on top of the hood.

"Surprise!" Heath, Max, and Silas all say simultaneously.

"This is for me?" I mutter in disbelief.

Heath sports a smirk. "You betchya."

"Thank you," I say, not knowing what else to say as I'm still stunned. "You keep lavishing me with gifts. It's gonna make me feel guilty."

"Don't be." Max places his hand on my shoulder. "Your bike has gotten you far, but you deserve something that doesn't make you work out like you're trying to get in shape for the Olympics."

"Silas pinches my waist. "Maybe then you'll finally be less of a twig."

"Ha-ha." I put my hands against my waist. "What a generous compliment."

"Don't mention it," Silas says as he slides his whole hand across my belly, creeping underneath my crop top. "Now let's go get us some burgers as juicy as these tits."

"Wow," I say, but I still laugh. "Your filth never ceases to amaze me."

His hand snakes its way up my crop top, all the way to my neck. "Good." He squeezes while whispering. "Keep it that way." His tongue darts out to lick the rim of my earlobe. "Now who's ready for a ride?"

"Wait, we can take it for a spin right away?" I mutter, completely distracted.

"Hell yeah," Heath says, opening the car door for me. "Jump in."

I'm too excited not to, so I hop in and slide behind the wheel, checking out the dashboard for all the fancy stuff.

"I don't wanna be rude or anything, but do you know how to drive?" Max asks.

"Yeah, my dad taught me before ... well, you know."

"Oh ..." Max mutters. "Well, you can put the skills he taught you to good use."

I turn on the engine and rev it a little.

"That sound is fucking nice," Heath says.

Someone taps the hood of the car, and I look to my left to see Caleb, Heath's dad, hovering over us. "Make sure not to crash it the first day. This baby deserves better."

"You got it, mister," Max says, saluting him.

"Of course, I'll drive safe," I reply.

He smiles. "Have fun."

I hit the gas, and we exit the parking lot of the car dealership. The wind flows through my hair the faster we go, and it feels so damn good that I don't wanna stop. If this is what true freedom feels like, I never want to exchange it for a damn thing.

We go to a burger joint somewhere in the middle of town and eat to our heart's content, or at least until Silas is done shoving fries down my throat. When I'm full, we jump back into the brand-new car and drive off into the night.

God, if I could only tell my past self where I'd be right now, she'd probably call me a liar.

"Where are we going?" Max asks.

"I thought we could drive out of town for a little. Do some sight-seeing."

Right as we head into the woods, my phone buzzes.

"Who's in your inbox?" Silas asks as he rummages around in my pocket. "It'd better not be some guy."

Heath snorts. "Like she doesn't have enough to deal with just being with the three of us."

"True," Max says. "Especially you two."

"I'm not interested in more trouble, thanks," I retort.

Silas hands me the phone before he turns his head to glare at Max, practically throwing darts with his eyes.

But all I can do is hit the brakes so damn hard the boys are nearly flung out of the car.

"What the fuck—this is a new car, be gentle with her!" Heath growls.

His words barely register with me while read the words on my phone up close ... and my whole body begins to quake.

"What's wrong?" Max asks.

"Silas." His face grows bleak when I look at him because I'm unable to hide the terror sinking into my heart. "Mavis is dead."

THANK YOU FOR READING!

Thank you so much for reading Boys Who Hunt. Please leave a review if you enjoyed!

You can stay up to date of new books via my website: www.clarissawild.com

I'd love to talk to you! You can find me on Instagram: www.instagram.com/clarissa.wild, make sure to click FOLLOW.

You can also join the Fan Club group on facebook: www.facebook.com/groups/FanClubClarissaWild and talk with other readers!

Enjoyed this book? You could really help out by leaving a review on Amazon and Goodreads. Thank you!

COMING SOON: BOYS WHO TAINT.
PREORDER VIA WWW.CLARISSAWILD.COM!

ALSO BY CLARISSA WILD

Dark Romance
Spine Ridge University Series
Beast & Beauty Duet
Debts & Vengeance Series
Dellucci Mafia Duet
The Debt Duet
Savage Men Series
Delirious Series
Indecent Games Series
The Company Series
FATHER

New Adult Romance
Fierce Series
Blissful Series
Ruin
Rowdy Boy & Cruel Boy

Erotic Romance
The Billionaire's Bet Series
Enflamed Series
Unprofessional Bad Boys Series

Visit Clarissa Wild's website for current titles.
www.clarissawild.com

ABOUT THE AUTHOR

Clarissa Wild is a New York Times & USA Today Bestselling author of Dark Romance and Contemporary Romance novels. She is an avid reader and writer of swoony stories about dangerous men and feisty women. Her other loves include her hilarious husband, her cutie pie son, her two crazy but cute dogs, and her adorable kitties. In her free time, she enjoys watching all sorts of movies, playing video games, reading tons of books, and cooking her favorite meals.

Want to be informed of new releases and special offers? Sign up for Clarissa Wild's newsletter on her website: www.clarissawild.com/newsletter

www.ingramcontent.com/pod-product-compliance
Ingram Content Group UK Ltd.
Pitfield, Milton Keynes, MK11 3LW, UK
UKHW021429271224
3869UKWH00041B/459